HELLFIRE

August, 1942. North Africa. The desert war hangs in the balance. Although the British Army's retreat has finally been halted, their morale is at rock bottom. When the commander of the Eighth Army, General Gott, is killed, it seems that foul play is at work. Jack Tanner, recovering from his wounds in a Cairo hospital, is astonished to receive a battlefield commission. Fit once more, he finds himself facing the full onslaught of Rommel's last offensive. *Hellfire* sees Tanner fighting his way through the most dangerous adventure yet, taking him to one of the decisive clashes of the entire war – the Battle of Alamein.

HELLFIRE

HELLFIRE

by

James Holland

Magna Large Print Books
Long Preston, North Yorkshire,
BD23 4ND, England.

British Library Cataloguing in Publication Data.

Holland, James
     Hellfire.

     A catalogue record of this book is
     available from the British Library

     ISBN   978-0-7505-3584-7

First published in Great Britain in 2011 by Bantam Press
an imprint of Transworld

Copyright © James Holland 2011

Cover illustration © Stephen Mulcahey by arrangement with
Arcangel Images

James Holland has asserted his right under the Copyright, Designs
and Patents Act, 1988 to be identified as the author of this work.

Published in Large Print 2012 by arrangement with
Transworld Publishers

Magna Large Print is an imprint of Library Magna Books Ltd.

Printed and bound in Great Britain by
T.J. (International) Ltd., Cornwall, PL28 8RW

For Rachel, Ned and Daisy

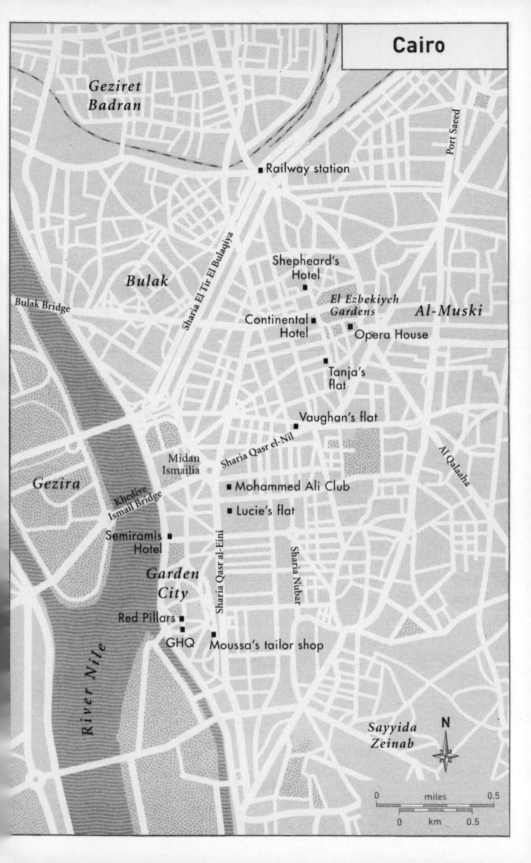

Cairo

Geziret
Badran

Port Saeed

■ Railway station

Bulak

Sharia El Tir El Bulaqiya

Shepheard's
Hotel ■

El Ezbekiyeh
Gardens

Al-Muski

Continental
Hotel ■

■ Opera House

Bulak Bridge

Tanja's
flat ■

■ Vaughan's flat

Sharia Qasr el-Nil

Al Qalaaha

Gezira

Midan
Ismailia

Khedive
Ismail Bridge

■ Mohammed Ali Club

■ Lucie's flat

Semiramis
Hotel ■

Garden
City

Sharia Qasr al-Eini

Sharia Nubar

River Nile

Red Pillars ■
GHQ ■

■ Moussa's tailor shop

Sayyida
Zeinab

N

0   miles   0.5

0   km   0.5

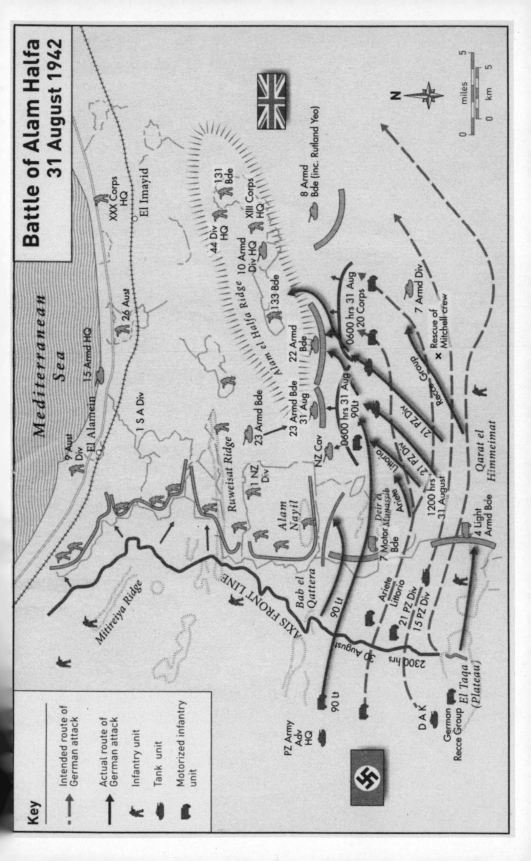

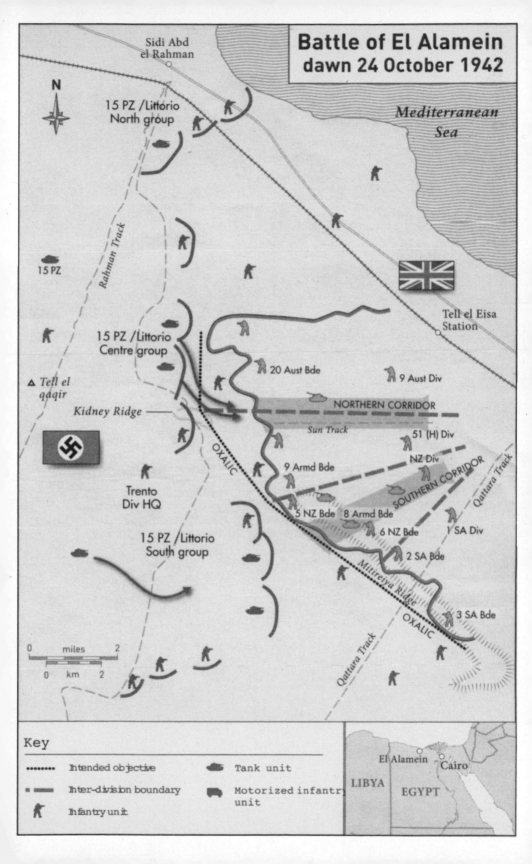

Battle of El Alamein
dawn 24 October 1942

N

Mediterranean Sea

Sidi Abd el Rahman

15 PZ /Littorio North group

15 PZ

Rahman Track

Tell el Eisa Station

15 PZ /Littorio Centre group

△ Tell el qaqir

Kidney Ridge

20 Aust Bde

9 Aust Div

NORTHERN CORRIDOR

Sun Track

51 (H) Div

OXALIC

9 Armd Bde

NZ Div

SOUTHERN CORRIDOR

Qattara Track

Trento Div HQ

5 NZ Bde

8 Armd Bde

6 NZ Bde

1 SA Div

15 PZ /Littorio South group

2 SA Bde

Mitireiya Ridge

OXALIC

3 SA Bde

Qattara Track

miles 2

km 2

Key

- •••••••• Intended objective
- Tank unit
- Inter-division boundary
- Motorized infantry unit
- Infantry unit

El Alamein — Cairo

LIBYA

EGYPT

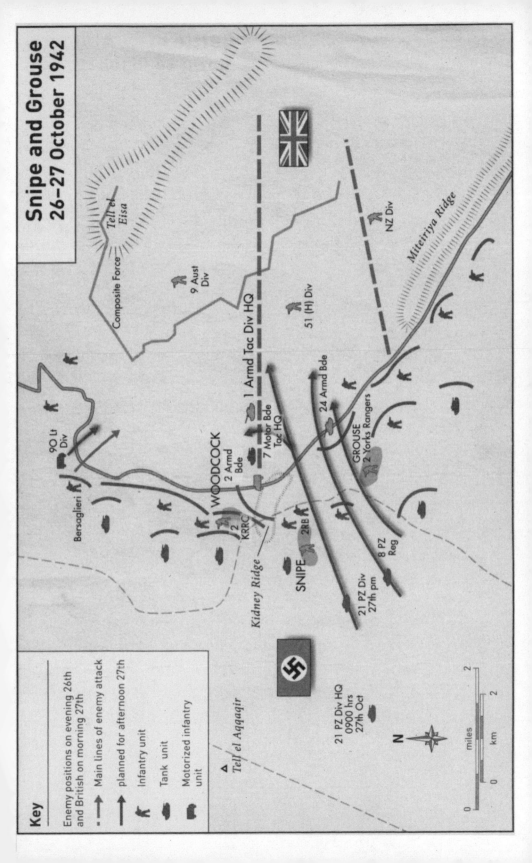

Snipe and Grouse
26–27 October 1942

Key

Enemy positions on evening 26th
and British on morning 27th

Main lines of enemy attack

planned for afternoon 27th

Infantry unit

Tank unit

Motorized infantry
unit

△ Tell el Aqqaqir

21 PZ Div HQ
0900 hrs
27th Oct

N

miles

km

2

2

0

8 PZ Reg

21 PZ Div
27th pm

SNIPE

2 RB

Kidney Ridge

GROUSE
2 Yorks Rangers

2 KRRC

WOODCOCK
2 Armd Bde

Bersaglieri

9O Lt Div

7 Motor Bde
Tac HQ

1 Armd Tac Div HQ

24 Armd Bde

51 (H) Div

9 Aust Div

Composite Force

Tell el Eisa

Miteiriya Ridge

NZ Div

Glossary

A and S – Argyll and Sutherland Highlanders
AOC – Air Officer Commanding
baksheesh – change, money
bundook – rifle
bawaeb – doorkeeper
bint – woman
blue, the – slang term for the desert
CIGS – Chief of the Imperial General Staff
COS – Chief of Staff
CQM – Camp Quarter Master
dahabiya – houseboat
DAF – Desert Air Force
dekko – have a look
DMI – Director of Military Intelligence
DMO – Director of Military Operations
effiyeh – cotton scarf, usually wrapped around
  head
feloose – money
FOO – Forward Observation Officer
GC and CS – Government Code and Cypher
  School
G(R) – branch of the DMO's office dealing with
  raiding parties, e.g. SAS, LRDG
GS – General Service, or General Staff
GSO(I) – General Staff Officer (Intelligence)
HE – High Explosive

iggery – hurry up, get a move on
intel – intelligence
IO – Intelligence Officer
ISLD – Inter-Services Liaison Department
ISOS – Intelligence Service Oliver Strachey
KRRC – King's Royal Rifle Corps
LRDG – Long Range Desert Group
LOC – Lines of Communication
MEIC – Middle East Intelligence Centre
MID – Mentioned in Despatches
MO4 – Military Operations, Department 4
M/T – motor transport
MTB – Motor Torpedo Boat
musquois – bad
OC – Officer Commanding
OP – Observation Post
QA – Queen Alexandra (Imperial Military
  Nursing Service)
RAMC – Royal Army Medical Corps
RASC – Royal Army Service Corps
RAP – Regimental Aid Post
2 RB – 2nd Battalion, Rifle Brigade
SAS – Special Air Service
Schmeisser – British term for an MP38 or
  MP40 sub-machine gun
SIME – Secret Intelligence Middle East
sitrep – situation report
SOE – Special Operations Executive
Spandau – British term for German machine-
  gun
suffragi – waiter, servant
Wafd – British-backed Egyptian Government
W/T – wireless telegraphy (radio)

CAIRO

August 1942

1

Friday, 7 August 1942, around eleven in the morning. The heat hung heavily over the city, like a shroud. However, in the first-floor flat just off Sharia El Maghrabi, which was home to the Polish Red Cross, the air was close and certainly hot, but not oppressively so. In part this was due to its position. Although east-facing, the apartment block stood in a small street behind the Continental Hotel. Since they were on the first floor, the grand nineteenth-century building shielded them from the worst of the morning sun, while by the afternoon it was almost entirely in the shade. The women had also worked out that by having the windows open, the shutters closed and both overhead fans whirring at full speed, the heat was manageable. One of the fans squeaked irritatingly, and the draught they made caused loose paper to flap listlessly, but this was a small price to pay.

The flat had four rooms: a living room, a single bedroom, a bathroom and a small kitchen. It had been donated anonymously the previous October, when General Sikorski had suggested that the few Polish ladies in Cairo set up their own Red Cross office. With countless Poles now freed from Russian internment, making their way south through the Soviet Union, then heading west towards the Middle East, it seemed only right that the tiny

Polish contingent in Cairo should do what they could to help their countrymen.

There were four full-time staff, led by Countess Sophie Tarnowska, and ten volunteers. Work began early, before the heat of the day. That was when the packages were made up in the bedroom – bundles of clothes, shoes, perhaps even some other basics, including tins of food, toothbrushes and cigarettes. When this was done, the women would spend their time writing letters, or purloining more supplies. As the central Allied hub in the Middle East, Cairo was about as well stocked with supplies as anywhere, but everything had to be donated, and there was a war on, and they were vying with the International Red Cross and numerous other charity organizations for what could be spared. They had quickly discovered that the personal touch worked best, collaring men of influence at parties, or even making appointments to see them during the day. Face to face, a bit of flirting, a generous display of leg and cleavage, and determined eye contact made all the difference.

It was because Sophie and her sister-in-law, Chouquette, had just set off to see the new United States assistant military attaché, and because the morning volunteers had already left, that only two of the staff remained in the flat. Both were at their desks in the main living room, writing letters to go into the packages. Boxes of goods filled the centre of the room, giving it a cluttered air that the rest of its contents did not: four differing tables made up as desks, four chairs, a tall metal filing cabinet, on which stood a tray of drinks, and a small chest of drawers. A signed picture of Sikorski and a map of

Poland hung on the whitewashed walls, and that was it.

Tanja Zanowski drew another piece of writing-paper from the drawer in her desk and placed it in front of her. It was white, with a stark red cross at the top, headed 'Polski Czerwony Krzyz' on one side and 'Polish Red Cross' on the other. She paused for a moment and looked up towards the window. She could hear outside the endless hub-bub of the city: the traffic, the horns, the *muezzin* making the call to prayer, his reedy, wailing voice carrying over the din. Yet the shutters muted the noise so that in the flat the air seemed quite still, despite the fans – so quiet that she could hear a fly buzzing noisily.

She looked down again at the paper in front of her. *My brave fellow countrymen*, she wrote, *please take heart that there are Poles here, in Cairo, working on your behalf. Working to help you. We know you have suffered under the cruel yoke of the Bolsheviks but you are free of them now*. They were lines she had written a hundred times before, but now, as the fly settled on her bare arm, she stopped and whisked it away.

'Hold on,' said Ewa, from the other side of the room. She stood up, clutching a fly swat, then moved towards the wall beside Tanja's desk, where she paused, her eyes following the fly. At last it settled, and she struck, with a loud crack. 'Got it!' she exclaimed, looking at the squashed fly stuck to the bare wall.

Tanja smiled. 'Good shot.'

The lone telephone rang, and Tanja started. Ewa was already standing so she stepped quickly

25

towards Sophie's desk and picked up the receiver.

'Polish Red Cross,' she said, in English. Pause. 'Yes, one moment.' She held it out to Tanja, and mouthed, 'It's for you.'

Tanja pushed back her chair, stood and took the phone. 'Yes?' she said.

'Hello, darling.' Her heart quickened.

'Oh, Harry, how lovely!' she said, smiling.

'Let's meet in the usual place. In half an hour?'

'But of course! I'll be there. Don't start without me!'

She put the receiver down, then glanced at Ewa, a smile on her face.

'A date?' grinned Ewa.

'Oh – just a man I'm having lunch with.'

'Who? Is it the one who was all over you last night at Madame Badia's?'

Tanja went back to her desk, picked up cigarettes, compact and lipstick and put them into her bag. 'Might be.' She flashed another grin at Ewa.

'He was very handsome. You are lucky, Tanja.' Ewa turned back to her desk, then added, 'I wish I had your looks.'

'Don't be silly, Ewa. Anyway, he's off duty earlier than he expected, so I'm going to join him. You never know, maybe he can fix some provisions for us.'

'If he's a cavalry officer, perhaps he can.' Ewa faced Tanja. 'At least tell me his name. It's hardly as though it's a state secret.'

'All right,' said Tanja, as she looked into the mirror of her compact and repainted her lips. 'He's called Harry Rhodes-Morton. I really don't know much more about him than that, but he seemed very sweet and he's offered me lunch and I'm not going to turn down a free meal. Not at the Continental, at any rate.' She shut her compact, put it back in her bag, said, 'See you a bit later on,' and walked out of the flat.

She sighed heavily. *Thank God for the Polish Red Cross.* A job in which slipping out to meet people – whether young officers or military attachés – was part of the brief. An additional rendezvous could easily be hidden...

Outside, the heat hit her like the opening of an oven door. She could feel it coursing through her flesh. She could smell Cairo too – the stench of animal dung and refuse, of scented smoke and dust – and the sound of the city, which had been clear yet remote in the flat, was now a dramatic cacophony. And there was the familiar stark hue, which seemed to be permanently washed over everything during the day: pounding sunlight filtered by smoke, dust and fumes. Cars and carts jostled with people. In front of her, a cart laden with green tobacco leaves rumbled past, the man whipping the mule and calling out to someone on the far side of the street. Several men in suits and tarbooshes walked past, while a street hawker in traditional robes squatted at the side of the road, a box of partly green oranges beside him. Across the road, several Australian troops, distinct in their wide-brimmed hats, were arguing with an Egyptian.

Tanja took a deep breath and walked on down Sharia El Maghrabi in the direction of the opera house. She was wearing khaki drill, a light shirt and narrow skirt that came down below her knee,

27

and on her head a soft peaked khaki cap. It was something Sophie had insisted upon when General Sikorski had asked her to set up the Polish branch of the Red Cross. She had done so because the light clothes were so well suited to the heat, and Tanja had been grateful, partly because they were, as Sophie had insisted, practical, but more because they made her inconspicuous, despite her striking looks. One barely could walk twenty yards in Cairo without seeing another serviceman or -woman. Khaki drill had become as common as the flowing white cotton *galabhiyas* worn by most Egyptian men.

Reaching Opera Square, she crossed the road and turned right, down Sharia Abdin, then after a hundred yards, she turned, at the edge of the old Islamic Quarter, down a narrow side-street, which was sheltered from the sun by the buildings either side and by the many canopies that stretched out from under the balconies above. The *muezzin* called again from a mosque as she walked past men and women sitting in doorways, past shops and yet more carts. A mule brayed, someone shouted, and the wail of the *muezzin* droned out once more. Good God, but it was hot. She paused outside a general store, saw a cat eyeing her suspiciously, then looked briefly around and stepped inside, heartbeat quickening. The smell of incense and food was strong. It was dark inside and cooler – much cooler. Stacked shelves lined the walls, while below the counter was piled with fruit, beans and nuts. Flies buzzed lazily.

The old man sitting silently behind it indicated that she should go through to the back of the shop. No one else seemed to be around.

She pushed through a beaded curtain into a room scented powerfully with incense. The floor was thick with rugs and lined with cushions, and lying against the far wall, smoking a hookah, was an Egyptian in a suit and tarboosh, about thirty years old with a lean, lined face and a neat, pencil-thin moustache.

'Madame,' he said. 'A pleasure as always.'

Tanja stood where she was. 'Hello, Artus. You have a message for me.' A statement not a request.

Artus reached into his jacket pocket and pulled out a folded sheet of paper. 'Here,' he said. 'I took the trouble to write it out for you first.'

Tanja took it, read it, reread it, then passed it back.

'You had better be quick,' said Artus. 'There's not much time.'

'No,' said Tanja. Without another word, she left. Back through the shop, out on to the street. Another quick glance either side. *Good. No one about.* She turned right, back the way she had come before rejoining Sharia Adli Pasha, then nimbly crossing the busy thoroughfare. Thirty yards further on, she turned down Sharia Al Khasa, a quieter residential street. A row of gum trees lined one side, providing dappled shade and sheltering the apartment blocks behind. Passing through a gate, Tanja trotted up a small path, climbed the half-dozen steps past the bougain-villaea and nodded curtly at the *bawaeb*, a beady-eyed old man who stared up at her from his mat just inside the entrance. A few more yards, and – *yes* – the lift was down. She wrenched back the lattice metal door, stepped inside and pressed the button 7. The lift began to rise, ticking as it did so, each floor passing as though in cross-section. Tanja tapped her feet and clicked her tongue against her teeth. With a jolt, the lift came to a halt, and Tanja stepped out, fumbling her key from her bag.

The dark corridor was deserted. Good. Key in the cream-coloured door, and then she was inside the familiar surroundings of her flat, with its odour of compressed heat and scent. She walked briskly into her bedroom and to the tall wardrobe. Reaching up, she felt about and pulled down the book – a comic German novel for children called *Hausboot Muschepusche*. Of course, the content was irrelevant: it was the pages, words and letters within it that mattered. She took it to the table in the kitchenette and began to work out the code.

It took a short while – five minutes – but with the numbers all written down in pencil on a scrap of paper, she returned to her bedroom and this time opened the wardrobe. The door creaked and from behind her dresses she pulled out a battered suitcase – it had accompanied her on the long, traumatic journey south from Poland nearly three years earlier. Back then, it had been stuffed with a few clothes, family photographs and treasures – jewels that had mostly been sold since. Now, however, it contained a small transmitter-receiver, around six inches wide and nine long, which she carefully took out and brought through to the living room. Setting down the case on the sideboard, she took out the small metal box, connected it to the accompanying battery pack, fixed the antenna, then took out the Morse tapper and screwed it in. It was a familiar process, but her heart was pounding and her hands were shaking. *Come on*, she told herself. *Calm down*.

She switched the set on, heard it buzz, checked it was tuned to the correct frequency, then held out her hands. They were still shaking, so she took a cigarette from the box on the table, lit it, inhaled and closed her eyes. Another deep breath. Then she began to tap out the numbers: *716, 713, 719, 717, 725, 715, 762.* GENERAL. *821, 817, 842, 864.* GOTT. *783, 744, 725, 743, 736, 762, 721, 753, 732, 783.* BURG EL ARAB. *638, 629.* ZU. *971, 972, 996, 922, 968, 8510, 967, 996, 915, 966.* HELIOPOLIS. It took a little time.

638.813.811.824. ZWEI.

735. 834. 952. 842. 921. HEUTE.

755.623.763.942.823.913. SIEBEN

919, 947, 954, 744, 767, 714. AUGUST

When she had finished, she switched the radio to receive, placed the flimsy headphones over her ears and waited.

A minute passed, then another. 'Come on,' she mouthed. 'Come on.' She tapped her fingers on the table. The flat was so still, so quiet. Dark too. Only faint light managed to force its way through the shutters. Outside the sounds of the city rumbled faintly.

Suddenly there was a crackle of static. Tanja snatched up her pencil, listening to the coded numbers: *811, 925, 617, 618, 927, 923, 821, 943, 923, 853, 863, 881, 911, 943, 982, 841, 864, 831, 951, 961, 975, 856.* The static stopped with a

31

whine and, after a moment, Tanja turned off the set. Taking the book, she began to decode the message, each set of numbers a single letter. EMPFANGEN UND VERSTANDEN, it read. *Received and understood.*

Five minutes later, Tanja was back down on the street, engulfed by the midday heat once more. She put on her sunglasses, tried to resist the urge to glance around and behind her, and instead determinedly looked straight ahead. She thought about the impact her transmitted message would have. She knew perfectly well who General Gott was: formerly the British commander of XIII Corps and, as of yesterday, the new commander of Eighth Army. The sweeping changes had been the talk of Cairo the previous evening. At Shepheard's and then Madame Badia's there had been talk of little else – until Harry Rhodes-Morton and his friends had descended on her. Even they had been unable to resist telling of their glimpse of the Prime Minister. Churchill had certainly shaken things up during his few brief days in the Middle East: Auchinleck fired, a number of other senior commanders fired, and now a new army commander and a new C-in-C Middle East.

She was wondering what von Mellenthin would plan to do with the information when she heard her name called. She looked around and saw Ewa hurrying towards her across Sharia Kamil Adli.

Surprised, Tanja instinctively put her hand to her chest, then immediately regretted it, knowing it revealed a guilty conscience. 'Caught you!' said Ewa.

For a brief moment Tanja froze, but then she

saw Ewa was smiling. *Relief.* 'Damn!' she said, with as much composure as she could muster. 'Yes, you have, rather.'

'Just thought you'd nip back home first?'

'Yes – a quick change of knickers. I'm sorry, Ewa.' She glanced at her conspiratorially. 'I suppose I didn't strictly need to but I'm just so bored of writing those letters. Is that a terrible thing to admit?' She placed a hand on Ewa's arm. 'Are you very cross with me?'

Ewa laughed. 'Of course not.'

'You won't tell Sophie, will you?'

'Really, Tanja! What do you take me for? In any case, I don't know what you're worrying about. Sophie would hardly have minded.'

'Maybe not, but I'd hate her to think I'm not pulling my weight. Or you, for that matter.'

Ewa smiled. 'Forget it. It's hardly the world's worst crime, is it?'

'Thank you,' said Tanja. Then, looking at her watch, she added, 'I must get going.'

'Do you think you'll still like him?'

'I don't know. Doesn't really matter if he can get us some more supplies, does it?'

'And if he pays for lunch.'

'Exactly.'

'Well, have fun. I'll see you later.' Ewa winked and walked on.

As Tanja crossed the road, her heart was still hammering. She was certain Ewa had suspected nothing – after all, why should she? – but that didn't stop her worrying. Thank God Ewa had not seen her stepping into the shop. *Come on, pull yourself together.* She reminded herself that she was following all the right safety procedures, and that the chances of anyone ever catching her out were surely small. She sighed. It was always like this: the rational side of her brain forever in conflict with the part that produced intense panic and fear.

By the time she reached the Continental, her heart rate had slowed and her panic had evaporated. She stopped briefly to check her makeup in her compact mirror, then sauntered into the canopied restaurant at the front of the grand old building. She scanned the faces and saw a hand waving in the air.

'Well done, you made it.' Harry Rhodes-Morton stood up as she drew near.

'Of course.' She smiled, offering her cheek. 'I was never going to pass up the chance of lunch with a handsome cavalry captain.'

Rhodes-Morton grinned and his cheeks reddened. He helped her into her chair, sat down opposite her and nodded to the waiter.

'Champagne?' he said, turning back to Tanja.

'Oh, Harry, how lovely!' said Tanja. 'Are we celebrating something?'

He cleared his throat. 'Well, I suppose so. It's our first lunch together, after all. And it's a new start for Eighth Army too. A new commander, and Jerry and the Wops held at Alamein. All our chaps think the same – that this time we really will send Rommel packing. And I rate Gott. I reckon he's got what it takes, you know?' He held up his glass.

Tanja lifted hers. 'So who are we toasting?'

'Would it be too forward to toast us?'

'Yes, definitely. We've only just met.'

Rhodes-Morton blushed again. 'Of course. How about to General Gott and Eighth Army, then?'

'All right.' Tanja smiled. The champagne was ice-cold, sparkling and delicious. *General Gott*. She wondered where he was now. Ah, well, it was out of her hands.

As it was, General Gott was fit, well, and looking forward to a couple of days' leave in Cairo. The last time he'd been there had been in April, some weeks before the Gazala battles; four months in the desert was a long time, and although he was well used to living in a tent, everyone suffered their fair share of privations, generals included. The lack of running water, latrines that were no more than a hole in the ground, and the millions of flies were the same for all ranks. Even in the last war, for all its ghastliness, Gott had never spent more than a few weeks without a hot bath; and only in summer, during an offensive, had flies been anything to worry about – even then their numbers were nothing compared to those in the Western Desert.

Even so, Gott had been determined to brief his new corps and divisional commanders who had, until the previous momentous day, been colleagues but were now his subordinates as well. Confidence was low. They had taken a hammering since the fighting had begun at the end of May. Eighth Army's battle plans had failed spectacularly. The Gazala Line had been overrun, British armour decimated, and Tobruk had

35

fallen – Tobruk, a coastal town of smashed buildings with a wrecked harbour of half-sunken ships, but a town in which much British pride had been invested. Although Rommel and his Panzer Army had been held at Alamein, there was no disguising the depth of the defeat.

Some had already been moved on, replaced as the Auk was being replaced. The PM and General Brooke had broken the news to Corbett, Dorman-Smith and Ramsden, but all the divisional commanders remained. There were personal tensions between them and national tensions too. Eighth Army might have been British in name, but in reality it was a polyglot force of Indians, Australians, New Zealanders and South Africans as well as British. Gott understood that these tensions needed ironing out, and fast. The new commander needed to clear the air, and if that meant delaying his leave by a few hours, then so be it.

Most important, he was conscious that the ongoing spat between himself and Dan Pienaar, the Afrikaner commander of the 1st South African Division, needed to be resolved. They had to put aside their differences. Eighth Army needed to gel once more, to fight as one. Pienaar had been the last to arrive at Eighth Army's Tactical Headquarters and their conversation had taken longest, as Gott had suspected it would – that was why he had postponed his flight back to Cairo.

Now, however, at a little after half past two, his last meeting was over. Some plain speaking and an apology had achieved his goal. The air *had* been cleared. He and Pienaar had even shared a joke or two before they had launched into a series of planning conversations that had certainly renewed Gott's confidence.

Seeing Pienaar's staff car rumble off in a cloud of dust, Gott felt both relieved and invigorated. He was only a week short of his forty-fifth birthday, yet just a few days ago he had felt washed-out – physically and mentally. Command was an exhausting business, but doubly so during defeat. When the Prime Minister and General Brooke had visited him, he had confessed as much to the Chief of the Imperial General Staff and had wondered whether it wouldn't be better to get some new blood in. He had even suggested it might be time for him to be sent home. He had begun to think about seeing his wife and children again – God only knew, it had been a long time since he had glimpsed their sweet faces.

But he had not been sent home. He had been promoted and made Army Commander, initially a daunting and forbidding prospect, but now it excited him, and seemed to have infused him with new energy and purpose. More tanks were on their way – new American models – as were more men, more aircraft, more vehicles. In the flush of bitter defeat it was easy to view matters from a half-empty cup but, he realized, there was now much in their favour. Rommel had been held: his lines of supply were over-extended and the RAF were making a damn good fist of ensuring that as little as possible reached the front. In contrast, Gott's own supplies had a comparatively short distance to run. Not only was there now no reason why Rommel could not be held, should he attack again, there was also every reason to believe the Panzer Army could be defeated once and for all. It was ironic, but the run of defeats had given them the chance of ultimate victory.

Gott smiled to himself, and rubbed his chin thoughtfully, then turned to one of his ADCs, hovering beside him. 'Right, Whitworth,' he said. 'I think it's safe for me to go.'

'That's good, sir,' said Whitworth, a young captain and Guardsman. 'The Bombay should be touching down at any moment.'

Gott looked at his watch. 'Gosh, yes – we'd better get a move on. We don't want to keep it waiting.'

'No, sir.'

Gott disappeared into his tent, grabbed a small suitcase, then strode out towards the waiting car. He would be at Heliopolis in under an hour, and safely ensconced at Shepheard's in two. A bath, a nap, then drinks and dinner.

As Tanja Zanowski proffered both cheeks to Lieutenant Rhodes-Morton after a delicious lunch at the Continental, a young nineteen-year-old sergeant-pilot was approaching the roughly cleared landing ground at Burg El Arab, some thirty-five miles along the coast, west of Alexandria. It had not been an easy flight. There was always plenty of turbulence over the Western Desert, but it was generally worse in the middle of the day, especially when it was sizzling hot and you were flying at only fifty feet off the deck in an ageing Bristol Bombay transport plane. Still, it was better to risk a sudden lurch and drop twenty feet at the hands of swirling thermals than it was to be shot down by marauding German fighters.

Sergeant Pilot Jimmy James eyed the landing ground, which was only just visible, thanks to the lines of old fuel cans marking out the strip and a few camouflaged tents and vehicles. Away to his right was the village of Burg El Arab – a cluster of mud-brick houses. The desert, as ever, looked impenetrable, sun-blasted and bleached. After a tight circuit over the landing ground, James brought the Bombay in to land with a light bump. Then came the familiar jolting as he taxied towards the few tents at the far end, and turned the aircraft ready to take off again. That was the golden rule: never switch off the engines. Keep them running, ready for an almost immediate departure.

James climbed down through the hatch in the cockpit floor and strode towards the operations tent to report to the duty operations officer, Flying Officer 'Jonah' Whale. Lorries and ambulances were already hurrying out to the waiting Bombay. Speed was imperative: the cargo was unloaded, then mailbags, personnel and wounded men were hoisted into the aircraft. The aim was to be airborne again in five minutes or less.

'You need to switch off,' Whale called, as James approached.

'What?' James replied. 'You know we're not allowed.'

Whale shrugged. 'It's orders.'

'Orders from whom?'

'Air HQ. You've got a VIP coming.'

Inside the operations tent, James took off his helmet and wiped his brow. 'Jesus,' he said.

'I know. Sorry, but orders are orders.'

James looked at his watch – *1438* – then glanced towards his second pilot and signalled to him to switch off. 'Damn, damn, damn,' he muttered, pacing up and down the stony sand outside the tent. Switching off the engines was a worry in itself. They quickly overheated when stationary in this kind of heat and could be bloody difficult to restart. Scanning the skies, he slapped at several flies that were buzzing around his sweating face, then strode back towards the Bombay.

'You'd better get the wounded off again,' he told the ground crew, who had just finished loading a number of stretchers on board. 'We don't want them to die from overheating in there,' he added, as one of the erks rolled his eyes with irritation.

James glanced at his watch again. It had been a frustrating day already. At six that morning he'd reported to the flight commander's tent at Heliopolis to be told he'd not be flying until after eleven. That was unusual in itself, but then eleven had come and gone, and still he'd not been ordered to take off. At noon, they'd been told to take a quick lunch, but an hour later, they still hadn't been given the go-ahead. Not until two that afternoon had James been given the orders to take off for Burg El Arab. Now it seemed it was a VIP who had caused all the delay.

He watched the wounded being unloaded, then ambled across to the ops tent once more, still scanning the skies above him. Was that a faint buzz in the distance? His heart lurched. *Nothing.* Just a vast empty expanse of blue. A phone rang in the ops tent and a few moments later, Whale

40

called, 'They'll be here in a short while. It's Gott, by the way – General "Strafer" Gott. He's the new commander of Eighth Army.'

Good God. James nodded acknowledgement, then ran back to the Bombay. He'd no sooner ordered the wounded on board again than two Humber staff cars drew up in a cloud of dust. A number of people got out, but he spotted the new army commander, who walked briskly towards the waiting plane.

'Are you the captain?' he asked James.

'Yes, sir,' James replied, suddenly conscious that he looked hot, sweat-streaked and – he had left his flying helmet on his seat. 'I'm sorry, sir,' he stammered, 'but I can't salute you without a cap.'

Gott smiled. 'Don't worry about that, my boy.' He glanced up at the ageing Bombay. 'Are you ready to go?'

'Yes, sir. We're just starting up the engines now.' No sooner had he said this than the twin propellers whined and clicked, then spluttered into life, whirring loudly, kicking up clouds of dust and rocking the airframe.

Gott turned towards the hatch just behind the wing, while James hurried forward to the cockpit. Clambering in, he glanced at Mackay, his co-pilot, wiped the sweat from his face, then hurriedly put on his helmet and plugged in his radio leads.

'Engine temperature's already rising horribly,' Mackay said.

James glanced at the dials. *Damn it.* 'Well, let's get going quickly then,' he muttered. Glancing down from the cockpit, he saw the ground crew signal his clearance to take off. He opened the

41

throttles, the Bombay began to roar and shake, and then they were speeding over the rough ground. James eased the control column towards him and the violent shaking stopped. The shadow of the great plane eased away and they were airborne. He breathed out heavily and glanced again at his dials. Engine temperature was still dangerously high. *Christ*, he thought. *This is not good.* And yet he had levelled out at just fifty feet – they were barely off the desert floor, and he dared not go any higher. They were within easy range of any roaming enemy aircraft. It was the middle of the afternoon and he had been stuck on the ground for more than half an hour. *This really is not good.* Sweat trickled down his face and back.

'Make sure you keep a sharp watch on the engines,' he told Mackay. 'If one of them seizes from overheating, I'm going to need to gain height quickly for cooler air.'

'I'm on it, Jimmy,' said Mackay.

James looked at the air speed. *One hundred and forty.* The desert spread either side of him. Far away to his left, he could see the vivid turquoise of the Mediterranean. Up ahead, nothing but bleached desert.

Suddenly there was a loud bang, a whiplashing noise and his starboard engine stopped dead.

'You fool!' James shouted at his co-pilot. 'I told you to–'

'But look!' Mackay screamed.

Cannon and machine-gun tracers were whooshing past the cockpit and over the wings. Flames leaped from the starboard engine, thick smoke billowing.

Christ. James felt paralysed, unable to think clearly, or move. His hands were glued to the control column and he was vaguely conscious that all sound had gone. A strange, unknown streak of yellowish-green seemed to enfold him, then run down the back of his head and through his body. His paralysis vanished.

'Get your head down, Mac,' he shouted, 'and get the medical orderly.' The cockpit was filling with smoke. He pulled back the Perspex window catch, then saw the port engine stop. Cursing, he pulled back the stick, hoping he might use what remaining speed he had to gain some crucial height. An enemy fighter plane hurtled past, then another. *Black crosses.* Frantically, James glanced around him. He could see at least two more and they were still firing. More bullets and cannon tracer whooshed past, clattering across the wings. A fuel tank was punctured. *A hundred feet, a hundred and twenty.* The ground still looked frighteningly close. He gasped and glanced back-wards. His wireless operator had been badly hit in the arm. There were a few flames now between the cockpit and the main body of the plane, but Mackay and the medical orderly managed to get past the bulkhead into the cockpit behind him.

'Get all the wounded off the stretcher hooks,' James ordered, 'and lay them on the floor.'

While the two men battled their way back into the fuselage, James watched as six Messerschmitts flew on, disappearing into small black dots ahead of him. The Bombay had no power at all; it was gliding. Scanning forward, James saw that the

43

desert sloped slightly downwards in a long, gradual descent. The ground looked far from even and there was also a difficult cross-wind, but he was able to glide the stricken aircraft lower and lower. Closer and closer came the desert floor until James tensed. A moment later, the wheels touched.

'Come on, come on,' he muttered to himself. 'Please, God.' The Bombay hurtled onwards, running forward down the desert slope, speed barely decreasing.

'Everyone's all right,' said Mackay, behind him. 'We've got them on the floor.'

'I can't get the damn tail down,' muttered James. 'The cross-wind's too strong.'

'What about the brakes?'

'I daren't use them. Not at this speed. It'll tip us over.' He grimaced, the muscles in his arms straining as he gripped the stick. 'Damn it, this is hard. Like driving a ten-ton truck through sand.' Smoke was still swirling around the cockpit, but there were flames now too. A sickly smell of burning hair and skin reached James's nose and pain now coursed through him.

But the Bombay was at last beginning to slow. 'All right,' he gasped, 'get back there again, and take off the door. Make sure it's completely off its hinge, and when I give the word, drop them out on to the sand.'

Smoke choked his lungs. His gloveless hands were reddening and blackening and he could feel his face burning – but then, with horror, he saw the Messerschmitts coming back, low, like a small swarm of wasps. *The bastards! They're going to attack*

44

again. 'Why?' he said out loud. The Bombay was down, it was clearly never going to fly again, and aircraft on both sides knew better than to hang around once an aircraft had been destroyed.

'Skip?' It was Mackay, with the medical orderly.

Ahead, the Messerschmitts were speeding ever nearer.

'Stand by!' James called. 'Get the hatch on the cockpit floor open!'

Mackay nodded. 'We've told them what to do back there.'

'Get the wireless operator out through the floor first, all right?' shouted James, looking back behind him into the main body of the Bombay. He could see Gott – the general raised a hand in acknowledgement. *Thank God.*

A whoosh of air and dust blasted into the cockpit as the hatch opened, fanning the flames further inside. James cried out in pain, but they had now hit some softer sand, and as he kept the control column close into his stomach, the Bombay slowed. *Thirty miles per hour, twenty-five, twenty.*

'Now!' shouted James. He slid off his seat and, as he did so, the enemy fighters opened fire again, bullets and cannon-shells tearing into the cockpit. The instrument panel disintegrated, bits of glass and metal shattering and zipping around the narrow confines. James crouched, then saw that the heels of his boots were on fire. Around him, the Perspex was melting. He needed to get out, and fast – *Mackay and the wireless op are out. Good* – but he knew he had to make sure the general was safe. *If I can just get into the fuselage...*

45

General Gott had had his fair share of close calls – during the last war, and on several occasions in the desert. As soon as the bullets had started to hit the aircraft, he had known the situation was critical yet the seconds passed and still the Bombay was airborne. Then the enemy aircraft appeared to have flown on by and it was quickly apparent that the young pilot was doing a superb job. When the great hulk touched down, Gott felt certain all would be well, despite the smoke and faint lick of flames coming from the cockpit.

'We're in good hands,' he said, smiling re-assuringly. 'We'll be all right. Soon out of here.'

The co-pilot and medical orderly appeared, coughing and spluttering.

'We need to get the door off,' said the co-pilot.

Gott turned to the two ground crew who had accompanied the flight. 'You boys know what to do?'

'Yes, sir,' they replied.

Like the pilot, they were young. *Barely men at all*, thought Gott. 'Good,' he said, then turned back to the co-pilot and medical orderly. 'You two get back to the pilot. He needs you more than we do. We're all right here.'

Gott watched as the two crewmen opened the door and latched it backwards, then sat down again. The Bombay was slowing but suddenly the aircraft lurched, the catch on the door broke free and the door slammed shut again.

'Damn it!' said one of the ground crew. 'Excuse my French, sir.'

Gott smiled. 'Let's just get it open again quickly.'

The young man stood but the handle would

not turn. A look of panic spread over his face. 'It won't budge, sir,' he said.

'Here,' said Gott, 'let me have a try.' He stood and gripped the handle, but it was no use, it was wedged. The sudden force of it slamming back had jammed it. 'Have you got a wrench or a hammer or something?' Gott asked.

His voice was drowned by another burst of bullets and cannon-shells raking across the aircraft, followed by the roar of planes hurtling past. Gott glanced up and saw a ball of flame erupt just a few yards away.

'Oh, no,' he muttered, and then the wall of fire was upon him.

The same ball of flame now engulfing the fuselage had forced the pilot backwards, and so, with his shoes still on fire, his face and hands blistering, he went down through the hatch in the cockpit floor just as the undercarriage buckled and collapsed. Groping his way through thick clouds of smoke and past a burning tyre, he managed to get clear into blinding sunshine only for there to be another bang and the Bombay collapsed. He had avoided being crushed to death by a few seconds.

Staggering towards the rear of the plane, he looked for the crew and passengers, but saw only four men: Mackay, the medical officer, the wireless operator and one soldier, all blackened and bloodied.

'What?' he mumbled. 'Where are the others? Where are they? *Where are they?*'

'In there,' said Mackay, pointing to the burning wreck.

The aircraft was now a ball of fire, changing shape before James's eyes. Melting.

'No!' he said. 'No!' He looked at the others, then at his smouldering boots, his blackened hands, his singed uniform. For a moment he could not take in what had happened. Then his mind slowly cleared. Turning to the medical orderly, he said, 'You do your best for everyone. I'm going to try and get help.'

North. He had to head northwards, towards the coast. Head north and, with luck, he might bump into someone. Above, the sun beat down. He felt light-headed, disoriented, but strangely no pain. *Come on,* he told himself, *it's your only chance.*

James staggered across the desert, once tripping over a stone he had failed to notice, another time snagging his shredded shorts on some desert vetch. Numbed and still in shock, he managed several miles until, cresting a shallow ridge, he stumbled again and fell, fainting as he did so.

As his senses returned, he looked up to see a Bedouin standing over him.

'Inglese,' rasped James. *'Inglese.'* The Bedouin put some water to his mouth, then hoisted him to his feet and helped him on to a camel. *Jolting.* James smelt the thick hide of the camel, then closed his eyes. When he woke again he was still moving, the sun still beating down mercilessly. He closed his eyes again.

He was awake. The camel had stopped. Beside him the Bedouin had taken off his turban and was waving it and shouting. James slid off the camel, staggered to his feet. The Bedouin was pointing furiously and there, a few hundred yards ahead, was a small cloud of dust and vehicle.

Thank God, thought James, taking off his shirt. It was completely red. The truck now changed direction and began moving towards them. James watched it approach, and then there it was, a miracle, stopped in front of them, men getting out.

'Christ!' said a man from the RASC. 'You've got no hair. Your face is burned and look at your bloody hands! What the hell happened to you?'

James sank to his knees. 'General Gott,' he muttered. 'Bristol Bombay shot down.'

'Shot down? Christ, where is he?'

'Still in the plane,' gasped James. 'He's dead.'

2

Jack Tanner was awake, conscious of a fly crawling across his back. He lay face down on the bed, the thin sheet covering his legs and backside. His back and arms were bare, his tanned torso still livid with ugly red scars. Above him, the fan whirred, a faint warm breeze wafting over him, but there was no escape from the afternoon heat, not even with the shutters closed. Outside, the city throbbed, but here, in this compact room, the air was still. The fly flew off, but Tanner lay still, his eyes open, watching Lucie wash herself in the adjoining bathroom.

He had been wounded more than a month before when a shell had exploded nearby. He had

49

been lucky not to be severely maimed – or even killed – but shrapnel had peppered his back and left arm and one piece had lodged just below his left shoulder-blade. At the time he'd felt nothing and although it had made a bit of a mess and there had been a lot of blood, he had not been anything like as concerned as the men who had picked him up and seen his shredded behind.

On the journey back by field ambulance the pain had kicked in. Jolting up and down across the desert had been torture, made worse by the man on top slowly dying, his blood dripping through the canvas on to Tanner's front. Eventually he had been transferred to an old Bombay transport plane, flown to Heliopolis and then had suffered another brutal ambulance ride. By the time he had reached the 9th Scottish General Hospital, he had been dipping in and out of consciousness, his wounds were beginning to smell, and for a day or so, it had been touch and go as to whether or not he would pull through.

But he had and, with the piece of shell casing safely excavated, had made swift progress. After two and a half weeks in hospital, he had finally been discharged, thanks largely to Lucie Richoux. Good God, he had hated that hospital. He did not mind the heat normally, but in there it had been oppressive, and it had smelt of carbolic, faeces and festering wounds – the kind of cocktail it was hard to clear from the nose. The place specialized in burns, and certainly most of those in the beds alongside him were either airmen or cavalry – men who had screamed by day and even more so by night. Others had lain silently, swathed in bandages, legs, arms, and parts of their heads blown away. Tanner was not squeamish, but to see those men cut down and helpless, their lives ripped apart, was more than he could stomach.

To make matters worse, streams of women had been constantly parading through the wards. Wives of Cairo dignitaries, some wearing bright dresses, others sporting VAD and Red Cross uniforms, pushing trolleys filled with sandwiches or books, and urging those fit enough to take up embroidery. Tanner knew it was all well meant but he groaned inwardly when he saw them coming. He had no intention of sewing – he did enough of that mending his uniform without being chivvied into more by some middle-aged woman with a plum up her arse. There had been one lady who had repeatedly singled him out. She had obviously been of a determined nature and was not going to be denied by a taciturn infantryman. Patiently, Tanner had explained that he was perfectly capable of sewing, that he had nothing against anyone who wanted to sew, but that he did not wish to spend his convalescence embroidering regimental badges. Despite this, she refused to give up, accosting him every time she came in, which was every other day. Eventually he had hidden in the toilet whenever he saw her coming.

The one consolation had been Lucie. They had met more than two years earlier, during the retreat to Dunkirk when she had been working as a QA nurse. With an English mother and a French father, she had been brought up mostly in France, and although Tanner had lost track of her following his return to England, they had met again at the end of May during the Gazala battles when Tanner and a patrol of Yorks Rangers had had to pull back to the Free French fort at Bir Hacheim. As the British line crumbled, so Bir Hacheim had been left isolated, but after ten long days, the entire brigade, medical staff and attached Rangers had made a successful break-out.

After safely falling back to the Alamein position, Tanner had left Lucie once more to rejoin the rest of the battalion, while she had made her way to Cairo. After he'd spent ten days in hospital, though, there she had been, dressed in a nurse's uniform and standing by his bed, smiling. She had heard he was wounded and had been looking for him. Following their escape from Bir Hacheim, General König had decided that women would not accompany the Free French in future – not even nurses. Having discovered that Tanner had been sent to the 9th Scottish, she had offered her services, which had been gratefully accepted.

'I've got to get out of here, Luce,' he had told her, as she had sat by his bed, squeezing his hand.

'Soon,' she had told him. 'I've just got to sort out my flat. As soon as I'm in, I'll get you discharged and you can convalesce there. They'll be delighted. There aren't enough beds as it is.'

That had been true. Nine weeks of the heaviest fighting the desert war had seen had stretched the medical services in the Middle East to bursting point. As Lucie had predicted, the doctors at the 9th Scottish had discharged Tanner with no more than a cursory examination and a scrawled signature on his medical notes.

Stiff-backed and aching, Tanner had gingerly put on a fresh uniform and, with Lucie's help, had made his way back out into the dazzlingly bright city, hailed a taxi and headed south-west through the pulsating streets to the Midan. From there he went south towards Garden City and the embassy. Just to the north, in a street edging the banks of the Nile south of the Kasr El Nil Bridge, Lucie's second-floor flat was in a block that was not even ten years old. It was small and compact, but modern enough to have its own toilet and bathroom. Short of being in Garden City, it was positioned in one of the best locations in all of Cairo. It belonged to an uncle of Lucie's – a British uncle – who had been posted back to England at the outbreak of war. It had been let ever since, but after a long and time-consuming exchange of letters, Lucie had been granted permission to terminate the lease on the existing tenant and move in.

'I've been rather lucky, haven't I?' she had said, as she led him out on to the balcony.

'Not as lucky as me,' Tanner had replied. 'The timing's been faultless.'

'It has rather. It should have been last week, but the poor man was struggling to find new digs and pleaded with me to let him stay on a few more days.'

Tanner had leaned on the metal balcony rail to look out over the city. He could glimpse the Nile and the Gezira Sporting Club to the left, while ahead and to his right, the city shimmered in the morning haze. In the desert there was nothing: vast, mostly featureless scrub. Patrolling in their stripped-down trucks, he and his men had often spent days without seeing a soul. Even in the heat of battle, there was still plenty of space. But in Cairo everything – people, beasts, buildings, vehicles – was crammed together. The contrast could not have been greater.

For the first week, Tanner had done as Lucie instructed. He had remained in the flat, resting and, for once in his life, reading. In hospital he had leafed through a few magazines and copies of *Crusader*, but he had never had much call to read. His boyhood education had been limited, and even in winter there had always been other things to do during the long nights and short days. With his mother gone, Tanner had preferred to help his father in his job as a gamekeeper. In winter that had meant spending much of his time outside.

Now, however, as he had begun to feel more himself and, accordingly, more restless, he had picked up the books Lucie had brought home. The first had been *Under the Greenwood Tree*, which he enjoyed with mixed feelings of nostalgia and regret: the descriptions of the Wessex countryside had reminded him of the home he had not seen in ten years, while he recognized some of the characters in the older folk he had known as a boy. Then Lucie had brought two more, *The Mayor of Casterbridge* and *Far From the Madding Crowd*. Again, he had experienced the same sensations of delight, yearning and regret. The books had also taken him away from the war. Ever since he had sailed for Norway two years before, Tanner had been in almost continuous front-line operations. Of course, there had been brief moments of leave in England and in Cairo, but for the most part he had spent his time with other soldiers, and the war had never seemed very far away. Passing idle days reading and walking, then lying close with Lucie at night had made him feel cocooned, as though he belonged to a different world in which he was not expected to fight.

He had recognized that his enforced convalescence had done him good, but now, ten days on, he was restless. Lucie had begun a two-week stint of night duty, and although he was happy to spend the day in her arms, he struggled during the long nights. His wounds ached, but not enough to dampen his mind. Suddenly the world seemed to be carrying on without him.

Salvation was at hand, however. The 2nd Battalion, the King's Own Yorkshire Rangers, had suffered less than some units during the recent fighting, but still had casualties of around a third. Since they had been at the front line continuously since the Crusader offensive of the previous November, they had now been withdrawn for refitting at Mena Camp, just outside the city, next to the Pyramids. The previous day, he had sent a note to his company commander and friend, Captain Peploe, informing him of his steady progress and his hope that he would soon be passed fit for active service. That morning a reply had arrived: Peploe would visit him that evening. Tanner was surprised by how much he was looking forward to seeing him.

Tanner lay still, watching Lucie. She had a slight frame, with dark hair cut at the shoulders, and a neat, compact face with full lips and large brown eyes. He had thought her pretty the first time he had laid eyes on her in that farmhouse in Flanders, and he had not changed his mind.

Sensing him watching her, she turned and smiled.

'You're very lovely, you know,' he said.

She blew him a kiss. 'Are you sure you feel up to going out tonight?'

'Yes. I won't go mad.'

She wrapped herself in a towel, then sat on the edge of the bed beside him and ran a hand over his shoulders. The towel fell away, revealing her naked body. 'I know you want to get back to them,' she said, 'so I really wouldn't overdo it. You're doing so well, but you could easily have a setback.'

'I might just have a drink with him here.'

She raised an eyebrow and smiled again, and Tanner reached out and pulled her towards him.

'Tempting though this is, I must get dressed.'

Tanner sighed and eased himself on to his side, so that he could watch her. Knickers, bra, white cotton uniform with claret shoulder pips denoting her rank as captain in the QAIMNS.

'It's rude to stare,' she said.

'I can't help it. You know I love a girl in uniform.'

Lucie laughed. 'What time is Captain Peploe coming?'

'He didn't say. Hopefully not too late.' He picked up the wristwatch from the small cabinet

56

beside the bed. The strap had been white once but was now grey with sweat and grime. 'Quarter past five,' he said.

She gathered her hair into a clasp. 'I must go. Have a good evening, Jack. See you in the morning.' She bent down and kissed him.

'Thank you,' he said, clasping her hand. 'I mean it. For everything. For these past days, for finding me in that hospital and rescuing me.'

'Trouble is,' she said, 'I know it's not going to last. You'll be off again soon and I'm dreading it. I'll miss you, Jack. You've been lucky so far and I'm worried you might not be next time.'

'I'll be all right. I've got a guardian angel – didn't I tell you?'

Tanner knew that Captain Peploe was not the most punctual of people, and had been preparing himself not to see his friend until much later. However, a little more than an hour after Lucie had departed, there was a knock on the door, and Tanner, already dressed, opened it to see Peploe standing before him, hair as dishevelled as ever and wearing the grin he had come to know so well.

'Well, you've landed on your feet!' he said, clasping Tanner's hand and making a quick visual sweep of the flat. 'How are you? Feeling better?'

'Much, thank you, sir.'

'Oh, less of the "sir",' said Peploe, slapping him on the arm. Then, seeing Tanner wince, 'Sorry about that.'

Tanner laughed. 'It's all right. Honestly, I'm almost as good as new. I'm hoping I might get signed off next week.'

'We're missing you, of course, but don't rush it.'

'You sound like Lucie.'

'She's right. You should listen to her.'

'Drink?' said Tanner.

Peploe clapped his hands together. 'Shall we go out? You're dressed so that means you must be feeling up to it.'

'I'd much rather, if I'm honest.'

'Good. We can go to the Union. No one will get sniffy about officers and NCOs drinking together there.'

They walked down to the embassy, then climbed into one of the gharries waiting there and headed across the bridge on to Gezira Island and round the edge of the Sporting Club. In twenty minutes they had reached the Union. Unlike the Gezira Sporting Club, which was Europeans and officers only, the Union Club had been created to promote friendship between the British and the Egyptians, although as they pulled up outside and walked to the front of the clubhouse, Tanner could see only a couple of Egyptians, deep in conversation, wearing western suits and red tarbooshes.

'I know, I know,' said Peploe, when Tanner pointed this out. 'But it's not as stuffy as some of the others. There are as many desk-wallahs and civvies as there are uniforms.' He nodded towards a table of three men a few yards away. 'And learned types with spectacles. At least Egyptians are *allowed* to come here.'

The grounds at the rear bordered the massive lawns of the Sporting Club, and were shaded by a row of vast, ancient trees. Peploe led Tanner to

58

a table, and sat down. He sighed and briefly closed his eyes. 'I know it's not the done thing to whinge about desert life, but you've got to admit this is rather pleasant.'

Tanner smiled.

'A decent bit of shade and birds chirping away merrily in the foliage above. I miss the lack of natural noise in the desert. It's all shouting and engines.'

'What about the flies buzzing?' asked Tanner.

'Very funny. You know what I mean.' A white-coated *suffragi* approached them. 'Two Stellas, please,' said Peploe. 'And put it on my tab, will you?'

They were silent a moment. Tanner pulled out a packet of cigarettes and offered one to Peploe, who took it. Having lit both, he said, 'So. What's the news from the battalion?'

Peploe exhaled heavily. 'Not much, really. Replacements are coming in, green as hell, but we're still understrength. Ivo's taken over D Company, which is re-forming. He wanted to take Mac, but I put my foot down about that.' He grinned. 'Said he could have Hepworth, but he turned his nose up at him.'

Tanner laughed. 'Good. I like Hep. Bloody whiner, but he usually comes good in a scrap. Who's taking over as second in command?'

'Dunno yet. I'm having to fend on my own, although Sykes is making a pretty good fist of being acting CSM.'

'Not too good, I hope. I want my job back.'

The beers arrived and Peploe raised his glass. 'Here's how,' he said. 'Good to see you up and smiling, Jack. You had us all worried there. How are you feeling – honestly?'

'Just a bit stiff and sore. My arm hurts when I raise it, but it's improving each day. I'm not worried, put it that way.'

'Good. It looks like we might be getting a few gongs, by the way. Croix de Guerres all round for those of us at Bir Hacheim.'

'Anything else?'

'I'm getting a bar to the MC and I think you're up for something too. You, Sykes and Brown. Might only be MID, though.'

Tanner pulled a loose piece of tobacco from his lips. 'Congratulations, but as we all know, it's a load of old bollocks, really.'

'Old Man Vigar keeps putting in for them. It makes his battalion look good. Still, I reckon we're as deserving as anyone.'

Their attention was caught by a couple of uniformed men hurrying over to one of the tables, followed by exclamations of astonishment.

'Christ, what's happened now?' said Peploe. One of the men turned and ran his hands through his hair in what seemed to be disbelief. 'Hey, I know him – I met him a few days ago at Mena House.'

'Who is he?' asked Tanner.

'A Kiwi squadron leader. Archie Flynn.' He waved and caught Flynn's eye. Flynn waved back, then came over.

'Archie,' said Peploe, holding out his hand. 'What the hell's going on?'

'Bad news, I'm afraid,' he said, pushing back his cap and wiping his brow. 'Strafer Gott's been killed.'

'What?'

'Yeah, poor bastard. Only made Eighth Army commander last night or this morning, or something. Must be the shortest appointment ever.'

'How?' asked Tanner.

Peploe sat there, incredulity written on his face, then remembered himself. 'Apologies,' he said. 'Archie, this is Jack Tanner. Jack, this is Squadron Leader Flynn.'

Flynn nodded at him. 'Seems like he was shot down this afternoon on his way up here.'

'Didn't he have an escort?' asked Peploe.

'No. Just jumped on a routine transport trip at the last minute.' Flynn glanced towards his friends. 'Look, I'd better get back. Sorry to be the bearer of bad news.'

The two men sat in silence for a moment. Then Tanner said, 'I wonder who'll take over now. Someone already out here, or someone from home?'

'Home,' said Peploe. 'I've almost forgotten what it's like. I don't know about you, Jack, but I feel so detached from home out here. The desert, our battles with Rommel – it's all pretty narrow, isn't it?'

'What do you mean?'

'Well – for us, the desert war is everything, but there's a much larger war going on in Russia, isn't there? There are all those convoys and now there's a war in the Pacific as well, but we don't know anything about that, do we? We just know our own little battles here. I mean, I have no idea what England's like now, after all this time. I know they've been suffering with the Blitz, but what do you think it's done to London and all those other cities? I wonder whether my parents have aged and what my sister looks like now. It's been nearly two years. Two years! That's a long time.'

'We've got to believe we're playing an important part here, though.'

'I'm sure we are, but don't you ever wonder where it's going to end? We've been back and forth across this desert, and every time there's a battle lots of good men get killed – but there never seems to be that one decisive action, does there? We can't keep up this ding-dong for ever. I just feel so in the dark, as though there's no real plan and no light at the end of the tunnel. I worry that the war will never end.' He drank some of his beer. 'By the way,' he added, 'have you heard who's taking over from the Auk?'

'Lucie told me.'

'Your old friend General Alexander.'

'That's good news, I reckon. He'll sort things out.'

'Maybe.'

Tanner took out another cigarette and lit it. 'I feel quite hopeful, really. I'm sorry about old Strafer, but I reckon it'll be all right now. Back at the end of June I really did think it might be all over out here, but we've held Rommel now and it'll be a hell of a lot easier to reinforce our lot with the front line just up the road than it will be for them. And the Yanks are in now. They've got to play a part soon. Actually, I heard there are some Yankee pilots in the Desert Air Force already. America's a big place, isn't it?'

'Certainly.'

'Lots of manpower, lots of factories.'

'Lots of money.'

'There you go, then.'

Peploe smiled. 'Maybe you're right.'

'You need a bit of leave. You should get yourself wounded and you'll get given convalescence. I recommend it.'

Peploe laughed. 'It helps when you've got a lovely popsie like Lucie to look after you and a swanky flat near the river. She doesn't have a sister, does she?'

They talked on, then had something to eat and decided to call it a day. 'There is one other thing, Jack,' said Peploe, as they walked out to the front of the club towards the waiting gharries and taxis.

'Yes?' said Tanner.

'The colonel wants to see you. Any chance you could get yourself out to Mena tomorrow?'

'Of course. What time?'

'Six o'clock sound all right?'

Tanner nodded. 'Fine. Do you know what it's about?'

'Yes, as a matter of fact, I do.'

'What, then?'

Peploe grinned. 'You'll have to wait and see.' He held out his hand. 'Good night, Jack.'

3

Saturday, 8 August 1942, around 7.45 a.m. The day always began early at the headquarters of Secret Intelligence Middle East, just as it did in all the offices of the sprawling General Headquarters, Middle East. Despite the fans that whirred from the ceilings, the shutters and blinds, it was only during the first few hours of daylight that the heat of the day could be avoided. By mid-morning, energy levels were ebbing, as was the ability to think clearly and cogently. That was why Major Alex Vaughan had already been in his office an hour and a half, at first reading the latest sitreps and the reports on the death of General Gott the day before, and now continuing work on a paper he had been preparing for a couple of weeks.

It was a proposal to establish coastal raiding parties. Working for SIME was interesting enough, but he was still only twenty-nine and had fully recovered from the wounds he had suffered back in February. He felt his age and front-line experience were wasted while he had to work as an intelligence 'operative', as Maunsell liked to call them, in Cairo. More than that, he was well aware that a number of his old Middle East Commando comrades had recently been having spectacular successes with their so-called SAS operations behind enemy lines. It had made him thirst for more obvious action.

He had talked to David Stirling about these raids several times. Rather than operating hundreds of miles south in the desert, Vaughan believed there was scope for using the new fast motor torpedo boats based at Alexandria in a similar fashion, on ports rather than the landing grounds that were the primary targets of the SAS. His idea was to put together small squads of four to six men, who would infiltrate Axis-held ports, blow up as much shipping and port facilities as possible, and get out under cover of the ensuing mayhem. A little more than a year before, on Crete, he had performed a not dissimilar action in the port of Heraklion. That had carried plenty of risks, but they had pulled it off. He saw no reason why it could not be repeated, and yet was well aware that there was no point in suggesting such a scheme until he had prepared his case thoroughly. There was much scepticism about special operations within GHQ: it was why Middle East Commando had been disbanded the previous year.

Admittedly, Stirling's SAS had been successful – spectacularly so just a few weeks earlier when they had smashed the landing ground of Sidi Haniesh – but many viewed Stirling and his band as little more than a bunch of unreliable mavericks. Then there was the Long Range Desert Group, and also the Special Operations Executive. None of those outfits could offer what Vaughan had in mind, but persuading the powers-that-be to back another special-ops force would not be easy.

But it was worth a try. He blew away a fly, then looked out of the window towards the high palms outside. His office was on the second floor of an old block of flats at the southern end of Garden City. To those in SIME it was known as Red Pillars, partly due to the brick entrance portico, and partly as a nod to Grey Pillars, the original GHQ building across the way in Tolombat Street. Vaughan lit a cigarette, but no sooner had he begun writing again than the phone rang. It was Brigadier Bill Williams, the director of Military Intelligence.

'Good morning, sir,' said Vaughan.

'I've just had RJ on the phone,' said Williams, 'asking to see the survivors from the Gott crash. Any idea what that's all about?'

'Er, no, but we haven't had morning prayers yet. You want me to find out?'

'Yes – sharpish. I need to be on top of this immediately, especially with the PM and CIGS still in town.'

'Of course, sir.'

Vaughan put the receiver down and leaned back in his chair. *Damn it*. Maunsell hadn't mentioned anything about it to him. He was supposed to be one of Maunsell's deputies – one of the senior officers in SIME – yet all too often he felt out of the loop. 'Christ, what am I doing here?' he muttered to himself. He'd been in the job two months now – it had been a sideways move from working as assistant to the then DMI, Brigadier de Guingand, at GHQ. That had always been a stop-gap and Vaughan, fully recovered from being wounded during Crusader, had found it frustrating in the extreme. He had liked de Guingand well enough, but being a desk-wallah, with the endless bureaucracy and red tape, had been more than he could

66

stomach. The chance to work for Maunsell had seemed like a step in the right direction.

He liked and respected Maunsell, who had shown nothing but cheerful encouragement from the outset. 'Most SIME operatives when first recruited,' he had told Vaughan, 'have had little or no experience of counter-espionage work and have to learn on the job. And, in my humble opinion, that's the best way. You'll be fine, Alex. It's all about common sense.' He had held up a pink folder and waved it at him. 'Judging from your file, you've got plenty of that.'

Even so, understanding the myriad components of SIME, who did what and under whom, had been a challenge in itself. After his experiences as an agent operating on Crete, he had believed he understood something of the arcana of counter-intelligence work, yet he soon discovered that counted for little.

SOE, with whom he had worked on Crete, were quite separate. 'A different beast altogether,' Maunsell had explained, over lunch at the Sporting Club on Vaughan's first day in the job. 'They're all about stirring up trouble in enemy-occupied territories. Our task is to catch any enemy should they come here. It's also to knock subversion on the head. We're fortunate that most Egyptians seem happy enough with the Wafd Government, but there are subversive elements – anti-British dissidents who are prepared to help the Axis if they feel it will support their cause. But I expect you know something of these types.'

Vaughan had nodded. 'Young Egypt, the Ring of Iron, the Muslim Brotherhood.'

67

'Exactly – those are the main ones. Mind you, they'd have an almighty shock if the Germans ever did take over Egypt. We don't have quite the same level of intolerance as the Nazis.'

There were other intelligence organizations, Maunsell explained: A Force, which was responsible for enemy deception measures; and the Inter-Services Liaison Department, which was, to all intents and purposes, MI6's Middle East wing, broadly responsible for intelligence gathering from within Axis-held territories. 'We help each other,' Maunsell had told him, 'but when it comes to counter-intelligence, we rule the roost, so to speak. It's important work. I hope you'll find it rewarding, too.'

Vaughan rubbed his eyes. *Ah, such hopes.* So much for racing down side-streets on the trail of enemy spies! Most of the active fieldwork – tailing suspects, handling informers – was carried out by Major Sansom's Field Security teams, based on the third floor. 'Our active arm in Cairo,' Maunsell had told him. True, Vaughan had interrogated a number of suspects, and had played a peripheral role in the recent Eppler case, but it was accepted within SIME that Major Tilly, Berlin born of English parents and an expert in German phonetics, and Captain Henry Krichewsky, a Sephardi Jew and Egyptian, as well as an old friend of Maunsell, were the masters of interrogation. There had not yet been an Axis suspect whom Tilly had been unable to break. It was also true that Vaughan had discovered the wife of a British general was sleeping with a known dissident member of Young Egypt, but he'd felt no elation in arresting both.

Rather, it had seemed sordid.

He had also discovered that while some of the defence security officers within SIME had distinct roles and areas of expertise, the four principal officers, of whom he was now one, had less specific roles and operated independently. 'Think of it as barristers' chambers,' Maunsell had told him. 'We're all here to help each other, we're all in it together, but we also do our own thing.'

As the new boy, Vaughan had found this frustrating because, rather than learning on the job, he felt he was left in the dark. And now de Guingand's successor, Bill Williams, had rung about the Gott plane survivors and he had known nothing. It was irritating. No, it was humiliating.

Vaughan stood up and walked out of his office, down a short stretch of corridor and paused by a wooden door with a brown plaque that said, 'Colonel R. J. Maunsell'. He rapped lightly.

'Come,' said a voice.

Vaughan entered to see Maunsell looking up at him expectantly from behind his desk. It was a simple room, but spacious and light; the shutters were back, the twin windows open. Outside, starlings chattered in the trees, while beyond he could hear the faint drone of the city, a near constant low rumble. On one wall, there was a large map of Egypt, and on another, a street-map of Cairo. The furniture comprised some filing cabinets, an easy chair and side-table, a desk surrounded by several teak and rattan chairs, and another desk, on which stood several trays, a jug of water, and an ash-tray crammed with cigarette stubs.

'Morning, Alex,' said Maunsell. He was a tall

man, and immaculately dressed in a dove-grey flannel suit, with a tie-pin in his green, red and brown Royal Tank Regiment tie, his only nod to an active soldiering past. Vaughan had rarely seen Maunsell in uniform, despite the regular commission he still held; he had let it be known that he did not mind what his team wore – civvies or uniform – but Vaughan preferred khaki drill. He liked to think of himself as a soldier still and felt the uniform helped. However, as Maunsell had told him when he had first joined, secret intelligence work was not at all like normal soldiering, and indeed, although there were a number of regular officers at SIME, most were not. One of Maunsell's informalities was his use of first names. Among his senior staff – and that included Vaughan – there was no saluting, no use of 'sir'. Maunsell was not 'Colonel' but 'RJ', as his wife and friends in civvy life knew him. 'There's nothing to be gained by having military-type discipline here, Alex,' Maunsell had told him, when he'd first joined. 'We've got RAF and RNVR types, civilians with honorary or temporary commissions, to say nothing of the extremely hard-working and efficient lady civilians – they're all part of the show and we all work together and for each other.'

'Come and have a seat,' Maunsell said to him now, proffering a chair in front of his desk.

'Thanks,' Vaughan said.

'What can I do for you?'

'I've just had the DMI on the phone.'

'Ye-es,' said Maunsell, an eyebrow raised.

'He says you've asked to interview the survivors from Gott's plane.'

70

'Yes. It seems there might be something rather fishy going on there.'

'Really?' said Vaughan. 'The report I've seen from Tac HQ suggested it was a chance encounter. It all seems rather cut and dried to me.'

Maunsell smiled, then extravagantly stretched his arm from his cuff and looked at his watch. 'Ten to eight. Look, Alex, tell you what, let's bring morning prayers forward. I'll give the others a ring.'

'All right. I promised Bill Williams I'd get back to him as soon as I could.'

'And you must. We don't want the poor fellow to burst a blood vessel. I know they're all rather twitchy at GHQ, and who can blame them?' He picked up his phone, smiled affably at Vaughan as he waited to be connected, then said, 'Could you ask Majors Jones, Maddox and Kirk to come here right away? Thanks so much.' Putting the receiver down, he said, 'Damn, I should have asked her to bring us some coffee too.' He began filling a pipe.

'I have to say, I felt a bit of a fool speaking to Bill, RJ,' said Vaughan. 'I hadn't heard anything about this.'

'Well, I apologize for your blushes, of course, but I didn't want all of you involved – not until we had something to play with. It all happened late last night. You weren't in your office so Paddy and I dealt with it. I thought I'd brief you all at morning prayers. No deliberate slight on my part, I assure you. Anyway,' he clapped his hands together, 'on a different tack, who do you think will take over from Gott, Alex?'

'My money's on an outsider.'

71

'I think you could be right.'

'Have you heard anything?'

Maunsell shrugged. 'A few murmurings. Montgomery's name has been bandied about. Apparently the CIGS favours him. I heard that he even wanted him ahead of Gott but the PM overruled him.'

'Monty, eh?'

'You know him?'

'Served under him in France. He's a funny cove. A rather thin, nasal voice – tiny too. Bloody good on the operational side. During the retreat, he moved the entire division to the back of another to fill a gap in the line in just one night.'

Maunsell looked impressed and was about to say something, when the door opened and Kirk and Maddox came in.

'Morning, George, Paddy. Come and sit down.'

No sooner had they done so than Major Jones tapped on the door and walked in. 'Morning, all, sorry to have kept you,' he said.

'You haven't, KJ,' said Maunsell. 'Now, first things first, can I get anyone a drink? Alex and I were planning on coffee.'

There were mumbles of agreement from the others. Vaughan drummed his fingers on his crossed leg.

'Coffee for five, Daphne, if you'd be so kind,' said Maunsell, into the telephone. Then he sat up, his fingers together. 'Hope you don't mind me bringing morning prayers forward a little, but Alex and I have been speaking with the DMI this morning. Obviously we don't really need his permission to interview the Gott crash survivors, but in the circumstances I thought it would be tactful to ask it. What with the VIPs in town, everyone's a bit on edge.'

'And Gott was the army commander, after all,' said Jones. 'They've a right to know what's going on.'

'As have we all,' said Vaughan. 'I'm still completely in the dark.'

'Me too,' said Kirk.

'But not for much longer now we're all here.' Maunsell beamed at them paternally and picked up his unlit pipe once more. He struck a match and puffed several billows of blue-grey smoke, which swirled around him but rapidly dispersed under the ceiling fan. He leaned back in his chair, which creaked. 'Do you want to explain, Paddy?' he asked Maddox.

Maddox glanced at Maunsell, then turned to Vaughan. He was in his thirties, a thin-faced man with gingery hair. 'We think there may have been foul play,' he said, 'which is why it is imperative that we speak to the survivors. The pilot especially.'

'Is this our Axis circuit?' asked Kirk.

'Maybe,' said Maddox.

'What Axis circuit?' asked Vaughan, his hackles rising once more.

Kirk smiled. 'An old chestnut of RJ's. You know, I'm still not very convinced about this.'

'All right, George,' said Maunsell. 'Just hear us out.'

Maddox cleared his throat. He was a softly spoken man, thin-lipped. *And tight-lipped*, thought Vaughan.

73

'First of all, let me say this,' he said. 'Since April, not one transport plane has been shot down, yet the moment General Gott gets into one, it's attacked by German fighter aircraft. And not only is it shot down, but utterly destroyed. Twenty-one people were killed, including Gott. That in itself is suspicious.'

'It got my alarm bells ringing,' added Maunsell.

'Possibly,' said Kirk.

'Have a look at these,' added Maddox. He took a buff envelope on his lap and passed it first to Vaughan. In it there were photographs, some taken from directly above, some oblique.

Vaughan was surprised. 'That was quick work. We only heard about Gott's death yesterday afternoon.'

'We have our wing-co to thank for that,' said Maunsell.

Vaughan examined the pictures, then passed them to Kirk and Jones. The wreck was still partially obscured by smoke, but the cockpit and wing ends could still be clearly seen. 'Looking at these, it's amazing anyone survived at all.'

'Yes,' agreed Maddox. 'It is, isn't it?'

'But what do you see on the wings?' asked Maunsell. He passed over a magnifying glass.

'A lot of damage.'

'A lot of bullet holes,' agreed Maunsell. 'It looks as though the plane was riddled with them. Quite a lot of effort just to knock out a slow and rather vulnerable Bristol Bombay, wouldn't you say?'

Vaughan stroked his chin. 'Yes,' he said at length. 'You may have a point there.'

74

'So we have two aberrations,' said Kirk. 'First, that a transport was actually shot down.'

'And second, that it was absolutely pummelled – more so than would seem necessary,' added Maunsell.

'Or than is usual practice,' said Vaughan.

Kirk passed the photographs back to Maddox. 'I concede you may have something there, but I don't see why this should be connected to your so-called Axis circuit. I thought we'd put that to bed.'

Vaughan was about to speak when there was a knock on the door and Daphne Lambert, Maunsell's secretary, came in with a tray.

All five men were quiet as she poured the coffee and passed around the cups.

'Thank you, Daphne,' said Maunsell, then waited for her to leave. When she had closed the door, he said, 'As you know, Alex–'

'Sorry, but hold on a moment, what Axis circuit?'

'You may well ask,' said Kirk.

'We're not sure exactly,' said Maunsell. 'It's something we've been wondering about for a while. Since you joined, there's been the Eppler case, various other things going on and, I'll admit, not much to arouse suspicion on that score. It's also true that, while we have our fair share of subversive elements here in Cairo, most, thank God, are amateurs, poorly connected. Even if they do get wind of stuff, it's generally low grade and their means of passing it on to the Axis are limited.'

'As we discovered with Eppler,' said Kirk.

'Quite so.'

'And we should also be clear here,' added Kirk,

75

'it's very difficult for enemy agents to get into Cairo or Alexandria. You can't cross the desert without transport, which would always be spotted if you did manage it, and once here, there are enough informers to get wind of anyone suddenly acting suspiciously. And, as I've always said, yes, agreed, there are thousands of officials, officers and their wives who, inflamed with cheap booze, might chatter about the war. But what do they know that's of any importance? And we're a hell of lot more secure here now that those various Axis legations have been shut down. The Romanian mission has gone, thank God.'

'Yes, yes, I accept all that,' said Maunsell, 'but it doesn't mean the cell doesn't exist.'

'Or that it does.'

Maunsell made a rare sound of exasperation. 'Just for the moment, George, let's assume that it does and that for the past couple of months it's been lying dormant.'

'What if the cell has been operating all the time?' said Jones, joining the discussion for the first time. 'The best intelligence is that which is used in tandem with another source that hides the original information.'

'Such as?' said Vaughan.

'Well, for example, your spy gleans some information about the movement of a convoy and passes that information on. The enemy then sends over a number of reconnaissance aircraft, one or more of which actually passes over the convoy. When the convoy is attacked, those in the convoy will think the reconnaissance plane is the source when, in fact, it is merely providing verification of the original information passed on by the spy.'

'Yes, all right, but what evidence have we got for a cell existing?'

'Very little,' said Kirk.

Maunsell sighed. 'Our role here is counter-intelligence. If there is so much as a whiff of the enemy receiving classified information and we have the power to prevent it, it is our sworn duty to do so. I agree that we have no actual proof yet, but I've been in this game a good while now and one thing I've learned is to trust my gut instinct.' He looked at Vaughan. 'I have a hunch, Alex, a hunch that has never gone away but which has most definitely been rekindled in light of the events of the past twenty-four hours. Now, I'm well aware that radio security in the field is not the best, and I'm also conscious that they have reconnaissance planes operating just as we do, and taken in isolation one could put down a lot of these "misfortunes" – for want of a better word – to nothing more than ill-luck and coincidence.'

'But add them together...'

'...and a rather sinister pattern emerges.'

'By interviewing the pilot and survivors,' Maddox continued, 'we might get a much clearer picture of what really happened.'

'And this might help us,' added Maunsell, 'not only in determining whether there really is an Axis circuit operating here, but if there is, it might be the chink of light we need to break it. As KJ has rightly pointed out, intelligence is best when backed up, but it may be that they've finally made a mistake. And, needless to say, if I'm right and it does exist, we need to break it as soon as possible.'

'I can see that,' agreed Vaughan.

'I don't need to tell you,' said Maunsell, 'that we have reached a critical moment – not just in the Middle East, but in the entire war. If we can break the Axis's grip on the Mediterranean, we'll surely knock Italy out of the war. If we do that – well, who knows? On the other hand, matters are finely balanced at the moment. Eighth Army has only just avoided annihilation, half the command has been sacked, the new commander's just been killed, the next C-in-C is yet to arrive, promised American supplies of tanks have not yet reached us, and confidence is, to put it mildly, pretty low at present. We know that – we've all read the morale reports.'

Vaughan nodded thoughtfully. 'An effective spy ring might just make all the difference.'

'Indeed. And particularly at key moments when victory or defeat balance on a knife edge,' said Maunsell. He leaned even further forward. 'As I've said to all of you before, the war out here is about supplies. I know there's been a lot of agonizing about German tactics, but to all intents and purposes our armies are pretty evenly matched. What it boils down to is who can get the most fuel and tanks and ammunition to the front at the critical moments. And that's where what we do plays such an important role. Gott's death is a tragedy and may yet prove an even bigger blow than it seems right now, but what's been worrying me is how much the enemy seems to know about our LOCs and when supplies are coming.'

'I don't disagree with you, RJ,' said Kirk. 'I just

think we're becoming too wrapped up in our own cocoon here. We're in the secret intelligence business so maybe we're seeing enemy spies when it's far more likely that there are none.'

'You said it was a hunch, RJ,' said Vaughan. 'You must have reasons for that.'

Maunsell relit his pipe and nodded. 'Take the Malta convoys. Usually no more than a handful of ships, making them hard to spot, even by reconnaissance planes. And the Mediterranean's a big place, you know. Four merchant ships and a few escorts on that vast sea – yet time and again, U-boats, Italian warships and aircraft seem to pick them up with ease. And now I've a hunch about Gott's death. It doesn't seem right to me. I agree with George that it can be tempting to see something suspicious and immediately think the worst when there's probably a perfectly innocent reason for that behaviour, but I am suspicious about this, and until I've been given good evidence to think otherwise, I think we should all treat it very seriously indeed.'

'I see,' said Vaughan.

'So it is of vital importance to find out as much as we can from the survivors of the wreck before it's too late.'

'Are there guards watching out for them?' asked Vaughan.

'Yes,' said Maunsell, 'but that's no guarantee of their safety.'

'In that case, hadn't we better get going?'

'Yes, Alex, you had.'

'Me?' said Vaughan, surprised.

'Yes. You and Paddy.'

'All right,' said Vaughan, 'but I should probably see the DMI first.'

'No – just ring him. No need for details, but tell him that in your judgement it's essential we see them now. We've been chinwagging here quite long enough. I think you chaps ought to collect Wing-co and get going.'

'Right,' said Vaughan. 'I'll ring him right away. And if I can't get hold of him?'

'Then go anyway. Look, George, Alex – all of you – if I *am* right, I hope you understand what's at stake here.'

'I do,' Vaughan replied, pushing back his chair and standing up. 'I see it very clearly indeed.'

The DMI, Brigadier Williams, had accepted Vaughan's judgement.

'All right, Vaughan,' he'd said, 'but go easy on those boys. From what I hear they're in a bad way. One of these days soon you can tell me all about it.'

They went in Maddox's car, leaving the wide, curving, verdant avenues of Garden City for the clamour and bustle of the centre of town. Vehicles and animals vied for space, but Maddox drove through the crowded streets with apparent imperturbability, accelerating when he could but always ready to jam on his brakes.

Vaughan knew a little about Maddox – that he had been an Intelligence Corps officer back in England and had been posted to SIME early the previous year. He was unmarried, spoke German and Italian. Drank little. They did not socialize.

'I've never asked, Paddy,' he said, as they

skirted around two camels. 'Do you like it out here in Cairo?'

'Hmm,' he replied. 'Do I like Cairo? I'm not sure I'd use that word. It's certainly a fascinating place. What about you?'

'That's not a bad way of putting it,' agreed Vaughan. 'It's an assault on the senses, particularly when you're coming back from the desert. And there's no blackout like there is in England. One can drink, party, play sport, eat reasonably well, find a woman.'

'All those things and more,' agreed Maddox.

'And there aren't as many flies here as there are in the desert – thank God.'

'No,' laughed Maddox. 'That's a blessing.'

'And yet,' added Vaughan, 'it's also a steaming hot, stinking cesspit and a long way from home.'

Maddox smiled. 'Oh, I'm pretty well acclimatized now.'

They reached the hospital and, after a few minutes' wait, were joined by a QA captain. 'Sorry to keep you waiting,' she said. 'Dr Carter asked me to take you to the men.' She held out her hand. 'I'm Captain Lucie Richoux.'

Very pretty, thought Vaughan. 'I'm sorry we've got to bother these men now,' he began.

'They're hardly in a state to be interviewed,' she replied. 'Could it not have waited?'

'Sadly, no,' said Maddox.

She led them up a flight of wide stairs, then along several linoleum-lined corridors that reeked of disinfectant and a sweet, sickly stench Vaughan knew all too well. Flies crawled over the windows and darted across their way. He flapped

81

his hand – a useless pursuit, as he was aware. 'It's almost as bad as the desert,' he said. Captain Richoux turned. 'The flies, I mean.'

'Oh, I see,' she said. 'Yes, I know. All this rotting flesh.' She led them into a ward of about forty men. Vaughan realized it was the very one he had been sent to back in February. *Ah, but it was cooler then.* Now he saw a sea of misery, badly wounded men struggling with the already rising heat.

'They're down here,' said the nurse, leading them through the doors at the end into another corridor. Halfway along, a sentry stood guard.

'We've arrived,' said Vaughan.

'How did you guess?' said Captain Richoux.

The guard snapped to attention. Vaughan saluted, then, with Maddox, followed the nurse into the room. The stench was powerful. Venetian blinds covered the two windows, ensuring the light was dim. There were six beds, three on each side, although only four were being used. A nurse was tending one of the men, cleaning his arm. Another was coughing, then cried out in pain. 'It's all right,' said Captain Richoux, to the other nurse. 'I'll see to it.' She picked up a glass of water and put the straw to the man's lips.

Vaughan was dismayed. All four men were badly burned, their wounds largely left unbandaged and glistening. A fan turned slowly above, while an electric one whirred from a cabinet between the windows.

'There're only four here,' said Maddox.

'One is having an operation.'

Maddox nodded. 'And the pilot?'

'Over here.' She pointed to the bed in the

82

corner on the left side of the room. He was sitting propped up, bandages wrapped across his shoulder; his hands, lower arms and legs were severely burned. The flesh was bare and red in places, blackened around the edges, blotchy and blistered. His hair had almost completely gone, with only thin tufts remaining, the skin purple and yellow, as were his nose and cheeks. His eyelids were swollen.

Vaughan swallowed and wished they could leave immediately.

'As you can see,' said Captain Richoux, 'he has severe burns, but has also taken a bullet through his shoulder. I'm afraid we've had to give him some morphine, so his senses are somewhat dulled.' She rubbed her face, then caught Vaughan's eye. 'I'm sorry. It's been a long night.'

'How long have you been on duty?'

'Since six yesterday evening.'

'A long shift.'

'It happens sometimes.'

Maddox cleared his throat and turned to the pilot. 'From the report I've read,' he began, 'you're clearly a remarkable young man. I sincerely apologize for having to barge in on you, but please be assured that we wouldn't have done so, were it not of vital importance.'

Vaughan watched the blistered lips move.

'It's all right,' rasped James.

'Good man,' said Maddox. He took out a pocket book and pencil, then turned again towards Captain Richoux. 'I'm sorry, but please would you and your colleague leave us for a moment?'

'I'd rather not,' she replied. 'These men are in

83

no fit state to be interviewed as it is.'

Maddox smiled thinly. 'Very well.' He turned back to Flight Sergeant James. 'How many aircraft attacked you?'

'Six.'

'And were they all German single-engine Me 109s?'

A nod. 'They shot out one engine and then the next.' His voice was barely audible, a slurred rasp. 'I was only at fifty feet. Setting one on fire was enough to bring me down. But they shot out both.'

'And you managed to land the Bombay?'

'Yes. Couldn't get the tail down for ages. Then it dropped as the 109s came back for another attack. But I was already down. The Bombay was never going to fly again ... covered with bullet holes, two engines on fire.'

'And this was unusual on their part?'

'Very. It's usually the machine you're trying to destroy, not the men inside. They would have known we had wounded on board.'

Maddox nodded. 'So you think they were deliberately trying to kill you?'

'It doesn't take six 109s and two sweeps to destroy a Bombay.'

Maddox smiled. 'Thank you – this is most helpful. We're nearly there, Sergeant. And why was the fuselage hatch not opened?'

'I gave orders for it to be opened. We had different ground crew on board – two new boys. I can only think they might have opened it but not lifted it off completely, which was what they were supposed to do. Somehow, it must have swung back and shut itself again. That's all I can think of, because they had signalled that it was open yet no one got out.'

'I see.' Maddox looked pensive. 'So then you went to get help?'

'Yes.'

'Do you know what time this was?'

'Just after three.'

'And do you have any idea what time it was when you reached the RASC headquarters?'

'Yes, because my watch was still working and I was amazed that it was. It was two hours later. Just before five o'clock.'

Maddox smiled. 'Thank you, Sergeant James.' He looked at Vaughan, then at the two nurses. 'That will be all.'

'What about the others?' asked Vaughan.

'We've heard all we need to know. Unless you have any further questions, Major?'

Vaughan shook his head. 'No. The sooner we leave these good men alone the better.' At the door, he turned and said, 'Good luck, all of you. I'm sure you're in the very best hands.'

Captain Richoux showed them out. Silently, they followed her back through the ward and down the long corridor to the main staircase. 'Captain Richoux,' said Maddox, 'I'd be grateful if you kept the conversation you heard to yourself.'

She nodded.

'In a time of war,' he added, 'the old adage of "careless talk costs lives" still rings true.'

'It's all right, Major,' she said. 'I understand.'

She shook hands and left them.

Neither man spoke as they trotted back down

the stairs. Outside, the sun was higher, the temperature rising. A number of boys ran up to them, hands outstretched, clamouring for *baksheesh*. The two men ignored them as they got back into the car, which was like a furnace. Hastily opening the window, Vaughan winced as his bare arm touched the hot metal frame.

'Let's get going, Maddox,' he said, a touch of irritation in his voice. Maddox grunted and pressed the starter. The car coughed into life.

'Well?' said Vaughan, as they moved off.

'Back to Red Pillars,' said Maddox.

'But what did you make of what he said?' persisted Vaughan.

'Let me turn that around, if I may. What did *you* make of it?'

'I think you and RJ are right,' Vaughan replied, 'but I don't see how we can possibly know where Jerry got that information. Nor can I see how you can possibly be any wiser about any enemy circuit operating here in Cairo.'

Maddox was silent for a moment, then said, 'Look, Alex, we'd better report back to RJ right away.'

'So there's more?'

Maddox, his face set, stared ahead. 'Yes and no,' he said. 'But I'll let RJ explain, if that's all right?'

Maddox's shutters had come down, and Vaughan said no more. *Cagey*, he thought. *Why?* Perhaps there was a lack of trust. And perhaps that was justified – he'd only been with SIME two months.

Maunsell was still in his office when Maddox and Vaughan tapped on his door. 'You're back sooner than I expected.' He beamed. 'Did you speak to them?'

'Only to the pilot,' said Maddox. 'He told us all we needed to know.'

'And how was he?' asked Maunsell.

'In a bad way but he'll recover. Apparently he had been given morphine, but he seemed perfectly cogent to me – a little slurred, perhaps.' Taking out his notebook, he relayed Flight Sergeant James's answers.

Maunsell listened, his expression pensive. 'Well that's pretty conclusive then, isn't it?' he said, when Maddox had finished.

'It is rather.'

Vaughan looked at both men. 'There's more, isn't there? Otherwise, I wouldn't say it's conclusive at all. Surely, as George suggested, the enemy could have intercepted some radio signals. God knows, our radio security is always horribly lax.'

'I don't think so,' said Maunsell. 'The information about General Gott's movements was relayed in top-security code – code that we're certain has not been cracked.'

'How can you be so sure?'

Maunsell smiled. 'Put it this way: if they had broken it, I don't think we'd be mourning the death of an army commander but the PM and CIGS instead.' He rested his hands on his desk. 'And there's one other thing,' he added. 'We intercepted a message from Mersa. Here.' He passed the pasted teleprint to Vaughan.

Neue Kommandant AOK getötet an diesem Nachmittag 1500 Stunden, he read. *New commander Eighth Army killed today 1500 hours.* 'My God,' he

87

said. 'So they know.'

'Yes. And have you noticed the time it was sent?' asked Maunsell.

'Fifteen twenty-five,' said Vaughan, quietly. 'But no one in Eighth Army knew the general had been killed until five o'clock.'

'No,' said Maunsell.

Vaughan ran a hand through his hair. 'How many people knew about the general's movements?'

'More than you'd think,' said Maddox.

'The AOC at Heliopolis for one, the commander of 216 Squadron for another.'

'You can't possibly think they would betray their country?' said Vaughan.

'Not intentionally. But they might have been a bit careless – someone there might have seen or overheard something. There are a lot of people at Heliopolis. The Egyptian Air Force has staff there.'

'A number of people at GHQ knew,' added Maddox. 'Admittedly only those on a need-to-know basis, but there are signals staff as well.'

'We knew of it,' said Maunsell. 'And I'm afraid there's more. The ISOS people picked up a signal sent from Cairo yesterday morning, and another from the Mersa area a few minutes later.'

'What kind of signal?'

'Numbers. All numbers. They have no idea what it means – but it's clearly a code of some kind. And the signal is equally clearly being received by a German signals team.'

'But that means,' said Vaughan, 'that someone in a position of trust is prepared to pass information to the enemy. Someone here in Cairo.'

'It certainly looks that way, yes,' said Maunsell. 'A traitor no less.'

'But *why?*'

Maunsell frowned. 'I have absolutely no idea. It's one of the reasons George is so sceptical. Motive – a crime always needs a motive. But just because we can't see what that motive is, it doesn't mean there isn't one.'

Vaughan rubbed his brow. 'And in the meantime this circuit is presumably still operating.'

'Presumably,' said Maunsell. 'But at least our suspicions have now been confirmed. Before, we could only suspect that a circuit was operating in Cairo. Now we can be sure. That's something. I want you two to lead the investigation. You have Sammy Sansom and his FS men at your disposal and any other operatives within the SIME organization you wish to use. But I want you to keep me fully informed. I'll do whatever I can to make your task easier. This is now our top priority. We must make it harder for the circuit to operate. Close a net around them. We will break them, Alex.'

'And quickly, before it's too late,' said Vaughan.

Maunsell smiled. 'God willing, yes.'

4

Tanner took the tram to Giza. A strong wind was blowing in from the desert so eddies of dust and sand swirled along the pavements. Shop signs swung, awnings flapped and billowed, while the ever-present throng of Egyptians and servicemen shielded their eyes. Only the camels and donkeys seemed unperturbed.

The tram was heaving with people. A group of men on leave were heading out to the Pyramids, grumbling about the wind.

'All that bloody time in the blue,' said one, a short man with a ruddy freckled face, 'and the first time I get out to the sodding Pyramids the wind gets up.'

'Bloody place,' said a second man. They were standing, clutching the straps that hung down.

'It's not so bad,' said another, who was taller, with ears that stuck out from under his field cap. 'It's hardly a full-blown *khamseen*. It'll probably die down soon.' He lowered his head and craned forward, peering out at the street.

'Oh, sure,' said the first.

'Stop being so bloody miserable. It'll be fine.'

Tanner agreed with the tall man. The wind outside was nothing – a blustery desert breeze. *Ignore it and get on with enjoying your leave.* They passed a cinema as a crowd of servicemen were pouring out, the film just ended. Street hawkers surrounded them, plucking at their arms and brandishing fly whisks, magazines, polarized spectacles and other goods.

A staff car overtook them, no doubt on its way to Mena. Tanner wondered who would take over now that Gott was dead, then thought about what Lucie had told him earlier. She had arrived back at the flat mid-morning, exhausted. First there had been the arrival of the survivors from the Gott crash and then the day sister hadn't turned up so she had volunteered to stay on.

'You've got to get your rest, though,' he had said, 'before you go back again tonight.'

'Yes, but first we were told to move the men into their own room, then guards arrived and finally a call came through that someone from GHQ wanted to interview them immediately.'

'Who?'

'A Major Maddox and a Major Vaughan. Anyway, those poor boys are severely wounded, and since I'd been with them when they arrived and helped get them into their separate ward, Dr Fisher was anxious that I should stay with them until the interview was over. I couldn't really say no. I wouldn't have wanted to in any case. Poor devils.'

'What did Major Vaughan look like?' Tanner asked her.

She thought for a moment. 'Average height, dark hair, broad shoulders and a square chin. Looked quite Mediterranean, actually.'

'That sounds like him,' said Tanner.

'Who?'

'Alex Vaughan. We were on Crete together. He used to be with Middle East Commando, but I'd heard he'd gone back to his regiment. I wonder what he's up to?'

'He didn't say much. Friendly, though, and polite.'

'He's a good bloke. Any idea what they wanted with your air crew?'

Lucie told him what the pilot had said. 'But Maddox told me not to tell anyone. Careless talk costs lives.'

'Did he say that?' Tanner grinned.

'Yes. And now I've told you, so clearly I can't be trusted. He was rather a serious man. Plain clothes. I don't know where he was from.'

'Probably some kind of intelligence-wallah.'

'Maybe. I suppose there's always going to be questions asked when a general gets killed in such a way.'

Yes, thought Tanner now, but it was odd that the enemy fighters had pressed home their attack so persistently. He had been thinking about it on and off all afternoon, and it was still troubling him. He'd seen those old Bombays plenty of times – and, of course, had had the misfortune to travel in one. They were old crates – obsolete to the RAF anywhere but in the Middle East. Slow and with no protection, meat and drink to a single 109, yet the pilot reckoned there had been six, who had made two sweeps, the second when the Bombay was already on the deck with both engines out. 'Are you sure that's what he said?' he had asked Lucie.

'Quite sure,' Lucie had replied. 'He'd been talking about it when he came in too.'

Tanner took out a crumpled packet of cigarettes. He tapped one out, pulling away a few strands of loose tobacco, put it between his lips and lit it. *Ah, well.* So the Germans deliberately killed Gott. So what? That was the point of war, wasn't it? To kill the other side? He exhaled a cloud of smoke and turned his thoughts instead to what the colonel wanted to see him about.

There was a little cause for worry there, too. Old Man Vigar was a decent enough bloke – didn't stand too much on ceremony, was prepared to fight his corner with Brigade and Division and was sensible enough to use his discretion when others in his position might well have been sticklers. Yet he hadn't shown much interest in the enlisted men: he was more comfortable in the company of officers, especially the public-school types. But now the OC was summoning him personally. He had initially hoped it was good news, but now he wasn't sure. After all, he'd been with the battalion a long time – ten years, not including the six months he'd spent with the 5th and then 1st Battalions. There was now a pause in the fighting; new men were arriving, others being promoted. Some of the old hands had been sent home, and the thought struck him that that might be his fate too: that Vigar would smile and shake his hand, thank him for all he had done and announce that His Majesty considered he had done his bit. 'You're going home, Tanner. The army needs men like you to instruct the next lot coming through.' Tanner cringed inwardly. He could see the scene so vividly: Vigar standing in his tent at Mena Camp, a grin on his face, and Peploe beside him. *I've just done you the biggest turn of your life.* He could imagine Peploe patting him on the back and saying, 'I'll miss you, Jack, but you deserve it.'

Tanner closed his eyes, conscious his heartbeat had started to quicken. He suddenly remembered what Peploe had said about Sykes, that he was doing a good job as CSM. And Tanner had retorted, 'Not too good, I hope. I want my job back.' But what had Peploe said to that? Nothing.

Nothing. He'd just smiled and raised his glass. *Oh, no*, thought Tanner. That was it, wasn't it? Not yet twenty-seven, but already he was being put out to grass. Didn't they realize he could think of nothing worse? Of course he'd like the war to end – neither did he have any wish to die – but the thought of leaving the life he had known for so long filled him with a profound sense of despair.

He glanced up and saw the Pyramids looming ahead, their colossal forms towering over the ramshackle streets of Giza. This was where Cairo and the western edge of the Nile Valley ended. It never ceased to amaze him how, with one step, one could pass from the green, palm-lined streets of the city into the desert. The tram halted and most of the carriage emptied. Tanner waited for the throng to disembark before stepping down. He stood there for a moment, gauging the strength of the wind, the sinking feeling of doom lying heavily in the pit of his stomach. Mena Camp was not far. In front of the Pyramids stood the Mena House Hotel; beyond was the camp – a vast tented base on the edge of the desert.

The wind was still whipping up the sand and dust, but was quite bearable. Tanner put on his polarized spectacles to protect his eyes and headed towards the camp. If anything, he welcomed the wind: although still very warm, it had a cooling effect. It meant he would reach the battalion still looking presentable, rather than with large dark patches of sweat on his shirt.

At the gate he presented his identity papers and was given directions to the Yorks Rangers' head-quarters. The various brigades, battalions and other units using the camp were all allocated different areas. Wide roads had been marked out, with either stones or sand-filled four-gallon flimsies along either side. Larger stones had been swept clear so that the routes through the camp were smoother than the rest. Near the entrance there were several buildings – Nissen huts, mostly housing ammunition and engineers' stores – but otherwise the entire camp was tented: row upon row of square tents, bell tents, mess tents and other canvas tarpaulins, some covered with sandy camouflage netting. Tanner set off down the main central thoroughfare, an endless number of jeeps, trucks and other vehicles rumbling past, more clouds of dust swirling into the air.

Eventually he found the Yorks Rangers, their encampment marked by two flags stuck into sand-filled oil drums, one with their own crest – a black and gold bugle with a York white rose on a dark-green background – and the other bearing the jerboa of the 7th Armoured Division.

A sentry snapped to attention. 'Good evening, sir.'

'Evening, Hopkins,' Tanner replied. 'Where's A Company?'

'Just there, sir,' said Hopkins, pointing to his right.

Tanner nodded and strode towards the collection of tents and vehicles. There were several carriers and more than a dozen stripped-down Bedford 15-hundredweights parked between the rows of tents. Wafts of cooking drifted on the breeze, which had lessened now. Here and there, lines of washed uniforms had been strung up between tents or vehicles. He heard laughter and felt a pang inside – of dread, of yearning. This was where he belonged – all the sights and smells were so familiar, yet he felt somehow apart from it. He was still convalescing, not back among the men. *Maybe I never will be again.*

'How did you do that?' he heard a man exclaim indignantly, followed by laughter.

'I can read you like a book,' came a familiar voice – not a Yorkshire accent, but Cockney. Tanner smiled. 'It's just brilliant. Every time I'm feeling short, a quick hand with Browner and I'm back in the money.' More laughter. Tanner moved round a Bedford to where the men were sitting at a makeshift table made from ammunition boxes.

'Browner,' he said, 'you should know by now. Never take on Sykes at poker.' The men all looked up, and Sykes's face broke into a wide grin.

'Well, look who it is – back from the dead!'

'Still fleecing the men, Stan?'

Sykes hurried over to him and pumped his hand. 'They're gluttons, sir, but then again, Browner's never been a great one for subtlety. I try to pass on the benefit of my wisdom, but what can you do? Anyway, how are you?'

'Fine. Getting there. Almost as good as new.' He clapped Brown on the back. 'How are you, Browner?'

'Bloody annoyed, sir. I've just lost six bob.' He stood up too. 'Are you back now, then, sir?'

'Er, no, not yet,' said Tanner. His stomach churned. 'No, I've got to see the colonel. Is the captain around?'

'In his tent, I think. I'll take you.'

Tanner clipped Brown lightly on the back of his head, then followed Sykes past more tents and vehicles. One truck had its bonnet up, a man tinkering with the engine. A little way off, some others were playing a makeshift game of football in a clearing. Tanner recognized most, but there were new faces too. *Bloody hell. It's only been a month.*

'So, how are you really, Jack?' said Sykes, using Tanner's Christian name, now that they were away from the others. 'You gave us a bloody scare, I can tell you. I really thought you were a croaker.'

'Nah – they won't get me. You should know that by now, Stan. And I'm fine – really. Arm's a bit stiff still, back's a bit sore, and I've got a few more choice scars, but otherwise...'

'So you reckon you'll be back soon?'

Tanner stopped by a parked-up carrier. He felt for his cigarettes, then tapped out two and passed one to Sykes.

'What?' said Sykes, alarm on his face. 'What is it?'

'I don't know. I'm worried. I've had this summons to see Old Man Vigar and I've got it into my head that he's going to send me home.'

'Don't be ridiculous.'

'I'm not. A lot of the old hands are being sent back. I've been with the battalion a long time. I reckon they're going to make me an instructor or something.'

'Jesus, of all the things to worry about,' said Sykes, scratching his head. 'Listen, you're getting your knockers in a twist about nothing. The battalion needs men like you. Honest, Jack – you

97

should see some of the new boys they've sent over. Vigar's not going to want to pass up the kind of experience you and I've got.'

Tanner drummed his fingers on the carrier. 'Maybe. Anyway, I'll know soon enough.'

'Come on, then, let's find the skipper.'

Peploe was in his tent, beamed cheerily at Tanner and abandoned the letter he was writing. 'Right, Jack, let's go and see the Old Man.'

Sykes left them and they headed back towards the battalion 'gate'.

'Are you all right, Jack?' Peploe asked. 'Seem a bit quiet.'

'I'm fine, sir,' mumbled Tanner.

'If you're sure.'

They walked on in silence, Tanner feeling more and more like a condemned man. At Battalion Headquarters, a guard snapped to attention.

'At ease,' said Peploe. 'Is the colonel there?'

'Yes, sir,' said the guard. 'He's in his tent.'

Battalion HQ was made up of a large rectangular tent, which was effectively the Rangers' command post and operations room, a mess tent for the officers, and a third, which was the commander's own. They were laid out along three sides of a square, facing each other.

The entrance flap to the colonel's tent was hooked up and they could see him inside, sitting behind the trestle table that was his desk.

'Peploe, Tanner!' he called. 'Come on in.'

Tanner ducked his head and followed Peploe. The tent was split in two, divided by a canvas wall. Out of view was the colonel's camp bed and canvas wash-stand, while in the main part there was his 'office' – a desk, field telephone, and a number of folding canvas chairs.

'My dear fellow,' beamed Vigar, standing up and shaking Tanner's hand. 'How the devil are you?'

'Mending nicely, thank you, sir. Nearly as good as new.'

'Good, good, glad to hear it.' He walked over to a second trestle table on which stood a couple of bottles and a few thick glass tumblers. 'Drink?'

Tanner looked at Peploe, who nodded, then said, 'Thank you, sir.'

The colonel was in his early forties, his wavy brown hair thinning, but with a clean-shaven, youthful face. 'Here,' he said, handing them both a shot of Scotch. 'Glasses a bit chipped, I'm afraid.'

Tanner felt his heart sink further. An NCO sharing a drink with the Officer Commanding. *Just spit it out and get it over and done with.*

'Anyway,' said Vigar, raising his glass, 'here's how.' He took a sip, then held out his hand towards the chairs. 'Do sit down.' He sat behind his desk, beamed again, then said, 'Well, it's jolly good to see you looking so fit and well, Tanner. Sounded like a nasty wound, but we should have known better than to think an old warhorse like yourself would be down for long, eh, Peploe?'

'He's made of stern stuff, sir, for sure.'

Tanner smiled weakly. *Get on with it.*

'Anyway, the fact of the matter is, Tanner,' said Vigar, shifting in his chair, 'that we've had a few changes since you've been away.'

Tanner tensed. His heart thumped.

99

'We lost a few, as you know,' Vigar continued, 'and some new chaps have come in. We've had to shift a few people around – you know how it is.'

Come on, come on. Tanner stared at him, waiting for the axe-blow he knew was now just moments away.

'In A Company there have been a number of changes, haven't there, Peploe?'

'Yes, sir,' said Peploe.

'You've been wounded for starters. Sykes has been filling your boots and, I have to say, been doing a damn good job of it, hasn't he, Peploe?'

'Very fine,' agreed Peploe.

'And we've had to put Captain McDonald across to D Company, which has left us with a bit of a hole. That's where you come in, Tanner.'

Tanner swallowed.

'Yes,' said Vigar. Tanner watched the colonel's left hand as it reached to the wooden in-tray on the desk and picked up a large buff envelope. 'You've been an exceptional soldier, Tanner, and an exceptional part of the 2nd Battalion. You've always exceeded expectations and all that has been asked of you. Good God, man, your record speaks for itself.' He was now tapping the envelope on the desk. 'Times are changing, you know, Tanner. The army needs always to move forward.' He cleared his throat. 'I've something here for you.' He extended his arm, holding out the envelope.

Tanner took it and swallowed again. He glanced at Peploe. Then, with fumbling fingers, he opened the seal and pulled out a single piece of paper.

'Well, go on, man,' said Vigar. 'Read it.'

Tanner looked down.

Middle East Headquarters, Cairo
2 August 1942

Dear Colonel Vigar,
I am happy to confirm that Warrant Officer Second Class John Tanner, DSM, MM*, should be granted a commission in His Majesty's Army, with the promotion to acting Lieutenant, substantive Second Lieutenant. Lieutenant Tanner has an outstanding record as a soldier and I agree that he deserves this opportunity. I also agree that in light of his experience and the current circumstances in which we find ourselves, there is little to be gained from sending him to O.C.T.U. His promotion is therefore effective immediately.

General Sir C. J. E. Auchinleck
C-in-C Middle East

At the end of the letter there was a hand-written line in blue ink: *Please pass on my personal congratulations and wish him all the very best of luck.* Tanner read it again, then looked up at Vigar.

'Well, Tanner?' He grinned. 'How d'you fancy becoming Peploe's second in command?'

'I–' Tanner began.

'Many congratulations, Jack,' said Peploe, offering his hand.

Tanner shook it, then took a deep breath and exhaled heavily.

Vigar laughed. 'Damn it, Tanner, you look like you've seen a ghost!'

'I–' he began again.

'And I know the Auk's been given the boot,'

continued Vigar, 'but that don't make a scrap of difference. The C-in-C has confirmed your commission and that stands.'

Tanner looked at the letter again. 'Forgive me, sir,' he muttered, then put his glass to his lips and downed the Scotch.

'Well, Lieutenant Tanner?' said Vigar. 'What have you got to say for yourself?'

Tanner shook his head. 'I can honestly say, sir, I feel utterly dumbfounded. I'm speechless, sir.'

Vigar laughed again, went over to the side-table, picked up the Scotch and poured another round. 'Actually, I've a further piece of good news, Tanner,' he said. 'You and Peploe have both been awarded an MC. It came through yesterday as an MM, but I've since had confirmation back that it's been changed to a cross, now that you're commissioned. So, congratulations again. I'm always pleased when our chaps get gongs. Reflects well on the battalion.' He raised his glass a second time. 'Here's to you both. Bloody well done.' He drank the shot back in one, then smacked his lips, and said, 'So. Any idea when you might be able to rejoin us, Lieutenant?'

'I'm seeing the MO in two days' time, sir,' said Tanner. 'I'll be pressing hard.'

'Well, take your time. We want you back, but we also need you fit and firing. We're due to head back up to the line around the twentieth of this month and I think we can manage all right without you until then.'

'I'd like to think I'll be back before then, sir. I'm feeling better each day.'

'Good show. One thing's for sure – we're on for

one hell of a shooting match at some point and we'll need you for that... Now,' he added, 'I'll let you and Peploe have a chinwag, and then I'd very much like you to join the rest of the officers in the mess. That sound all right?'

Tanner downed his drink, then stood and saluted. 'Thank you, sir. It's a great honour. You've made me a very proud man.'

'Good!' Vigar glanced at his watch. 'It's getting on for eighteen thirty now. Shall we say nineteen hundred in the mess?'

Outside, Peploe clapped Tanner on the back. 'I'm thrilled, Jack, thrilled. Really. I'm bloody lucky to have you as my second-in-command – I so wanted to tell you last night.'

'And I thought I was going to get the chop.'

'The chop? Why on earth would you be chopped?'

Tanner shrugged, suddenly feeling rather foolish. 'I don't know. I've been in the battalion a long time. I got it into my head that I'd be sent back home to instruct.'

'No wonder you were so quiet.' Peploe chuckled.

'I was nervous as hell,' Tanner admitted. 'It was the longest trip out to Mena I've ever had.'

'Honestly, Jack. That's absurd.'

They reached Peploe's bell tent and, once inside, Peploe reached under his camp bed and pulled out a cardboard box. 'Here,' he said, 'consider it a congratulations present from me.'

Tanner eyed him, grinning sheepishly, then opened the lid. Inside was a new shirt, complete with shoulder tabs, two lieutenant pips on each, and an officer's cap. Tanner picked it up and looked at the black Rangers cap-badge.

'I hope it's the right size.'

'Thank you, sir. Very good of you.'

'My pleasure. And you don't need to call me "sir" any more either, Jack. Oh, and I know I could have just got you the shoulder tabs, but, well – I thought you could do with a new one.'

'You're right. This is the only one I've got. The other never made it out of that RAP.'

He took off his old shirt, wincing as he pulled back his sore arm, grimacing as he put on the new shirt, with its half-front buttons.

'Jesus,' muttered Peploe. 'Your back.'

'Looks worse than it is,' he said.

'And what about that arm? No false bravado, Jack. How bad is it really?'

Tanner felt a flush of irritation. 'As I said, it's improving daily. Another week and it'll be fine.' He hoped it would be: in truth, the pain and stiffness had remained fairly constant the past few days. He fastened the bottom button, tucked the tail into his trousers, then put the cap on his head. The fit was perfect. He felt strangely self-conscious.

'Every inch the officer,' grinned Peploe.

'Thank God I don't have to do OCTU,' said Tanner.

'Utter waste of time for someone like you. You don't need any training.'

'Except in how to be a gentleman.'

Peploe waved dismissively. 'Oh, I wouldn't worry too much about that. I've hardly ever been one for decorum. You'll be fine. Look, Jack, the world's moving on. We British are moving on. We've had to. The old order is dying and, frankly, about bloody time too. Army officerhood can't be the sole preserve of public schoolboys any more.'

Tanner took off his cap and looked at it again, fingering the stiff band and the silk lining. *Lieutenant Tanner*. He chuckled. If only his father could see him now.

He'd left the battalion at just after eight, well before the ten o'clock curfew and considerably less drunk than he might have been, had he enjoyed a piss-up with the lads. And that was the point, he thought ruefully, as he sat on the tram, going back into Cairo. His life was different now: no longer one of the men, but an officer – and an officer who did not fit the mould. In the mess tent, his new fellows had been generous in their congratulations, but their camaraderie had been different. He had felt unable to swear and rib them as he would have done with Sykes and the rest of the boys. He had worried, too, about doing and saying the right thing, his mind and body on edge all the time. It was a singular honour to be awarded a battlefield commission – with an MC too – and he was proud, thrilled and excited. And yet, and yet... He was not what was considered a gentleman, for all Peploe's talk of social change. Most officers *were* from public schools, institutions that had turned out generations of officers and officials, instilling in them the necessary codes of behaviour and discipline expected of them. *I'm the son of a gamekeeper.* Damn it, he had barely been to school.

The tram rumbled on. The carriage was busy but not as packed as it had been earlier. There was a strong smell of sweat, dust and stale tobacco. Tanner peered out: the sky was almost black, but the streets were lit with a brightness that would, he guessed, seem alien to anyone in Britain. The focus of his eyes shortened and he now saw his reflection in the glass: his officer's cap, the pips on his shoulders. The extra pay was certainly not to be sniffed at – and, anyway, he could read and write, and he knew a damn sight more about soldiering, human nature and leadership than most of the young subalterns who arrived on the boat from England. And while it was true that he understood little of the codes of behaviour expected of an officer, he had been brought up to understand the importance of good manners; rudeness, his father had drummed into him, was inexcusable, no matter what your station in life. Tanner had taken it with him into the army and had adhered to it ever since.

And then there was Lucie. She, the daughter of middle-class parents, was lowering her social standing by being with a man from the ranks. It hadn't seemed important that dark, sinister night in France more than two years before. It had seemed even less important while they were holed up in the God-forsaken fort of Bir Hacheim, in the heart of the Libyan desert. Neither had it mattered while Tanner was convalescing. But it *would* have mattered when they began stepping out in Cairo together. The city was segregated: there were places for the ranks, and places for officers, but very few that allowed both. It had troubled him, for he had sensed that the time would come when the social gulf became too great. She had always denied it, had told him that she didn't mind whether he was a private or a general, but he had known that it would break them eventually.

Now, however, he could take her to Shepheard's or the Sporting Club along with the best of them. Now he and Lucie might have a future together, after all. As the tram reached the Midan, Tanner stepped down in as good a mood as he had known for a while. God only knew what would happen in the war in the desert or what part he would play in it, but right now, the future seemed full of hope and promise.

5

Sunday, 9 August. A phone call to her flat early in the morning: that same voice, light and conversational. What switchboard operator could ever suspect a thing? This time the address was in the Moski, it being the day of rest for the Europeans in the city; no need to be close to the Polish Red Cross office this time. The rendezvous was eight thirty a.m., the perfect time for a young woman to go shopping in the bazaars of the old Muslim city. Nothing suspicious about that.

Tanja washed, dressed and, a little after half past seven, set out. It was already warm but nothing compared to what it would be later. She was wearing a light blue cotton dress with a belt round her waist, coral lipstick, a plain, wide-brimmed straw hat and polarized glasses. Normal attire for an off-duty European woman.

She walked to the Opera House and then, feeling hot, took a gharry. The driver, a small man with silvery hair and a large moustache, stepped down, offered his hand to help her and nimbly jumped up beside her. He cracked his whip and they drove forward. There was a clump of leaves for the mule at the driver's foot, which implied the beast was better looked after than its protruding ribs suggested. Already the streets were busy – pullulating with people, animals, trams and other vehicles.

At the edge of the Moski, their way was barred. A car had evidently hit a cart laden with watermelons, most of which had rolled off on to the street. Men were shouting and gesticulating. Tanja began to fret: she did not want to be late. Then a whistle blew and several Egyptian policemen arrived. A few minutes later, car and cart had been moved to the side of the road, the fruit retrieved, and the way was clear once more.

A short distance further on, the gharry turned and the open streets of the city were replaced by a web of narrow, overhung lanes, the delicate iron balconies above so close they were almost touching. They enclosed Tanja in a different world, one that always reminded her of the *Arabian Nights* stories. The gharry inched its way forward, through a sea of bobbing turbans, deep red tarbooshes, and black yashmaks. The lanes were lined with an array of brightly coloured shops and stalls, pots and pans hanging from one, fruit in another, then a line of dead fowls hanging above cages of live ones, right next door to a jewellery shop that glittered gold and silver against the cavernous black interior. And the smell! The exotic aroma of spice and animal dung. The lanes seemed to go on for ever, a true labyrinth that made the great Khan al Khalili bazaar appear almost magical in its size. A place one could easily get lost in. A place ideal for spies.

At a crossroads, familiar to her by the shops rather than the Arabic names, she asked the man to stop, paid him ten piastres and continued the last part of her journey on foot. It was now twenty past eight; she had made good time, after all. Tanja walked slowly, pausing here and there, ignoring the imploring sales patter of the shop-owners, occasionally casting glances to ensure she was not being followed.

At half past eight exactly she slipped into one of the many jewellery shops in the bazaar, took off her glasses, nodded at the old man sitting in the gloom and went through a door at the back, up rickety stairs to a room that was lined with rugs and cushions, and heavily scented with frank-incense.

As always, Artus was waiting for her, sitting cross-legged in the corner, sipping coffee and smoking a hookah.

'Punctual as ever, Madame Zanowski,' he said, making no effort to get to his feet. 'The Muslim Brothers are, as ever, eternally grateful to you.'

Tanja tapped the end of a cigarette against her small tortoiseshell case. 'I'm not doing this for you.' She put the cigarette between her lips and lit it. 'Well,' she said. 'What is the message this time?'

Artus raised a hand. 'A moment, please. Why the hurry?'

Tanja sighed. 'Just give me the message.'

Artus did not move, instead taking another sip of his coffee. 'You want coffee? Tea?'

'No, thank you. I just want the message.'

Artus smiled. 'Why do you do this?'

'I'm beginning to wonder.'

'But, like us, you hate the British?'

'No.' She exhaled a cloud of smoke, one arm crossed over her chest.

'Then why?'

'Please,' she said, 'the message.'

Artus nodded. 'The British are sending through another convoy – a big one – but there is one ship above all that must be sunk. Malta needs fuel and only one ship can deliver enough for the British there.' He felt inside his jacket, pulled out a slip of paper and held it towards her. Tanja snatched it and read the typed instructions:

Fourteen ship convoy PEDESTAL passing through Straits of Gibraltar tonight 9 August to Malta. Fuel ship OHIO must be sunk. Half escort leaving convoy Cap Bon.

'When should I send this?'

'As soon as possible.'

Tanja nodded. 'And now I have a message for you to pass on.'

Artus raised an eyebrow. *Oh, yes?*

'I want to see Orca.'

Artus smiled. 'I'm not sure that will be possible.'

110

'It has to be.'

'You know as well as I do that the chain of command has to be kept secure. If it is compromised, then so is the entire circuit.'

'Arrange it, Artus.'

'And if he does not agree?'

'Make sure he does.' She turned and left the room.

Monday, 10 August. With Lucie back at the flat and already asleep, Tanner had headed to GHQ armed with his letter of commission and a further note from Colonel Vigar. Now that he was an officer, he needed new papers: an officer's identity card and an amended pay-book. He had only been to Grey Pillars once before, not long after he had first arrived in Egypt. Now, walking through the curving boulevards of Garden City, he was surprised by the vast compound enclosed by curls of wire. General Headquarters, Middle East no longer occupied just one *belle-époque* building, but a number of villas, apartment blocks and other houses.

He approached the main guardhouse, braced to make a lengthy and frustrating explanation as to why an apparent warrant officer was wearing the pips of a lieutenant. Despite the seemingly tight security measures, however, and much to his relief, he was saluted and waved on through. More sentries had been placed outside Grey Pillars, but again Tanner saluted casually and walked on past, up the steps and straight into the building. He would never have got in so easily had he still been a mere NCO.

In the hallway, he was directed to the Army Administration Office, accessed via several long corridors and doors in another building. A number of questions, his accompanying letters handed over for inspection, followed by a short wait on a bench in the corridor outside the office, and then he was called back in and his photograph taken in a cubby-hole of a room.

'We won't keep you too long,' said the civilian clerk, a middle-aged woman. *Egyptian?* Not European, at any rate, but wearing European dress.

Tanner nodded. 'While I'm here,' he said, 'I don't suppose you can help me find someone?'

'Army?'

'Yes. I know he's in Cairo somewhere but I'm not sure where.'

She looked at him sceptically.

'He's an old friend,' Tanner added. 'Alex Vaughan. Captain last time I saw him, but that was over a year ago.'

'What regiment?' said the woman, a pencil poised over a scrap of paper.

'Middle East Commando – before that Coldstream Guards, I think.'

'I'll see what I can do. You can wait in the corridor.'

Tanner thanked her and did as he was told. Half an hour later, he was called back in to collect his new officer's identity pass and amended pay-book. Tanner looked at it, the stamp across the photograph, and the words 'John Tanner, Lieutenant' in ink: *Height: 6 6'. Colour of Eyes: grey. Colour of Hair: dark brown. Other Distinguishing Marks (if any): scar on face, broken nose.* His nose had been broken twice, but not badly; and the scar – well, it barely showed.

'Your friend is a major now,' said the clerk. 'He works in the Defence Security Office.'

'Thanks,' said Tanner. 'Any idea where it is?'

She shook her head. 'Ask at Reception.'

Tanner did so and was given directions by the duty sergeant. 'It's beyond the guardhouse, almost dead opposite, with the red pillars at the front.' He chuckled. 'Almost anyone could walk into it – it's supposed to be the security office around here but it's outside the wire. Where's the logic in that?'

Sure enough, it was beyond the vast barbed-wire barrier that protected the GHQ compound, and was guarded by a lone Egyptian policeman. Flashing his new identity card and receiving a curt nod, Tanner stepped into the hallway, to be met by a legless Egyptian sitting on a wheeled square of wood.

'Excuse me, sir,' said the man, 'please may I see your papers?'

Tanner stopped, startled. He was further surprised to see the man wore a shoulder holster and an army service revolver. 'Here,' he said, handing over his card.

The man eyed him carefully, glancing up and then down at his card. 'Who are you here to see?'

'Major Alex Vaughan.'

'All right,' said the man, handing back the card. 'Take the stairs to the second floor and ask one of the secretaries. Major Vaughan is in at the moment.'

At the second-floor landing he found a civilian

secretary typing at a desk. In her thirties, Tanner guessed, no doubt an officer's wife.

'Good morning.' She smiled. 'How can I help?'

'I'm here to see Major Vaughan.'

'Is he expecting you?'

'No.'

'Not to worry. What is it regarding?'

'I'm an old friend.'

'Oh, that's nice.' She flashed him another warm smile, then lifted the phone on her desk. 'May I take a name, please?' she asked him.

'Lieutenant Tanner.'

She stared at the wall for a few moments, then said, 'Hello, Alex, there's a Lieutenant Tanner here to see you... Yes.' She glanced at him. 'Yes, that's him.' As she put down the receiver she said, 'He's just coming. He sounded very surprised.'

Tanner smiled. 'It's been a while.'

'My God, Jack!' said Vaughan, seconds later, as he pumped his hand vigorously. 'What have they done to you? A lieutenant in His Majesty's Army!'

'Scraping the barrel, I know – I think they'd killed all the others, sir.'

Vaughan laughed. 'Come into my office.' He led Tanner back down the corridor and into an airy room with whitewashed walls, simply furnished. There was an old wicker chair and a side-table in one corner, which he offered to Tanner, then sat at his desk. 'So, tell me, Jack, how have you been? What's happened to you since Crete?'

'Rejoined the battalion. It was still being brought up to strength and retraining, but we got back up into the blue in time for Crusader.'

'Me too,' said Vaughan. 'I rejoined the Guards after Middle East Commando was disbanded and was given a company.'

'Crusader?'

Vaughan nodded. 'A horrible fight. I was wounded at Sid Rezegh.'

'Bad?'

'Shell blast. Head was a bit sore and I've a nice scar on one of my arms, but I was lucky. Got away with it. I'm fine now. You obviously came through it?'

Tanner nodded. 'And the retreat back to Gazala – the retreat from there too. Always bloody re-treating. It's the story of my life.'

'I missed that.'

'You did well. I've witnessed some cock-ups in my time, but that was a bloody disgrace. Clueless, those generals were. We should never have lost.' He shook his head. 'We have Tobruk sitting there with all its wire and minefields and defences and we go and put our line fifteen miles to the west of it in the middle of the sodding desert, all spaced out in boxes and the Frogs right at the bottom. Rommel goes round the bottom, attacks in the middle and picks off the boxes one by one. We all thought it was bloody nonsense – and if we could see it was a crap plan, why couldn't the generals?'

'I don't know, Jack. But things are changing. You've heard that Alexander's taken over as C-in-C?'

'Yes – a good move, I reckon.'

'And Montgomery's taking over Eighth Army.'

'I hadn't heard that. He was in France, wasn't he?'

'Yes. He's no-nonsense and decisive.'

'Good – that's what we need.'

'So you've come through unscathed, have you?' He took out a packet of cigarettes, helped himself to one, then threw another to Tanner, which he caught.

'Thanks,' he said. 'No, I was wounded at Alamein at the beginning of July. Shell blast too. Buggered up my back and arm. It's why I'm here now – I'm still convalescing.'

'You look fit enough.'

Tanner lit his cigarette. 'Mm,' he said, then flicked out his match and exhaled. 'My arm's a bit stiff, but I'm hoping the MO will sign me off this week. If I'm honest, I'm looking forward to getting back.'

Vaughan sighed. 'Yes, I know how you feel. I'm a soldier – I shouldn't be sitting here in this office.'

'Defence security – an important job, though, I should think.'

'Yes, well, actually I'm working for SIME.'

'Which is what?'

'Secret Intelligence Middle East. When I recovered I was offered a job as assistant to the DMI over at Grey Pillars, but it wasn't really my scene, and then Colonel Maunsell asked me to come and join his lot here. It's not quite what I imagined.'

'I liked your security guard.'

Vaughan laughed. 'Abdu – yes, he's quite a character. We've only been in this building three months or so, and he came with it – he's sharp as a pin. Speaks English, French and Italian and is as canny as they come.'

'What happened to his legs?'

'A tram when he was a child. Sliced them clean off, apparently. Anyway, RJ's had him vetted and he's now an official *ghaffir*.'

'I saw the revolver.'

Vaughan sighed. 'I know. It's a bit eccentric here. First-name terms, and dress how you like.' He leaned back, arms behind his head. 'Anyway, how did you find me?'

'Ah, yes. Well, you see, you were spotted. I've been staying in the flat of a lovely girl called Lucie Richoux. She's a QA nurse. A captain, in fact.'

'At the Ninth Scottish?'

'Yes. She told me about the survivors of Strafer Gott's crash coming in and mentioned that a Major Vaughan had been to see them. The description was right, so I guessed you must be in some intelligence job here in Cairo. When I got my papers, I asked them to look you up.'

Vaughan smiled. 'We could do with that kind of detective work around here.'

'What do you mean?'

'Oh, I don't know, really. We're a mixed lot. Some boffins, some who've lived in Egypt all their lives. Regular army officers, honorary commissions. None of us have been specifically trained in counter-intelligence work, as far as I can make out. It's a question of learning on the job. I'm not sure how much I've learned so far.' He paused. 'By the way, did your pretty nurse tell you why we were there?'

Tanner looked sheepish. 'Not really, sir.'

117

'Less of the "sir", Jack. It's Alex. And what do you mean by that? It's all right – you can speak plainly.'

'She did mention you suspected Gott might have been deliberately killed.'

'And what did you make of that?'

Tanner shrugged. 'Not much. How he died is irrelevant. He's gone, and now we've got Montgomery. Presumably Jerry picked up some radio traffic.'

Vaughan nodded thoughtfully. 'So if you get the all-clear you'll be back with the battalion at the end of the week?'

'Yes.'

'But you're kicking your heels until then?'

'Yes – Lucie's on nights, so she sleeps most of the day. I'm bored stiff.'

Vaughan leaned forward. 'Look, I've got to get on, but are you around this evening?'

'Yes.'

'Good – I'll meet you at Shepheard's at, say, eighteen thirty?'

'I don't know – I'm not sure about that place.'

Vaughan grinned. 'Come on, Jack. You're Lieutenant Tanner now. It's a great place. Dinner on me. There's something I'd love to talk to you about. A plan I've got.'

Tanner got to his feet. 'All right,' he said. 'Eighteen thirty it is.'

At four o'clock, as the car jerked its way back through Cairo, Vaughan felt the weight of the city compressing him. His shirt was dark with sweat. Every time the car halted when a cart or a camel

118

blocked their path, the heat soared. Then they were away again, jerking forward, a faint breeze providing a glimmer of relief.

Beside him sat Wing Commander Walker, an RAF Reserve officer attached to SIME. Another desk-wallah – he'd not flown in years – he had useful links to Air House, the headquarters of Air Marshal Tedder, the AOC-in-C in the Middle East. It was Walker who had arranged for SIME to have call on a couple of aircraft whenever required, which was why a Blenheim had been sent to photograph the Gott crash almost as soon as they had heard about it. In this city of endless bureaucracy and red tape, men like Wing-co Walker were worth their weight in gold.

A busy day. Briefings with RJ and Paddy Maddox, then a visit upstairs to see Sammy Sansom and Francis Astley, the two men running the Field Security sections in Cairo. They had around sixty men directly under their command, and Sansom had recruited a number of agents and informers, but until they had a solid lead, there was little they could do. 'Find me something or someone,' Sansom had told him, 'and we can get busy.'

But how to get that lead? He and Maddox had agreed with Maunsell that first they would try to establish a list of those who had definitely known about the general's movements. Maddox was to concentrate on those at GHQ, Vaughan on those at Heliopolis, and, with Walker to smooth the way with the RAF, Vaughan had headed out of the city towards the airfield.

Close the net, Maunsell had told them. It would be a process of elimination to begin with.

The first person they had spoken to had been the station commander, Wing Commander Robinson. In his office next to the control tower at the aerodrome, he had patiently answered all of Vaughan's questions as innumerable flies had crawled over the whitewashed stone walls. Yes, he had known that Gott was going to be on board. Normally, he had explained, transport flights took off early, before the heat made flying – and life – more difficult. He had resisted telling Squadron Leader Attwell, commander of 216 Squadron, but had felt obliged to inform him when the Bombay and its crew were stood down at 1100 having been waiting at dispersal since 0700. Apparently they had been getting frustrated and somewhat agitated by the delay. The only other person who had known was the cipher clerk who had received the original message from Tactical Headquarters, Desert Air Force, at Burg El Arab, then two further communications updating them on Gott's likely departure time. As far as he was aware, Squadron Leader Attwell had not told his pilot or crew the reason for the delay.

The wing commander had then summoned Squadron Leader Attwell, who had confirmed that he had not told a soul that Gott would be on board, least of all the pilot. 'They were bloody annoyed by the endless delays,' he told them. 'It does happen from time to time, though.' Attwell's testimony tied in with what Flight Sergeant James had told them.

Next had been the cipher clerk, who had been at the station for at least a year, with an unimpeachable record. There had been other clerks in the signals office and they all testified that they had not seen him speaking to anyone other than those in the office all day. There was a signals log, which they showed to Vaughan and Walker. Apart from the encrypted messages received, there was no outgoing cipher traffic.

So that was that. The leak could not have come from Heliopolis.

The following day, they would fly down to Burg El Arab and find out exactly who had known of the general's movements at both Air and Army Tac HQs. That agreed, they had then driven back to Cairo in silence, Vaughan immersed in his thoughts. There had been nothing untoward in anything the men had said and, in any case, there was no motive. RJ's argument that they might not know what that motive was held true – but only to a point. He supposed they would have to check up on Robinson's wife, but Attwell had no family in Egypt and neither did the cipher clerk. All three would be properly vetted but Vaughan instinctively knew that none of these men was responsible. And there had to be a motive. Suddenly he felt a surge of hope. Someone would stand out, he was sure of it.

They reached the railway station, heaving, as always, with troops, trams and hawkers. Walker drove on, weaving a passage through, and suddenly the traffic lessened as they travelled down the long, straight stretch of Sharia El Tur'a El Bubaqiya, along the canal and towards the cathedral and the Egyptian Museum.

'A bit more like it,' said Walker, leaning his head

out of the open window.

'At last,' agreed Vaughan. 'I'm surprised we haven't melted.'

He wondered whether Maddox had made any progress, and whether there was any news on the convoy heading towards Malta. What would happen if Malta fell now? *Bloody hell.* There was so much at stake with that convoy. Get the fuel through, and the island would be safe, her forces operating against the enemy sea lanes once more. Fail, and only God knew what would happen. If Malta fell, the knock-on effect could be catastrophic. What it boiled down to was whether the handful of men manning that tanker and those protecting it could get the ship to the island, and whether those comparatively few enemy pilots and seamen could sink her. For all the vast manpower now lining up in the desert, the war might be turned on the efforts of a handful of people.

As they passed the barracks at Kasr El Nil, the sight of large numbers of troops made him think of Tanner. What a surprise that had been! It had been good to see him. He had liked him well enough when they'd been on Crete, but it was more than that: Tanner was so dependable. Honest, too, with the kind of intelligence that was rooted in sound common sense and more experience than most men had had in a lifetime.

A thought struck him. Tanner was kicking his heels in Cairo for the rest of the week and they had a potential crisis on their hands. He might be able to make good use of him. It was already his intention to talk to him that evening about his coastal raiding party idea, but now he wondered whether he should ask RJ if Tanner might be briefly seconded to SIME.

They reached Garden City, the hubbub giving way to the calmer tree-lined boulevards, and then Walker was pulling up outside Red Pillars, and there was Abdu on his trolley, peering out of the doorway.

If there's a role for him, Vaughan thought, *there's room for Tanner too.*

It was a little before six and Vaughan was about to leave to meet Tanner when the intercom on his desk buzzed.

'Alex, it's RJ. I think you'd better come here.'

What was it? Vaughan hurried out, down the corridor, tapped lightly and walked into Maunsell's office without waiting for a reply. Maddox was already there, as was another man, a major in khaki drill, whom Vaughan recognized as Rodney Dennys, in charge of all SIS signals operations in Cairo.

Maunsell was standing behind his desk. 'Alex, good chap, there you are.'

What's going on?

'You've met Rodney Dennys?'

'Yes, of course,' said Vaughan, extending his hand.

'His team have intercepted another message,' said Maunsell. 'Here.' He passed him a piece of thin pink paper on which the message had been typed.

'Numbers again.'

'There's a clear pattern,' said Dennys. 'Three, sometimes four, figures. We're pretty certain this

123

is a book code. The first number represents the page, the second the line, the third the number of the letter on that line.'

'Hence three numbers,' said Vaughan. 'But what about when there are four?'

'It might be a less common letter that simply doesn't occur within the single-digit option.'

'Eppler was using a similar code, wasn't he?'

'Yes – it seems a popular method among Axis spies,' agreed Dennys. 'And with good reason. Without the book it's almost unbreakable because no one letter corresponds to a single number, making it almost impossible to get a pattern. And a pattern, of course, is key to breaking the cipher. The GC and CS people back home are already working on it, but it's extremely doubtful that they'll get anywhere.'

Vaughan looked at the sheet of paper again. 'Sent yesterday. What happened yesterday?'

'Alexander arrived late the previous evening,' said Maddox.

'Pedestal passed through the Strait of Gibraltar last night,' said Maunsell. 'If my theory's right, it could refer to that.'

'And tonight the PM and CIGS leave for Tehran,' said Vaughan.

'Yes.' Maunsell looked grim.

For a moment no one spoke. Vaughan handed back the cipher sheet to Maunsell. 'But we know this message was sent from Cairo, do we?' he asked.

'Quite definitely,' said Dennys. 'Somewhere within three to four miles.'

'In other words, any part of the city,' said

Maddox, rubbing his eyes. 'Any one of nearly two and a half million people could have sent it.'

'Yes, that's true,' said Dennys, 'but we can do better than that from now on. The message was picked up by our Y Service in Britain and the response from the Mersa area by our chaps in Alexandria. But we can fix up a listening post here in the city. If our spy sends another message, we'll be able to pin the signal down to a few hundred yards. It's not perfect, but–'

'It's a damn sight better than three miles,' agreed Maunsell.

At just before half past six, Tanner walked past a bowing *suffragi* and up the steps to the terrace of Shepheard's Hotel. He had passed this place, one of the best known landmarks in all of Cairo, numerous times, but it was only now, as a commissioned officer, that he was able to set foot inside. Far from relishing the prospect, he felt absurdly conspicuous and uncomfortable. *I don't belong here.*

At the top of the steps, he stood still. *Come on, you bugger, be here.* He glanced around. A sea of people: civilian suits and uniforms, mostly men, but a fair few ladies as well, sitting in wicker chairs around small, square-topped tables. Half were under the hotel balcony, the rest jutting out overlooking the street, penned in by an elegant iron railing. At the piano, a man was tinkling Cole Porter numbers. A captain sitting on his own nearby mouthed the words to himself, but otherwise no one seemed to be listening.

Tanner noticed that none of the officers there

125

were wearing their caps so he took his off, then wiped his brow and whisked away a fly. 'Yes, sir?'

Tanner turned to see a *suffragi* beside him, dressed, like the others, in a long white robe, tarboosh and maroon sash. 'I'm looking for a friend, but he doesn't appear to be here yet.' He was not sure what to do next – whether he should choose a table and sit down or whether he should be seated by one of the staff.

'Shall I take you to a table, sir?' said the man.

Good. 'Thank you.'

The *suffragi* led him to one under the shade of the balcony, not far from the piano. There were four empty chairs, two with their backs against the wall. Tanner took one of these, which gave him a good view. He would be able to spot Vaughan the moment he arrived. He glanced at his watch – *six thirty-five* – then drummed his fingers on the table.

At the next table there were two young lieutenants, one obviously good-looking, with fair hair slicked back and sharp, refined features, the other rather red-faced, with deep-set eyes that were too close together. The fair-haired one was also sitting with his back to the wall, a few feet from Tanner. They were drinking champagne, the bottle standing in a cooler on the table.

The fair-haired one glanced at him and Tanner nodded, then glanced around. *Christ. Look at this lot.* He took out his cigarettes and lit one just as a different *suffragi* came over. 'Yes, sir?'

'I'll have a Stella, please.' The man nodded and left him. Tanner glanced again at his neighbours and saw the dark-haired one looking at him as he

126

spoke in a low voice to his friend. He felt a flush of irritation.

'Excuse me,' said the fair-haired man, a smirk on his face, 'but I couldn't help noticing your accent.'

Tanner saw that the other was trying not to laugh too. Anger welled within him. His West Country burr had been more pronounced as a boy, but over the years had softened considerably. It was still there, though – and Tanner had always spoken in a soft, measured way, unless riled, which was also different from most. The officers from public schools tended to speak in a clipped way, the vowels sharp and precise.

'What did you notice about it?' said Tanner, looking the man square in the eyes.

The man chuckled. 'Forgive me, I suppose I just don't recognize it.'

'Ah,' said Tanner, still holding the man's gaze. He inhaled deeply on his cigarette.

'Well? Aren't you going to tell us?' said the dark-haired one.

'It's not a *patois* I've often heard in an officer, I must say,' added the other.

'You have now.'

'He's not going to say,' said the fair-haired man. 'We've offended him.'

Had Tanner been having this conversation in the street, he would have warned them to shut their mouths immediately. But he was on the terrace at Shepheard's and threatening other officers was, no doubt, unappreciated here. *Where the hell are you, Vaughan?* The *suffragi* returned with a large bottle of beer and a glass.

127

He placed them on the table.

'A beer,' said the fair-haired man, as he brought his champagne glass to his lips. 'A man of the people, clearly.'

The dark-haired man sniggered, and Tanner briefly closed his eyes.

'Somerset,' said the fair-haired man. 'I bet he's from Zummerzet.'

'I think you're right, Harry.'

They were silent for a moment, then the fair-haired one turned to Tanner again, still smirking. 'Excuse me,' he said, in an overly polite manner, barely able to contain his laughter, 'but what school did you go to?'

At this the other could contain himself no longer and began laughing uncontrollably.

Tanner had had enough. Moving his chair, he brought himself closer to their table, put his right arm around the shoulders of the fair-haired man and, pretending to laugh too, reached out his left hand, grabbed the man's crotch and gripped tightly.

'You're being rude,' Tanner said quietly, his hand still gripping the man's testicles. 'Very rude.'

'What the hell do you think you're doing?' said the dark-haired man, not laughing now.

'Ssh,' said Tanner, still smiling. 'Now listen, you tit, unless you want your bollocks ripped off, I want you to pay your bill and leave. I'm meeting a friend in a moment and I don't want to have to sit next to you any longer.'

'How dare you?' gasped the fair-haired man, his face turning puce with agony.

Tanner tightened his grip, and the man let out a

cry of pain. 'You're picking on the wrong man,' Tanner hissed. With his arm still around the man's shoulders, he took the identity card from his breast pocket and opened it. 'Henry Rhodes-Morton, Lieutenant,' he read aloud. 'Unit: the Rutland Yeomanry. Never heard of you. Must be new.'

A civilian at the table next to them shot them an anxious glance and a *suffragi* came over. 'Is everything all right, sirs?' he asked.

Tanner smiled and stared at the dark-haired man. *Well?*

'Yes, thank you,' he said.

'These gentlemen need their bill,' said Tanner. 'Don't you, lads?' He tightened his grip again.

The fair-haired man winced.

'Yes – our bill,' said his friend, his face reddening with humiliation.

The *suffragi* looked at them uncertainly, then bowed and left.

'Good,' said Tanner. 'Very sensible. I know who you are now, Blondie, and if you ever talk to me like that again, I can promise you that you'll regret it for a long time after. Is that understood?'

Both men were silent, so Tanner moved his arm up a little and tightened his hand around Rhodes-Morton's neck. 'Is that understood?' The man nodded.

Tanner released his hands and Rhodes-Morton sat back, spluttering. 'Christ, we were only having a bit of fun.'

'At my expense.'

'For God's sake,' said Rhodes-Morton. 'I'm supposed to be meeting my popsie.'

'You've got a girl already, have you? How long

129

have you been out here?'

'A month,' said the dark-haired man.

'I'm meeting her here at seven,' said Rhodes-Morton.

'Then I'll tell her you had to go. What does she look like?'

The *suffragi* returned with the bill.

'She's a cracker,' said the dark-haired one.

'Who is?' said a voice behind Tanner.

'Alex,' said Tanner. 'Where've you been?'

'Sorry. Got held up.' He looked at the two other men. 'Friends, Jack?'

'No, they're just leaving.'

Rhodes-Morton stood up.

'Go on,' said Tanner. 'Hop it.'

'For God's sake,' said Rhodes-Morton again. 'No wonder they don't let oiks like you into the cavalry.'

Tanner pushed back his chair, but Vaughan moved in quickly between him and Rhodes-Morton. 'If I were you,' he said, 'I'd be very, very careful what you say in front of this gentleman.'

'Gentleman?' said the other. 'That's a joke.'

'Leave now,' said Vaughan, quietly. 'And that's an order.'

'All right, all right,' said Rhodes-Morton, 'but if you see a tall blonde lady in her twenties, tell her we're at the Continental. She's foreign. Polish.'

'Just go,' said Vaughan.

Tanner moved his chair back to the wall and mopped his brow. A few people were looking at him, and at the two officers making their way out. *Damn it all.*

Vaughan took the bucket of champagne and

130

one of the glasses, and sat down. 'Don't worry,' he said, 'no one's really looking. They're too wrapped up in their own conversations. Anyway, they've probably seen far worse here.'

Tanner sighed. 'It's true, though.'

'What is?'

'I'm not a gentleman. I'm just the son of a gamekeeper.'

'Come on, Jack. I'm not going to let you feel sorry for yourself for being awarded a commission. Who were those two, anyway?'

'Just a couple of cavalry officers fresh out here.'

'There you are then. They'll learn. Probably go and get themselves killed first time in action. Forget it. What did you do to them, by the way?'

Tanner told him.

'Ouch.' Vaughan laughed. 'What you need is something to do rather than whiling away your time feeling resentful.'

'And you've got just the thing for me, have you?'

Vaughan grinned. 'Yes, as it happens, I have. I want you to come and work with me for a week – or until you're passed fit to go back to your battalion.'

'I thought you didn't like it much where you are. I got the impression you found it dull.'

'Well, I *did*, but not any more. Something's come up.' He leaned in closer. 'I can't say much, but we've suddenly got a hell of a case on our hands – something potentially rather serious – and we need to crack it pretty damn quickly. If this wasn't so important and, frankly, worrying, it would all be rather exciting.'

'But I don't know anything about your line of work.'

'You know enough to help me. You're street-wise, Jack. You've been around. And you've got common sense in bucketfuls. That's all it is, really.' He tapped his head with a finger. 'Using a bit of nous.'

Tanner eyed him carefully. 'What does your boss think?'

'He trusts my judgement.' Vaughan had been to see Maunsell about Tanner after his return from Heliopolis – the colonel had needed little per-suading: the idea was right for the now entirely autonomous and *ad hoc* nature of the SIME organization that Maunsell had established. 'We'll have to have him vetted first,' RJ had said, 'and he'll have to sign the Official Secrets Act. Assuming he's in the clear, I'll want to interview him as soon as possible. But he sounds like a good man, Alex. And a pair of fresh eyes can often make all the difference. Our absolutely top priority is to break this circuit. If you think he can help, then let's use him.'

The vetting process had not taken long: Maunsell had spoken to Colonel Vigar, who had provided him with a reference and authorized him to use Tanner until he was fit to return to active duty. That, as Vaughan now explained, had been all there was to it.

'Bloody hell,' muttered Tanner. 'I'd always thought GHQ was a minefield of red tape.'

'Not if you know how to circumnavigate it.' He looked at Tanner. 'Well?'

Tanner took a swig of his beer. 'All right,' he

said. 'Why not? I'll take your word for it, Alex. If you think I can help, that's good enough for me. I'm curious, I'll admit, but the moment I'm given the all-clear, I'm off.'

'Understood.' He clapped Tanner on the back. 'Good man, Jack.'

The pianist broke off, dabbed his brow with a handkerchief, had a drink, and was then joined by a violinist. With a nod from the pianist, the duo then struck up a version of 'Cheek to Cheek'.

'This place,' mused Vaughan. 'It's full of madmen and eccentrics – a melting pot of refugees and *émigrés*, Arabs and Jews, Turks and Hungarians.'

'And servicemen,' said Tanner.

'Yes, thousands of them, but how many are British?'

Tanner shrugged.

'Actually,' said Vaughan, 'it's only with the new divisions that have been arriving that British have outnumbered Imperial troops.'

'Is that so?'

'Well, think about it: Eighth Army's got a Kiwi, Aussie, South African and Indian Division, and half the Desert Air Force is South African. It's an extraordinarily mixed bag.'

Tanner's eyes were on the steps to the terrace. 'Look,' he said, 'do you think that's the girl?'

Vaughan turned in his seat. A tall, elegant young woman, with shoulder-length fair hair, stood there, clearly looking for someone.

'It's got to be, hasn't it?' said Vaughan. 'She's a cracker, isn't she? Surely she can do better than that blockhead of a cavalry lieutenant.'

'Like a decorated Guardsman major?'

Vaughan pushed back his chair. 'Exactly.'

Tanner watched him hurry through the crowded terrace and saw her turn as he reached her. A brief conversation, her face indifferent, and then she smiled. Vaughan pointed to Tanner and she began to move towards him, Vaughan following.

Tanner stood up as she approached. 'Good evening,' he said.

'We were right, Jack,' grinned Vaughan, as they reached their table. 'She was looking for Rhodes-Morton, but he's called Harry, not Henry. I've persuaded her to have a drink with us. After all, she's only just got here. Who wants to turn around and head off to the Continental?'

She laughed. 'Not me.'

Tanner eyed her: high cheekbones, pale blue eyes, neat, straight nose and full, reddened lips. Striking, certainly. He held out his hand. 'My name's Tanner. Jack Tanner.'

She took it and held it lightly. 'And I am Tanja. Tanja Zanowski.'

6

Tuesday, 11 August. Lucie arrived back just before six thirty a.m., just as Tanner was preparing to leave. She looked exhausted, so he held her tightly in his arms, then carried her to the bed and laid her down. He sat beside her and stroked her hair.

'Mmm, don't stop,' she said.

'Do you want me to run you a bath?' he asked.

'No. Just lie with me for five minutes.'

Tanner looked at his watch. He had time. 'All right.'

She kissed him. 'We're like ships passing in the night at the moment, aren't we?'

'Can't be helped, though, can it?'

'Four more, then I'm back on the day shift, but you'll have been given the all-clear and will be back with the battalion.'

He kissed her.

'I hate this bloody war,' Lucie said, into his chest.

'It won't go on for ever.'

'Won't it? It seems like it will. Do you have to take this job?'

'Yes, if they want me.'

Lucie sighed. Tanner pushed her over gently and began to unbutton her white uniform. 'How was it?' he asked her. 'Last night.'

'Quieter. Now that the battle's stopped for a bit, there are fewer coming in. I think they've cleared all the RAPs and field hospitals.'

Tanner undid her belt. 'And the Gott crash survivors?' he said, easing each arm out of her dress so that she wore nothing but her underwear.

'They'll be all right. Do you really have to go?'

'Yes.' He rolled her over, lifted the freed uniform, then unclipped her brassiere. He moved close behind her, his hands cupping her breasts.

They lay together for a few minutes, and then he said quietly, 'Lucie, goodbye, sweet girl.'

'Will you be back before I have to go again?'

'Yes, if they don't want me.'

'But they will.'

135

He kissed her shoulders and then her neck. 'Get some sleep.'

Outside, the sun was rising, casting a pink and orange glow over the city. There were already cars on the streets, trams too. Shops were beginning to open, tables of fruit brought out from the cavernous depths behind. Tanner found himself following a number of uniformed men and women heading towards GHQ. *There's hundreds of them.* There were always jokes about the desk-wallahs when the men were on leave and it certainly seemed true that for all those soldiers in the firing line there were plenty in Cairo and Alexandria who never went anywhere near the sharp end.

He reached the leafy suburbs of Garden City, the scent of jasmine strong on the air. From the dense foliage above birds were singing, a constant cacophony that rose above the noise of any passing traffic. He heard doves, sparrows and even a raven, with its low, distinctive cawing. A truck went by, a whirl of dust from the road in its wake. Tanner looked at his watch, saw that he was ahead of himself, cursed for not staying longer with Lucie, and slowed his step. *No bad thing:* he didn't want to arrive with damp staining his shirt – it was already warm and sweat was pricking at his back and brow.

His thoughts turned to the previous evening. Tanja Zanowski had been good company. She had deftly cajoled them into explaining what had happened to her cavalry officer and had laughed. 'He's just a kid,' she had said. 'He's very full of himself, but he likes to buy champagne, so what's a girl to do?'

Vaughan had been captivated, and had asked her to stay for dinner. She had made her excuses, but as she had left, Vaughan had jumped up and walked with her to the terrace steps. When he returned, it had been with a broad grin on his face.

'She said I could call her,' he had said, then sat down again. 'What a girl! Bloody gorgeous, funny, and with a fabulous accent.'

Good luck to him, Tanner had thought, although he'd been quite glad she'd left them to it. There had been something else Vaughan had wanted to discuss and Tanner had wondered about it all day.

At Tanner's prompting, Vaughan had brought up the matter as they'd sat down to eat in the dining room.

'It's something I've been working on for a while,' he said, then told him his idea for small coastal raiding parties. 'The thing is,' he explained, 'the SAS travel bloody miles over tough desert terrain to get to their targets. Hitting airfields and supply columns is a great help to us and causes all sorts of havoc for the enemy, but it would be good to hit the ports as well. You know as well as I do that this fight's all about supplies.'

'Rommel's overstretched himself, if you ask me,' said Tanner. 'I've no idea what his current supply situation is, but it can't be great, otherwise he wouldn't have called off the fight. What I do know is that Alexandria is a hell of a lot closer to the front than even Mersa Matruh – and that's a pretty small port. Tobruk's bloody miles away and Benghazi's even further. He must be using half the fuel they land just getting the rest to the front.'

'Which is why it's so important to destroy as much as possible before it gets there.'

'Aren't our bombers hitting the ports?'

'They are – but how accurately?'

Tanner had nodded. 'I wouldn't know, but I take your point.'

'We've also got the RAF attacking enemy ships at sea, but their efforts are hampered by the range and by the fact that Malta isn't operational at the moment. It's why this latest convoy is so crucial – and why these raiding parties could make such a difference.'

'But you couldn't destroy any ships, Alex. Not a four- or six-man team. First, how would you get the explosives on to them? And second, we couldn't carry enough to do the job.'

'I understand that, but we could carry enough to destroy a stack of stores. We could time our runs with the arrival of ships coming in. A few carefully placed packets of HE2 would soon get rid of any fuel that's been freshly unloaded.'

'Yes.' Tanner nodded. 'Those MTBs are pretty quick, aren't they?'

'And they've got decent firepower. They carry out mine-laying operations along the coast as it is.'

They had discussed the idea at length. They would take folbots with them on the MTBs – small, collapsible canoes that would get them to the coast silently. Then they would put on German uniforms and infiltrate the ports. The operations would always be at night – the RAF's bombing ensured all Axis-held ports would be blacked out.

'When will you submit the plans?' Tanner had asked.

'As soon as I've got them typed up and I can get an audience with the chief of staff. This week, I hope.'

Tanner had thought Vaughan's idea was sound, although whether anyone in GHQ would authorize it was another matter. Vaughan had told him of how David Stirling had bulldozed his way to see General Ritchie, then Auchinleck's chief of staff.

Now Tanner saw he had reached Red Pillars. This time there was not even an Egyptian policeman outside, while on the other side of the road coils of wire and sentries barred the way to GHQ. *Red tape and staff officers*, he thought, as two prim-looking men walked past, their shoes polished and socks neatly drawn up to their knees. If Vaughan's plans were turned down – and he would put money on it – it wouldn't be the first time that initiative had been stifled by the desk-wallahs.

It was eight thirty, and Tanner was now Maunsell's latest 'operative' at SIME. He'd been interviewed by Maunsell and Maddox together, he'd signed the Official Secrets Act, and was now a temporary intelligence officer. *Just for a few days*. And he'd been fully briefed. *Jesus*. Spies, the Secret Intelligence Service: it was a world he'd barely considered, yet he was now caught up in what Maunsell had just described as one of the most critical counter-intelligence operations ever mounted in the Middle East theatre.

They were in the colonel's office: he, Vaughan, George Kirk and Paddy Maddox.

'So, Jack,' said Maunsell. 'What do you make of

what we've just told you? What's your gut reaction?'

'That I want to know how they're getting their
information. And I want to know what those
numbers mean.'

'We're all agreed on that.'

'But you still don't have hard proof, do you?
Not really – not until you can read that message.'

'George would certainly agree with that
viewpoint.'

'All right, but assuming we do have a mole in
GHQ, then why don't you just arrest all those
who knew about Gott's movements?'

Maunsell glanced at the others. 'If only that
were possible, Jack.'

'But surely you're only talking about a handful
of people.'

'There are a couple of difficulties here,' said
Maddox. 'The first is that those who would know
would all be GSIs and the C-in-C, the DMI and
their staff. However, it might be possible that
their secretaries and clerks also know. Then there
are the cipher and signals people.'

'So the numbers are mounting already,' said
Maunsell.

'Second, as you know, we find ourselves at a
delicate moment, with new commanders coming
in, defeat still lingering heavy. You weren't in
Cairo for the Flap, but there was panic here at
the beginning of July. It was pretty ugly.'

'What happened?' asked Tanner.

'Rumours spread that Rommel was about to
reach Alexandria. A large number of staff officers
believed it was all over and started burning

140

official papers.'

Tanner shook his head. 'I had no idea.'

'It hardly reflected well on GHQ.' He cleared his throat. 'In any case, if we start suggesting there's a spy at the very heart of GHQ, at this moment in time, I'm not certain how well that would go down.'

'Especially when we don't have any hard proof,' added Kirk.

Maddox bowed his head. 'Exactly.'

'We need to work from the outside in,' said Maunsell.

Tanner looked thoughtful. 'I'm not really sure how a spy circuit works,' he said. 'Does it have to be a circuit? Could it not be just one person?'

'It could,' said Maunsell, 'but it's unlikely.'

'When were the number messages sent?'

'At about eleven hundred hours on the seventh of August, and at around ten a.m. two days ago.'

'And if the information is coming from GHQ, presumably he, whoever he is, couldn't just head out and make a radio transmission without arousing suspicion.'

'He could,' said Maddox, 'but not repeatedly, no, and in any case he or she would be most likely to cover his or her tracks.'

'So it would be safer for him to send a message to someone else, who would then make the radio transmission?'

'Probably,' said Maunsell.

'All right,' said Tanner. 'This is what I'm thinking. I agree it looks very likely there is a spy network operating here. The coded messages, the nature of the attack on Gott's plane, the timings

141

and so on – it all adds up to something, doesn't it?'

'It does rather, yes.'

'I'm trying to imagine what I would do if I were an enemy spy. We need to start somewhere, so I'm going to assume that I'm within GHQ where I get to see lots of highly confidential information. But sometimes, such as with General Gott taking a flight back to Cairo, I need to tell my Axis contact pretty damn quickly. How do I do that? I can't telephone the information because someone on the switchboard will hear it and I'll be arrested right away. So I have to give the information to someone. I have to do it face to face, don't I?'

'Yes,' said Vaughan.

Maunsell said, 'Go on, Jack.'

'Someone who's easy to get hold of without arousing too much suspicion,' said Tanner. 'Who is that person going to be?'

'Well, assuming the source is within GHQ, it's going to be someone nearby but outside the wire,' said Vaughan.

'Like who?'

'A tobacconist, a barman, a newspaper seller,' said Vaughan. 'Someone who's always there.'

'That's what I'd have thought,' continued Tanner. 'A wink, or some such signal, and a piece of paper slipped in a folded pound note. That sort of thing.'

'And then,' said Vaughan, 'that person nips to the back of the building, gets out a radio set and makes the signal.'

'I think this is the right approach,' said Maunsell, 'but I also think that there would be some

142

further person involved. To be sending radio signals from just outside GHQ seems too risky to me.'

'But you're suggesting, are you not,' said Maddox, turning to Tanner, 'that outside GHQ the next person in the chain is an Egyptian – or a non-European at any rate?'

'I suppose I am,' said Tanner.

'And his motive is that he's a dissident,' said Vaughan. 'It might be completely wrong, but it's a starting point.'

'It's the most obvious, I reckon,' said Tanner.

Maunsell leaned back in his chair. 'You're right,' he said. 'That's as good a way to look at this as any. Sound common sense – it's what we need.'

'What we need is a chink, a foot in the door,' said Vaughan. 'We should have a look at all the traders around GHQ.'

'I'd talk to Sammy's lot upstairs first,' said Maunsell.

'And what about Burg El Arab?' said Maddox. 'Are you still planning to fly down there?'

'I think you should,' said Maunsell. 'As I said, it's a process of elimination. Satisfy yourself that nothing's being leaked from our army and air HQs at the front – narrow the field a bit further.'

'You can still go,' said Maddox. 'I can pay a visit to Field Security.'

'All right, but what about Tanner here?' asked Vaughan.

'Can't he go with you and Walker?'

'No,' said Maunsell. 'Jack, I'd like you to meet Sammy. Alex, you go to Burg El Arab and, Jack, you spend the morning with Paddy. All right?'

'Of course,' he said.

'I'll be back by the afternoon,' said Vaughan. 'I can meet up with you and Paddy then.'

'And you should speak to Rolo,' said Maunsell.

'All right,' said Vaughan. 'Good idea'

'Rolo?' said Tanner.

'Lieutenant Rolo,' said Maunsell, 'is the Defence Security officer dealing with Egyptian politics and subversive activities.'

There was a light knock at the door.

'Come,' said Maunsell.

His secretary entered. 'This just came through, RJ,' she said, passing him a piece of signal paper.

'Thank you,' said Maunsell. His brows knotted immediately.

'Bad news?' asked Maddox.

'It's the convoy,' he said quietly. 'They've sunk *Eagle*.'

Tanner knew of the ship – it was one of Britain's few aircraft carriers.

'That means we've lost twenty-five per cent of our air strength already,' said Maddox.

'What it means,' said Maunsell, 'is that we haven't a moment to lose.'

Major Sansom was a short, fleshy man, with dark hair brilliantined on to his scalp and a trim moustache that made him look middle-aged when in fact he was still in his early thirties. He wore khaki drill, with a polished Sam Browne, although his revolver lay on his desk, as casually placed as a pen. The contrast with Maddox – thin-faced and slight – could not have been greater. Sansom's office on the third floor was almost identical to

Maunsell's, although there were several more filing cabinets, and the view from his large metal-framed window was better.

'I've heard of you,' said Sansom, as Maddox introduced Tanner.

'Really?' said Tanner. 'How's that?'

'One gets to hear things in this line,' he said, with a wry smile. 'There are not too many men as decorated as you. Men on leave will tell the world their stories when they've had a skinful.'

'There's not much that gets past Sammy,' said Maddox.

'That's good,' said Tanner. 'But I'm a bit in the dark here. You're Field Security, but you're not Defence Security?'

'No, we're a part of SIME but we're at the coal-face of the counter-intelligence operation. We're the ones out on the street.'

'So how many men do you have?'

'Five sections of twelve. Each section is led by a lieutenant with a warrant officer as his number two, and then ten NCOs, but I've also got a number of agents and informers. I try to make it our business to know what's what in this city. There's not much going on that we don't know about, which is why I'm a bit surprised about this Axis spy circuit you seem to think you're on to.'

'You don't think it's real, then?' asked Tanner.

'I'm not saying that. I'm saying it would be very difficult for any Axis network operating in Cairo to get any meaningful information. I've lived in this city all my life, Jack. I was born here, I speak Arabic better than English, and I know these streets and the people who live here very well.

Since I took charge of Field Security at the end of 1940, we've caught a number of Axis spies and not one of them has ever managed to pass on any really critical intelligence – neither have they shown much aptitude for the task.' He chuckled. 'Frankly, they've been a rather cack-handed bunch, to be honest. Female *émigrées* ensnaring sex-starved GHQ desk-wallahs and Egyptian subversives, mostly. And then there was Eppler.'

'I've heard that name mentioned a few times,' said Tanner. 'Who is this bloke?'

'A German spy,' said Maddox, 'caught by Major Sansom and his men last month.'

'It seemed like a feather in our cap at the time,' said Sansom, 'but, really, the more I think about it, the more I realize what a hopeless spy he was. Eppler was as German as I'm British but had also been born and brought up in Egypt, spoke Arabic fluently and had the kind of tanned skin that enabled him to pass as an Egyptian – and, although he'd been born a Catholic, he'd converted to Islam. Then war comes along and he buggers off to Germany to fight for Hitler. Anyway, he was sent here by Rommel. The obvious problem for any spy is how to get into Egypt – it's not so easy – but they had a pre-war Hungarian explorer, a certain Count Almásy, to lead Eppler and his radio operator, a character called Peter Sandsetter, across the desert. Incidentally, we know quite a lot about Almásy because he knew all those LRDG types in the thirties. Anyway, they eventually reached the Nile some way to the south and caught a train to Cairo. Our radio monitoring people picked up an unidentified

146

transmitter in the Cairo area, which came on air every night without fail at around midnight, and was sending out brief coded messages. We couldn't decipher them but agreed that we'd try to jam any future messages. That same day, I got a call from a British officer who was in the Turf Club and wanted to report some suspicious behaviour. It seemed there was a King's Royal Rifle Corps officer, who kept buying people drinks. Nothing very unusual in that, you might think, but it turned out he'd been paying for them in English pound notes.'

'Rather than Egyptian ones,' added Tanner.

'Exactly – everyone knows you pay in Egyptian money in Cairo rather than sterling. So that was a big mistake. Second, when we recovered some of the notes we quickly realized they were counterfeit, so that was mistake number two.'

'There can't be that many KRRC subalterns on leave at any one time.'

'Quite – so it was straightforward enough to discover that there was no one answering to his description. Mistake number three.'

'But then he went to ground,' said Maddox.

'It later turned out that that was the last time he posed as a British officer. He kept sending short messages every night but we still couldn't locate the transmitter. Until we had a really lucky break. A couple of Hun signallers were captured in the desert and had copies of an English novel, even though neither spoke any English. Anyway, those books still had the Portuguese price tag on them.'

'So we contacted Lisbon,' said Maddox.

'Who in Lisbon?' asked Tanner, surprised.

Maddox smiled. 'We have an embassy there – and where there is an embassy or a legation, we also have intelligence services. Anyway, we soon got a message back saying that the wife of one of the German Embassy staff had bought six copies of the same novel, all in English.'

'The novel was the codebook,' said Tanner.

'Yes,' said Maddox.

'But, actually, we caught him part by hunch, part by chance and part by his own stupidity,' said Sansom. 'There were reports of an Egyptian trying to use dud British five-pound notes, so I started going to various haunts in town and eventually caught up with him at the Kit Kat Club. He was sitting at the bar lighting a cigarette with one of these fivers. Incredible, really.'

'What a bloody idiot,' said Tanner.

'So I befriended him and eventually went back with him and a belly dancer friend of his, called Hekmat Fahmy, to a houseboat on the Nile.'

'So then you had him.'

'Yes, but we had the houseboat watched for a few days so that we might round up any contacts he had. Eventually we went in at two one morning and got him, his radio man, Hekmat Fahmy and one of his Egyptian contacts in the Muslim Brotherhood.'

'And we also cracked the code,' added Maddox. 'They were about to send some details of troop movements and that sort of thing, but nothing to compare with the details of Gott's flight or the latest Malta convoy.'

'This Eppler bloke sounds like a complete half-wit to me,' said Tanner.

'He certainly made a number of mistakes,' said Sansom, 'but it still took six weeks to track him down. It wasn't easy, Tanner.'

'And did he ever send anything meaningful at all?'

Maddox shook his head. 'No. Eppler was on the outside. He arrived in Cairo with a deep knowledge of the city but not of any top-grade intelligence.'

'I suppose it's a different kettle of fish if our spy is already on the inside,' said Tanner.

'Have you got any hard evidence yet that he is?' asked Sansom.

'Enough,' said Maddox.

Sansom scratched his cheek absently.

'Look,' said Maddox, 'Tanner's suggested that we have a starting point. A set of assumptions, if you like, that we're going to work with.'

Sansom looked at them doubtfully, then took out a cigarette from a small silver case. 'So what's your first assumption?' he said, cigarette between his lips.

'That the information is coming out of GHQ and being delivered face to face to someone in the circuit,' said Tanner.

'Why assume that?'

'Because,' continued Tanner, 'in the case of Gott's movements, he wouldn't have had time to fix up a meeting. He'd have learned of the general's movement plan, then had to act quickly. The decision to fly Gott was made last minute, right? Our man wouldn't have been able to phone because obviously the switchboard operator would have heard what he said, and nor would he

149

have been able to go to a prearranged meeting point or assignation.'

Sansom leaned forward, his interest clearly rising. 'Go on.'

'So there must have been someone he could pass this information to quickly,' Tanner continued. 'Someone nearby to GHQ. Someone that our mole could visit without arousing suspicion. A tobacconist, for example. Our mole nips out for a packet of cigarettes. What could be less suspicious than that?'

Sansom nodded thoughtfully. 'There are no shops in Garden City itself. The nearest would be on Sharia El Fasqiya.'

'I agree,' said Maddox, 'but what about the Nile? There are always hawkers along the riverbank.'

'But how often would staff officers buy things from street hawkers? It's troops on leave who do that sort of thing. I think we should have a look at Sharia El Fasqiya first.'

'How far is that from GHQ?' asked Tanner.

'No distance,' said Sansom. He stood up and went over to the window. 'Just over there.' He pointed. 'Hear that rumble of traffic? That's Kasr El Aini, which runs parallel. Four or five hundred yards. A five-minute walk.'

'So he could be back in less than fifteen minutes,' said Tanner.

'Yes, he could,' agreed Sansom, still standing by the window. The smoke from his cigarette wafted lazily outside. 'One thing I would say is that most people are less suspicious than you might think. I know GHQ is surrounded by wire and guards

150

but I think that gives them a false sense of security.'

'You're probably right,' said Maddox.

'I'll tell you something,' said Sansom. 'When I first took over here, my number two, Captain Astley, and I conducted a little experiment. The city was swarming with troops, just as it is now, but we wanted to gauge how security-minded most were, so we got two of our men to put on ordinary German Army desert uniforms and walk about town until they were stopped.'

Tanner grinned. 'Let me guess – they weren't challenged once?'

'No, not once in the two whole days they tramped the streets.'

'Incredible,' said Maddox.

'Well, yes, it is, but it proves that this mole, if he exists, probably has less to worry about than he might think. He could slip out and no one would think it at all suspicious because, as you say, a man needs his cigarettes, or newspaper, or morning coffee or whatever, and second, no one's on the look-out because it wouldn't occur to most that there could possibly be a traitor in their midst.'

'Like Major Kirk,' said Maddox. 'He's been citing lack of motive.'

'There has to be one, though,' said Tanner.

Sansom nodded. 'Absolutely, although God knows what.' He flicked his cigarette stub out of the window. 'So, shall we go over to Kasr El Aini now?'

'Are you beginning to feel less sceptical?' asked Maddox.

'Put it this way, I agree that it's certainly a

151

starting point.'

They walked down Tolombat Street until they reached Sharia El Fasqiya. Along the nearside, the buildings were the same ornate *belle-époque* designs that were a feature of Garden City, and the road was lined with high palms and other trees. The other side looked less salubrious, shops and offices running along its length. They strolled along slowly, noting each building in turn. There was a mixture of services and artisans: the ubiquitous fruit seller, with his half-green oranges, dusty strawberries and huge water-melons; a dentist and doctor in a shared building; a tiny coffee-house, or *ahwa*, with a few old men inside smoking hookahs; a general store; another fruit seller; a butcher; a tailor; and then a cut-through to the main thoroughfare of Kasr El Aini. Beyond that, heading north up the street, there were no other shops for a hundred yards or more.

'So, what now?' said Tanner.

'We should just watch for a bit,' said Sansom. 'See how many staff officers come and go and who goes where. We'll soon get some idea of whether or not we're barking up the wrong tree.'

The *ahwa* had two rickety wooden tables outside, both empty, so they sat down. Tanner looked up at the endless blue sky. The street ran north–south, and although the buildings and trees were of sufficient height for them to be shaded, the heat was rising. Tanner adjusted his cap and wiped his brow, then took out his cigarettes and offered them to Sansom and Maddox. Sansom declined, producing a silver case. 'No offence, but I prefer Turkish.'

'You can still get them?' asked Tanner.

'You can get almost anything.'

An elderly Egyptian came out, a thick white moustache on his upper lip, the rest of his face flecked with white where he had not shaved. Sansom spoke to him and the man shrugged, then pointed inside. Sansom asked him another question and he pointed again, first one way up the street then the other, before shuffling back inside.

'I was asking him whether British officers from GHQ ever use his coffee-house,' Sansom explained.

'And what did he say?' asked Maddox, flicking away a fly.

'"Not often." Apparently it's mostly the old men who come here. Then I asked him which shops our chaps used, and he pointed to the general stores and to the tailor.'

'I've used the tailor in the past,' said Maddox. 'He's a Copt. I expect he does a good trade with the GHQ staff.'

'Well, let's see,' said Sansom. 'I'm also quite interested to know whether anyone appears to be using Kasr El Aini. It's got shops and services all the way along it and it's only fifty yards behind us.'

They remained there for an hour and a half until the heat and the flies became too much. The fruit on the street stall next door seemed to wilt before their eyes. At the top of Sharia El Fasqiya, the road shimmered. Yet they had learned something. Twenty-four people, all but two British staff officers, had used the general stores; none had remained inside for more than a few minutes. Two British civilian women had bought fruit, and five officers had called in at the tailor's. Not one person had travelled further than the row of shops opposite the junction with Tolombat Street where they had been sitting. A number of cars and gharries had gone past, but if that ninety-minute period was anything to go by, staff from GHQ used this small collection of stores and services and no other on this side of Garden City.

'Rather telling, if you ask me,' said Sansom, pushing back his chair noisily.

'I suppose it stands to reason, though,' said Maddox. 'In this heat one wants to use the easiest and nearest. No point travelling further than one needs to.'

'I'd like to have a good look at all these places,' said Tanner. 'If there is someone receiving our man's messages, why not let them know we suspect them?'

'I can get one of my sections to do that,' said Sansom, dabbing his brow with his handkerchief.

'I'd like to have a look at them myself.'

Sansom shot a quick glance at Maddox, then nodded. 'Very well,' he said. 'You're right, Tanner. We should.'

They went inside the *ahwa*. The old men had barely moved. It was dark inside, and much cooler than out. A tiled floor, a worn counter and a sharp smell of tobacco smoke and spices. Just a few tables along one wall. The old men glanced up from their cards, pipes still burning gently.

Sansom asked the barman a number of questions, making notes on a small pad he had produced from his shorts pocket. Tanner watched the Egyptian carefully, but saw no darting eye movement, no shift of position; no sign of alarm.

'It's his *ahwa*,' said Sansom, as they went back out into the dazzling brightness of the street.

'He's called Mahoud Ibrahim and is forty-seven. His son runs it with him but is not here today. His parents live with him and his wife above the bar, and also two children. This is entirely typical, I should add. Families tend to stick together – or, at least, the male side of the family.'

'Can you verify this?' asked Tanner.

'Absolutely. Later, I'm going to have this part of the street watched, the places searched and the inhabitants vetted.'

Next door, in the general store, they entered another darkened, cool room, stacked floor to ceiling with shelves of tins, packets, bottles and other supplies. It had a similar distinctive smell of smoke and incense. Behind the wooden counter there were stacks of cigarettes, mostly cheap Egyptian brands. There were two men – one elderly, the other in his late twenties or possibly early thirties. They were, they told Sansom, father and son. Their wives were in the rooms beyond the store, as were the younger man's children. Tanner again watched the men carefully: he detected their slight unease at being accosted by three uniformed men but nothing more.

It was a similar story with the fruit shop and the butcher's, both of which appeared to be family-run concerns. The doctor was away – and had been for some time, according to the dentist, a portly, middle-aged man who was both gracious and co-operative.

Tanner was beginning to wonder whether they were barking up the wrong tree, after all. At the tailor's, a British officer was collecting a shirt. It was a small place: a wooden door, a dusty glass front, and a room crammed with cloth of various colours and textures. There was a sewing machine, a table, a small desk and a wooden icon. The tailor looked to be in his late thirties. His hair and moustache were flecked with grey, and a pair of wire spectacles sat on the bridge of an aquiline nose.

'There you are, sir,' he said in English. 'That will be one pound, please.'

The officer glanced at the three new arrivals, grunted and delved into his pocket for his wallet. Having paid, he squeezed past them and left without a word.

'We're just making a few enquiries,' said Sansom.

The tailor smiled benignly.

'Good morning,' said Maddox.

The tailor bowed. 'Yes, indeed, sir.'

'Could I take your name, please?' Sansom asked.

'Certainly. It is Gyasi Moussa.'

'Date of birth?'

'May the twenty-first, 1902.'

'Does anyone else live here?'

'Sadly, no.'

'Do you employ anyone?'

'Masud Efrahim. He is my apprentice.'

'Where is he now?'

'In the next room, cutting. Shall I fetch him?'

'Yes, please.'

The tailor went to a curtain at the back of the room, opened it and called. A moment later a young man in his twenties appeared. 'Yes?' he said.

Sansom asked him a few questions, noted the answers, then said, 'Thank you. You've been most helpful,' and turned to leave.

'Excuse me, sir,' said Moussa, 'but may I ask what this is regarding?'

Sansom turned back. 'It's something rather serious, actually. But don't worry. If you've nothing to hide you've nothing to worry about.'

At that Tanner, who had been watching him closely, saw the tailor glance out of the window. It was a spontaneous momentary reaction that passed in an instant. But it was a look Tanner recognized immediately. He had seen it in men's faces many times.

Fear.

7

At the offices of the Polish Red Cross, Tanja Zanowski was helping to make up supply parcels to send to Polish troops, now building strength and training in northern Iraq, when the telephone rang. Sophie was in the main office and picked up the call.

'You want Tanja?' she said. 'Yes, all right. Please wait one moment.'

She called, but Tanja was already through. 'Who is it?' she asked.

Sophie's hand was cupped over the receiver. 'Major Vaughan?'

Tanja smiled to herself and took the receiver. 'Hello, Major,' she said. 'How nice. And what can I do for you?'

'Oh, nothing very demanding, I assure you. Just allow me to take you out to dinner.'

'Hmm, well, I'm not sure that I should, you know.'

'Really? Why not?'

'I barely know you.'

'Which is why we should have dinner. Then you can know me a little bit better.'

'You have a point, I suppose, Major.'

'I'm glad you agree.'

'When were you thinking?'

'This evening, actually. About seven o'clock.'

'So soon?'

'Why wait?'

'All right,' she said. 'Where?'

'Where would you like to go?'

'Not Shepheard's and not the Continental.'

'How about the Union? Nice fresh air there.'

'That sounds lovely.'

'Perfect. I'll pick you up. What's your address?'

'No,' said Tanja. 'No – I'll meet you there. Seven o'clock.'

'I'll be waiting for you in the garden.'

She replaced the phone, smiled at Sophie and began walking back towards the other room.

'A date, Tanja?' Sophie asked.

'Yes. A free dinner – but I have a feeling I might

158

rather like him. He's good-looking and seems funny and nice.'

'He sounds marvellous,' laughed Sophie.

'I hope so,' Tanja replied.

An hour later, she was walking back to her flat. As she crossed El Maghrabi, a tram hurtled past and she lurched backwards. She gasped and put a hand to her chest. It had missed her by a hair's breadth, but her mind had been elsewhere, thinking about the message she had been asked to transmit that evening and about the meeting she had just had with Artus. That morning he had deliberately bumped into her as she had been on her way to work, slipping a note into her hand as she had made her way through a busy throng of people. It was not the first time he had contacted her in that way, but she didn't like being caught unawares. The note had been terse: *Five o'clock. Zawass.* Zawass. That was the shop in the alley close to the Polish Red Cross office.

He had been waiting for her, as he always was – as oily as ever. He had told her the message immediately.

Tanja had repeated it back to him.

'Good,' he had said. 'So Rommel had better get a move on. The British now have American muscle. Those tin cans they used to have will be history soon.'

'What about Orca?' Tanja had asked.

His smile had vanished. 'Why do you want to see Orca?' he asked, his voice sharp. 'You know you must never break the chain and yet you always ask. Why? Why?'

159

'Oh, for goodness' sake,' Tanja said, 'because I'm sick of getting my messages from you. Because I want to know that what I'm risking my life for is worth it.'

Artus had regained his normal composure. 'I am sorry.' He took a step towards her and held out his arms. 'But it is not possible. Not now at any rate.'

The faceless man, she thought, now safely across El Maghrabi. Or, *the man with no name*. And who was Artus? She knew so little about him too, except that he had been working against the British for years, part of an organization called the Ring of Iron. What Artus's role was within it, she had no idea. All she knew was that somehow, via Orca, Artus managed to obtain highly sensitive top-secret information that would materially help the Axis.

As she reached her flat, she said good evening to the *bawaeb* and climbed the stairs to her door, her heart pounding in the now familiar way, while nausea gripped her stomach. She shut and locked the door behind her, took out the copy of *Hausboot Muschepusche* and, with a pencil and a piece of paper, began to work out the message. She jotted down what Artus had told her: *Three hundred and seventeen new Sherman tanks arriving in the first week of September. More Shermans to follow.*

Artus was right. Soon it would be too late for Rommel. He needed to strike soon. Very soon.

At the same time, a short way across the city, Tanner was sitting in the corner of Vaughan's small office reading reports and notes about the various dissident organizations active in Cairo. On their return to SIME that morning, Sansom had, as planned, sent a section to watch the street. A government-owned flat opposite had been temporarily requisitioned in impressively quick time, and from there, Sansom's men had set up their vigil. Everyone who came and went was to be noted: staff from GHQ, the owners of the shops and various services. Meanwhile, all the names they had taken were passed on to the Egyptian secret police to be vetted and verified. Tanner had found it a considerable eye-opener. He was a soldier; up until now what had happened behind the scenes had just *happened*, as far as he had been concerned. It had not been something to which he had given much thought. This was an entirely different part of the military machine – a clandestine world, in which a handful of people rather than great armies and vast amounts of weaponry played what appeared to be a crucial part as well. And while he was glad his secondment at SIME was for a short period only, he had found the experience more exhilarating than he had at first imagined he would.

The working hours were agreeable too. At one o'clock, he had been sent home. 'Unless it's absolutely critical,' Maddox had told him, 'we tend to take a couple of hours off. We rather feel it's too hot to think clearly at this time of year. Get some sleep, and come back around four.'

Tanner had been surprised: the war in the desert never stopped for a siesta, but he could see the logic in it. Start early before the cool of the night had worn off, work through the morning, sleep through the worst heat of the day, then work some more in the late afternoon and evening. He was happy with that, and so was Lucie, who had not expected to see him again that day. Two hours in bed, one of which had been spent sleeping with her in his arms, had been most restorative.

He had returned to Red Pillars to find Vaughan back from Burg El Arab. As they had expected, he and Walker had found no obvious gaps in security. Eighth Army Tactical Headquarters had initially spoken face to face with Air Headquarters, who had then transmitted the signal regarding Gott's movements. As Gott had then twice been delayed, this information had been passed between headquarters by field telephone, but the messages had been oblique. *Arrival now 1200 hours.* Then, *Delayed. New arrival 1430.* No German listening in would have been able to understand what was being said without having had an original tip-off signal from Cairo. Moreover, the number of people who had known about the general's movements at either headquarters had been few. Furthermore, there had been no obvious way in which anyone there would have been able to inform the enemy.

So a leak from the desert had been discounted. It was a process of elimination, Vaughan had reminded them. *Closing the ring.*

'What now?' Tanner had asked Vaughan and Maddox.

'Sammy's men are in place. We watch, we wait,' Vaughan had replied. 'Do you have any other ideas, Jack?'

Tanner had, as it happened. Not *ideas* as such, but a line of enquiry, certainly. He had not told anyone of the look he had seen on the tailor's face; he had felt it was not something he could explain convincingly. *I saw something in his eyes. What exactly? A glance. It was just for a moment, but I saw it.* No, he decided to keep that to himself, but it occurred to him that if this man was somehow involved – and he had to admit the chances were that he wasn't – it would be worth trying to discover a motive; after all, it was motive that Kirk believed was lacking.

It was why he had been reading up on subversion in Egypt. The tailor was a Copt, Sansom had said, an Egyptian Christian, and certainly there had been a Christian painting on the wall. Tanner had also seen a crucifix hanging around Moussa's neck, yet from what he had read the main subversive organizations – the Muslim Brotherhood, the Grand Mufti of Jerusalem, Young Egypt – were all strongly Islamic. There was one other, the so-called Ring of Iron, but, according to the reports he was reading, it was finished.

Outside, beyond the quiet calm of Garden City, he could hear the faint hooting of taxi horns and a donkey braying plaintively. He looked at the wall beside him, where several flies were marking time, then at Vaughan, who was at his desk, working on his coastal raiding party proposal.

'When will you finish it?' he asked.

'Tomorrow morning, hopefully.'

'Then straight round to GHQ?'

Vaughan nodded. 'How are you getting on?'

'Are there any non-Islamic subversive groups?'

163

'I'm not sure. You'd need to ask Rolo. What are you thinking?'

Tanner rubbed a hand across his chin. 'I'm not quite sure yet. Didn't RJ say we should see Rolo?'

'Yes, he did. Well remembered. We could see if he's there now, if you like.'

Paul Rolo was at his desk. He was young, in his twenties, and had been recruited by Maunsell a year earlier. He had lived in Egypt before the war and had been lecturing at the university. 'I still consider myself more of a historian than an intelligence officer,' he said, 'but in wartime one must do one's bit. I'd like to think I'm helping in some small measure.'

'You can maybe help me,' said Tanner.

'I'll certainly try,' said Rolo, pushing his spectacles back up the bridge of his nose.

'It's about the subversive groups operating here. Do they all have strong Islamic tendencies?'

'Well,' said Rolo, picking up a pencil and scratching the side of his head with it, 'the Muslim Brotherhood obviously does. And that's the main one, although we have that pretty tied up now. They've been infiltrated so we pretty much know who's who and what's what in that organization.'

'And there's the Grand Mufti of Jerusalem,' said Tanner.

'Yes, but he's in Jerusalem. He's a pro-Axis Palestinian agitator, but although he has his supporters here, they're not a very organized body. Young Egypt is most definitely Islamic in nature – their leader is a rather unsavoury fanatic called Ahmed Hussein – but the movement has no real support. The Ring of Iron was led by General

Pasha El Masri.'

'Former chief of staff of the Egyptian Army,' said Tanner.

'Yes, indeed,' said Rolo, 'and always quite explicitly anti-British and pro-Axis but, thankfully, he's now interned. When he went, the Ring of Iron rather went as well.'

'But was it an Islamic organization?'

'No, no, not at all. Well, that is to say, a number of its members were Muslim, but it was a military organization. I think elements of the Egyptian armed forces want us out and Axis support for their military government, headed, presumably, by General Pasha El Masri. But we think it has largely died. With El Masri out of the picture the movement has no leader. A number of Egyptian Army officers have also joined the Muslim Brotherhood.'

'Which we've infiltrated,' said Vaughan.

'Yes. We're not very worried about them, to be honest.'

'But the Ring of Iron – it could still exist?' said Tanner.

'It could, I suppose, although we have little intelligence to suggest that it does. We have so many informers now, it's hard to know how it could possibly have any great substance without us knowing it.'

'And its goals,' said Tanner, 'are to overthrow the British, run the country as a military dictatorship and make a treaty with the Axis?'

'That's about the sum of it. At one point last year they seemed quite a threat. You couldn't go anywhere in Cairo without seeing posters calling for revolution and leaflets all over the place.'

'But cut off the head...' said Vaughan.

'That's the theory,' said Rolo. 'Without leadership a movement dies.'

They left him, but once in the corridor, Vaughan said, 'Come on then, Jack – let's hear it.'

'It's supposition,' said Tanner.

'What, then?'

Tanner said nothing until they were in Vaughan's office with the door closed. *Sod it*, he thought. *I'm going to tell him.*

'It was that tailor. Moussa,' he said, in a low, conspiratorial voice. 'I saw something in his eye this morning. I reckon he knows something. I'm not saying what – but something.'

'What did you see?'

'A flicker, the briefest glance.' Tanner was standing in the centre of the room and began pacing. 'It was fear, Alex. He was scared. He hid it immediately, but it was there. I know what I saw.'

'Why didn't you say earlier?'

'Because it would have sounded stupid. I don't know Maddox or Sansom, and I wanted to find out whether it was likely that a Copt could be a secret revolutionary. But now, listening to Rolo, it suddenly seems possible. If the Axis are getting help running a spy circuit, then which underground organization are they most likely to turn to? A bunch of Muslim fundamentalists or the Egyptian military? I've read the reports on General El Masri – he clearly had contact with the Axis through the Romanian mission, if nothing else. I saw what RJ wrote about that. He reckoned the Romanian Legation was a nest of spies and

166

that it even had its own radio transmitters. It's funny how El Masri's attempt to stir up trouble occurred when it was still fully operational.'

'It's shut down now, though.'

'Yes, but it could have put everything in place with this spy racket when it was still there. For all we know, it might have been operating all that time. RJ made the point, didn't he? That the best intelligence is that which is fed with something else. This circuit might have been feeding information about convoys for the past year and a bit, only no one's noticed.'

'RJ's suspected for a while.'

'He's an old hand at this, isn't he? He can smell a rat at fifty yards. But it wasn't until Gott was shot down that his suspicion became something more solid. That signal about Gott might have been their first mistake. Maybe they thought it was worth the risk to kill the new Eighth Army commander.'

'Time will tell.'

'Not much time. I reckon Rommel's going to have to have a pop at us before long. Then we'll see whether this new lad's up to much.' He paused and lit a cigarette, clouds of smoke swirling up to the ceiling. 'But, as I say, it's all supposition, isn't it?'

'Yes, but it all fits bloody well. And if it all fits, there's a decent chance you might be on to something. What we need to do now is have another look at this tailor.'

'There must be records from the time when El Masri was stirring things up?'

'Of course. Probably Sammy's the person to go

to. FS keep files on everyone.'

'Let's go and see him now, then.'

Vaughan looked at his watch. 'All right.'

'You've got your date with the blonde bombshell, haven't you?' said Tanner.

'Er, yes,' said Vaughan, 'but this is rather more important.'

'Look,' said Tanner, 'let's see Sansom, find out what he's got, and if there is anything, I'll stay and start going through it. Lucie's on nights so I'm not missing anything.'

Vaughan clapped him on the back. 'Thanks, Jack. Let's just see what Sammy has to say first.'

Sansom was in his office with Captain Astley. Unlike Sansom, Astley was tall, lean, and with a full head of dark hair, which was still quite wavy despite a liberal amount of brilliantine. A pipe was wedged between his teeth.

'How d'you do?' said Astley, his voice clipped and precise. 'Do call me Bones. Everyone else does.'

'Jack,' said Tanner. 'Jack Tanner.'

'Don't usually have genuine fighting men around here,' smiled Astley, genially, 'Alex being the obvious exception.'

'The trend we discovered this morning has been maintained,' said Sansom. 'Mostly the stores. A water-seller pitched up this afternoon. A few more visited the tailor too. He's got a good little business there.'

'What about the vetting?' asked Tanner.

'Not back yet.'

'We're quite interested in the tailor,' said

Vaughan. He turned to Tanner. 'Do you want to explain?'

Tanner did so. 'It's only a hunch, nothing more,' he said, when he had finished.

'But it fits, doesn't it?' said Vaughan.

Astley nodded.

'Yes, I'll admit that,' agreed Sansom.

'So, do you have any files on people associated with the Ring of Iron?' asked Vaughan.

'Or any subversive activity from early last year? I mean, are there photographs, or reports on suspicious people? How does it work?'

Astley cleared his throat. 'All of those things. We write up incidents, and we have some photographs. Of people we arrest, obviously, but also of suspects. The quality isn't always very good, but we should definitely have another look through everything. It may be that this tailor crops up. Who knows? It's got to be worth a bit of graft through old files.'

Tanner saw Vaughan glance at his watch. 'Go, Alex,' he said. 'I mean it. I can do this.'

'I'm afraid I'm needed in GHQ shortly,' said Sansom.

'I can stick around for a bit,' said Astley. 'I'll show you what we've got.'

Vaughan gave an appreciative smile. 'Well, thanks. I, er, owe you both.'

'After you,' said Astley, opening the door for Tanner. 'We keep the files locked in a separate room.' He led him along the corridor to a small, narrow room with shelving from floor to ceiling against two walls, filled with endless box files and card folders, and a small desk at the far end beneath a single window. 'Sorry it's a bit cramped.'

It wasn't just cramped, but hot as well – Tanner immediately felt a line of sweat run down his back.

'Let's look up personal files first,' said Astley, 'and see if we've got anything on him. He's called Moussa, you say?'

'Yes, Gyasi Moussa. Born May 1902, I think he said.'

'They should be filed alphabetically,' said Astley. He ran his fingers along a shelf, then pulled one out, looked at it, pushed it back. 'Ah, here's M.' He looked through each. 'Moham-med, Mohmet, Mustafa, Myoti. No Moussa.'

'What about reports?'

'How far should we go back?'

'When did the Italians kick off? June '40, wasn't it? How about then?'

'All right. There's a lot of them.'

'I'm in no hurry.'

Astley pulled down two box files, one each for June and July 1940, and together they began to look through them, searching for any references to either Moussa or the Ring of Iron. Tanner scanned reams of thin paper, most with typed reports but some in pen or even pencil. Most were accounts of suspicious behaviour – people acting oddly or furtively.

'Usually there's nothing to it,' said Astley. 'It's often sex related.'

Tanner chuckled. 'Really?'

'Troops are starved of it in the desert. They get to Cairo on leave and hit the brothels.'

'I know all about that,' grinned Tanner. 'But

most of the blokes I know aren't exactly embarrassed about it.'

'No, but you do get shy ones. A lot of young men have never been with a woman before so they start acting furtively, hoping no one they know will spot them.'

'Actually, now you mention it, I can think of a few lads like that.'

'But it's mostly officers rather than enlisted men,' added Astley. 'Officers, of course, are not supposed to use brothels – or, at least, certainly not those frequented by ORs. It's quite absurd that we continue with this pretence that no proper gentleman would ever consort with a prostitute.'

'There's one here,' said Tanner, reading through one particular report. 'Suspect acting suspiciously, constantly glancing behind him. Then there's a line saying, "Suspect is Lieutenant Milner, RASC, known to have visited Betty Borango."'

'Ah, yes, Betty,' said Astley. 'She's Sudanese. The words "buxom" and "Betty" go together very neatly. You know, we once paid her to have sex with Italian prisoners.'

'Really? How was that?'

'These half-dozen Wops had promised to co-operate fully but only if they could have a woman. Sammy was asked to find six prostitutes for these men so he went to Betty. She offered to see to the lot. Her bill was exorbitant.'

Tanner laughed. 'Quite a lady.'

'Yes. She's a mercenary, all right. She'll do anything for money – but, actually, she's quite likeable. Bright and with a good sense of humour.'

'But not someone to–'

'God no. Probably riddled with VD. Actually, I think Sammy felt a bit funny about acting the pimp. We've often wondered what the cost went down as in the army books.'

Tanner chuckled again. 'I never knew Field Security work could be such a good laugh.'

'Oh, it's pretty tedious and sordid at times, but we like to think we do a good job.'

The files were fatter with every passing month. For March 1941 there were several reports of young Egyptian Army officers having been spotted visiting General Pasha El Masri, deposed by now as chief of staff of the Egyptian Army, but still living quite openly.

'Tell me,' said Tanner, as he pored over one report after another about disaffection within the Egyptian armed forces, 'how bad was it? I was out here in early '41 but at the front we knew nothing of this.'

'You have to remember,' said Astley, 'that we'd had all that success against the Italians and then Rommel arrived. Suddenly we were being thrown back again. Then lots of troops were withdrawn to Greece and that made the situation worse.'

'I was one of those. Our battalion got out there, marched inland and then fell back. It was bloody terrible. One of the worst times I can remember.'

'Well, of course, we were following what was going on in Greece. Our forces were spread too thinly. There were signs of agitation in Palestine, Iraq and Iran. Rommel's Afrika Korps seemed an impressive foe and, of course, the *Luftwaffe* and Regia Aeronautica had air superiority. From where we were standing, here in Cairo, it was all looking pretty damn bleak, I can tell you. What had begun as rumblings within the Egyptian armed forces was becoming a major threat. We honestly believed they would have risen up the moment the signal was given.'

'Jesus,' said Tanner. 'I had no idea.'

'The mistake had been showing El Masri our plans when he was chief of staff. We all knew he was pro-Axis but, of course, once we knew he was passing on information to the enemy he had to go. But his sacking was at our insistence and the Egyptians didn't like that. Egypt is not officially a British vassal state, and the army didn't take kindly to having one of their senior generals forced out by us. It was a damned tricky situation, because we couldn't be seen to be making the matter worse by flinging him in jail, but at the same time, he was becoming a focus for anti-British sentiment with the Egyptian armed forces, and beyond.'

'How dangerous was the threat?'

Astley thought for a moment. 'That I don't know. We interned El Masri eventually, and as Rommel ran out of steam and the desert war stabilized, the fire went out of the dissidents and everything calmed down again. As the summer wore on, Syria fell, the Iraq uprising was quashed, then the one in Iran.'

Tanner leafed through more papers, then saw a report written by 'Major Hussein' in which he suggested the Ring of Iron was formed of a number of cells: 'They work in cells like the Communists,' he had written, 'with each member knowing only the other members of his cell.'

Tanner passed it to Astley. 'Major Hussein is a childhood friend of Sammy's,' he said. 'He's in the Egyptian Army. He wants us out of Egypt too, but is sensible enough to realize it'll be a damn sight worse under the Axis. Islam is also a Semitic religion. Ultimately the Nazis would want to be free of Muslims as much as Jews.'

A moment later, Tanner came across a report of a conversation picked up at the Central Telephone Exchange. As he read it, his heartbeat quickened.

Bernard: 'I've just listened to the conversation between an Egyptian officer and his father. The officer was calling from the Egyptian Officers Club in Zamalek. The son wanted money to pay his mess bill, but the father would not give him any unless he lands him a British Army contract for making uniforms. Let me read back to you what the father says: "In your own interests you would do better to get that contract instead of involving yourself in crazy plots that are bound to fail."'

Kirk: 'Did you get their names?'

Bernard: 'Only that of the son, but presumably the father's is the same.'

Kirk: 'What is it?'

Moussa. The name was Moussa.

8

Vaughan reached the Union Club ten minutes late, having hurried back to his flat, washed and changed into a fresh shirt and trousers. He had then hurried across the river to Gezira and the Union Club, conscious that he was late, which was never a good thing on a first date, but also aware that it was a bad idea to hurry anywhere in Cairo in August. So, it was with some relief that on reaching the Union he discovered Tanja had not arrived ahead of him. Finding a free table on the lawn near the large old trees at the edge of the garden, he was grateful to have a few minutes to dab his brow and compose himself.

Listening to the cicadas in the trees and the low murmur of voices around him, he felt a twinge of guilt at leaving Tanner back at Red Pillars. He wondered whether his friend would manage to discover anything that would help them. But then he saw Tanja drifting towards him across the lawn and a pulse of excitement coursed through him that made him put all thoughts of work and catching spies out of his mind. She was wearing a simple one-piece dress, her fair hair parted, with one side tucked behind an ear. Her lashes had been darkened, her lips were red, and Vaughan wondered whether he had ever seen a more ravishing vision.

'You look absolutely wonderful,' he said, standing and stepping forward to kiss her on each cheek.

'Thank you,' she said. She glanced around her and sat down as Vaughan pushed in her chair. Another glance, then a quick smile as he returned to his own seat. Somehow she didn't seem quite as self-assured as she had the previous evening. *Well, I feel a little apprehensive too.*

He ordered champagne; a bit reckless, perhaps, but what the hell? It seemed to do the trick: Tanja relaxed, the conversation flowed. They talked of the heat, of Cairo, of wishing they could see more of Egypt. She wanted to take a felucca and travel downriver to Edfu and Luxor.

'I've seen lots of Egypt,' said Vaughan. 'More than I'd like, really – but, sadly, not the interesting bits. Only the desolate parts. And, trust me, once you've seen one stretch of unending desert, you've probably seen all you'll ever need to see. But it would be wonderful to travel down the Nile.'

'One day.' Her smile was sad. 'What do you think will happen here?'

'I suspect Rommel will attack before long. He has to.'

'Has to? Why?'

'Because his lines of communication are so long and ours are now so short. The fighting has stopped because both sides have run out of steam. But as time goes on, we'll get stronger and stronger. The enemy cannot hope to keep pace, so if Rommel is to defeat us he needs to do it soon.'

Tanja was thoughtful for a moment, then said,

'Tell me, do you think he can still win? Do you think the Axis will still take Egypt and the Middle East?'

Vaughan shrugged. 'I'd like to think not, but who knows? Montgomery is taking command of Eighth Army but whether he'll be better than Cunningham and Ritchie – or even Gott – I don't know. He was a good divisional commander in France two years ago, but that's not quite the same thing.'

'Gott – I heard about that. It was sad.'

'He was a good man – and to be burned alive like that. It's a horrible way to go.'

Tanja shuddered.

'These are troublesome days. The war out here hangs in the balance.' He clapped his hands together and, brightening, said, 'So let's enjoy ourselves while we can. *Carpe diem*, and all that. And that means making the most of what this city has to offer, not least half-decent grub.'

The dining room was busy, as it usually was, the normal smattering of khaki blending with the flannel suits and printed dresses, and with *suffragi*, in long, white *galabhiyas*, flowing between the tables, large trays of drinks and food held aloft.

Vaughan ordered wine, they chose from the menu, and then he leaned towards her. She had seemed so confident the previous evening, and on the telephone earlier she had been playful and flirtatious. Now she seemed quite vulnerable – troubled, even. 'Are you all right, Tanja?'

Another quick smile. 'Yes. Yes, of course.' She looked around. 'So many uniforms. So many

177

soldiers. I want to do as you say – have a jolly time and forget the war, but it is not easy.'

'And here am I, wearing my uniform too.'

'Tell me, Alex, what do you do? You haven't said.'

'Strictly speaking, I'm a Guardsman. An officer in the Coldstream Guards. But I was wounded a little while back, and when I was recovering, I was given a staff job here at GHQ.'

'But you are better now?'

'Absolutely. Fit as a fiddle. But this staff job keeps me from the front, unfortunately.'

'Unfortunately? Why unfortunately? What is it about you boys that you always want to get to the front and risk being killed?'

Vaughan sighed. 'It's not that I want to get killed or even wounded. Of course, I don't. It's more a question of guilt, really. I'm an experienced soldier, and experience counts for everything. Anyone can suffer bad luck and get hit by a shell or a bullet, but the more you know of war and fighting the better the soldier you become.' He smiled bashfully. 'I'm sorry – I'm not explaining myself very well.'

She looked at him. *Go on.*

'I see all these young, fresh-faced chaps – like your friend Rhodes-Morton – and I wonder what hope they have. And then I think about how fit and able I am and it seems wrong that my knowledge and experience are being wasted here in Cairo while those fellows are being sent out into a fight they cannot possibly begin to understand.'

'But they probably need your experience at GHQ, don't they?'

'Hm, I often wonder, to be honest.'

'So what is it you are doing?'

Vaughan offered her a cigarette, which she accepted, then took one himself and lit them both.

'Nothing very exciting,' he said. 'Planning work, mostly.' He exhaled, smoke billowing into the air above them. 'Anyway, I want to know about you. It's obvious why I might be out here, but not a Polish girl. I met a few Poles in Tobruk, and there are people from most places here in Cairo, but I've never met a Polish lady.'

'It's true, there are not very many of us, only four at the Polish Red Cross. If there are any others, I do not know of them.'

'It must be difficult,' he said. 'Egypt is very different from Poland.'

'So is Britain.'

'True. But although it might be a bit battered, it is still Britain. It's still British. My people are still living in the same family house.' He paused. 'The same can't be said for your country.'

She blinked a few times, swallowed, then touched the corner of an eye. 'No,' she said. 'No, it cannot.' She looked at him and was about to say more when a *suffragi* arrived with the soup. A pause as the bowls were set in front of them.

'I am sorry, Alex,' she said, stubbing out her cigarette. 'I get upset just thinking about it.'

'Then tell me something that doesn't upset you. If we're to be friends, I need to know something about you, don't I?'

A smile. 'Perhaps.'

'Tell me, when you reached Cairo, how you joined the Polish Red Cross.'

'I got here in May last year. From Jerusalem.'
She laid down her spoon. 'I got to Cairo and I said
to myself, "Enough." I had been running and running, always on the move. Always running away.
Really, I can scarcely believe it. Europe was in
turmoil. I left Poland and crossed into Romania,
but then there was change in the wind again and I
could see which way it was blowing, so I kept
heading south. My God, it was bleak, and all the
time I was getting further and further away from
home.'

'It must have been terrible.'

'It was difficult, certainly. But all of Europe was
on the march in those days. I'm hardly the only
refugee in this city.'

'But what of your family, Tanja?'

'My family,' she said, her eyes moistening once
more. 'We were all scattered to the four winds.
The Germans on one side, the Russians on the
other. I couldn't find them but I knew I didn't
want to die. I wanted to survive. There were
many times when I came close to giving up. After
all, what was the point? My country was ripped
and divided, my family gone, but – I don't know.
I kept telling myself, "You're only young, Tanja,
and who knows what the future holds?"'

'So you kept going?'

'And here I am.'

'I'm sorry,' he said. 'I can't even begin to imagine what you must have gone through. But I'm
glad you didn't give up.'

She smiled at him, then held his hand, which
was resting on the table. It surprised Vaughan,
but thrilled him too.

'I was already in the army in September '39,' he said. 'I'd been to university, but I decided to join up because I believed it was essential that we stood up to Hitler. Nazism is evil, Tanja. It needs to be stopped. I fight because I believe it's our moral obligation to do so. As far as I'm concerned, this is a crusade. A crusade for the free world.'

Tanja took her hand away. 'And where is Poland now?' she said. 'Where were you British in September 1939?'

'We went to war for you.'

'You didn't. You went to war for yourselves. You promised to help us and you did nothing – not when the Germans invaded, or when the Russians poured into Poland. Poland has been torn in two, our people imprisoned and murdered. You say Nazism is evil, but what about Communism?'

She sat back and flung her napkin on the table. 'And now the Russians are your ally – the people who took my home. This is no moral war, Alex, and no crusade. No one who consorts with the devil can claim any moral high ground whatsoever. It is just like any other war, brought about by a few and suffered by the many.'

Vaughan stared at her, aware of the blood rising to his cheeks, as stung as if he had been slapped. 'Tanja–'

'I'm sorry, Alex, but I have to go.'

Vaughan nodded. He wished she wouldn't – but what could they say to each other now? Too much had been said too soon for them to revert to cosy chats about future holidays. Instead he watched her push back her chair and get to her feet.

She looked at him as though she was about to say something, then briefly laid a hand on his shoulder and walked away.

At a little after eight p.m. Kirk had still been in his office, although as Tanner had laid the report in front of him, the major had seemed more than a little irritated by the sudden intrusion.

'What is this?' he said, his eyes scanning the typewritten sheet.

'It's a report of a telephone conversation, sir, that you received in May last year.'

Kirk frowned. 'And what of it?'

'Sorry, sir,' Tanner said, 'I just wondered whether you can remember anything about it.'

Kirk sat back in his chair, and held the paper up in front of him. 'No need to call me "sir", Jack,' he muttered, as he read the report again. 'George is fine.'

'It's this bloke, Moussa, I'm interested in,' said Tanner.

'Moussa, Moussa,' said Kirk. 'I do vaguely remember. It was during the trouble with El Masri. Have you looked at the rest of the files?'

'Not yet, sir – George.'

'Then I suggest you do. This was quite a while ago now and you'll appreciate that one receives a lot of these calls, and especially back then. But my guess is that a watch would have been put on the father, and the son brought in for questioning. There should be reports on both.' He continued to hold the paper a few inches away from his face. 'Hold on a moment,' he said. 'This chap is the tailor just down the road, isn't he?'

'I'm guessing so.'

'Moussa is not an uncommon name for Egyptians, but I don't suppose there are too many who are also tailors.'

'That's what I was hoping.'

Kirk passed him back the report. 'You'll be able to confirm that too.' He eyed Tanner with curiosity. 'Does this mean you've got some kind of a lead?'

'Possibly,' said Tanner. 'Less a lead, more a possible line of enquiry.'

Kirk chuckled. 'One day in the job and our soldier is already talking like a seasoned detective.'

Tanner hurried back up to the third floor, and returned to the file room.

'Was he there?' said Astley, still sitting at the table.

'Yes. Doesn't remember it much, but said there should be a file on the son and that a watch would probably have been put on the father. He reckoned there'd be a report on that too.'

'I'd had the same thought, which is why I've been looking for a report on that suspect watch, but I've found nothing. And there's no file on the son either – which is also odd as there should be if he was interrogated.'

'Damn,' muttered Tanner. 'Perhaps no one put a watch on the tailor after all.'

'Well, the thing is, I do faintly recall it happening. I didn't remember the name at first but it's coming back to me now.'

'Sansom didn't mention it this morning.'

'I wouldn't read anything into that. There was a

183

lot going on then. Sammy probably had nothing to do with the watch – it could have been any of the sections, or even the Egyptian secret police. But the curious thing is that I can't find anything. It's even odder that there's nothing on the son.'

'Perhaps we should have another look,' said Tanner. 'One file might have got caught in another.'

'Always possible, I suppose.'

Tanner pulled out each file in turn, starting at 'Mamet' and working his way through, one by one. There were photographs – mostly police head shots – as well as transcriptions of interrogations, letters, related messages and papers – but no missing Moussa file. Tanner then took down a buff file entitled 'Mustafa, Eslem', because it was fatter than the others, brought it back to the table and sat down.

'What have you got there?' asked Astley.

'Eslem Mustafa.'

'I remember him. He was an El Masri acolyte. Major Tilly interrogated him, but got nowhere. We tailed him for a while and then he disappeared, never to be seen since.'

Tanner leafed through the file. Mustafa had been a squadron leader in the Egyptian Air Force and had been seen not only visiting El Masri but also the Romanian mission, which was why he had been initially tailed and subsequently arrested. The interrogation had revealed little. Tanner glanced at the typed transcript. Of course he wanted the British out, Mustafa had told them, but he was hardly unique in that. In any case, there was no crime in *wishing* something.

He had visited the Romanian mission because he had been seeing a secretary there. So it went on: a stream of questions and accusations, each of which he had batted back. 'Subject is highly intelligent,' someone had written in ink at the end of the interrogation, 'and quick-witted and is clearly guilty of plotting against the British and of stirring anti-British sentiment, although there is no hard evidence to support this.'

There was a list of Mustafa's alleged contacts, reports on the Ring of Iron and the Muslim Brotherhood, and written allegations that Mustafa had purloined the aircraft in which El Masri had unsuccessfully tried to flee to Iraq. Mustafa had also been present at a lunchtime meeting between El Masri and Lieutenant Colonel Thornhill of the SOE in May 1941. When later questioned by Sansom's team, El Masri had told them he had intended to go to Iraq to help quell the rebellion there, not inflame it. Colonel Thornhill, he said, had known about it and had supported such a move.

Tanner showed this report to Astley. 'How the hell did that happen?'

'Let's just say we weren't quite so communicative with one another at the time. We were all livid, as you can imagine. We were trying to prepare treason charges against El Masri, only to find bloody SOE had kyboshed the whole thing.'

A canny bugger, thought Tanner. There were also Mustafa's discharge papers from the Egyptian Air Force, then several sheets of paper in Arabic, followed by a translation that had been paperclipped together. It was a report by the

Egyptian secret police outlining how they had tailed Mustafa but had repeatedly lost him: 'It is our opinion that Eslem Mustafa has many connections both high up and among the criminal underground.'

'The criminal underground?' Tanner said. 'Is there one in Cairo?'

'Is that an Egyptian report?' asked Astley.

'Yes.'

'There are criminals, of course,' said Astley. 'Cairo's full of thieves and ne'er-do-wells, but that just means the lower classes. The uneducated impoverished mass. Street urchins and the like.'

In June 1942, Mustafa seemed to vanish entirely. There was speculation as to where he had gone. One reported sighting suggested he was up-country, south of Luxor, another that he was hiding at St Catherine's monastery in the Sinai. Kirk had written a conclusion the previous August, two months after Mustafa was last known to be in the city:

Numerous sightings have been made of Eslem Mustafa but, frankly, none is credible. Knowing as we do that most Egyptians are endemically corrupt and will happily lie if they think it will make them money, none of these sightings is to be taken seriously. Most likely, the subject has fled to Palestine where he is known to have connections, or has been killed by his own. Since the stabilizing of the front and the lessening of the Masri faction, the risk to security posed by the Ring of Iron and Muslim Brotherhood is now considered slight.

In other words, thought Tanner, *who bloody cares*

where he is?

At the back of the file there was a green envelope with a metal fastener. Tanner opened it and discovered a number of photographs, which he let slide out on to the desk. A set of police shots showed a handsome man with oiled black hair, a trim military moustache and pale, intense eyes that seemed to be laughing at – mocking, even – the photographer. There were others, most taken from a distance, of Mustafa at various places in Cairo – presumably from when he had been tailed. Tanner shuffled through them, one by one, until suddenly he stopped. He looked again. The picture was slightly out of focus, but it seemed to be of Mustafa emerging from a building and glancing to his right as he did so.

'My God,' he said.

'What have you found?' asked Astley.

'Have a look at this,' said Tanner.

Astley took it and squinted. 'Looks like Mustafa,' he said.

'Yes,' said Tanner. 'But look where it is.'

Astley stared at it again. 'Of course,' he said, after a moment, 'that's Sharia El Fasqiya.'

'Exactly, but look at the building he's coming out from.'

Astley peered closer.

'There,' said Tanner, pointing. 'You can just see the wording on the board above. 'I-L-O-R. I recognize it. I was bloody well there this morning.'

'And the missing letters are T-A.'

'Yes,' said Tanner. 'That's not any old tailor. That's Moussa's place.'

187

With Tanja gone, Vaughan had lost his appetite. He finished his soup, drank his wine, paid his bill and left, walking away in the darkening but still warm evening. He felt ashamed – of his insensitivity and his grandstanding. An image kept repeating itself in his mind: of himself sitting there, saying that line about it being a moral war. *So bloody pompous. A crusade!* Who the hell did he think he was? It was no wonder she had felt insulted and patronized. 'Damn, damn, damn!' he cursed. She was a beautiful, interesting – *intriguing* – girl, and he had ruined what had been shaping up to be a wonderful evening.

Vaughan sighed and paused to light a cigarette. The glow of the lights from the Gezira Sporting Club shone out over the lawns and playing fields as he walked slowly south towards the Khedive Ismail Bridge. Somewhere not far away across the Nile, several car horns hooted. And perhaps she had been right, in any case. It had not occurred to him that any Pole might feel less than grateful to Britain, yet he knew that the material aid to Poland during the invasion had been negligible. Of course Britain's move had been self-interested: she had guaranteed Poland's independence in an attempt to dissuade Germany from attempting further land grabs; and why did Britain want to deter German expansionism? Because an increasingly strong Germany, led by a despotic, murderous dictator, might one day threaten her sovereignty. It had had nothing to do with altruism towards Poland.

As he reached the bridge, a tram rattled past, full of troops heading back to Mena Camp. He still believed in the rightness of Britain's cause: Nazism was evil, and the Nazis had to be defeated, not just for Britain's sake but for the world's. But the Communists? He instinctively disliked Communism, but had never thought the Stalinist regime was as bad as that of the Nazis. Since the German invasion of the Soviet Union, Uncle Joe had been depicted as a friend, yet Russia *had* invaded Poland and hundreds of thousands of Poles had been sent to labour camps in Siberia. He had chosen to put that to the back of his mind, as most British had. Indeed, if he was honest, he had barely given it a thought. Their task was to beat the Axis, not worry about the moral fibre of Stalin and his regime.

Now he wondered what had really happened to Tanja. She had somehow reached Cairo alone, her family split up, her home gone. She had not said what had happened to them, but perhaps she didn't know. There had been anger in her words, and pain. Another wave of shame engulfed him.

On the other side of the bridge, he paused. He had thought to return to his flat and drink at least half a bottle of whisky, but now realized there was little sense in that. He had been feckless and arrogant: drowning his sorrows wouldn't help. Crucially important matters were at hand within SIME and he had already abandoned Tanner. Far better that he head to Red Pillars and see whether there were any developments. If not, he could continue work on his proposal until the 2200 curfew. At the very least, it would be a welcome distraction.

Nearing Red Pillars, he saw Tanner and Astley

189

heading out and called to them.

'Alex,' said Tanner. 'What are you doing here? Shouldn't you be whispering sweet nothings?'

'Don't ask,' he said, jogging over to them. 'I fluffed my lines rather.'

Tanner grinned. 'Oh dear.'

'Who was she?' asked Astley.

'Only a stunning blonde Polish girl with a lovely accent,' said Tanner.

'But temperamental, eh?' said Astley.

'Justifiably so,' said Vaughan. '*I* might be a little sensitive if I'd lost my home and family to the Bolsheviks.'

'Ah,' said Astley.

'Send her some flowers tomorrow,' said Tanner, 'and say you're sorry. She'll probably come round. After all, she liked you well enough yesterday to agree to dinner tonight.'

Vaughan shifted his feet. 'Yes, well... But enough of my romantic failures. What are you two doing?'

'Going to bring in the tailor for questioning,' said Astley. 'We've had a breakthrough.'

'Really?' said Vaughan, brightening. 'Tell me all.'

'First, have a look at this,' said Tanner, passing him the photograph of Mustafa outside the tailor's shop. They stood under a streetlight; insects swirled and flitted above them.

'Who is this man?' asked Vaughan.

'Eslem Mustafa. A former squadron leader in the Egyptian Air Force; he was heavily involved with El Masri and the agitation last year. He's also had dealings with the Ring of Iron and the

Muslim Brotherhood.'

'But since last summer he's gone to ground,' added Astley.

'And Moussa's son was involved in subversive activities at the same time.'

'Bloody hell, chaps – good work. Have you told Paddy and RJ?'

'Just RJ – Paddy's not in the office,' said Astley.

'I know it's still not hard evidence of any link between the tailor and our mole,' said Tanner.

'But it's something. There's a clear thread.'

'Which is why,' said Astley, 'RJ told us to bring him in.'

The flat the Field Security section had requisitioned was in a block built into the wedge between the end of Tolombat and Sharia El Fasqiya Streets. The entrance was in Tolombat Street. Taking the stairs to the first floor, they found the flat and knocked at the door. An FS sergeant opened it and led them into a lit hallway. From the darkened living room, the section commander, Lieutenant Matherson, emerged and saluted.

'Any movement?' asked Astley.

'Not really, sir. It's been pretty quiet.'

Astley nodded. 'And the tailor? He's still there?'

'Yes. He was shut for most of the afternoon. He went next door for a coffee, returned about half an hour later and didn't open up again until nearly seventeen hundred. He's been working ever since. Look.' He led them into the darkened living room. There was a small balcony, and although the glass doors leading out were closed, the shutters were open. In the shadows either side of the door, two men sat watching.

Tanner could see the faint light of the tailor's shop, although Moussa was hidden by the awning that had been drawn down over the front. 'Has anyone been to see him since he opened up again?' he asked.

'Two GHQ staff and one Egyptian.'

'Did you get a good look at the Egyptian?'

'No – but he was pukka,' said Marriott. 'Suit, tarboosh.'

Tanner felt in his pocket for the head-and-shoulders shots of Mustafa. 'Was it this man?'

Marriott took the pictures, one face-on, one in profile.

He shook his head. 'I couldn't say. Possibly.'

'Was any of your men using binoculars?' asked Tanner.

'Not at the time. I was watching with Sergeant Crosby.'

Tanner sighed, then rubbed his chin thoughtfully.

Vaughan glanced at his watch. 'Shall we get him now? It's nearly nine.'

'Sir!' said one of the sergeants by the balcony. 'The tailor's shutting up shop.'

'We'd better get down there,' said Vaughan.

'He's opening the front door,' said the sergeant.

'Let's be quick then,' said Vaughan. 'Bones, Jack – come on!'

Tanner followed him out of the flat, then the three ran along the corridor, down the stairs and out into the warm evening air. At the corner of Tolombat Street and Sharia El Fasqiya they paused.

'There!' Vaughan pointed to the lone figure walking away from them. They crossed the road quickly, then slowed their pace. The tailor was some sixty yards ahead – and suddenly disappeared to the right.

'Damn!' hissed Vaughan, and they broke into a trot. Reaching the cut-through between Sharia El Fasqiya and the main thoroughfare of Kasr El Aini, they saw the tailor once more, silhouetted against the busy street ahead, but then he turned left and vanished once more.

'Come on!' said Vaughan. 'We can't lose him now!'

Reaching Kasr El Aini, they looked around. Although it was after nine, it was still busy. A group of drunken soldiers were staggering towards them singing 'A Long Way To Tipperary' as though it were a dirge.

'Get out of the sodding way,' muttered Tanner. A tram hurried past, its bell ringing. Cars and taxis hooted. Where the hell was the tailor? Tanner spotted him on the far side of the road. 'There!' he shouted and ran forward, dodging a cyclist, then a car, which screeched to a halt with a blaring horn. The driver yelled, but Tanner ignored him. Now the tailor was turning down an alley and Tanner glanced back – Astley and Vaughan were mid-way across the street, waiting for a couple of gharries to pass. He saw Vaughan catch his eye, then hurried on after Moussa. The alley was full of shops and stalls still open for trade. Awnings stretched into the street, while pyramids of produce lined the pavements. Tanner saw men and veiled women shopping, talking, walking. Another *ahwa*, busy with men playing cards, had spread on to the pavement.

'Where the hell is he?' said Vaughan, now beside him.

Tanner scanned ahead: Moussa was passing the *ahwa*.

'He's forty yards away,' said Tanner. 'Come on. Let's see where the hell he's going.'

They followed him to the end of the street where he turned right, and briefly disappeared again. Hurrying forward, they spotted him taking yet another turning.

'Where the bloody hell is he going?' muttered Tanner. The road darkened as the shops began to thin. They were passing a series of warehouses, and at the end of the street, Moussa stopped, silhouetted against a faint light coming from one of the buildings, and looked around. He seemed to see the men, then calmly turned right.

Reaching the end of the road, they could just see him ahead, but then he was gone again. Quickly, they followed, but the wide open streets of modern Cairo, with its grand, ornate buildings and blocks of flats, had been left behind. The tailor was leading them into the old quarter of Zenab, with its labyrinth of narrow lanes, alleyways and densely packed buildings of scavenged limestone and mud-brick.

'Damn it!' cursed Tanner, as they turned into a busy lane. It was after nine, with the curfew less than an hour away, but the narrow streets were still busy with people, animals and mule-carts, the many shops still trading. Tanner reeled at the stench of effluence and rotting food. A moment later, as they pushed their way through a throng of people outside a small mosque, he could smell only strong coffee, tobacco smoke and incense.

Another *ahwa*, tables and people spilling out on to the street, but there was Moussa, still ahead, his dark jacket standing out against the sea of white and soft-coloured *galabhiyas*. Tanner hurried forward, conscious of Vaughan and Astley beside and behind him. People were watching them; it was obvious they were after someone. Tanner saw Moussa glance backwards, and quickened his pace. A pyramid of watermelons, then a stack of rough cages filled with chickens; flickering lights shimmered from within booths. A small crowd – an argument, a man with his hands raised in outrage. Tanner hurried on, Moussa just thirty yards away. Suddenly the tailor slipped into a side-street and Tanner began to run, pushing past several people. He heard Vaughan apologizing behind him, but when he reached the turning it was to find the alleyway deserted.

There was no sign of Moussa.

9

As luck would have it, a number six blue bus had been approaching the Anglo-Egyptian Union just as Tanja walked outside, so she had hailed and boarded it. With a gust of exhaust fumes it trundled forward, the driver grinding slowly through the gears. It drove over the Bulaq Bridge, a cluster of houseboats and sails, and back into the hubbub of the city.

She closed her eyes, angry with herself for losing control. She had no doubt that Alex Vaughan had meant what he'd said. He was a good, kind-hearted man – deluded, maybe, but his convictions were well intentioned. Yet, like most British, he was either oblivious or blind to the reality. Russia's role in the invasion of Poland had been either ignored or forgotten, Soviet barbarity brushed aside. But she had seen it with her own eyes: the burning villages, the ransacked family homes, the wagons of men and women shunted east. And she had read the accounts of some of those who had survived and made it to Iran and Iraq. Such hypocrisy! How could Britain and America object so strongly to the Nazis yet ally themselves with Stalin and the Bolsheviks? The Communists should be brought down, not aided and abetted. She was no lover of Hitler or the Nazis, but if only the Allies would back down, they could be left alone to rid the world of an even greater threat.

She looked out of the window. *Cairo*. This hot, impossible city, the beating heart of a free country that was not free at all. Britain, with her much vaunted democracy, ran Egypt like a dictatorship – the vast numbers of troops were testimony to that. Even now she could see several British soldiers arguing with an Egyptian water-seller.

She got out at the Tipperary Club, where a number of drunken British officers were singing, and quickly crossed the road. Her flat was only a few minutes' walk away. The streets were still busy, but as she moved through the throng, she thought of Vaughan again. He was a good-looking man, decent, intelligent, and with a sense of humour she could appreciate. It should have been a good evening – she had been looking forward to it. Yet now there would be no friendship between them; in truth, she had hoped for something more.

Desolation descended on her. She was alone in this vast city, her former life gone for ever, and entangled in an operation that she had begun to question. Yes, she hated the Communists and despaired of the Allies, but she was tired of fighting; tired of living a lie; tired of loneliness and isolation. She wished she could be elsewhere, far, far away, the war, the Nazis and the Communists an aberration that had long since ceased to be. Perhaps then there might be a chance for her and Alex Vaughan.

She crossed El Maghrabi and turned into her street. A few yards from the entrance to her block, she paused to look in her bag for her key. A car pulled up alongside her.

'Hello, darling,' called a voice.

Orca. My God.

'Jump in.'

She turned and saw that the front passenger door was open, but the voice had come from the back, through the open window.

'In you get,' said the voice, as charming and easy as ever.

She did as she was told, her heart pounding. The car reeked of leather and stale tobacco.

'Madame.' Artus was behind the wheel.

Instead of replying, she turned to the man in

197

the back, and saw only shadows: it was getting dark and was darker in the car. A hat low over the face, dark glasses. *Impossible to tell.*

'Face the front, Marlin,' he said, the voice now cold and firm. 'I have a pistol pointing at your back.'

'You wouldn't dare shoot me.'

'Oh, yes, I would. Without a second thought.'

'Why have you come?' she said, as Artus released the clutch and the car moved forward. She glanced out of the window, hoping to see someone she knew – the *bawaeb*, perhaps, but there was no sign of him.

'We've a problem.'

'What kind of problem?' she said, her heart quickening once more.

'Your signal about General Gott was picked up and has aroused suspicion.'

'But that's impossible. No one could break the code without the book.'

'They haven't broken the code, but the pilot and several of the crew survived the crash and confirmed that the Germans knew about Gott's death before the British. They suspect a mole within GHQ.'

Tanja fumbled in her bag for a cigarette.

'Unfortunately they've worked out who my go-between is.'

'Have they arrested him?' She put a cigarette between her lips. Artus reached across and lit it.

'Not yet, no. But he will talk if he's interrogated.'

'How do you know? Who is this go-between anyway?'

'He'll talk because he's not strong enough to resist. British interrogation techniques are superb. But, hopefully, we won't need to worry about him. Fortunately, Artus managed to visit him this afternoon without arousing suspicion. His place is being watched, but our man is going to slip out before the curfew. Artus has arranged to meet him in the Old Town where it should be easy to give the British the slip.'

'So we need to close the circuit down,' said Tanja. 'Lie low for a while.'

'No,' said Orca. 'This is the key moment in the campaign. But we have to face facts: a link in the circuit has gone, and it will no longer be possible to react immediately to any information we receive.'

'How will you get information to me now?'

'Through planned meetings with Artus.'

'I do not need to know any of this, so why are you telling me?'

'We need to warn Cobra. First I want you to contact them and get instructions.'

Tanja exhaled. 'And second?'

Orca chuckled. 'It's a small world, isn't it? Here we are in a city of millions, yet you manage to befriend Major Alex Vaughan.'

Tanja felt a stab of alarm. 'What about him?'

'You don't know who he is, do you?'

'Stop playing games with me.'

'Major Vaughan is one of the key officers investigating this case.'

Tanja closed her eyes. *No, no, no.*

'He's a Defence Security officer with Secret Intelligence Middle East, MI6's counter-intelligence organization here. Fortunately for us, he's still quite new to the job and would far rather be on active service at the front.' He paused for a moment. 'But we can use this to our advantage. I want you to cultivate your friendship with Vaughan. Become his lover, Marlin.'

'Why? Surely it would make more sense to disappear from his life.'

'On the contrary. You may be able to learn some important intelligence from him. Keep him close to you, Marlin. That's an order.'

Tanja bit her lip. 'What about the transmitter?'

'What about it?'

'I can hardly keep it in my flat while I'm entertaining Alex Vaughan.'

'It's small, isn't it? Make sure it's hidden properly. That's your job, Marlin.'

'But it will be your problem if I am caught.'

'You won't find any trace back to me. The radio is best kept with you. If, however, there is an urgent reason to move it, we will find somewhere for you to take it.'

'And what about the go-between?'

'You don't need to worry about him.'

They had driven south, towards the edge of the Old Town. Artus now pulled over on a busy street, beside a cart filled with tobacco leaves.

'And how will I pass on any instructions to you?' Tanja asked.

'We will contact you in the same way as before.'

Tanja sat still for a moment, wondering whether to lean back and make a grab for those glasses and his hat. Would he really shoot her? Perhaps it would be better if he did.

'Good night, Marlin,' said Orca. 'We still have very important work to do. All will be well. Now leave us.'

Tanja opened the door and stepped out, then turned and looked through the passenger window. But she could see nothing: just a dark, featureless figure. *But I know your voice.* That, at least, was something.

Thursday, 13 August, around eight twenty a.m. There was still no sign of Moussa the tailor. The mood during morning prayers had been tense – tetchy, even. The convoy to Malta was suffering – *Ohio* had clearly been targeted – and progress on the spy circuit had ground to a halt. Meanwhile, Axis convoys had successfully reached Tobruk and Benghazi, and another transmission of coded numbers had been picked up.

Vaughan had returned to his office to find Tanner standing at the window, smoking a cigarette and staring out over Garden City, while on his makeshift desk, a rickety table pushed up against one wall, there was a mass of files and reports. 'You're looking very pensive, Jack.'

'I reckon I'm too impatient for this lark. My old dad used to din into me the importance of patience, but it's deserted me. This is so bloody frustrating. Anyway, what's happening with the convoy?'

'It's not good news. They've suffered three separate attacks. Last night it was by E-boats. *Cairo, Nigeria* and *Ohio* all torpedoed in the first attack.'

'And sunk?'

'Only *Cairo*, but *Ohio's* in a bad way. It's clearly being targeted. A short while ago, sixty Stukas turned up, all concentrating on the tanker.'

'But she's still afloat?'

'God knows how. According to the message RJ received, one Stuka crashed on her deck. Amazingly, the fuel hasn't fireballed yet.'

'Jesus.' He sighed heavily. 'Does RJ think she's being targeted because of intelligence they've received?'

'Absolutely. He's convinced of it. I tell you, Jack, I've seen pictures of *Ohio,* and she doesn't look that different from the other merchantmen in the convoy.'

'Bloody hell. And *Cairo?* She's a cruiser.'

'Oh, that wasn't all. Another cruiser's gone too – *Manchester* – and three of the merchantmen. Two set on fire and abandoned, and another sunk. Apparently she went down in three minutes – with most of the crew.'

'Poor bastards. Christ, I'm glad I never joined the bloody navy.'

'I'm glad I didn't join the *Merchant* Navy. Half the escorts have buggered off back to Gib. How the hell the rest of the convoy will get through, God only knows.'

'Sounds like a bloody massacre.'

Vaughan digested this, then said, 'There's been another signal too.'

'When?'

'On the afternoon of the eleventh, from Cairo, and a message sent in the same code a few moments later from the Mersa region again.'

'Bloody hell,' muttered Tanner. 'And what

about the signal from Cairo? Any idea where it came from? Although I'm guessing you'd be looking a bit more cheery if you did.'

Vaughan shook his head. 'Major Dennys's signals people can narrow it down to around a mile and a half from the centre of the city but that's the best they can do.'

Tanner stubbed out his cigarette. 'Very helpful – only around a million people to choose from.' It was already growing warm outside so he closed the wooden shutters, the room darkening.

'Any news from upstairs?' asked Vaughan.

'I'm afraid not.' Tanner had seen Astley and Sansom half an hour earlier, but although they still had a section watching the tailor's place, Lieutenant Matherson's men had reported nothing of interest. Moussa's assistant had turned up on two separate occasions but, getting no reply, had trundled off again.

'Come on,' said Vaughan. 'Let's get out before the heat gets too unbearable. I want to hand in my proposal, then we'll get some coffee at Groppi's.'

Vaughan was just putting his proposal into an envelope, when there was a knock on the door and one of the secretaries came in. 'This just arrived for you,' she said, handing a letter to Vaughan. 'It came over from GHQ.'

Vaughan thanked her, then saw the stamp of the Polish Red Cross on the back of the envelope and tore it open. 'It's from her,' he said, his face lighting up. It was handwritten, and dated the previous day.

Dear Alex,
I hope this reaches you. I want to apologize for my
outburst last night. It was very wrong of me and I
know you meant well by what you said. I should not
have reacted in such a way, but it is painful to think
of what has happened to Poland and to my family
and many others who were once dear to me. I hope
that you can forgive me and that we may still be
friends. And if you are not busy perhaps I could buy
you a drink tonight? I do not have your address but
you can find me here, at the Polish Red Cross.
Tanja Zanowski

He folded the letter and smiled.

'She still loves you, then?' Tanner grinned.

'Come on,' said Vaughan. 'And after we've been to GHQ, maybe we'll go to Groppi's Garden instead.'

'Oh, yes? A bit closer to the Polish Red Cross, is it?'

'Perhaps.' Vaughan laughed.

While Vaughan headed into GHQ, Tanner waited outside the wire, sheltering under several large palms. He watched the kites wheeling high above, then the traffic heading in and out of GHQ. He'd heard there were some six thousand staff officers there. It was a hell of a number, and certainly in the twenty minutes he was kept waiting, he saw a steady stream – most in neatly pressed shirts and shorts, socks pulled up just under the knee. He looked down at his own attire – khaki trousers, battered suede boots – and wished he could be back out with the boys in the desert. *Fingers crossed.* That afternoon he'd have his medical. By the end of today, he would know his fate.

Vaughan reappeared, a broad grin on his face. 'You'll never guess who I've just seen.'

'Who?'

'Only the C-in-C!'

'General Alexander?'

'The very same. Only he's not officially C-in-C yet – not until the fifteenth.'

'Well done, mate. How come?'

'He was with the new COS. I went in and saw Brigadier Bill. He was with Peter Fleming, who seemed very taken with the idea and took me straight away to see General McCreery. We knocked on his door and there, sitting on the edge of his desk, was General Alexander.'

'What did they say?'

'Peter said I had an excellent idea for them, repeated what I'd just told him and then the general said, "Very interesting. We were just talking about something along those lines." He thanked me and said they'd have a good look at my suggestion.'

Tanner clapped him on the back. 'I told you he was a good bloke. I've always rated Alexander. When I was out in India on the North-west Frontier, he was a brilliant brigade commander. Last man off at Dunkirk, too. He's not stuffy. Always open to ideas. If he thinks it's got legs, he'll do it, I'm sure.'

They took a taxi to Groppi's Garden, Tanner watching the rush of the city from the open window. He could sense that Vaughan was distracted

– there was much to think about – but was happy to leave his friend to his thoughts. It was only a little after nine, but already the temperature was rising. Tanner was less bothered by the heat in the desert, where for the most part the air was clean and empty – if anything, the freezing cold nights of winter were more of a hindrance – but the city, with the smoke and the mass of people, beasts and machines, was appreciably hotter and more oppressive.

He thought again about his medical, and prayed he would be given the all-clear to return to the battalion. It was time. Detective work was not for him, and he yearned for the camaraderie of the men he knew so well. He'd missed Sykes these past weeks, and for all the good that this period of recuperation had done him, and the pleasure he had gained from his time with Lucie, he was impatient to return to what he knew best. He rolled his shoulder and pumped his arm. It felt all right – bit of a twinge, perhaps, but nothing he couldn't hide from the doctor.

Groppi's Garden was on El Maghrabi, the rather bland coffee-house leading out into a walled garden filled with brightly coloured umbrellas that shielded every table. The scent of jasmine, coffee and freshly baked pastries wafted across the tiny oasis. Tanner and Vaughan found an empty table and sat down. They ordered thick, sugary Turkish coffee – so different from the ersatz variety they were given in the desert – and lit cigarettes.

'At least we're making progress,' said Vaughan. 'Our spy circuit must know we're on to them. That's going to make it harder for them to continue sending messages. RJ always said it was about closing the ring around them and that's what we're doing. If the tailor's been involved, he's certainly out of the picture now. I wonder where he's got to. Lying low?'

'Perhaps,' said Tanner.

'And while everyone had forgotten about Eslem Mustafa,' continued Vaughan, 'now the whole of FS and the Egyptian secret police are looking out for him. If he is still around, there's got to be a good chance of catching up with him. And if he's involved, it'll be harder for him to continue.'

Tanner nodded slowly. 'I feel certain he is. I think we're dealing with an operation that's been going on for some time. I reckon this circuit's been operating without anyone realizing, and that it was set up by the Romanian mission before they got the boot. All the connections with El Masri and Mustafa point to that. But I bet that's how they got their radio set, or whatever it is they're using. I'd also lay good money on that Eppler bloke being sent as a decoy.'

'Eppler?'

'I read through all those reports and, bloody hell, he was useless. No properly trained spy could be quite so bloody obvious. All that non-sense about dressing up and spending fake fivers. So we're all busy looking for him and getting on his trail, and all the while the proper spies are operating right under our noses.'

'I hadn't thought of that,' mused Vaughan, 'but it's certainly possible.'

'I doubt Eppler was in on it. He probably

thought he was as cunning as a snake, but he never once managed to send a single meaningful message, did he?'

'All he transmitted were signals trying to establish a connection.' He laughed. 'Maybe you're right, Jack – but don't tell Sammy. Those FS boys are terribly pleased with themselves for capturing him.'

'I think you should keep this between us anyway. After all, we've still not got the proof we need, have we?'

'Sadly not.'

Tanner leaned forward, and spoke quietly: 'But then our real spies go and do something they haven't before. They send a specific signal, which could only have come from here in Cairo. They probably hoped the shooting down of Gott would be passed off as a chance encounter, but the pilot miraculously survived, and suddenly what was a suspicion that might otherwise have been dismissed is now ringing major alarm bells. It all fits. It's just tying it down – getting that proof – that's the headache. That's what's so bloody frustrating.' He wiped his sleeve across his brow. 'But I feel certain Mustafa holds the key. I'm sure of it. If we can find him, we might at last begin to get somewhere.'

At just before five o'clock, Tanner was sitting in the 9th Scottish General Hospital, waiting to see the doctor. The air was heavy with the smell of sweat and carbolic. Flies crawled across the wall opposite as he jiggled his leg and glanced at his watch. *Still not five o'clock.* A little further down the corridor a VAD nurse sat behind a desk. She had told him Dr Chawley would not be long, and no one else was waiting.

Tanner rolled his arm again. It was getting better, there was no doubt of it, and he was certain he'd be able to raise his arm and fire a rifle if necessary. Hopefully he wouldn't have to for a week or so yet: the moon wouldn't be full until the end of the month, and a full moon was what the enemy would most likely want for any attack.

A buzzer sounded on the VAD's desk.

'Yes, Doctor?' she said. 'Yes... Of course.' She turned to Tanner, who sat up expectantly.

'Dr Chawley will see you now. Second door on the left.'

Tanner loosened his shoulder and arm once more, then walked the few yards along the corridor and knocked.

'Come!'

Tanner went in, conscious that the air in the doctor's room was noticeably cooler. Two large ceiling fans whirred above him, and the smell of disinfectant was sharp. Unlike the wards, there was no stench of decay and sweat, only an impression of cleanliness. The doctor, a colonel in the RAMC, looked to be in his fifties, with thinning grey hair and a moustache. Stethoscope around his neck, he was sitting upright at his desk, reading some notes.

Tanner stood to attention and saluted, at which point the doctor looked up and smiled. 'Lieutenant Tanner,' he said. 'You've been promoted?'

'Yes, sir.'

'Congratulations. Army needs more chaps who

know what they're doing, rather than young boys straight out of school, which is the kind of subaltern we mostly see in here.'

'Thank you, sir.'

Chawley put the notes down and leaned back in his chair, fingers together. 'So, how are you feeling?'

'Fine, thank you, sir. Fit as a fiddle.'

The doctor smiled. 'I remember when you first came in, Tanner – you were in a hell of a mess. I'm surprised to see you so soon.'

'I've been well looked after, sir.'

'Well, let's have a look at you. Shirt off, please.'

Tanner slipped it over his head as Chawley came around to him, perched on the edge of the desk and turned Tanner around.

'Hmm,' he said, 'the scars are healing well, but they still look a bit livid.'

Tanner felt his heart sink. 'I can't feel them, sir,' he said.

'Not bothering you at all?'

'No, sir.'

'And what about this arm? Lift it for me, will you?'

Tanner clenched his teeth and raised it.

'A bit higher.'

A stab of pain shot down Tanner's side, but he managed to hide it.

'And down and round.'

Tanner did as he was told. The doctor took his arm and rolled the shoulder. 'And you can move this freely, can you?'

'Yes, sir,' said Tanner. But not without pain. *No point mentioning that.*

210

Chawley put the stethoscope into his ears. 'I'll just have a quick listen to your heart.' Tanner felt the cold metal on his chest. 'Perhaps a little fast.'

'I'm nervous, sir,' said Tanner.

'Nervous, boy? What about?'

'Failing this medical, sir.'

Chawley took the stethoscope from his ears and returned to his chair. 'Tell me, Tanner, why are you so desperate to get back to the front? You could easily sit out a few months here in Cairo. For all I know, you might even be able to get yourself a ticket home.'

'I feel I'm letting the boys down, sir. I'm a soldier. It's what I do best. I've appreciated the chance for a rest, but now I feel it's time to get back.'

The doctor looked at him a moment, then took out a piece of paper and a fountain pen. He began to write. Tanner watched him in silence. Did that mean he'd been passed fit? He couldn't tell.

Eventually Chawley folded the paper and put it into an envelope. 'All right, Tanner, you can rejoin your battalion.'

'Thank you, sir,' said Tanner, brightening.

'But give it another couple of days.' He passed over the envelope. 'It's Thursday the thirteenth, now, so I've put Saturday down. It gives you the rest of this week.'

'All right, sir. Thank you.'

Chawley eyed the tall young man in front of him. 'I hope you haven't persuaded me against my better judgement. You know, Tanner, earlier this year I had a similar case. Young chap, desperate to get back to his men. He'd been decorated,

211

too, but rather like you, his wounds could have kept him out of the fray for a good long time, if not for ever. Sadly, that young man was killed almost immediately, and I know that's what happens in war, but I've always regretted giving him the all-clear. He'd still be alive if I hadn't.'

'I'll be all right, sir,' said Tanner. 'And if I'm not, I promise I won't hold it against you.'

Chawley smiled. 'All right, Lieutenant. Off you go. Good luck, and God speed.'

Tanner saluted and left.

Thank God, he thought. *Thank God for that.*

Tanner had not gone back to Red Pillars that evening. Instead he had waited at the main entrance to the hospital for Lucie to arrive and had told her the news. She had smiled weakly, kissed him, and he had promised to take her out the following evening, her first night off and their last together for God only knew how long. Then he had taken the tram to Mena to tell Peploe that he would be returning in a couple of days. A few beers later, he headed back into Cairo, in a better mood than he had been all week.

His conscience had taken him to Red Pillars. There was no sign of Vaughan, but Tanner had guessed his friend was with Tanja Zanowski. Instead, he had continued to go through the piles of reports he had borrowed from upstairs, trying to piece together a trail around Eslem Mustafa: every place he had been spotted, every person known to have been seen with him.

He had been at his desk a little under an hour when Maunsell put his head around the door.

'Ah, Jack – you're on your own, are you? Why don't you come and have a drink with me and Paddy? Only in my office, I'm afraid, but I've a half-decent bottle of Scotch. We're celebrating.'

'Really? Good news?'

'Three ships have safely reached Malta.'

'That's something,' said Tanner. 'What about *Ohio?*'

'She's still afloat, about a hundred miles out. And while she's afloat, there's always hope.'

He followed Maunsell down the corridor and into his office. Maddox was sitting there, fingering a glass tumbler.

'Malta, Malta,' said Maunsell, walking over to the side-table on which stood a tray of glasses and several bottles. 'Ever been there, Tanner?'

'Only for a couple of nights on the way to India. But that was years ago.'

'A tiny place, and there it is, slap-bang in the middle of the Mediterranean.' He jabbed at the island on his large wall map. 'You know,' he said, pouring Tanner a generous glass, 'I've never been able to understand why on earth the Huns went for Crete when they could have had Malta for the taking. You were on Crete, weren't you?'

Tanner nodded. 'With Alex Vaughan.'

'A bad business, but it's proved next to useless for the Huns. More of a hindrance, really. A bit humiliating for us, but no long-term disaster – one thing less to worry about, really.'

'We lost a lot of ships and good men there.'

'Yes, and that was obviously a terrible waste, but strategically, Jack, it's a dud for the Axis. Now Malta, on the other hand, had Hitler tried a bit

213

harder there, that really would have been catastrophic. I don't think it's over-stretching things
to suggest that if the Axis lose in North Africa it'll
be down to their failure to capture that island.'

'They haven't lost yet, RJ,' muttered Maddox.

'True, and I suppose Malta might still fall,
although I think that's unlikely as we have three
ships unloading in Grand Harbour. The island
won't starve now.'

'But Malta can't strike at the Axis shipping
lanes without that fuel on *Ohio*,' said Maddox.

'No, and that might make all the difference as
to whether or not Rommel can attack successfully. Armies run on fuel – without it they grind
to a halt.' He put his pipe into his mouth. 'I fancy
we're looking at Rommel's last chance. He's *got*
to strike soon. If we survive that, then I think the
tables really will have turned.'

'Actually,' said Tanner, 'I'll be one of those facing Rommel's forces. I've just been passed fit for
active duty.'

'You're pleased?' said Maddox.

Tanner nodded. 'I'll be glad to get back to
fighting an enemy I can see.'

'Better the enemy you know, eh?' said Maunsell. 'Well, good for you, Jack, although I'm sorry
we're losing you so soon. You've done some in-
valuable work this week. Quite a breakthrough,
really.'

'I'm not so sure about that. Really, we've only
confirmed what you'd already suspected. I'm not
sure we're any closer to catching the buggers.
Our mole's still sitting pretty, isn't he?'

'We're getting there, Jack. I've been in this

business a long time, and it can be frustrating, but we've made great strides at a critical time. If I was that mole, I'd be feeling pretty damn twitchy at the moment – wouldn't you agree, Paddy?'

Maddox shifted in his seat and crossed his legs. 'Absolutely.'

'And if, by what we've done this week, we've made it harder for him and the circuit to operate effectively and, more importantly, to pass on important information, we've already played a key part in the battle to come.'

Tanner took a sip of his Scotch. He wanted to ask them something, but wondered whether he should. *Sod it. Where was the harm?* 'I keep thinking about who our mole might be,' he said. 'We've been assuming he's in GHQ, but doesn't it worry you that it might be someone here? We knew about Gott's movements at SIME, and presumably they did at MEIC too.'

Maunsell lit his pipe. 'Of course it worries me. We're all under scrutiny, as are our colleagues at ISLD and MEIC. But tell me this: have you seen any new top-secret information this week?'

'No.'

'And neither have many others. We've already implemented a new clampdown, further limiting access to top-secret information. And, actually, I've got a further development I can report.'

Maddox looked up. *Oh, yes?*

'Earlier I met the new C-in-C over at Grey Pillars. It wasn't just me, I hasten to add, but all the intelligence chiefs.'

'How was he?' asked Tanner. 'The general, I mean?'

215

'Looking fit, well and mustard keen to get stuck in. Anyway, he's been here a few days now, and I've got to say he's not that impressed with what he's seen around Cairo. He reckons it's all a bit slack. Says there are too many staff officers, too many distractions in the city, and that the General Staff need a proverbial kick up the backside.'

'No disrespect, RJ, but I'd agree with that,' said Tanner.

Maunsell bowed. 'Obviously we need to stay in the city, but he's moving most of the staff out to Mena. He's setting up a new camp there for GS bods.'

'And does that include all the GSI chaps?' asked Maddox.

'Absolutely. It might make life a bit more difficult for our mole, don't you think, stuck out on the edge of the desert?'

'Maybe,' said Tanner. 'If he's one of those being moved.'

'Look,' said Maunsell, 'as I said to you before, Jack, it's all about tightening the ring. Making it harder for our circuit and our mole to operate. Whoever it is, we will catch him, maybe not to-morrow, maybe not this week, but one day. Rest assured of that.'

This time, there had been no disagreements, no cause to walk out early. And not because of what Orca had told her, but because she had found Alex Vaughan to be good company. He had apologized for being a prig and for his insensitivity, and had done so with a graciousness that had impressed her. After that, he had carefully kept off the subject. The drink she had suggested had developed into dinner, at Shanti's in the Ezbekiyeh Gardens, and for a blissful couple of hours, Orca, Artus and the web of deceit that was her life had been put to one side. She had laughed, too, more than she had in a long time; Alex had been a good raconteur.

At a little after half past nine they had left the restaurant, and she had allowed him to walk her to her flat.

'So this is where you are,' he said, as she stopped by the entrance and looked in her bag for her key. 'A convenient place to live. Very central.'

'Yes. I've been lucky.'

They were silent for a moment, then Vaughan said, 'Tanja – thank you. I've had a lovely evening. I'm glad we're friends again.'

'Me too.' She looked up at him, his strong features half in shadow from the streetlight. *Not this time.* 'Thank you for dinner. And for walking me home.' She leaned towards him and kissed him, not on the cheek, but on the lips. Then, brushing his arm, she headed inside. When she turned back, she saw he had already begun walking away.

Once in her flat, she pulled off her earrings, kicked off her shoes and lay on her bed, her mind a jumble of conflicting thoughts. *What to do?* She had yet to make contact with Cobra; indecision had paralysed her. Orca had repelled her: the bullying, hectoring tone; the threats; the contempt he had shown her. And what of the go-between? What would happen to him? She dared not think.

217

Her motive had always been to help overthrow Stalin and the Communists, yet the iron certainty, the conviction that this was the single course she should follow, now seemed open to question. Polish men were training in Iraq to fight against the Germans, not the Reds, which meant she was actively working against her countrymen. And yet they were still a long way from the front line. The 2nd Polish Corps now being formed would not see action this year, or possibly even next. They were too ill, too weakened, for that. That meant Germany might defeat the Soviet Union before the Polish Corps entered the fray.

She lay there, staring at the featureless white wall. Not for the first time in recent weeks, she felt overwhelmed by the situation in which she found herself. She was suffocating. Anger, grief and desolation had fuelled her decision to spy for Germany, but now she faced a wall of doubt. What would happen if she told Cobra the circuit was compromised? What would Orca do if he found out? There had been something rather crazed about his insistence that they continue feeding information to Cobra. Reason, she was certain, dictated they should lie low, yet Orca was seemingly prepared to risk all.

She wondered what would happen if that tanker, *Ohio*, failed to reach Malta. She wondered what would happen if Rommel attacked and failed to smash through the British defences. And she wondered what would happen if she offered herself to the British as a double-agent. What would Alex Vaughan think of her then? Alex, who was a secret-service agent himself.

Would spying for the British help rid Poland of the Reds? Perhaps, if the Western Allies could smash the Nazis. Would they then insist Poland be returned? Might Britain honour her pledge after all?

The answers to these questions, which she had asked herself over and over again, were no clearer to her. She closed her eyes, clenched her hair in her hands and felt tears prick her eyes. There was only one thing about which she was certain: that she no longer wanted to be a spy – not for Germany, not for anybody. *I can't do it any more.* She wanted to work for the Polish Red Cross, help her countrymen, and begin a love affair with Alex – not because Orca had told her to, but because she wanted to be with him. A good, decent man, who made her laugh and who would make her feel safe. *I can't mourn for ever.*

She shuddered. 'Be strong, Tanja,' Tomas had told her. 'Never give up.' She wiped her face, stood up and went to the small leather box on her chest of drawers – she had had it since childhood and had carried it with her all the way from Poland. Opening it, she took out the single gold ring and clutched it. Then she took out the photograph. A young man, laughing, sitting beneath a tree, a lake beyond. Four years ago, almost to the day, she realized. *August 1938.*

She looked at it for several moments, then put it, with the ring, back in the box, went into the living room, poured herself a brandy and lit a cigarette. She sat at the table, thinking hard and forcing herself to clear her mind. Smoke swirled into the still air. Brandy seared her throat.

Then, at last, resolution of sorts. What happened in the desert or at sea was now out of her hands. She would respond to messages from Orca with her normal swiftness; she would appear to Artus as committed as ever. She now had something on Orca, but to get out of this mess, she needed to know more – much more. From now on, Alex and his colleagues would not be the only ones trying to unravel the spy circuit. She would try to find out who Orca and Artus were.

Friday, 14 August, around six a.m. Tanner was just completing his morning shave when there was a bang on the door of Lucie's flat. Quickly wiping his face, he hurried to the door and opened it. One of the Field Security men was standing there.

'Morning, sir,' he said, slightly breathless. 'Sergeant Ellis. Sorry to call so early, but Major Vaughan and Captain Astley sent me to get you.'

'Give me a moment, will you?'

A minute later, his shirt on, belt and pistol fastened around his waist and cap hastily shoved on his head, he was shutting the door behind him.

'Did he say what it's about?' asked Tanner, as they hurried down the stairs.

'No, sir. Captain Astley just told me to get you and take you to Old Cairo.'

'Old Cairo? Bloody hell.'

They left the apartment block. Parked outside was a black Austin 10. 'That's ours, sir,' said the sergeant.

Tanner got in beside Ellis and they set off down past the university and turned south on Kasr El

Aini. There was already traffic about: trams jangling up and down, and carts laden with fruit and other produce heading into the city. The car rattled and spluttered, jerking both men in their seats.

'Sorry about the car, sir,' said Ellis. 'We've been promised some jeeps, but the priority's the desert.'

'Doesn't bother me. Just so long as it gets us there.'

'It's not far. A couple of miles at most.'

The city briefly gave way to mud-coloured shacks and small fields of maize and sugar cane. Tanner glanced to his right and saw the Island of Roda, with its dense groves of date palms, hazy in the early-morning light. He watched the tramline turn over the bridge across the Nile that led to Giza and Mena Camp. Tomorrow he would be taking a tram along that line himself, on his way back to the battalion. *But first this.*

Ellis took the road down to the harbour. Warehouses lined the quayside, which was already busy with boats, newly docked and already unloading rice and grain from Upper Egypt. Ellis wove through carts and trucks right up to the edge of the quay, where they saw Captain Astley, who waved.

'Morning, Jack,' said Astley, as Ellis brought the car to a stop.

'What's going on?'

'Jump out and I'll show you.'

Tanner thanked Ellis, and got out. The quayside was alive with the shouts of merchants and dockworkers.

221

'This way,' said Astley. 'We're right down by the river.'

He led Tanner down a broad flight of some forty or so steps to the water's edge, where Vaughan stood, with several FS men and Egyptian police gathered around him.

Vaughan turned as he approached. 'Hello, Jack. Guess who washed up in the river this morning?'

'I've got a pretty good idea.'

An FS man stood back to let him through, and Tanner peered down at the dead man stretched out on the stone. The corpse was pale, with a swollen gash across his throat, his shirt covered with blood.

It was the tailor, Gyasi Moussa.

THE WESTERN DESERT

August and September 1942

10

Tuesday, 18 August 1942. The column trundled slowly north-westwards, a stream of some hundred sand-coloured vehicles into which the entire 2nd Battalion was crammed: a combination of Bedford 30- and 15-hundredweight trucks and at least thirty universal carriers, all rumbling along at a steady twenty-five miles an hour. The road, an unmetalled track, hugged the edge of the Nile delta, so that although the view ahead was mostly of the dust kicked up by the vehicle in front, at either side they could see the endless desolation of the desert to the left, and the lushness of the delta to the right.

It was still quite early, a little after eight, and they had been driving for more than an hour. The air was still fresh. Tanner sat up front, next to Private David Brown, who was driving. The truck was a Bedford 15-hundredweight, an MWD, six-cylinder, 72-horsepower, and around two tons unloaded. It was basic as hell, all glass and doors stripped off, with just a single roll-bar between the cab and the body. Although the engine sometimes played up, the radiator was sturdy and reliable even in the extreme heat of the desert, and the gearbox was as strong as an ox. With five men in the back, rifles, a Bren, ammunition, rations, water and fuel cans, plus all their individual kit bundled up and strapped to the sides, the MWD was home to the seven and would remain so throughout their time in the desert.

The truck hit a pot-hole, causing groans behind, and knocking Tanner in his seat.

'Jesus, Browner!' cursed Tanner. 'Watch where you're bloody going.'

'Sorry, sir,' said Brown. 'My goggles must be a bit dusted up.'

'Well, give them here, then.'

Brown took them off and passed them to Tanner, who poured a small amount of water from his bottle over the lenses. Once the grit was washed away, he dried them on his shirt and passed them back.

'Cheers, sir,' said Brown, putting them back on. 'Ah, yes, that's much better.'

Tanner cuffed him gently on the back of his head. 'Bloody hell, Browner. Next time just ask, all right?'

Despite being jerked and bounced in his seat, Tanner was in a good mood. Things were back to normal. Browner was beside him, his old mate, Stan Sykes, was behind with Hepworth and Smailes, with whom he had served for more than two years, then Mudge and Phyllis, two new lads. It no longer mattered that he was now Lieutenant Tanner rather than CSM: the differences in rank could more easily melt away out in the desert.

The same could not be said of camp life. For the past three days, Tanner had found it difficult to adjust to his new status. He did not feel he belonged in the mess. Officers swore, but not in the same way that he used such language. Table manners were different too. His father had taught him how to behave, but during dinner at Mena House with Peploe and the colonel, he had been at sea with the array of knives and forks, unsure which to use and when. He had also struggled with some of the conversation. It often seemed to be about people they all knew but he did not. And there was also his sense of social inferiority: he did not feel a lesser man, but was keenly aware of the huge gulf between him and his fellow officers – all but Tanner and one other in C Company had been to public school. Lieutenant Marsden was a grammar-school boy; Tanner had barely been to school at all. Strangely, he had felt less conspicuous when he'd been with SIME. Maunsell's relaxed ship, the eclectic group of operatives and the fact that he had barely been out and about socially had shielded him.

Most of his fellow officers had been friendly and accepting towards him; only one or two, including a couple of young subalterns in B Company, seemed to be steering clear. He was aware that the problem was mainly of his own making, and recognized that it was up to him to come to terms with his new status, but it was not something he could resolve in a few days. It would take time.

What he had found even harder was feeling like an outsider among the men. He could no longer share his meals with Stan and the other lads, or enter the sergeants' mess for a beer. An invisible barrier had been drawn up. Even Stan had initially seemed a little wary, as though not wanting to appear overly familiar now that Tanner was an officer. Eventually Tanner had told him to cut it out and, armed with several bottles of Stella, they had walked up to the Pyramids and had the kind of easy chat that had done so much to sustain them both during the past two and a half years.

That had helped, because after three days back, Tanner had been feeling quite deflated. It had reminded him of when he'd first joined the regiment, ten years before, as a boy soldier. He, a Wiltshireman with a West Country burr, had been surrounded by Yorkshiremen, mostly from the industrial cities of Bradford and Leeds. He'd felt like an outsider then too.

Now those feelings had melted away. This was the life he had known since they had become fully mechanized the previous autumn. Their role was to roam the desert, to patrol and cajole the enemy, not hold any static position or the dreaded 'boxes' that had done for Eighth Army back at Gazala in May. Each company worked as a team, and each six- or seven-man section lived, slept and fought together.

Captain Peploe was in the lead truck with six men from Company Headquarters, followed by Tanner with six men. Then came six more trucks per platoon, except for 2 Platoon, who were in carriers. Tanner leaned out and gazed back at the long column as it trundled forward along a wide curve in the road. It reminded him of a goods train. He breathed in the smell of dust, oil and metal, and smiled to himself.

'This is more like it, isn't it, sir?' said Sykes, behind him.

'Too bloody right, Stan.' Tanner grinned. It was

good to be back on track with Sykes – they'd been through so much together. Sykes was from Deptford, in south London. When they'd first met, back in early 1940, Tanner had sensed a kindred spirit immediately, not least because Sykes had been another outsider among the mass of Yorkshiremen. After nearly three years of war, the battalion was not quite so full of home-grown soldiers as it had once been – Mudge, for example, was from Suffolk – but the early ties that had drawn the two together remained. Men came and went in any company and battalion – whether killed, wounded, promoted or posted – and Tanner knew that, at some point, the chances were that he and Sykes would be separated. It was something he chose not to dwell upon. They would be serving together in the battle to come; for the time being that was good enough. *Never look too far ahead*. It was a mantra Tanner had always lived by.

Sykes had also proved his worth as a friend: after Tanner had been wounded he had saved both his rifle, with its special fittings for a scope, and his German sub-machine gun, the latter taken the previous year on Crete. He had presented these weapons back to him as though they were long-lost family heirlooms on his arrival back with the battalion. Tanner had been very grateful, allowing himself more effusive thanks than he would normally have demonstrated, for he valued both weapons and had assumed they had long since become casualties of war. The rifle he had had since returning to England early in the war. Most were now the Number 4 Short Magazine Lee Enfields, but his was the earlier

Number 1 Mark III, which not only had fittings for the old 17-inch sword bayonet, which Tanner preferred, but also had special pads and mounts attached for fixing a telescopic sight, which he had had fitted on the quiet before heading to Norway. He still had the Aldis scope – most of his personal belongings had thankfully made it with him on the long journey back to Cairo. It had been his father's in the last war and was one of his most treasured items, partly for sentimental reasons, but principally because it had repeatedly proved itself a life-saver. That scope had helped him get out of more scrapes than he cared to remember.

The sub-machine gun was an MP40, taken from an enemy paratrooper on Crete. Beautifully balanced and superbly made, Tanner preferred it to the Thompsons that were now staples of the British Army and thought it a far superior weapon to the smaller, lighter Sten, which, although easy to carry about, lacked the velocity of either the MP40 or the Thompson. Nor was getting ammunition for the MP40 a problem: it shared the same 9mm-calibre rounds as the Sten. He had put several boxes of it in the truck.

Some thirty yards ahead, Peploe's truck swerved to avoid a donkey and cart, kicking up a bigger swirl of dust. Tanner squinted behind his sunglasses and ducked his head as the cloud rolled over them.

'Just ease back a bit, will you, Browner?' he said. 'Don't want everyone to choke to death before we get up to the blue.'

'Sorry, boss,' said Brown.

The road now climbed on to an embankment and Tanner looked out over the sprawl of delta. Away to his right he could see the Nile, the sails of feluccas clearly visible between the date palms and banana plantations. There were fields, too, small dark-green rectangles. A farmer was ploughing with an ox, the blade turning furrows of rich, chocolate-coloured earth. The sun beat down, but unlike in Cairo, where the taxis were mostly dark, enclosed vehicles that drew the heat, the open Bedfords, travelling at twenty-five miles per hour, provided a warm breeze that shielded them from the scorching sun.

Cairo had been left far behind. Glancing back, he saw the city as a grey smudge in the distance. He would miss Lucie and he had been sorry to leave her, but he'd vowed he would be back. The thought of returning to her was something he could relish. He had also been sorry to say good-bye to Vaughan. As they had shaken hands, and wished each other luck, he had seen the envy, regret, even, in his friend's face. He wondered whether the general would take up his coastal raiding party idea. He hoped so – it seemed a good one to him, particularly now when Rommel's LOCs were so much longer than their own. If the raiders could sabotage supplies coming into Tobruk and Mersa, the enemy's closest ports, they might make a big difference.

The convoy rumbled on towards Alexandria. His thoughts turned to the mole and whether they would ever catch him. Moussa had been cut from ear to ear – such an unnecessary way to kill someone. Quiet, yes, but all that blood: it would have been a messy business. Paul Rolo had suggested that an Islamist had killed him – cutting the throat was an Islamic way of delivering death. Perhaps. But if there had ever been any doubt about the circuit, the murder had clinched it. Even George Kirk had conceded that.

Ah, well. It was out of his hands now, and already the importance of catching the spies had receded. *Ohio* had made it, limping into Malta's Grand Harbour, despite having been hit innumerable times. Two destroyers had strapped themselves to her sides, and a third had led. A miracle. Four other merchantmen had got there too – five out of the fourteen that had begun, but Malta was saved. There was now apparently enough fuel for the island to launch offensive operations once more. It meant that bombers could fly from Malta, attack a convoy, fly on to Egypt and vice versa.

Maunsell had been so jubilant he had sent one of the secretaries to buy several bottles of champagne from the Semiramis Hotel and they had all toasted the success of the convoy and gallant *Ohio*. 'In the battle to come,' Maunsell told them, with uncharacteristic gravity, 'this really could make all the difference.'

The convoy had succeeded, despite the enemy spy circuit operating from Cairo. GHQ had started moving to Mena, which might well narrow the field of suspects, should another signal be picked up. New clampdowns were in place, making top-secret information even more need-to-know. One of the circuit – or an associate – was dead, and continued efforts were being made to track down the elusive Eslem Mustafa. Maun-sell had repeatedly said they must tighten the noose around the spies to make it far more difficult for them to obtain intelligence of real value. After all, any spying operation was only as good as the information it passed on.

Tanner thought of the eccentricities of Maun-sell's organization: only a few, like Maunsell and Maddox, were proper intelligence men. It had struck him as odd that Vaughan, or even he, could be drafted in with little or no prior grasp of coun-ter-intelligence work. And yet, as Maunsell had said, so much of it was about common sense. He supposed he had been able to bring a bit of that to it. He chuckled to himself. *A strange experience.*

The road led them further into the lush vege-tation, and after a couple of hours the desert to their left had vanished. By half past ten Hep-worth, especially, was restless.

'Surely it's time to brew up, sir. We've been going nearly four hours already.'

'What do you want me to do about it, Hep?' said Tanner. 'I'm sure the colonel'll give us a halt in a while.'

Hepworth was quiet for a bit, but as another ten minutes passed, even Sykes was beginning to grumble. 'I really thought Old Man Vigar under-stood the importance of char,' he said. 'I'm bloody gasping.'

'I'm hungry too,' said Phyllis.

'You're always bloody hungry, Siff,' said Sykes. 'Is there ever a time when you don't think about scoff?'

'Yes,' said Phyllis. 'Course.'

'When's that, then?'

'When I'm thinking about that Egyptian bint I had last week.'

'We all know about that one, Siff,' said Sykes. 'An absolute beauty once you got past the moustache.'

'She didn't have a moustache, she–'

'Siff, he's taking the piss,' said Tanner. 'I'm sure she was gorgeous.'

'Have you checked yourself, though, Siff?' asked Brown. 'You know, that your tackle's still functioning.'

'Course it is.'

'Only I've heard you can catch something awful from those native bints. I mean, you wouldn't want to get syphilis, Siff, would you?'

They all laughed, then passed another cart, this time with a young Egyptian girl sitting on the back.

'There, Siff, what about her?' said Brown.

'Nah,' said Phyllis. 'Not my type.'

'Just because she didn't have a 'tache, Siff,' said Sykes.

More laughter.

'Oh, I get it,' said Phyllis. 'It's take-the-piss-out-of-Siff day, is it?'

'I thought that was every day,' said Brown.

The banter tailed off and they were silent for a few minutes. Then Hepworth said, 'I'm even more parched now. This is getting ridiculous. Hey, Stan, couldn't we try and brew up while we're going along?'

'I knew a bloke who tried that once.'

'What happened?' asked Phyllis.

'Did you notice I used the past tense, Siff?'

'Yes, but what happened?'

'Well, just think about it, Siff,' said Tanner. 'A moving truck, full of ammo and fuel.'

'So he killed himself?'

'That's a wonderfully quick brain you've got there, isn't it, Siff?' said Sykes. 'Yes, he was brown bread. Well, actually, if you really want to know I made it all up, but no one's brewing anything while I'm sitting here.'

'Well said, Stan,' said Tanner. 'Sorry, lads, you're just going to have to hold on. Anyway, look on the bright side. If we keep making good progress, the colonel might feel we deserve a little swim in the sea.'

'Do you think so?' asked Smailes.

'He might,' said Tanner. 'I heard talk of it.'

'That'd be great,' said Smailes.

'I'd love a swim in the sea,' said Phyllis.

'All that salt water would do your old fellow good, Siff,' said Brown.

'Shut up, Browner.'

'I mean it. Salt water's good for the clap, isn't that right, sir?'

'I wouldn't know, Browner.'

Around eleven Tanner spotted a red flag being hoisted on the lead vehicle, some way ahead but just visible as the convoy snaked along a curve in the road. 'There you go, Hep,' he said. 'We're stopping.'

Sure enough, one by one, the vehicles ahead began pulling off to the side of the road, until at last it was their turn to halt too.

Tanner hoisted himself out, stretched and lit a

235

cigarette. He watched Hepworth and Mudge gather three large stones as a makeshift hob, while the others scavenged for dried leaves, sticks and bits of scrub. These were flung together between the stones and then an old four-gallon flimsy with the top sliced off was filled with water. The fire was lit, the flimsy placed on top, and Mudge carefully added a handful of leaves, sugar and condensed milk, then gave it a quick stir.

The men now stood around, smoking and chatting. Tanner wandered down towards Peploe. It was searing hot now that they had stopped. In the sky above, kites were circling, mewing to each other in their strange plaintive cry. They reminded him of the buzzards that had drifted in the sky at home, when he'd been a boy.

'We seem to be making good progress,' said Peploe. 'Nearly at the edge of Alexandria.'

'How long are we stopping? Are we expected to have tiffin now?'

Peploe glanced up the road. 'I'm not sure. It's a bit late for a tea break and a bit early for lunch. Don't know what Vigar's thinking, to be honest.'

'I'm all for keeping going. The lads are keen to have a dip in the sea. It'd do 'em good, before we get out into the blue.'

Peploe nodded. 'I'll go and see what's what.'

He strode off towards the head of the column and Tanner sauntered back to his men. The char was boiling, so Mudge began to pour it into the line of enamel tin mugs.

Tanner leaned against the wooden side of the truck. The lads already looked tousled and a bit weathered. It was too hot to wear tin helmets –

they avoided them as much as they could – and although Sykes and Smailes wore their field service caps, the rest were bare-headed, their hair already thick with dust.

Peploe returned with the news that tiffin was to be eaten *en route*, and that if they continued to make good progress, they would stop near Burg El Arab for an hour, when there would be an opportunity to swim.

'Sounds good to me,' said Tanner.

'I agree. Pass it on, will you?' said Peploe.

'Of course.'

Peploe wiped his brow. 'I'd better get back. The blue flag's going up in about five minutes.'

Tanner and his men finished their char, kicked out the fire and got back into the truck.

'Bloody hell, it's hot,' muttered Brown. 'My seat's like a flipping hob and the steering wheel's going to blister my hands.'

'Stop whingeing, Browner,' said Tanner, 'and be thankful the skipper doesn't make you wear shorts like the rest of the battalion.'

The entire company wore trousers, rather than shorts. Tanner had always avoided the shorts that were standard issue in the Middle East. They were comfortable enough and, of course, used less cotton so were cheaper to produce, but it was all too easy to get sunburned legs, even with long socks, and bare skin was also exposed to cuts and scratches. In the desert, a minor injury could lead to infection and even gangrene. Tanner had explained this to Peploe when they'd first been issued with shorts in Crete the previous year, and since taking command of A Company, the captain had insisted all his men stick to this principle.

Ahead, the blue flag had been raised and engines were coughing into life. Brown pushed up the ignition switch in the centre of the dashboard, then turned the knob and, after a few languid whirrs, the engine burst into life.

'Off we go again,' said Sykes, cheerily. 'Next stop, the blue.'

In Cairo, the heat was suffocating. Everyone had been sucking ice cubes most of the morning, and despite closing the shutters, Red Pillars had sweltered. In his office, Vaughan had found it hard to concentrate, although in truth, the heat was only partly responsible. Like Tanner, he was finding the spy case frustrating. No signal had been picked up and no sighting of Eslem Mustafa had been reported. It had been the same story for the past three days. Sansom's FS men had searched extensively in the Islamic quarter where they had lost Moussa a few nights earlier, but had found nothing. No one had seen him. No one had heard anything. A wall of silence.

Then there was the matter of his coastal raiding party proposal. He had hoped to hear something by now, and feared it had disappeared among a sea of other requests and demands. As each day passed with no word, the thought that he might now be stuck in Cairo, a largely desk-bound counter-intelligence officer, gnawed away at him.

The only consolation was Tanja. Beautiful, alluring, enigmatic Tanja. He had had plenty of girlfriends in the past, but never one who had consumed him so quickly. Barely a minute

238

passed without her crossing his mind. A week ago he'd not even met her; now, he could barely imagine life without her. It was no wonder he was finding it hard to concentrate on his work.

Now he was on his way to meet her: a drink, a little lunch, and then back to his flat, where they would make love and sleep a while. Yesterday, he had stretched it out until half past four before heading back to Red Pillars. He shouldn't have done – *but what the hell?*

Outside, as Vaughan had stepped clear of the entrance hall, he had been hit by a blast of hot air. It burned his nostrils and his ears as he stood searching desperately for a taxi. When eventually he hailed one, he almost burned his legs on the back seat. Well over a hundred degrees, he reckoned.

Not until he reached the Mohammed Ali Club, with its high ceilings and shaded rooms, was there any relief. When Tanja arrived soon after, she was fanning herself furiously. 'Ah,' she said, collapsing into her chair, 'this is like a cool oasis. And always so quiet. In here I feel as though I have escaped the city.'

They lunched, then braved the heat again to walk the short distance to his flat, which was just off the Midan El Azhar. It was small, simple and, with the shutters closed, dark. Kissing her, he led her to his bed. Her face was in shadow, close to his. A faint smile, lips parted, then her fingers were tugging at his belt, undoing his shorts, while his hands fumbled at the buttons of her shirt and tugged it from her skirt.

Ah, yes. He no longer cared how hot it was.

He had been back by twenty past four, but this time his late return had been noticed. Maunsell wanted to see him.

'Sorry, RJ,' Vaughan said, as he knocked at the door and walked into the colonel's office.

'There you are. Where've you been?'

'I'm afraid I had a siesta and overslept. The heat's somehow worse in the city than it is in the desert.'

Maunsell smiled. 'That's perfectly all right, Alex. Just let someone know, eh? In case we need to get hold of you urgently.'

The lightest of reprimands.

'Anyway, you've been summoned. General McCreery wants to see you about your coastal raiding parties.' He looked Vaughan in the eye. 'Obviously thought I knew all about it.'

Vaughan felt himself redden. *'Mea culpa*, RJ,' he said. 'I wasn't trying to be furtive. There just didn't seem any point in mentioning it if nothing came of it. And I didn't think anything would.'

'Would you like to tell me now?'

Vaughan did so, then went on, 'It's what you were saying about supplies that convinced me. Stirling's mob seem to be dealing with enemy aircraft. We could hit the fuel coming off the ships.'

'And if you could get into Mersa you might be able to find out something about those messages.'

'I hadn't thought of that, but yes. Mersa Matruh is not a big place.'

'It might be worth mentioning that to General McCreery.' He leaned back and began to fill a pipe. 'Look, Alex, I know perfectly well that you don't want to be stuck here for the duration. Chaps like George, Rolo and Tilly are made for this sort of thing but you're cut out for a more physical role – I appreciate that. But two things: first, what you're doing here is of vital importance and don't ever think otherwise. Second, I'd like to think you know me well enough now to feel you can always come and talk things through. My door is always open.'

A second reprimand but, as ever, done with the lightest touch.

Vaughan smiled sheepishly. 'Yes, I know. And I'm sorry, RJ. You're quite right.'

Maunsell looked at his watch. 'Well, you'd better get cracking. McCreery's expecting you at five thirty in the Semiramis. Come and report back to me afterwards, though, will you?'

It was not far – just a short ride up through Garden City and past the British Embassy. Vaughan took a gharry, which brought him to the Semiramis with a quarter of an hour to spare. He didn't want to walk in with sweat on his brow and dark stains on his shirt, so he was grateful to feel a faint breeze whipping up off the Nile.

The Semiramis Hotel was a vast white end-of-century edifice along the banks of the Nile just south of the Ismail Khedive Bridge, Cairo's largest hotel by some margin. However, its proximity to Garden City and the embassy had ensured that it had been taken over long since as digs for the senior staff at GHQ, although it remained every bit as luxurious as it had been when tourists had flocked to it before the war.

Having asked for Major General McCreery, Vaughan waited in the lobby, knocking his hands together and jiggling his foot impatiently. Like the Mohammed Ali Club, the Semiramis seemed to be a place of refuge: cool, calm and quiet, shielded from the hubbub of the city. Oriental jars stood beneath high, ornate columns. Occasionally someone would enter or walk out briskly, and *suffragi* would glide across the marble floor, their white *galabhiyas* not unlike the sails of boats drifting down the Nile beyond.

A naval commander – Vaughan recognized him vaguely – trotted down the staircase and walked towards him. 'Major Vaughan?' he said.

'Yes,' said Vaughan, standing.

A hand was thrust towards him. 'Bill Williamson. Have we met? I think perhaps we have. Hello, I'm General Alexander's senior ADC but I was also General Auchinleck's.'

'I was MA to the DMI for a brief period.'

'That must be it, then. Thought our paths had crossed.' He led Vaughan up to the first floor, opened a door and walked into what had clearly once been one of the finest suites in the hotel but was now an office with desks, clerks and telephones. High french windows opened out to a balcony; beyond it, there were date palms and the Nile. The room was warm, but not overbearingly so.

Having briefly absorbed the grandeur of the room, Vaughan saw two generals before him, one he immediately recognized as the Commander-in-Chief, and the other whom he guessed must be McCreery. Alexander stood up and offered his hand. He was a slight man, with a gentle face, laughter lines stretching from the corners of his eyes. His uniform was unembellished by rows of medal ribbons and red tabs but looked immaculate. McCreery, taller and thinner, was similarly attired.

Alexander led him towards a circle of armchairs and held out an arm for him to sit. 'Drink?' he said.

'Iced water, please, sir.'

'Yes,' said Alexander. 'I'll have the same. What about you, Dick?' he said to McCreery.

'Maybe some lemonade?'

A guardsman, standing by, nodded and hurried off.

'How are you finding Cairo, General?' Vaughan asked, as they all sat down, Alexander and McCreery next to each other, Vaughan opposite. An interview, but a relaxed one.

'Very interesting. Actually, I was here in June, although only briefly and busy with meetings, but I arrived nearly ten days ago and only took over on Saturday so I had a little time to myself. It's given me a chance to look around. Get a feel for the place. It's a wonderful city but one could be forgiven for thinking there were more servicemen here than at the front. I know that struck the Prime Minister very keenly.'

'I can see how it must seem that way, sir.'

'I've been driving around a bit in my official car, and it's quite obvious it's the Commander's car, with little flags on it, and it's also really rather smart and official-looking too. But I've not been saluted once.'

'I'm sorry to hear that, sir. Men on leave are notorious for not noticing what's going on around them.' He told the general the story of the two Field Security officers who had dressed up as Germans and were not challenged once in two days.

Alexander laughed. 'Good Lord. Well, that tells me a great deal. I think, Vaughan, that we need to sharpen up, don't you?'

'Most certainly, sir.'

'It's why I'm moving my headquarters out into the desert.' He looked around at his apartment. 'This is all very fine, and were I here on holiday I should think it a wonderful place to bring my wife and family. But this is no place from which to conduct a campaign. There are too many distractions. One cannot concentrate properly. We're in the process of building a small camp out at Mena. Much better to be closer to things. Of course, the great administrative services need to remain here, but not my staff, Major Vaughan. I'm hoping this will be my last night here.'

The guardsman returned with the drinks. Alexander thanked him, then said to Vaughan, 'Tell me, how do you think morale is? Generally, I mean.'

'Honestly, sir? Most people are a bit fed up. Those of us who have been out here any length of time have been back and forth across the desert to such an extent that there's been a loss of confidence in it ever being any different. It's a shattering experience to fight so hard for something, to lose so many good men in doing so, and to push forward only to lose that very same piece of ground again a couple of months later. It makes one think it's all been for nothing.'

Alexander crossed his legs and put a finger to his chin, as though in deep thought.

'To lose Tobruk, which had held out for so long, and then to lose even Sidi Barrani, the Halfaya Pass and Mersa Matruh has been devastating, sir. I wasn't even there this time around, but those were hard blows to take.'

'I'm sorry to say, Vaughan, that you're not the first to point this out. However, I believe that confidence and morale can be boosted. Very soon, Rommel will attack. We will stop him. I've already asked General Montgomery to make it absolutely clear to the men that there will be no further retreat. The Axis advance will go no further than the Alamein Line, and once we've secured that, we'll prepare to take the attack to him. Fortunately, this time, we have much in our favour. Our strength is growing at a far greater rate than that of the enemy, and we now have the United States, whose material strength we're beginning to feel to a much greater extent. I know the situation still seems very grave, but I feel genuinely confident that our fortunes are about to turn, Major.'

At that moment, there was a light knock on the door, which was opened by one of the ADCs. In walked the director of Military Operations, Brigadier Davy.

'Brigadier,' said Alexander, getting to his feet. 'Good of you to come.'

He saluted, then shook hands and sat down.

'Anyway, Major,' said Alexander, turning back to Vaughan, 'we've asked you here primarily to

talk about your proposal, which General Mc-
Creery and I read with great interest.'

'Yes,' said McCreery. 'Your views on Rommel's
extremely shaky supply lines mirror ours exactly.'
He glanced at Alexander. 'Intelligence suggests
he needs at least a hundred thousand tons of
supplies every month. For the past three months,
with Malta more or less completely out of the
picture, his supplies have been reaching Tripoli
and Benghazi unscathed. The problem for Rommel, of course, is that Tripoli is thirteen hundred
miles away and Benghazi eight hundred, which is
why Tobruk and Mersa are so important to him.
These are much smaller ports, but they're a heck
of a lot closer, as you well know. Our chaps in the
RAF have been doing their best, attacking all his
ports, but obviously aerial bombing can only
achieve so much. It's always much more effective
when it can be used hand in hand with other
means of attack.'

Vaughan nodded. 'Absolutely, sir.'

'Malta is about to go on the offensive again, with
both the RAF and the navy targeting the Axis sea
lanes very heavily. They'll be doing their level best
to ensure that Rommel doesn't get anything like
the tonnage he needs,' McCreery ended.

'Here's something to give you confidence,
Vaughan,' smiled Alexander. 'We know that the
enemy needs his supplies just to keep the Panzer
Army Africa on its feet, but we are currently unloading a hundred thousand tons of *fuel* per
month.'

Vaughan whistled.

'Quite something, eh?'

246

'It certainly is, sir.'

McCreery leaned forward. 'We're fairly certain Rommel will attack before the month is out, Major, and at present, stopping him is our first priority. However, as the C-in-C has just said, we're confident we can do so. Our air forces are primed, the Army Commander has drawn up a good defensive plan, and blocking an attack is more straightforward than winning outright. What's more, Rommel cannot outflank us as he did at Gazala.' He cleared his throat. 'Afterwards all our minds will be concentrated on delivering that knock-out blow.' He turned to Davy. 'Do you want to explain, Brigadier?'

'Of course, sir,' said Davy. 'Our naval and air forces will be continuing their assault on Axis shipping, but we also want to hit enemy supplies once they're unloaded. Now, as it happens, we've already been thinking about launching a co-ordinated raid on Benghazi and Tobruk, using the LRDG, Stirling's SAS, and some naval forces as well.'

'That's where you might be able to help, Major,' said Alexander.

'You were part of Middle East Commando,' Davy continued, 'and we also now have the Special Boat Section, which has been a hit-and-miss affair, but has recently been put largely under operational control of Major Stirling's SAS. However, we think you can help Stirling. You have all the right experience, your record is first class, you're a fluent German and Italian speaker, and your thinking is spot on.'

'Thank you, sir,' said Vaughan.

247

'So – the mechanics. We're proposing you should command C Detachment of the Special Boat Section.'

'An irresistible pun,' interjected McCreery.

'Exactly so,' said Davy. 'This will place you under operational command of Stirling. It will be up to you to form this force but we're looking to keep it quite small and somewhat *ad hoc*. In other words, you'll be used for specific operations.'

'May I suggest targets and operations, sir?' asked Vaughan.

'Absolutely. And you will do this through the DMO's branch at GHQ. We're proposing to install a staff officer at GHQ working under me. His task will be to co-ordinate all future raiding operations. I'm having a conference next week, which you'll attend and at which I'm hoping to square this away.'

'Do you have any ideas, Major?' asked McCreery

'Yes, sir. As I'm sure you're aware, at SIME we've been trying to break an enemy spy circuit operating here in Cairo.'

Alexander nodded. 'We talked to Maunsell about that.'

'The messages they've been transmitting have been received at Mersa. In order to attack the port facilities there effectively, it will be necessary to go under cover – to pass ourselves off as German or Italian. It might be possible to gather intelligence as well as destroy enemy supplies.'

'Possibly, yes,' agreed Davy.

'It's something to consider,' said McCreery, 'but in the meantime, Vaughan, we'd like you to concentrate on planning and preparing for a double-fisted raid on Tobruk and Benghazi.'

'Of course, sir. Am I to leave SIME, sir?'

'Only temporarily. For the time being, this is a secondment. I've already spoken to Maunsell, and he wants to keep you at arm's reach, especially while this Axis spy circuit is still active.'

So RJ already knows, thought Vaughan.

'But I'd also like you to help with planning,' added Davy. 'And you'll need to go up to Alexandria and talk to Admiral Harwood and the 10th MTB Flotilla. You should also get together with David Stirling.'

'Yes, sir. When were you thinking we should launch the raids?'

'With a bit of luck, around the second week of September. It's going to need very intricate planning because the SAS and LRDG will have to set off a number of days beforehand – certainly before your lot set sail from Alexandria.'

'It all depends on when the Panzer Army attacks,' added Alexander. 'When we've stopped Rommel, and seen off his advance, then we go on the offensive. These raids, Major, will be part of our preparation for the decisive battle to come.'

Five minutes later, Vaughan was back outside the hotel. It was bathed in golden light as the sun was already lowering in the sky to the west. He smiled to himself as he clambered into a waiting gharry. *Active service again*. It was what he had wanted, and incredibly, he had the backing of both the C-in-C – Alexander himself! – and the chief of staff. Yet apprehension stabbed inside him. It was what he had hoped for, but such operations were fraught with danger. Furthermore, the eyes of the senior generals in the theatre would be on him and the raids; the responsibility was enormous. He experienced a niggle of doubt. He was still only twenty-nine, his highest command that of a company some six months before. He looked across the river, towards the desert. He thought of Tanner, who would be out there now, back with his battalion. That was who he needed. Sykes, too, the tough little Cockney who had proved such a dab hand with explosives on Crete.

But first there was a battle to be fought. Despite the C-in-C's confidence, Vaughan was keenly aware that the outcome was still far from certain.

11

The men had been allowed a swim. At around two o'clock, as the heat rose off the metalled coast road, shimmering and causing mirages ahead, the red flag was raised, the column had halted, and the men had run the three hundred yards to the sea. Stripping off, leaving their boots and clothes in small piles, they had enjoyed a brief, cooling respite in the iridescent waters of the Mediterranean.

Forty minutes later, they were on their way again, joining a supply column heading up to the front. Other vehicles began passing them on the way back towards Alexandria. To their right, the sea twinkled in the afternoon sun; ahead and stretching for ever to their left, the desert, that desolate, unvarying landscape of scrub, sand and stone. Hummocks of vetch stood up between the sand and rock, giving it a mottled biscuit complexion. A short distance away, Tanner watched a Bedouin boy with his goats, then spotted a small camp – russet cloth over a few rough wooden poles.

'Good to be back, sir?' asked Brown.

'I thought it was,' Tanner replied. 'Now I'm not so sure.'

'It's quite boring, isn't it, the desert?' When Tanner did not reply, he added, 'Well, we can be thankful for one thing – at least we're not Bedouins.'

'What, Browner?' said Hepworth. 'You mean you don't fancy living out here all your born days with nothing but a bit of cloth and some goats to keep you company?'

'I'd rather get blasted to hell.'

'We're not going to this time, Browner,' said Sykes. 'Haven't you heard?'

'D'you think it'll be different, then, sir?' Hepworth asked Sykes. 'Or will it be the same old story? I remember before Gazala everyone was so damn sure we were going to have Rommel beat. And look what sodding well happened there.'

'That's what I love about you, Hep,' said Tanner. 'Glass always half empty, isn't it?'

'All I'm saying, sir, is that I'm not getting too excited just yet. I know we've got new generals, but who says they'll be any different?'

They drove on along the road until the lead

251

vehicles turned off and began rumbling across the desert, clouds of dust following in their wake. As their own vehicle slowed and dropped on to the rough track, Tanner looked ahead and saw the rail stop of El Hammam – a solitary rectangular building the same shade as the desert – and away to his left, a large number of tents and camouflage nets under which were lines of fighter aircraft. A battery of anti-aircraft guns had been dug in around it. The column slowed again as each vehicle rolled over the railway line. At the edge of the landing ground there were more ack-ack guns and behind them more netting. *A fuel dump*, thought Tanner.

He put his sunglasses back on to protect his eyes. The track was marked by oil barrels, painted and filled with rocks and sand. For a while the going was reasonably smooth, but suddenly they hit a rockier area, the truck jolting and rattling, the men cursing. The track was leading them south-west along the edge of a minefield. Rough signs had been put up, skulls and crossbones on each, with warnings written in English, Italian and German. Tanner took out his map, freshly issued the day before with the latest minefields marked in pencil. This one was some fifteen miles from the forward positions but running south-west, a relic from July when the Auk had clearly been worried about enemy encirclement.

Desultory gunfire boomed not far to the west, while scattered in the desert around them were vast numbers of tanks and other vehicles, most in loose groups for as far as the eye could see. Most were stationary – army reserves and support units – but others were moving, clouds of dust marking their way. Away to their left, near the Alam Halfa ridge, Tanner spotted bulldozers scooping out gun pits. He had never seen them out in the desert before. They appeared to be making light work of it. 'Jesus, will you look at this?' he muttered. 'It's like a bloody lorry park.'

'We've had reinforcements since we were last out here, though, sir,' said Sykes.

'You can say that again.' Tanner took his binoculars from the pack at his feet and peered at some of the clusters of vehicles, careful not to point the lenses in the direction of the sun. Closest was an encampment of heavy supply lorries and Matadors, their tracks criss-crossing over the desert. They were all the same buff sandy colour, but painted with a logo he had not seen before. 'Which unit uses a rhinoceros?' he said. 'Where's the bloody jerboa?'

'Dunno, sir,' said Brown beside him.

The ground gradually, almost imperceptibly, rose until suddenly they were on a ridge and looking south towards the Qattara Depression, where dramatic escarpments dropped several hundred feet into what had once been a large lake or sea. A single vehicle like a jeep could get up or down at certain parts, but it was impassable to any massed formation of tanks or trucks. It was what made the Alamein Line unique. There was no other position between here and Benghazi that Tanner had ever seen where both flanks were covered. That had been one of the major flaws of the Gazala position to the west of

Tobruk. The British line had stretched some forty miles, just as it did here, but without an impassable escarpment, Rommel had been able to send his forces around the bottom. He would not be able to do that now.

The large numbers of vehicles began to fall behind them as they continued south, bumping across the desert until, once again, the red flag was raised and one by one they ground to a halt.

'What now?' said Hepworth, exasperation in his voice.

'Two to one we're lost,' said Sykes. 'They can't find Brigade.'

Sure enough, a moment later, one of the lead trucks peeled off and began beetling across the desert to the east. Tanner peered through his binoculars again, but although the ground seemed flat as a board, he could see now that it rose gently towards another ridge. Within a few minutes the truck had disappeared.

'Now where's he bloody well gone?' said Hepworth.

'Calm down, Hep,' said Tanner, lighting a cigarette. Flies were circling above, so he exhaled a cloud of smoke at them. 'It's always the same every time we come out here, fart-arsing about trying to find things. We'll get there eventually.'

'I'm hungry again,' said Phyllis.

'I reckon Siff's got worms,' said Brown.

'Nah, he's just a growing lad, aren't you, Siff?' said Sykes.

'Have we got time to brew up, d'you reckon?' asked Mudge.

'No, leave it,' said Sykes. 'It won't be long now.'

A low rumble came from the east, which grew louder rapidly. Suddenly, above them, they saw a formation of medium bombers.

'Go on, lads!' called Sykes, waving at them. 'Give 'em hell!'

They roared over, only a few thousand feet up, Bostons. There were sixteen of them in loose formation, and higher, much higher, a number of fighters, black dots in the sky.

Soon afterwards, Tanner saw a cloud of dust on the horizon. 'Here we go,' he said, training his binoculars back towards the east where the scout truck was reappearing. They watched it scurry towards them, then halt. Someone got out, a brief conference, maps being studied, arms pointing.

'He's found Brigade,' said Tanner.

'Hoo-bloody-ray,' said Hepworth.

A minute later, the blue flag was raised, engines started up again, and the column moved forward, this time heading eastwards over the ridge.

They arrived at 7th Armoured Brigade Head-quarters a short while later, a cluster of vehicles, tents and flags sprouting from oil barrels. Tanner wiped his brow as more flies buzzed, circled and landed when they dared. It was always the same: stop, start, stop, start. He got out, stretched, had a pee, then climbed back into the truck, until eventually he could see people striding about. Soon after, the Chinese whisper of orders arrived, passed from one vehicle to the next. They were to leaguer for the night and head up to the front line the following evening.

The phone call had come through at about half

255

past five. The same distinct voice.

'Hello, darling, how are you?'

'Fine, fine,' Tanja had replied. 'How lovely to hear from you.'

'Can we meet tonight, darling? I really want to see you.'

'Yes, of course. I'd love to.' She glanced across at Sophie, then smiled into the receiver.

'Usual place? Seven thirty?'

'Yes, all right. I'll be there.'

For more than an hour and a half she had continued with her work at the Polish Red Cross, chatting with the girls, acting as though everything was perfectly normal. Both Sophie and Ewa were intrigued by the new man in her life – the telephone call had prompted a gentle interrogation.

'But what about your cavalry-officer friend?' asked Ewa. 'Harry – wasn't that his name?'

'Oh, Harry – he was sent to the front. But he was just a boy. Alex is–'

'More of a man,' said Ewa, smiling coyly.

'Exactly. He is. A little older, certainly. Two years older than me, which is how it should be.'

'And works in Cairo?' asked Sophie.

'Yes – something very hush-hush at GHQ.'

'They all say that,' said Sophie. 'It's to hide the boring desk job.'

'You're probably right, but I don't care. I really like this one. I don't want him heading up into the desert.'

She left at a quarter past seven, walking up towards Opera Square, then crossing the still busy road. Carts, donkeys, cars and buses – it

256

never stopped until the curfew, when suddenly the city closed down and the only noise was that of cats screeching or dogs barking. Tanja turned down Sharia Abdin, the entire street now in shade. She wondered what the message was this time. She'd not yet sent a signal to Cobra, despite Orca's instructions. Several times she had thought to, then had stopped, unsure what she should say. Perhaps she should have done, though, especially since she had told herself she should appear to be acting normally. She put a hand to her forehead. A headache. The world pressing down around her. *I feel so trapped.*

When Vaughan had returned to Red Pillars, Maunsell had been as genial as ever and had suggested they go for a drink at Shepheard's, where, he had explained, he was due to be dining at seven. They had taken a taxi and, on reaching Shepheard's, had sat inside, clear of prying ears.

His dinner guest had arrived shortly before seven – Brigadier Cuthbert Bowlby, head of the Inter-Services Liaison Department, or ISLD as it was known, and MI6's organization in the Middle East, and the Middle East Intelligence Centre. As such, Bowlby was very much the SIS supremo in the Middle East. Maunsell had introduced Vaughan and had insisted he stay for another quick drink, so it was not until around ten past seven that he had finally left them to their dinner.

He had walked down Sharia Kamel towards Opera Square, intending to call in on Tanja, first at the Polish Red Cross, and then, if she was not there, at her flat. For once, he had not noticed the hustle and bustle of the city: he was too busy thinking of all that had happened that afternoon. He felt buoyed, excited by his new directive, all the more for the dizzying way in which it had been conveyed. He remembered that David Stirling had told him of a similar conversation he had had with the Auk when he had proposed his idea for the SAS, but certainly it was not every day that one found oneself talking face to face with the C-in-C.

The idea to strike Tobruk and Benghazi simultaneously worried him, though. His idea for C Detachment had been to operate in very small numbers – teams of four or six men and no more. Maunsell's suggestion, which he had just outlined, of using C Detachment not only for sabotage but also for intelligence work, seemed to tie in much more closely with what Vaughan had had in mind.

'You'll have to do this raid,' Maunsell had told him, 'but after that it'll be up to you to make of it what you will. They've given you the authority to create this special-operations unit. You must show them what it can achieve.'

Vaughan smiled to himself. Maunsell was a canny old bastard. He wanted Vaughan to remain within the SIME fold, and had suggested he try to attend morning prayers once a week. And introducing him to Bowlby: clearly, it had been his intention all along. ISLD ran a number of double-agents, in Greece and the Balkans, and Maunsell was keen to do this too. 'Indirect counter-intelligence,' he had called it. *But counter-intelligence all the same.*

Vaughan glanced at his watch – *nearly twenty past seven* – then at the corner of the Continental Hotel, glanced down towards Opera Square and saw what appeared to be Tanja waiting to cross the road. *Is it her?* She was wearing khaki uniform, had blonde hair of the right length, but she was a couple of hundred yards away so he couldn't be sure. Quickening his step, he walked past the Continental, keeping his eyes on her as she crossed Opera Square and headed on down Sharia Abdin. He was getting closer, although she was still some way ahead of him, but from her walk he was certain it was Tanja. He wondered where she was going – certainly, it was a long way round to take to her flat. *Oh, well*, he thought, glad to have spotted her. A piece of serendipity.

Then, suddenly, she turned off down a narrow street. *Where the hell are you going, Tanja?* A network of narrow streets in the old Islamic part of the city. He was struck with curiosity.

Tanja fought off the urge to walk quickly, or to look behind her. *Act normally.* That was the key. It was why meetings were always during the day, and never at night. It was quite possible to avoid being seen at night, but why defy the curfew? To do so was to act abnormally. Abnormal behaviour aroused suspicion. Normal behaviour did not.

Outside the shop, a scrawny cat stood on a table still piled with watermelons and oranges. She stepped inside, nodded to the shopkeeper, then went on through the beaded curtain to the room beyond.

'As punctual as ever,' said Artus, rising to his

feet and stepping towards her. 'I am going to be quick. Why have you not sent a message?'

Tanja was startled. *How does he know?* 'I will. I have been wondering what to say. How to phrase my signal.'

He stepped closer still, until he was just inches away. She could smell his cologne, could see his dark eyes fixed on hers. 'Do it. Do it right away.'

'Very well. I will.'

'You know Aladdin was found dead?' he said softly. 'Dumped in the river. I would hate that to happen to you.'

'Do not threaten me,' said Tanja.

He ran a finger across his throat.

'You wouldn't dare. This circuit is nothing without me.'

Artus smiled. 'Go now, Marlin. Send that signal to Cobra.'

Tanja turned, her heart thumping, pushed through the beaded curtain and went out on to the street, where she paused, her eyes closed.

'Tanja!'

She froze. *Alex. Think. Think quickly. And act normally.* Her heart was in her mouth and her hands were shaking. *Artus, my God.* She turned towards Vaughan and her face lit up with a smile. From the corner of her eye she saw Artus in the doorway. He stepped back inside.

'Alex!' she said, hurrying towards him. 'How lovely!' She put her arms around his neck and kissed him. 'Have you been following me?'

'I have, as it happens.'

She laughed. *What did he see?*

'A bit off the beaten track, isn't it?' he said.

'I suppose,' she said, looping her arm through his and gently steering him back the way she had come.

Don't look back.

'I like the older parts of town. The bazaars. The back-streets. I was looking for some Turkish Delight,' she said. 'That kind of shop is just the type that sells it.'

'But not that one?'

'They didn't have any. So,' she said, 'does this mean you are now mine for the rest of the night?'

'Yes,' he grinned, 'if you'd like me to be.'

'I would, actually.' She gripped his arm tighter, leaning her head against his shoulder.

'Where first? Some dinner?'

'Perfect. Near your flat?'

'All right. This way, then,' he said, wheeling her around. As they turned, she saw Artus leaving the shop, with a furtive glance in their direction, then walking away from them. Tanja's stomach lurched. She wanted to turn round again, to lead Alex away from Artus, but she knew she could not: the risk was too great. *Act normally.*

'Where do you think, then?' she asked. Vaughan did not answer, so she looked up at him, and saw, with mounting dread, that he was frowning, his brow pinched, staring after the man.

'Alex?' she said. 'Where shall we go?'

'What?' he said. 'Oh, um, how about the Mohammed Ali Club again?'

He looked back towards the disappearing figure, striding between numerous passers-by and under awnings, until the red tarboosh and the dark head disappeared from view.

'Are you all right, Alex?' she asked. 'You look as though you have seen a ghost.'

'Actually, Tanja, I think I just may have done.'

A dull weight filled her stomach. *He recognized him. He knows Artus.*

12

Wednesday, 19 August, 0755. The large mess tent smelt of dust, canvas, tobacco smoke and a faint residual whiff of beer. *So they've had some Stella brought up.* Tanner supposed the proximity to the base depots had its advantages: it wasn't only plentiful supplies of fuel and ammo that could be quickly amassed, but beer too. And it certainly helped keep the men in good heart. A light breeze had got up, drifting across the Sahara, so the camouflage netting was flapping.

Tanner glanced around at his fellow officers, some twelve in all, himself included: the OC, the 2i/c, Major Tom Arliss – new to the battalion since Tanner had been away – the company commanders and their second in commands, all gathered for a briefing by the commander of 7th Motor Brigade, Brigadier Tom Bosville. He was not there yet; in front of the map, Colonel Vigar was talking in hushed tones with the brigade intelligence officer. Behind, at the back of the mess, a large sketch map had been unfurled, the sea to the north, the Qattara Depression to the south, with various lines, coloured symbols and other markings drawn on it.

The previous evening, Tanner had assumed they would be going straight up to their forward positions and had felt a flush of frustration when they were told they would be leaguering for the night; having reached the front, a large part of him wished they could get on with the task in hand. However, he had soon accepted that this was not to be, and now realized that a further day of preparation for the front line was no bad thing. A day of travelling took its toll. Vehicles needed to be checked over and serviced; two of the carriers in A Company needed replacement sections of track. It also took time to acclimatize to the living and operating conditions of the desert. It was one thing being based at Mena Camp, but quite another at the front. As much as anything, it took a day or two to get used to the hordes of flies. They were a minor nuisance back at Mena, but out at the front, during the heat of the day, they were a constant source of discomfort. The dead were always buried quickly, but even so, the flies were quick to gorge on and breed in the many chunks and gobbets of flesh that had been blown to smithereens throughout the recent fighting in July.

Tanner had been thinking about these things when the brigadier strode into the tent and made his way to the front.

'Good morning, gentlemen,' he said, 'and welcome back to Brigade. We're certainly very pleased to have you with us once more, refreshed, replenished and ready to send Rommel and his Panzer Army packing.' He paused and looked at the assembled Rangers officers in front of him.

263

The two Rifle Brigade battalions, he went on to explain, had already retrained as semi-mobile anti-tank gunners and were positioned towards the southern end of the line in the low ground of the Munassib. It was to be the role of the King's Royal Rifle Corps and the Yorks Rangers in the coming battle to act as the fully mobile arm of the brigade.

'Your task,' the brigadier told them, 'is to patrol the southern half of the line alongside 4th Light Armoured Brigade, and should the enemy attack in our sector, to lure him towards our waiting anti-tank screen.' He pointed to the map, on which had been marked the principal minefields and Eighth Army's dispositions. The main line ran roughly north to south, but then halfway down, and curving back in a great sweeping arc up to the coast, there was another set of interrupted minefields, running along the base of two ridges, first the smaller Alam Nayil, and then the longer, more pronounced Alam Halfa Ridge.

'Most of our armour is dug in along and between these two ridges,' said Bosville. 'For all Rommel's supposed tactical brilliance, experience so far has suggested that he likes nothing more than a good outflanking manoeuvre, so the Army Commander is confident he'll try it again. A feint in the north seems most likely, followed by an assault with his armour in the south here, where you chaps will be.' He pointed to the less extensive minefields across the southern stretch of the line. 'Of course, he's welcome to try in the north, if he likes, but he'll hit something of a brick wall if he does.' A collective chuckle. 'Thick with minefields and our infantry dug in – in depth too. Here, though,' he continued, pointing to the southern end of the line with his stick, 'the minefields are not laid in such depth, and the going is pretty good, lots of light gravel – ideal for the Deutsches Panzer Korps to try and exploit. Let's assume he does attack here. He sweeps through and he's then got all our chaps dug in firing at his flanks, so he's going to have to attack those positions head on. The difference is that our boys are dug in and his won't be. So long as our chaps stay where they are and don't follow them, we'll beat him.'

The 2i/c from Ivo McDonald's D Company put up his hand.

'Yes?' said the brigadier.

'What if Jerry tries to go round the back of the line, sir?'

Brigadier Bosville smiled.

'Sorry, sir,' said Vigar. 'Lieutenant Ramsay is new to the battalion.' Another laugh. Tanner watched the young lieutenant reddening.

'Would someone like to explain?' Bosville looked around and spotted Tanner. 'Yes, Lieutenant,' he said, 'you're an old hand at this kind of caper. Would you kindly explain to Lieutenant Ramsay?'

'If they do that they'll soon find themselves cut off from the rest of the Panzer Army, and probably by us. With their supply lines cut, they'll run out of fuel and ammo and we'll destroy every last one of them. Sir.'

'Bravo. Exactly that,' said Bosville.

Now Tanner put up his hand. 'Excuse me, sir,'

he said, 'but has our armour been specifically ordered to stay put? I've noticed there's a tradition of our tanks racing after the enemy the moment they see them falling back and then they always get knocked to hell.'

'A fair point,' said Bosville. 'I'm glad to say that I think something of a sea-change is taking place out here. We've had the pleasure of seeing the new Army Commander down here at Division, and I can tell you, he means business. He's insisting that if and when Rommel attacks, we fight a defensive battle only. Push Rommel back, then build up strength until we can deliver a knock-out blow. Not send him back to Mersa or Sidi Barrani or Tobruk, but out of Africa altogether. That's the plan. So he's issued very strict orders that all our armour is to remain hull-down and not be lured out into the open. A damn sensible idea, if you ask me.' He clapped his hands together. 'So,' he said, 'you'll be heading up to the front line tonight. I want you to do what you do best. Patrol, reconnoitre, capture a few Jerries and Eyeties, and then, when Rommel attacks, as we're all expecting him to do any moment now, take a few pot shots, and lead him back to our guns. The Rifle Brigade will hold them up as much as they can, then they'll be pulling back too. Keep your distance, but make life as difficult for them as possible. Clear?' Nods, and *Yes, sir. Simple, when you put it like that.*

A short while later, Tanner and Peploe walked back out. Brigade and Divisional HQ were almost as one: a cluster of tents and lorries in a very shallow bowl in the middle of the desert, all draped with camouflage netting. Wires and telephone cables littered the ground, running from the brigade commander's tent to the signals lorry and the operations tent, then to Division, a little further away. Brigade and divisional flags fluttered lightly in the breeze. The men of the 7th Armoured Division were the original Desert Rats, and the jerboa, the symbol that had come to mean so much, was there for anyone to see. Not for the first time, Tanner marvelled at the sheer logistic effort of keeping and maintaining such an army in the field.

'Sounded like a good plan to me, Jack,' said Peploe, as they stepped over wires and headed back to the company encampment.

'I agree. If they stay put. I know what these cavalry boys are like, though. They still think their tanks are chargers. They see a panzer on the run and they think it's bloody Waterloo all over again.'

High above, more aircraft flew over.

'Ours?' said Peploe, squinting in the sun.

'I reckon so. Haven't seen a single enemy plane since we got here.'

'They're saving themselves. It's all about fuel.'

Clangs and hammer sounds could be heard as maintenance work was carried out. A jeep drove past. Somewhere to the north, guns boomed.

'Do you think I could take some of the boys on a recce?' Tanner asked Peploe, as they approached the company. 'I could take my truck with someone from each of the platoons. If we're going to be operating mostly by night, it would be good to give them some markers, particularly up around Alam Halfa. Get a feel for the lie of the land and who's where.'

Peploe nodded. 'Good idea.'

They reached their tent, hastily erected the previous night. Tanner was used to wrapping himself up in a greatcoat and tarpaulin; he couldn't remember once having slept under canvas up in the blue, but as an officer, he shared this standard GS tent with Peploe. He doubted they would have much opportunity to use it again before they were next out of the line, but it had been produced from Peploe's truck, not his, so he wasn't complaining.

Inside, Tanner grabbed his kit to take back to his truck, then paused, looking again at his map. He could envisage Rommel's Afrika Korps sweeping through this southern end of the line, and he could also picture the battalion then falling back further, towards the edge of the Depression, and from there snapping at the heels of the enemy as they faced up to the onslaught from the Alam Niyal and Alam Halfa ridges. No, he could see there was logic to the plan. *As long as we don't get carried away.*

A restless night in Cairo. Was it the heat, or a troubled mind? Vaughan had woken at nearly four and been unable to get back to sleep. Beside him, breathing softly, lay Tanja. He was losing his heart to her. Last night they had walked arm in arm to the Mohammed Ali Club, but then had changed their minds and eaten at the French restaurant, Au Petit Coin de France, in Sharia El Maghrabi. A nice meal – good food, and Tanja as clever, funny and attentive as ever. Since that first disastrous date they had had barely a cross word between them. Back at his flat, she had made love with a passion that made him feel quite lost with desire. No English girl had ever consumed him so, or seemed so open towards him, and yet in other ways, she was not really open at all. He still knew so little about her. Poland, her home, her background – it was off-limits, an unspoken acknowledgement between them.

But the man he had seen. He was sure it had been Eslem Mustafa. If only he had been twenty yards closer! *I know it was him. I'm sure of it.* And walking out of the same shop from which he'd seen Tanja emerge, looking, he had first thought, slightly – what was the word? – *shaken.* But then she had turned to him and seemed so genuinely happy to see him. Nothing she had said or done during the rest of the evening had, in any way, suggested something was wrong, or that there was anything to cause him even the slightest concern. And yet he was concerned. It had nagged away at him. Or perhaps he was just paranoid. Perhaps it was as Kirk had suggested: that if one worked in the world of secret intelligence, one started to view everything with suspicious eyes. More often than not there was a perfectly rational and normal reason for most things. Perhaps Tanja really had been looking for Turkish Delight. Why not? Surely it was more likely than her being an associate of Eslem Mustafa?

Good God, there was still no hard evidence even that Mustafa was directly involved in the spy circuit. It was all circumstantial. He cursed to himself. There was nothing. It was all hints, suggestions, chance meetings, tenuous links. Flitting shadows, nothing more.

These thoughts rolled round his mind, one part of his brain acting as defence, the other as prosecutor. Neither won. Stalemate, prompting repetition. Gradually, night gave way to the first streaks of dawn and Tanja was still sleeping peacefully, the crumpled sheet covering her legs and buttocks. She did not look tormented as she slept. She looked quite at peace – *and beautiful*.

Round and round, getting nowhere. But had it really been Mustafa? Eventually he got up, moved next door and took his briefcase to the battered desk he had bought some months before. Inside it he had put a copy of some reports on Mustafa, plus several photographs of him. Vaughan stared at them: the dark, oiled hair, the dark eyes, narrow nose, and neat pencil moustache.

When he heard movement behind him, he hastily thrust the file back into his briefcase. Turning he saw Tanja, naked, walking sleepily towards him, her hair dishevelled. She draped her arms around him, her breasts pressing against his back. 'Are you all right?' she asked.

'Yes. Just couldn't sleep.'

'Come back to bed,' she said, her lips on his ear.

Of course he'd said nothing. Instead he had carried his doubts around like a heavy case. He had called in on SIME on his way to GHQ, catching Maunsell and Maddox to tell them he was sure he had seen Mustafa the previous evening. He had not mentioned the shop, although he knew he should have done. Instead he would visit it himself.

He was not only troubled about Tanja. The plan to attack Tobruk and Benghazi simultaneously was a massive distortion of his original coastal raiding party plan. Whatever concerns he had had on first hearing about the plan had been stifled by his excitement over his new directive, and by finding himself face-to-face with the C-in-C and his chief of staff.

Now, though, it seemed a very different proposition. Taking even half a dozen men, as he had originally envisaged, was fraught with risk, but experience had shown that such operations were possible. Brigadier Davy had been talking about something much larger, and that was quite another matter. Neither were his fears allayed when he met up with David Stirling at GHQ. Stirling had been issued with Operation Instruction Numbers 139 and 104, for the attacks on Tobruk (Operation AGREEMENT) and Benghazi (Operation BIGAMY), both of which he had shown to Vaughan at the MO4 offices.

'Have a look at these, Alex,' he said to Vaughan. The orders were to block the main harbour, sink all shipping and lighters there, and destroy all oil facilities and pumping plants. That alone was more than Vaughan had ever reckoned possible, and to achieve it, Davy and his planning team were proposing a considerable force – or, rather, series of forces. For Benghazi, there would be attacks from the land side by the SAS, reinforced with the LRDG, and simultaneously an assault from the sea by a combination of SBS and naval forces and two Stuart light tanks. The SAS would not be directly involved in the attack on Tobruk. That would be left to another combined attack from three separate forces, including one that would be dropped along the coast from the town and would attack from the landward side, while naval forces attacked from the sea. Vaughan's role was to be part of Force C, which would include a number of recently arrived Argyll and Sutherland Highlanders, detached from 51st Division. This was to be their first combat operation since most of the division had been destroyed in France two years before. They would be delivered to the headland at the harbour's entrance by MTB. And that was not all. While Force X, led by Stirling and including his SAS with a patrol of the LRDG, were attacking Benghazi, another column, Force Z, made up of a battalion of the Sudanese Defence Force, would march from British-held Kufra, an oasis deep in the southern desert, to Jalo, another desert fort but held by the Italians. With this captured, Stirling's X Force would make good their escape from Benghazi and head straight to Jalo, whence they would carry out further attacks on Benghazi and Darce, the other port in the Cyrenaica bulge.

Vaughan felt giddy just reading these elaborate orders. 'You don't think this is a little ambitious?' he asked Stirling.

'Just a bit, yes,' he said. 'They're madness – far too many people involved. The Benghazi plan is bad enough but the one for Tobruk... Look, I'm hungry. Let's go and get some lunch.'

They went to the Gezira Sporting Club – in Stirling's jeep, into which he managed to fit his six-foot-six frame with remarkable dexterity. But on the journey there and as they sat down for drinks in the bar, they talked little about the proposed raids. Vaughan liked Stirling and had known him for years – they'd been at school together, had joined the army, gone through Sandhurst together and later joined the Commandos. Vaughan remembered Stirling had slept most of the way out to the Middle East. He'd been nicknamed 'the Great Sloth'. And while Vaughan had always taken his military career seriously and had immediately been posted to Crete, Stirling had done nothing to improve his reputation. He was a hopeless case, a party boy, not to be relied upon. His appearance hadn't helped: soldiers were not supposed to be six-foot-plus giants. And there was the slight stammer. Vaughan remembered Stirling once saying, 'Actually, i-i-it's rather fashionable.'

Out of the blue, he had channelled all his undoubted intelligence and charisma with his seemingly dormant willpower into creating L Detachment, the SAS. No more was he the Great Sloth. Now he was the 'Phantom Major', the commander of some of the most daring and outrageous operations of the desert war. He was a half-colonel and one of the most celebrated soldiers in the British Army.

After they had finished lunch and Stirling had ordered whisky and cigars in the drawing room, they discussed the operations to come.

'No point in spoiling a good lunch getting depressed,' said Stirling, 'but, really, Alex, these raids are a load of old cock. It's bloody Haselden who's behind it. He's been bending Davy's ear, and Davy's fallen for it, hook, line and sinker.'

'Haselden used to be with me in Middle East Commando, but I thought he'd gone native and was out in the desert with the Arabs.'

'He was – but he put this scheme to Montgomery the moment Monty pitched up at Eighth Army Tac HQ. He liked the sound of it and sent Haselden to talk to Davy'

'The basic aim is right,' said Vaughan. 'The more of Rommel's supplies we can get the better.'

'Yes, but Davy's talking about two hundred and forty men, forty supply trucks and another forty jeeps just for Benghazi – and that doesn't include the seaborne attack. Surprise is everything with these operations, but with that many men and vehicles, we haven't a hope of achieving it. And while we're blowing up Benghazi, Haselden wants the Sudanese Defence Force to take Jalo.' He shook his head. 'I'm all for daring operations and ambitious schemes, but one force, one plan, one commander. Keep things simple.'

'I agree. And I think these ops require small numbers of highly trained, experienced men. For the Tobruk raid the only ones with any experience of this sort of thing are the LRDG patrol and myself and, hopefully, the men I'm intending to recruit into C Detachment.'

'I wouldn't have anyone in the SAS unless they've been through rigorous training first. I have no idea why the A and S are involved. They've only just reached theatre and are green as peas.'

'They've never even been to Tobruk. And Davy's proposing to land them at night.'

Stirling blew out a cloud of cigar smoke. 'I didn't like the sound of it when I was called back from the desert, and I like it even less now. There're lots of young chaps in MO4 who are very keen to make Rommel's life as difficult as possible, and good for them, but this is not the way. So what are we going to do, Alex?'

'Present a united front. I'm the new boy at the DMO's office, but I know Haselden. We should suggest a smaller operation – you leading your boys at Benghazi at a time of your choosing.'

'Hear, hear. The success we've had so far has largely depended on striking when the opportunity has presented itself. It doesn't work sticking to a prearranged schedule. In fact, the whole b-bloody plan goes against every principle on which the SAS was founded.'

'And against every principle I put forward for C Detachment,' said Vaughan. 'But, David, we've still got a chance to fight our corner. Davy's got a planning conference on the twenty-third of August. Are you going to be there?'

'Yes – as are Guy Prendergast and another of his LRDG chaps.'

'Right. Let's work out a good alternative plan and present it together. We've got a few days.'

Stirling took another puff on his cigar. 'Some of the other chaps are back this week, so come over to the flat and meet some of them on Friday. We're having a little party.'

'That would be fun. Thank you.'

'And do bring a friend.'

'I will.'

Stirling raised a quizzical eyebrow. 'Does she

have a name?'

'Tanja Zanowski. She's Polish.'

'*Très exotique.*'

'She is rather.'

Stirling took another sip of his whisky. 'Alex, it's a shame you never joined my little enterprise. The door will always be open, though.'

'Well, I rather felt I ought to do a stint with the regiment, and then I went and ruined it all by getting myself wounded.'

'And now you're a spy hunter, I hear.'

'A bit of intelligence work, that's all.' *How the hell does he know?*

'A bit more than that, I gathered. An Axis spy ring operating here in Cairo, or so I've been told.'

'Well, there was one rather hopeless spy, but we caught him and his radio operator last month.'

'Of course you can't say. Wrong of me to fish. But I hope you get him – or her.'

Vaughan said nothing, but he was disturbed that David Stirling knew so much. Perhaps the new clampdown would make a difference.

Walking back to his flat, he was filled with disquiet. He wished he could forget about Mustafa, the mole and the incomprehensible cipher messages, and throw all his energy into C Detachment, but he was convinced the proposed raids on Tobruk and Benghazi were ill-conceived. If he and Stirling could not persuade Davy and Haselden to change the plan, disaster loomed. And there was Tanja. He was in love with her, yet there was that seed of doubt – and only one way to get rid of it. Somehow he would have to find out the truth.

The battalion moved out at 1930 hours, as the sun was sinking on the horizon. After a day of unending blue, the Rangers were treated to a sky of magical beauty as they rumbled forward in open formation across the southern end of the line. Suddenly cloud lined the horizon and hung suspended, like strips of mercury, across a sphere of deepening red, with islands of gold and silver. The desert was changing too, from the dun shade of biscuit that was its daytime hue, to pink. Ahead, marking the southern end of the line, stood the weird Himeimat Feature, tall and jagged.

No one said much as they began the fifteen-mile journey to the line, most deep in thought at the prospect of returning to combat. Ahead and to the north, desultory artillery fire boomed, followed by counter-battery fire, but it was landing nowhere near them. Tanner saw Brown flinch as one enemy shell crashed to their right at the foot of the Alam Halfa Ridge, but it was still some distance away. The skies were clear too. Jerry hadn't changed that much, Tanner thought. *He never did like flying in the evening.*

He was glad they had made the recce that afternoon – three trucks, with a sergeant or lieutenant from each of the company's platoons to familiarize themselves with the lie of the land and take stock of their own dispositions in the area. The New Zealanders were covering the Alam Nayil Ridge, then the bulk of XXX Corps between and on the Alam Halfa Ridge. Tanner, driving for a change, had led them to the edge of the Munassib, where they were due to go into the line, had dodged some inaccurate and light artillery fire, and headed back towards Brigade HQ. They had spotted a flight of Italian Macchis, but as they'd dived to attack, they had been bounced by a squadron of Kittyhawks. One Italian had been shot down, the rest had scarpered. The men had cheered, and again as one of the Kittyhawks, gleaming shark teeth clearly visible under its engine cowling, had buzzed them and performed a victory roll. Tanner was glad they'd seen that. It seemed that the Desert Air Force ruled the skies at present, which boosted the men's confidence.

At one point they had met up with the Rutland Yeomanry, now part of 8th Armoured Brigade, out on exercise from their base to the south of Alam Halfa. Tanner had ordered the three trucks to perform a mock attack, circling the formation, then speedily withdrawing. As he had expected, the Yeomanry tank crews had risen to the bait, a squadron of Crusaders breaking off and heading towards them.

Tanner had slowly driven up alongside and halted.

'Bang, bang, you're dead,' said a captain from the lead Crusader.

'Oh, I wouldn't be so sure, sir,' said Tanner. 'We were leading you into a nest of anti-tank guns, you see.'

'Where?' said the captain, looking around.

'Camouflaged, sir.' He heard the others begin to laugh.

'Who the devil are you lot anyway?' said the captain. Another Crusader inched forward, and Tanner saw Lieutenant Rhodes-Morton sticking half out of the turret, wearing a black beret, his field glasses in his hand.

'They're the Yorks Rangers, sir,' said Rhodes-Morton.

Tanner dabbed his fingers to his brow. A casual salute.

'You know them?' said the captain, in a tone of incredulity.

'Lieutenant Tanner and I have met, sir.'

'Really, Harry,' said the captain, 'I thought you'd keep better company.'

'That's not very friendly, sir,' said Tanner, pulling out a cigarette. 'I was only trying to add a bit of realism to your exercise. Jerry likes luring our cavalry out into the open.'

'Look here, who the devil are you?'

'Lieutenant Tanner, sir. A Company, the Yorks Rangers, and these men are some of our platoon commanders and sergeants.'

'He's from Zummerzet, sir,' said Rhodes-Morton. 'Promoted from the ranks.'

'Good God!' spluttered the captain. 'Well, thank goodness the cavalry still has its standards. I've a good mind to report you to your commanding officer, Tanner.'

'Why, sir?' asked Tanner. More laughter from behind him.

'For gross insubordination.'

'I was only trying to help, sir,' said Tanner, 'you being new to the desert and everything.'

'My squadron doesn't need advice from the likes of you. Good day!' He raised his arms. His Crusader crunched into gear and lurched forward.

'What an arsehole,' said Sergeant McAllister, sitting behind Tanner.

'Now, now, Mac,' said Tanner, 'let's not be rude.' He grinned at the men. 'Come on, lads, let's get back. We know when we're not wanted.'

He smiled to himself now. *The stuck-up prigs.* But they'd learn – no doubt at the loss of a fair few lives. The cavalry were always the same and especially the Yeomanry. Part-timers and country squires used to lording it on their horses, looking down at others. The top brass might be giving infantrymen like him commissions in the field, but that didn't mean the traditional class divisions would be broken down any time soon. But as far as Tanner was concerned, class was irrelevant. It was respect that mattered. If he respected a man, he didn't care where that person came from.

Half an hour after setting off, with the first stars twinkling above them, they reached Deir el Munassib, a strange lunar landscape beneath the Alam Nayil Ridge, full of sudden sharp escarpments, some just a few feet deep and others as much as forty. Odd islands of sandy rock sprang up, while in other parts, the desert floor was flat. The Munassib was difficult terrain for any large formation to pass across, but offered the perfect place for a battalion of motorized infantry to hole up during the day. Directly to the south, the desert levelled again into a gravelly plain, the going about as firm as any part of the line. It was through here that they would carry out their nocturnal patrolling.

They passed through the gap in the western

280

edge of the British minefield, then pulled up near the Guide Post, a spot marked on the maps at the edge of the Springbok Track, an old Bedouin trail roughly marked out with stones, which ran the length of the line. While Battalion Headquarters made contact with the Rifle Brigade along the front of the line, the companies settled into their lying-up positions. A Company found a hollow beneath a fifteen-foot escarpment and parked their vehicles. The men jumped out and began to brew up. Guns thundered up ahead, making the ground shudder. *The front*, thought Tanner. *I'm back at last.*

At around 2130, after a conference at Battalion HQ, Peploe returned with orders for A Company to send out a fighting patrol right away. 'This has been an Italian-held section of the line,' he told them, as they gathered around the back of his truck, the tailgate down and the map spread out. He had Sykes hold his German torch over it, with the blue filter over the bulb – it threw enough light to see, but lessened its range. 'The Littorio and Ariete Divisions, apparently. However, the 2 RB boys reckon some German troops are now there. They've been patrolling recently and have reportedly heard German sappers along the enemy minefields. They've also noticed the shelling has intensified in the past few days.' He pointed to a more clearly defined route that ran south-west. 'This is the Qattara Track,' he said, 'and it's about twelve miles due west. The edge of the enemy minefield is halfway, so about six miles west. Our job is to identify the enemy directly in

281

front of us.'

'I'll lead, sir,' said Tanner.

'Thank you, Jack.'

'What are we talking about? A patrol of eighteen men? Three sections?'

'Yes, but no more. Three trucks. This landscape continues, so pass through the minefield gap, then park here.' He pointed to a trig point on the edge of the gravel flats, five miles due west. 'You can see from the map that's there's an escarpment running along there. Use that to cover your approach, then set out on foot for the last mile or so. The enemy have definitely got some forward positions up there near the edge of the minefield, so you can expect wire, mines and MGs.'

'Are we to try to take some prisoners?' asked Tanner.

'Just have a dekko, Jack. If the opportunity arises, yes, but err on the side of caution. This is primarily to identify the enemy. We don't want casualties ourselves.'

Tanner nodded. 'All right,' he said. 'I'll take the boys in my truck, and perhaps two sections from 1 Platoon. Is that all right with you, Jimmy?' he asked Lieutenant Shopland.

'Of course,' said Shopland. He was only twenty-two, but had been with the battalion since March and had shown some initiative and plenty of courage. He was a platoon commander Tanner rated. 'I'll take one section,' he said. 'McAllister can take the other.'

'Good,' said Peploe. 'Get yourselves ready and then head out.' As the officers dispersed, he gripped Tanner's shoulder. 'Jack – no heroics, all right? I need you back.'

'Of course,' Tanner replied. 'Intelligence gathering, that's all.'

13

They set off just after ten o'clock, moving forward slowly – quietly – in line astern, skirting the southern edge of the Munassib, then passing several Rifle Brigade anti-tank guns and driving on through the gap at the edge of the outer minefield. It was dark – only a sliver of moon – but the air was so clear, and the canopy of stars so bright, that there was light enough to navigate.

'It doesn't seem right, sir,' said Sykes, behind him, 'driving one after the other like this. I prefer it when we can spread out a bit.'

'It's better this way, Stan,' Tanner replied. 'We can keep together. Anyway, we'll be parking soon.'

They were now in no man's land. Tanner kept his eye on the looming, ragged escarpment to the right, some twenty to thirty feet high in places. Several enemy shells hurtled overhead, hissing through the night air and exploding moments later some distance behind, but otherwise the enemy was quiet. The curve of the escarpment arced to their right, and by following it, Tanner found the trig point Peploe had pointed out on the map.

'All right, Browner,' he said quietly. 'This'll do. You can stop here.' The edge of the escarpment loomed darkly over them.

There were a few chinks and scrapes as the men clambered down from the trucks and gathered around him.

'All right, lads,' said Tanner, in a loud whisper. 'We'll move forward in a wide, flat V, but each of you make sure you can see the man next to you. Use that to judge the distance between each other. I'm going to halt you regularly, but use your ears as much as your eyes. We'll walk normally to start with, but watch out for my signal to hit the deck. Sykes? Where are you?'

'Here, sir.'

'Good. I want you next to me. Mac, you come on my right with your section and the Bren. Lieutenant Shopland, you attach your other section to Mac's. Everyone got enough ammo?'

Nods, 'Yes, sir,' muttered under the breath.

'Good. Let's go.' He grabbed his rifle from its rest between the front seats and slung it across his back, then hung his MP40 around his neck. On his belt he had half a dozen grenades and his Sauer pistol, and in his pack, a number of clips of ammunition for the rifle and the sub-machine gun. Between them, they also had three Brens, spare magazines, and Sykes was carrying several packets of HE No. 2 and Nobel's 808 Explosive.

Clear of the escarpment, the desert was as flat as a board, but Tanner soon found a sandy seam where it was possible to tread quietly. His heart was thumping strongly. Their surroundings seemed so still, so empty. Occasionally a shell was fired, but otherwise there was nothing, just a vast expanse – yet ahead the enemy had forward positions, just as they had forward positions, and their various units and headquarters, and supply dumps and endless lines of wire stretching back, all just as they had on their own side of the wire. Tanner's ears and eyes strained for any sign of life.

After a hundred yards, he raised his hand and paused to listen, then led them forward another hundred yards. Pause, listen, move forward. The sand remained, but now he led the patrol slowly back to the edge of the rising ground, which might offer them a dark backdrop for any enemy observers watching for them. No dramatic escarpments now, only one of several feet: the ground rose away from them and he was confident they could not be seen clearly in silhouette. On again, pause, listen. Nothing. Tanner reckoned they had moved fourteen hundred yards from the trucks – and then he heard it. A click and a murmur. He froze and raised his arm, then lowered it: the signal for the patrol to get down.

Very slowly, very carefully, he led them forward again, crouching. He gripped his MP40 tightly, wincing at the faint sound of every step. Another fifty yards, he raised his arm again and listened. Voices, a low murmur, then someone laughed quietly. Not in front of them but ahead and away to their right, on the higher ground. A conversation – that meant more than one person. A pair at least, so probably an MG post. Jerry Spandaus were always manned by two men – one to fire, one to feed the belts of ammo. A tap on his shoulder. He turned to see Sykes next to him.

'An MG post a hundred yards at three o'clock,' whispered Tanner.

'And a cigarette at ten o'clock.'

Tanner stared and saw a pinprick orange glow. And something else. The faintest sense of a dark shape. What was that? A sangar? *A gun?*

He turned to McAllister and pointed towards the voices. 'Get your Bren covering that post and call Shopland.' A faintly discernible nod, and a few moments later, Shopland was beside him.

'I think there's something at ten o'clock,' he whispered to the other lieutenant. 'I'm going to move fifty yards to the left and have a dekko with Sykes. I also think there might be an MG post at two o'clock, but Mac's got it covered.'

Shopland nodded.

'Stan,' said Tanner, 'follow me.'

Slowly, he moved away from the others, crouching low, with Sykes almost soundless behind him. They had gone perhaps fifty yards when Tanner stopped and again strained his eyes. Above them, a million stars, and ahead, he now saw, silhouetted against the sky, enemy wire, just ten yards or so away, and the ever-present wooden boards that were now becoming such a feature of the line. Here was the edge of the enemy minefield. But beyond that, seventy or eighty yards off, was a gun, its long barrel slightly elevated, a sangar of stones and sand built up around it. The cigarette they had seen had been from one of the gun's crew.

They crouched there, Tanner staring ahead, weighing up their options.

'What are you thinking, sir?' whispered Sykes.

'A diversion. We set up one of your time pencils. Get it ready here, inch forward, leave it at the wire, then get back to the others. Boom – the explosive detonates, the enemy's confused. Mac's section take out the MG post, we disable the gun, get one or two of the crew, then bugger off.'

Sykes nodded. 'Sounds good to me.' He delved into his pack, pulled out a cartridge of HE No. 2, then a tin of detonators. He fixed a detonator into the top of the cartridge, then produced a time pencil.

When he was ready, he tapped Tanner's shoulder and they began inching forward. Every footstep made Tanner wince, but he kept reminding himself that a German gun crew wouldn't hear that fifty yards away – and most likely not even when they were closer than that. It was late – nearly midnight. Only one or two of the men would probably be awake, and even though someone would be on guard, that didn't mean they were expecting British troops to appear.

As they reached the wire, a German machine-gun opened fire, a sudden *brrp* that cut the night apart, tracer flashing low across the desert away to the right. Tanners heart hammered. Was the aim wide? McAllister hadn't returned fire. *Good lad.* Then another burst, followed by German voices – and the machine-gunner was firing in a wide arc. Now the Bren returned fire, and was joined by another.

'Damn it!' Tanner grabbed Sykes's shoulder as a flare pistol was fired.

'I'm going to throw it.' Sykes threw back his arm and hurled the stick of explosive.

Tanner heard the flare hiss into the air. 'Chuck a packet of Nobel's, Stan.' He cocked his MP40. The flare burst and crackled, and suddenly the desert was lit by a milky white glow. Tanner glanced back towards the others, now lying on the deck – *they're all right* – then saw the packet of Nobel's thirty yards ahead, and opened fire. Bullets burst from the gun. *One second, two seconds, three seconds*. Nothing. 'Bugger it,' he muttered, frantically pulling the magazine out and fumbling in his pack for another, but before he had put the second in, Sykes had lobbed a grenade. After a moment, it exploded, followed by a second, larger detonation. There was a burst of livid orange flame, a man cried out, and now the MG was turning its attention towards them, tracer flashing over them, bullets whizzing above their heads. Tanner glanced across and saw the low profile of his men moving forward. He felt for his wire cutters and, lying on the ground, began slicing at the wire in front of him – just a single coil. *Easy*. Another explosion as the HE detonated, then two more. *Mines?* Tanner ducked as sand and grit showered down on them, then felt for the last piece of wire and snapped it. Away to their left, another MG fired, then rifles too.

'Stan? You all right?'

'Yes.'

'On three we dash for the gun, all right?'

Sykes nodded.

Tanner waited for the flare to die. 'Sod it, let's go!' He scrambled to his feet, machine-guns still chattering. A stumble, a trip. Falling to his knees, then up again, forward, and as another flare burst into magnesium brightness he was standing by the gun, and looking down at three Germans cowering in the dug-out scrape.

'Perfect timing,' said Sykes, breathlessly, beside him.

Tanner jumped down into the scrape and roughly pulled the first man to his feet. 'Get up!' he said. They stood, crouching, hands half raised. The machine-gun to the right had stopped, but the Spandau to the left was still firing, mostly too high. Someone was shouting further ahead, and wild shots were being fired into the night, as Tanner and Sykes shoved the three men clear of the gun.

'Get going, Stan!' said Tanner. One man groaned nearby; another, he saw, was dead. Taking a grenade from his belt, he pulled out the pin, shoved it down the barrel of the gun, and ran forward. A couple of seconds later, the grenade blew and the gun rocked back, the end of the barrel splayed.

The flare fizzled out as they began to run back, the three prisoners in front of them. 'To the others!' he hissed at Sykes, as they ran, half crouching.

'Where are they? I can't see!' said Sykes. A machine-gun was still firing intermittent bursts, the odd rifle shot cracked out and then another flare went up.

'Hit the ground, Stan!'

They dived, pushing the prisoners down with them. The flare burst and crackled, showering them once again with white light.

'Very good of 'em,' said Sykes. 'Now we can see the others.' He pointed towards the rising ground where they were prostrate, just thirty yards away. As light flooded the line, McAllister, Braithwaite and Lewis opened up with the Brens once more, while the others were firing their rifles.

Tanner looked back. It was hard to see much: some wire, some minefield signs, tracer, but beyond that nothing, just inky darkness. *Outposts only*. A few guns, widely spaced MG posts, but not much more. But it was time to get the hell out.

The flare died, and he scrambled up, yanking the prisoners to their feet, and forcing them in a low crouch towards the others.

'There you are, sir,' said McAllister. 'And with some fresh Jerries too.'

'Come on,' said Tanner. 'Let's go. Mac, Ron, Taff – cover us with the Brens, moving back in turn.'

They began to retreat, still crouching, hugging the edge of the rising ground to their left, with bursts of Bren fire, but the enemy had not put up another flare, and as they melted into the darkness, the firing died away. 'All boys, hold your fire,' Tanner called.

They were standing tall now, jogging with the rising escarpment on their left. Suddenly one of the prisoners made a run for it, veering wildly away from them, but Lieutenant Shopland ran after him and brought him down. 'Get up,' he snarled, grabbing the man's collar.

'*Nein – nein! Scheiße!*' cried the man, as Shopland shoved him back towards the others.

Twelve hundred yards from the enemy wire, the desert seemed vast and empty once more. Tanner blinked, his eyes getting used to the night again. Shapes were becoming clearer, the men more defined. *Nearly there*, he thought, recognizing the shape of a lone rise in the ground, like a wedge sticking up, just ahead. And then there they were, the three trucks, just as they had left them – how long before? Half an hour? An hour?

The men began to chatter – they'd all made it. Tanner knew that release of tension well. He felt it now, the adrenalin coursing through him, his body still alert. But they were not back yet.

'Keep it down, boys,' he said. 'We've still got to get back through our own lines. One prisoner in each truck and let's go.'

Tanner leaped into the front of his Bedford, the engines coughed into life, and they were on their way, following the route they had come, the night now silent but for their three-truck patrol as the rubber tyres sped over the gravelly ground.

A small hold-up at the British wire, and then they found the tracks and were through. Tanner breathed a sigh of relief: he'd known the gaps to be closed while he'd been out on patrol. *But not tonight.* He wiped a sleeve across his brow, took off his tin helmet and lit a cigarette. A Pak 75 anti-tank gun destroyed, three prisoners taken, and not a single man down. He was pleased. Mission accomplished.

Around a hundred and fifty miles away, as the crow flew, Tanja Zanowski awoke, and turned towards Alex, lying beside her silently – so silently that she leaned closer to make sure he was breathing. He was. She could hear him – and smell him, for that matter: the rather sour whiff of alcohol, which was unsurprising, considering the wine and whisky he had drunk. She had encouraged it.

Was now the moment? She lay on her back and sighed heavily. She could feel tears building behind her eyes. It was getting hard to know what was reality and what was part of the charade. She was sure she was falling for Alex, but she had been instructed to become his lover. The day before, when he had so nearly caught her red-handed, she had been horrified to see him but her heart had quickened with joy too. Had that been real happiness when she had embraced him? Or had it been part of the act? She rubbed her eyes. And tonight they'd had another lovely evening. She'd enjoyed being with him – but at the same time she'd been hoping he'd get tight, so that he would sleep more heavily and she could look through his briefcase. It was a photograph she had seen him hurriedly put away yesterday morning. She had got a glimpse, not enough to see clearly who it was, but she was convinced it had been of Artus. If she could just find out who Artus was...

She knew the briefcase was in Alex's living room on the armchair. All she had to do was slip out of bed, walk in, open the catch and look. It would take – what? A minute? Maybe less.

Maybe they were both acting. Maybe Alex was pretending he had seen nothing, just as she was pretending that there was nothing for him to be suspicious about. She leaned her arm across her forehead and closed her eyes. *I don't want it to be like this.*

She had signalled Cobra early that morning – after leaving Alex and before going to work: 'British intelligence knows of Axis spy operation in Cairo. Please send instructions.' A reply had come through almost immediately: 'Has Operation Cobra been compromised?' Not yet, Tanja had transmitted by return. 'Only contact if information of vital importance,' had come Cobra's second reply. But that was hardly a new instruction – that was the golden rule of espionage, drummed into her during her training. Neither Orca nor Artus had tried to make contact that day, but she dreaded they would. She was tempted to lie – after all, her whole life felt like one – and tell them Cobra had ordered them to keep silent for a while, but perhaps that was too obviously false. They had already begun to doubt her. One wrong move and she would be dead. They would kill her, she knew, just as they had killed Aladdin. Artus had meant what he had said.

She shuddered, goose-bumps prickling her skin despite the heat. She was dead if she was caught by the British; dead if she tried to trick Orca and Artus. Not for the first time a wave of despair swept over her. She felt so trapped. Could she confess to Alex? To the British Secret Intelligence Service? Offer to work for them instead? But the risk seemed so great. *I'm damned.*

Damned unless I find out who Artus and Orca are. And only a few steps away she might find part of the answer. *But if Alex wakes...* The thought terrified her, not because it would lead to her arrest but because it would mean losing him. She had lost so much already – and her feelings for him were not an act. *I love him,* she thought, but by looking in his case, she would betray him.

She leaned over him again, then ran her hands over his cheek and through his hair. He did not

293

move. *He must be asleep*. She moved away from him, slid her legs off the bed and padded into the living room. Darkness. She stood there for a moment, then switched on the light and waited. Would he come through? A minute passed, then another. There was the case – within touching distance. The flat was still. She glanced back at the bedroom. No sign of Alex stirring, no indication that he was lying there, secretly watching her, had been awake all along.

A deep breath, and then she was standing over the chair, one hand on the leather handle, fingers at the metal catch. Suddenly a screech. *What was that?* She recoiled, her heart pounding. Another screech. *A catfight. It's only a catfight.* Outside somewhere. Tanja gasped, her hand to her brow. She listened again, but Alex was still asleep. Blissfully asleep. She stood over the briefcase again, felt for the clasp, prised it open and lifted the leather flap. Inside were just a few papers, and a buff folder. She pulled it out and there was the photograph she had been hoping for: a head-and-shoulders shot. Quickly she put it back and scanned the papers inside the folder. 'Suspect has been seen...' 'Interrogation of Suspect...' A name, a name. Where the hell was the name? And then she saw it. *Eslem Mustafa.*

She swallowed, her heart thudding so hard she thought it would burst. Carefully, she put the folder back between the sheets of paper where she had found it and, with trembling fingers, shut the clasp, then took another deep breath.

Eslem Mustafa. She switched off the light, left the living room and slid back into bed.

14

It was Saturday, 29 August, and they had been invited for a brew at the front with an anti-tank gun crew from 2nd Rifle Brigade. Much of A Company had been out on patrol work at various stages of the night, but as Tanner and his men had returned through the wire, they had been invited to join the Riflemen for some char.

'A cuppa before the flies come out,' said the sergeant, cheerily.

'Go on, sir,' said Brown, beside him. 'I'm gasping.'

'Thanks,' said Tanner. The sun was rising behind them, the desert lightening rapidly, as they parked the Bedford. At the back of the gun scrape, men were sitting around two four-gallon flimsies, one full of sand and burning petrol, the other filled with near boiling water.

'So what d'you think then, sir?' said the sergeant, who had introduced himself as Albert. 'We heard a rumour that Rommel was going to attack three nights back.'

Tanner shrugged. 'Any night now, I'd say. When's the full moon? Tomorrow?'

'Definitely tomorrow,' said Hepworth.

'Then tonight or the next two nights, I reckon.' Tanner clapped his hands and rubbed them together. 'I hope they do come through here. Let's give 'em a spanking.'

'They've got to, haven't they?' said Albert.

'Looks like it,' agreed Tanner. The prisoners they had captured more than a week before had been from the German 90th Light Division. At their initial interrogation at Battalion, they had revealed that the Deutsches Afrika Korps were moving down to the southern end of the line and that the Italian Littorio and Ariete Divisions were still there. The former was fully motorized, the latter armoured. That meant all Rommel's panzer and motorized divisions were massing in the south.

With the tea boiled, the brew was poured into mugs from the truck.

'How are you getting on with the six-pounders?' Tanner asked, as he stood looking at the gun.

'Pretty good. Nice bit of kit,' said Albert. 'Good against soft-skins and most Eyetie tanks.'

Tanner grinned. 'And it looks like that's all you've got directly in front.'

He lit a cigarette, then one of the Riflemen said, 'Oi, oi, who's this coming in?' A truck had heaved into view, emerging from around the edge of the low escarpment up ahead.

'A Dodge,' said Brown.

'Who's driving them round here? The KRRC?'

One of the Riflemen scrambled down to the area of flat ground to show the approaching truck where the entrance to the fence line was, despite the numerous tracks funnelled there.

Tanner watched with mild interest, then saw that one of the men in the truck was standing on the running-board, clutching a submachine gun.

'What the hell?' he said, and at the same moment the Rifleman cried out, 'They're bloody Jerries!' and tried to swing his Thompson as the German on the running-board opened fire. The burst missed but the Rifleman hit the ground. Tanner now saw that in the back of the Dodge there was a machine-gun. He already had his rifle off his back and pulled back the bolt, aiming as the machine-gun opened fire towards them with a short burst. Bullets pinged and ricocheted as men dived for cover, but Tanner was already in position with a bead on the man. He held his breath and felt his finger squeeze the trigger. The butt thumped against his shoulder, and the machine-gunner lurched backwards off the truck, tumbling on to the sand.

The Rifleman by the wire had also opened fire, making the man on the running-board duck. With their machine-gunner dead, the driver now careered round in a wide arc away from them. Another man in the back was scrambling up to take over the machine-gun, swinging the barrel towards them, but Tanner already had him in his aim, and squeezed the trigger again. He saw the German's right shoulder jerk backwards. *Not dead, but that'll hurt, all right.* Others were firing their rifles now as the Dodge swerved away, speeding back across the desert in a cloud of dust.

'What the hell was the point of that?' said Sykes, standing beside him.

'I suppose they thought the truck would get them close enough. Brave lads, but pretty reckless, I'd say.'

'Good shooting,' said Albert, clambering down

297

towards his fellow Rifleman, who was now on his feet and dusting himself down.

Tanner followed with Sykes, and made his way through the wire to the German lying prostrate some hundred and fifty yards away.

When they reached him, he was on his front, so with his boot, Tanner rolled him over. A large stain of dark blood had spread across the dead man's chest. His face, too, was dusty, and he was only young. His cap had fallen off, revealing a mop of thick hair. Tanner bent down and patted the man's pockets. In the shorts he found what he was after: cigarettes – almost a full packet. 'Bloody idiot,' he said, then turned and walked away.

Later that day, around seven o'clock in the evening, A Company was back at its operating base in the Deir el Munassib when the ration wagon arrived. That was one of the many advantages of being stationed along a fixed line and closer to the Delta: instead of long weeks of hard-tack biscuits and bully beef, there were tins of Maconochie's stew, tinned fruit, even corn flakes, as well as condensed milk and cigarettes.

Each section had men with particular roles, tasks that naturally fell to one person rather than another. In Tanner's truck, Mudge was the cook, with Smailes as his assistant, while Sykes, despite his elevated position as CSM, still considered himself the best brewer of tea. Now Mudge and Smailes hurried to collect the food. From his seat up front in the truck, Tanner watched them. He was about ready for some scoff, but there were still plenty of flies around. It would be better to wait another half-hour, by which time the temperature would have started to drop, the sun would be setting and the flies would be calling it a day.

Tanner, who had been reading the last of the Thomas Hardy novels Lucie had bought for him, flicked a fly off his face. They had been particularly bad that day – he'd had his tiffin earlier with his mess tin an inch from his mouth and a cotton *keffiyeh* he had bought in Cairo over his head and the food, but still the flies had got through. God only knew how many he'd eaten since first arriving in the desert. Even after the food had been cleared away, they buzzed about the men's faces, landed on their arms, and crawled over the vehicles. It was impossible to be free of them, and brushing them away was almost a full-time job, arms swishing like a horse's tail.

Peploe wandered over. He was capless, his strawberry-blond hair wild and thick with dust. Seeing Tanner whisk away more flies, he said, 'They're bad today, aren't they?'

'Bloody awful. It was better when we had the run of the desert, wasn't it?'

'In that respect, yes. By the way, did you know that the flies out here are different from the ones we have back home?'

'Really? They look the same. I thought a fly was a fly,' said Tanner.

'Not according to Tom Arliss.'

'He's an expert, is he?'

'It would seem so. I was talking to him earlier after seeing Old Man Vigar. He was saying that the common European housefly is much bigger – *Musca domestica*, to give it its proper name.'

Tanner raised an eyebrow.

'*Musca* what, sir?' said Sykes, sitting beside Tanner.

'*Domestica.* Latin was never my strong point at school, but it means "house". *Musca* – fly. Major Arliss was saying that the desert fly is smaller, hardier and aggressive. *Musca sorbens*, apparently.'

'He didn't mention a way to get rid of them by any chance?' said Tanner.

'I asked him that too. He said, "Yes. Stop the war."'

Suddenly the air was filled with a rushing whine. Tanner and Sykes leaped out of the truck and, with Peploe, pressed themselves against the escarpment as others hurled themselves to the ground. The shell landed some short distance behind them, but was immediately followed by several more. The ground trembled with every explosion while dust, grit and stone erupted into the air, much of it landing on the A Company positions, showering the men and pattering on to the vehicles. There was coughing, cursing, and an open tin of stew was ruined – but no one was hurt.

'Something's up,' said Peploe, crouching beside Tanner.

'Too bloody right,' said Tanner. 'They've got to attack any moment now. They've just got to.'

Several more shells landed nearby and then the enemy fire moved further to their right. They heard the New Zealanders' guns from Alam Nayil firing counter-battery barrages, the ground shuddering.

'I think they're done with us for the moment,'

said Tanner. 'Shall I tell the lads to get on with supper, sir?' he asked Peploe.

'Might as well.'

Tanner stood up and dusted himself down. 'Flies have gone,' he said. 'They might be aggressive but they're cowardly little bastards too. A couple of shells and they scarper.'

The shelling lessened as the sun began to set. Tanner had asked Peploe if he would like to join them for supper, an offer he accepted. As Mudge and Smailes prepared the meal, the rest sat in the truck or stood around smoking and chatting.

'What have we got, then, Mudge?' asked Peploe. 'Any surprises?'

'Tinned potatoes and beans, sir,' Mudge replied, as he squatted by the two stoves – one, a fuel can of petrol-soaked sand, the other a Primus. 'And some Maconochie's.'

'What about pud?'

'Tinned pears and condensed milk,' said Mudge, 'unless you'd rather have Mudge's Special Burgoo, sir.'

Peploe thought a moment.

'Mudge's burgoo is usually pretty good, sir,' said Sykes, 'but it's always worth checking his biscuit and jam source before you make a decision.'

'They're Peak Frean's biscuits, sir,' said Mudge, 'and Egyptian jam, probably strawberry. It's red, at any rate.' He suddenly looked up, his face brightening. 'I know! How about burgoo with pears?'

'It's not every day we entertain the company commander, Mudgy,' said Tanner. 'You should pull all the stops out on this one.'

'Well, I wouldn't want to be greedy,' said Peploe.

'It's fine, sir,' said Mudge.

'I've got a few extra tins stashed away,' said Sykes.

'Course you have, Stan.' Tanner grinned.

They ate the stew as the desert changed colour, like a chameleon, from dun to amber to pink. A few of the braver flies had returned, but the hordes had gone.

''Ere,' said Sykes, 'I 'eard a good one this morning from one of those Rifle Brigade lads.' The others looked at him expectantly. 'I was cursing those Jerries that tried to shoot us up out of the blue, and he was saying that not all Jerries were bad. And then he told me this story. At one point they'd been dug in for a little while, and he was saying about how it was small things that made the desert bearable. Anyway, for him it was his enamel plate. It was a really nice one: beautiful white, dark blue trim, barely a chip on it. All the other lads had their battered old mess tins but this chap had his enamel plate. He was always very careful about washing it afterwards and making sure he looked after it. Anyway, Jerry attacks one day and they get pushed back. It's when they stop again that he realizes he's lost his plate. Fair gutted he was about it. And you know how it is: little things take on greater importance than they should. Well, a little while later they counterattack and retake their old positions, and there, the other side of this little ridge, is a stove and a number of old tins and so on. And there's his plate – the same one – but there's a little stone on

302

it and underneath a note.' He looked at the others and grinned. 'It says, "You left this behind last time. Thanks for the loan. All the best, Fritz."'

Everyone laughed.

'He swore blind it was true,' said Sykes.

'I wouldn't want an enamel plate,' said Phyllis.

'No? Why not?' asked Peploe.

'I prefer the mess tin.'

'No refinement in Siff, is there?' said Brown.

'I've got enough to worry about out here without thinking about enamel plates. As long as they don't get me they can have any of my kit.'

'Not your bundook, though, Siff,' said Tanner. 'Lose that and it's the glass-house for you.'

Phyllis looked worried. 'Is it? Really?'

Tanner shook his head. 'Siff, where did they get you from?'

'Leeds. Well, Horsforth, actually.' He was typical of many of the Yorks Rangers: small, wiry, undernourished as a kid. Most of them came from the twin cities of Leeds and Bradford – they were working-class boys, where growing up had been hard. Tanner had noticed that it was the ones who had been in the battalion longest – men like McAllister, Smailes and Hepworth – who were the biggest and fittest. Hepworth was quite tall, McAllister was not, but they'd filled out since he'd known them. Hepworth had grown up on a farm, but the other two were from Bradford. McAllister, he knew, had grown up living four to a bed, eating bread and dripping, meat once a week if he was lucky. The only fruit were apples and even those were rare. The army had done them good. They complained about the monotony of the food but at least they were given three square meals a day – for the most part, at any rate, which was better than most of them had had growing up. They were fit and, on the whole, healthy too. They'd had meat, vegetables and fruit most days since they'd been back in the line, plenty of exercise, and cleaner air to breathe than there was in any of those industrial cities at home. Phyllis was still a skinny runt, Tanner reflected, but so long as he survived the fighting, he would grow into a strong young man.

There was a pause while Mudge prepared his pudding. The packet of Peak Frean's biscuits was crushed finely and poured into a billy-can of condensed milk, which was heated over the Primus. He added some sugar and the jam and stirred it into a thick, pink, syrupy sauce, or burgoo. Sweet-smelling steam rose from the billy-can, while Sykes brewed more tea.

Eventually, satisfied that the burgoo had reached the right consistency, Mudge dished it out, encouraging them to help themselves to the open tin of pears in syrup.

'Well, sir?' said Mudge, as Peploe took a mouthful.

His eyes widened and he clutched his throat. 'Argh!' he said. 'It's musquois!'

Mudge's face fell, then Peploe laughed. 'Sorry, Mudge. A cheap trick. It's delicious.'

Mudge's face relaxed.

'It'll certainly weigh me down,' said Brown.

'Careful, Browner,' said Tanner. 'Insult the chef and you'll be cooking your own.'

'Sorry, mate.' Brown looked sheepish. 'It's

bloody beautiful. My mam couldn't have made it better.'

'Maybe Mudgy should become a housewife when he's older,' said Phyllis. 'You could stay at home and look after the nippers while your missus goes out and works the shift.'

'I'd love that,' said Mudge. 'Cooking and looking after the kids would be brilliant. I'd hate the scrubbing, though. It's bad enough cleaning my bundook.'

'Well, who knows what the world will be like when we all get home?' said Peploe. 'The old order changeth – and about time.'

'It certainly is,' said Tanner. 'I never thought I'd get a commission.'

'Will there be a revolution, sir?' said Sykes.

'I don't think so. But social change – yes, I'm sure. After all, the women are working now, aren't they? We've got Land Girls on our farm back home and my old man reckons they're doing a bloody good job too. They can drive tractors as well as the next man.'

'We've got 'em on our farm an' all,' said Hepworth.

'All these women in the factories and on the land and manning airfield control rooms might like working and may not want to give it up,' said Peploe.

'But they worked in the last war and everything went back to how it was,' said Sykes.

'True. But we're a quarter of a century on,' replied Peploe. 'Society moves forward. Look, I've got no crystal ball, Stan, but this war will change things. I'm certain of it.'

They were all silent for a while, until Hepworth said, 'Anyway, we've got to get through this yet. We might all be dead this time tomorrow.'

'Bloody hell, Hep, you miserable bastard,' said Tanner.

'Yes – thanks for that cheery thought, Hepworth,' added Peploe.

'Can't help it,' said Hepworth. 'I've survived this far but I keep thinking my luck's bound to run out.'

'Stick with me, Hep, and you'll be fine,' said Tanner.

'I just wonder how we're ever going to beat Rommel,' Hepworth continued. 'He seems so much better than any of our generals.'

'That's almost treacherous talk, isn't it?' grinned Sykes.

'You should have killed him when you had the chance, sir,' Hepworth told Tanner.

'When was that, sir?' said Phyllis.

Tanner smiled. 'In France, a couple of years back. I had him in my sight. A bullet was going to go right through his temple but then some aide moved and he caught it instead. Actually, I had another chance a few minutes later, but if I'd fired then we'd have betrayed our positions and probably all got ourselves killed. Stan here stopped me.'

'Do you ever wonder whether you should have done it anyway, sir?' Phyllis wanted to know.

'It's crossed my mind once or twice, but not really. Not now, anyway. If you ask me, he's busted his flush. Another Jerry general might have had a bit more sense and stayed around Tobruk but he's a reckless one, Rommel. He's got to attack us here, and as long as those cavalry idiots stay put, as Montgomery's told them to, and don't go racing after the enemy the moment they look like they're pulling back, he's going to lose. And we've got the RAF. Those boys rule the roost, these days, and that's a beautiful thing to see.'

'Too right,' said Sykes. 'You remember Norway and France? It's nice to know Jerry's getting it in the neck for a change.'

Tanner put a cigarette in his mouth. 'If you ask me,' he said, striking a match with his thumbnail, 'we're going to be eating Rommel's bollocks for breakfast.'

Colonel Maunsell was of much the same opinion. Vaughan had been unable to join him at morning prayers that day, but had received a call from Maunsell asking him to drop in that evening and had done so. Maunsell was in a celebratory mood and, even after another sweltering day in the city, looked as immaculately urbane as ever in a white silk suit and what Vaughan recognized as a Charvet tie.

'Ha!' said Maunsell, lighting his pipe. 'The Huns must be ruing the day they failed to take Malta. We've learned, Alex, that the Italians have ordered nine fuel-carrying ships direct to Tobruk and Mersa, leaving Taranto and Naples over a period of six days. Apparently, Rommel's desperate for them. His fuel supply is critical. Enough for one last push and that's it, but if these tankers don't make it, he really will find himself up the proverbial creek without a paddle.'

'You always did say it was a war of supply, RJ,' said Vaughan.

'Anyway, we got wind of the first convoy of three ships and they've been attacked by Malta-based submarines and aircraft and two are already at the bottom of the Med.'

'That's the most marvellous news,' said Vaughan. 'So the submarines are back on Malta too?'

Maunsell grinned like a schoolboy. 'Incredible, isn't it?' he said. 'A fortnight ago, the island was staring down the barrel.'

'Our spies must be cross,' said Vaughan.

'I should say so.'

'I don't think we need to worry too much about that any more,' said Maunsell. 'Obviously we want to catch them, but as long as they're not passing on vital information, they're not doing any harm.'

'I suppose not,' agreed Vaughan. 'Have there been any more signals?'

Maunsell shook his head. 'One just over a week ago – a signal, then a reply, then another signal and reply, all in the space of twenty minutes or so, but nothing since.'

'That's good. And Mustafa?'

'Lying low is my guess. Sammy and Bones are still very much on the case, though. As I said to you before, Alex, these things can take time. We've done bloody well to get where we've got with it.' He beamed. 'However, there has been a development, which is why I asked you over this evening. The others don't know yet, either.' He pressed the buzzer on his desk. 'Daphne,' he said, 'could you round up KJ, George and Paddy for me? Thanks awfully.' He looked up at Vaughan. 'They'll be along in a minute. Tell me, how's planning going?'

Vaughan sighed. 'Not good, I'm afraid. Anyone who's got any experience with these operations is against using such large, disparate forces. David Stirling's against it, so is Guy Prendergast.'

'I've always wondered whether Stirling's a bit of loose cannon,' said Maunsell, 'but Prendergast is as sound as they come. He's been a friend for years.'

'It's not just them. I'm with them completely and so are the SAS and LRDG chaps in Cairo at the moment. But Brigadier Davy's set on it and so is Colonel Haselden. They feel that unless we attack strongly we'll never have the weight of fire to destroy the harbour installations. They're arguing that if one or other of the forces involved doesn't succeed, it's not the end of the world, so long as we go in hard and cause as much havoc as possible.'

'In other words, chuck a load of mud at the wall and hope some sticks.'

'Exactly. But what they're failing to understand is that there's little chance of any mud sticking at all, because it'll be almost impossible to maintain any kind of surprise once we get even remotely close.'

'Indeed. And we also have to hope our dormant spies don't get wind of it and tip off the enemy.'

'Well, yes, there is that too, although hopefully it's now sufficiently dormant not to add to our woes.' Vaughan rubbed his chin. 'I just hope my crew get back safely and that I'll then have the chance to implement what we discussed.'

Maunsell raised his glass. 'I'll drink to that, Alex. I know Bowlby is of much the same opinion as you about this raid. He's been trying to put some pressure on the COS to put the kybosh on the whole thing.'

'We don't need to kybosh it entirely. We just need to scale it down and lessen the objectives.'

'In any case,' said Maunsell, 'you and I need to get together with Bowlby sooner rather than later.'

There was a knock at the door and Maddox entered, followed by Jones and Kirk. They sat in their usual chairs in front of Maunsell's desk.

'I would have kept this until morning prayers, but I wanted Alex in on it,' he said, once he had poured everyone a drink. He cleared his throat, then said, 'The boffins at GC and CS have had something of a breakthrough. They've picked up some signals sent by Rommel's head of intelligence at Panzer Army Africa Headquarters in Mersa Matruh – a Major von Mellenthin. However, what is of interest to us is an intercepted signal relating to Operation Cobra. GC and CS became suspicious when the message started referring to agents and using what were blatantly codenames. They forwarded this to MEIC, who recognized the terminology immediately from Axis spy circuits operating in Turkey and elsewhere. Cuthbert Bowlby immediately passed it on to me.'

'That's terrific,' said Vaughan.

'Have you got any details?' asked Maddox.

Maunsell nodded, and lit his pipe, his face briefly disappearing behind swirls of curling smoke. 'Yes. It seems Cobra is a four-man team, headed by a fellow codenamed Orca. The signal made reference to one of the team, Aladdin, having been "eradicated".'

'Moussa,' said Vaughan.

'One can only presume so,' said Maunsell.

'And the other two?' asked Maddox.

'Codenames Artus and Marlin.'

Kirk smiled ruefully. 'How could I ever have doubted it?'

'And Marlin is the radio operator.'

'Anything else?' asked Maddox.

'Yes. The message is a warning that Cobra is in danger of being compromised and may have to be closed down.'

'It said that?' Kirk looked surprised. 'Well, well. I don't suppose there's much more to worry about on that score, then.'

'We mustn't take our eye off the ball, though,' said Maunsell, then added, 'And, sadly, there's been no reply as yet. Still, it's a great leap forward. We now have confirmation of the circuit's existence, a name, agent codenames, and we now know that we've been on the right trail. Well done, all of you, but to Paddy and Alex, particular credit is due, not to mention the part played by Jack Tanner, wherever he might be.'

'Out in the desert, waiting for Rommel to attack,' said Vaughan.

'As are we all.' Maunsell smiled, then raised his glass.

Vaughan left them soon after, stepping out into the warm evening air. He decided to walk to Tanja's flat rather than take a taxi or gharry, and headed past GHQ, the smell of jasmine heavy on the air, then across Sharia El Fasqiya. The *ahwa* was busy, elderly men spilling out on to the pavement, but the tailor's place was empty, a large padlock on the door.

He had done much to quell his doubts about Tanja. What a long time a week could be! He smiled to himself, thinking of how he had gone back to the narrow street where he had followed her. He'd felt quite nervous going into the store, convinced he would find endless boxes of Turkish Delight, but they'd had none – just as she had told him. He had even had a check done on her at SIME. It had come back clear: a Polish refugee, she had reached Egypt via Palestine in May 1941 – just as she had told him.

He had still not mentioned to Maunsell or Maddox what he had seen: the breathless expression, the glimpse of Mustafa soon after. The possible connection. He had not questioned the owner of the shop, or shown him photographs, but even in a week he had begun to see that his grounds for suspicion were unfounded. It had been a coincidence. Tanja was not a spy. He had been guilty of paranoia, his mind clouded by having allowed himself to become too consumed by the case.

And so he had left it, concentrating on his new job instead, and as the days passed, his doubts about her had melted away. He had been busy, and forming C Detachment had taken up a great deal of his time. During the past week he had been to Alexandria and had met with the commanders of the two MTB flotillas there. The 10th Flotilla had been earmarked for the Tobruk operation, but Vaughan had struck a rapport with the commander of the under-strength 15th, Lieutenant Commander Jim Allenby, a young but experienced naval officer who had impressed Vaughan with his knowledge of the North African coastline. The flotilla was due to be merged with the 10th, and Allenby was anxious to find a role for himself since command would go with the 10th. Vaughan had accompanied him on a two-day patrol up the coast, during which the two men forged a strong working relationship. Vaughan had returned to Cairo, his enthusiasm rekindled.

Then there had been the process of recruitment. Eight men – that was all he needed. A small, tight squad and nothing more. Men with experience, and, crucially, different skills. He would have to wait for Tanner and Sykes, but the other five he needed to recruit right away. Conversations with various people, David Stirling and Guy Prendergast among them, had given him a start. The first to join C Detachment had been Johnny Farrer, a Scotsman Vaughan had known from his time in Middle East Commando, and who, like him, had got stuck at GHQ. Farrer was also a German and Italian speaker, and a man Vaughan liked and trusted.

Next he had visited the large training camp of Geneifa in the Canal Zone, and there he had found the other four: a South African called Pete de Villiers, a former estate manager in the Trans-

313

vaal and a German speaker; a New Zealander called Sam McInnes; and two Englishmen, Sergeants Len Ferguson and Tom Walsh, both of whom had seen action in India before the war as well as in North Africa. Currently instructors at Geneifa, they were bored and frustrated with training recruits, and had been among the large number of volunteers who had stepped forward. Ferguson and Walsh had stood out from the rest. They both had the right levels of experience but other skills as well: Walsh was an unarmed combat instructor, while Ferguson was a signals expert with the technical knowledge Vaughan reckoned they would need.

He had had neither the time nor the inclination to think too much more about enemy spy circuits, or the whereabouts of Eslem Mustafa – that was for Maunsell and Maddox, Sansom and Astley and their men. Moreover, while he had been away, he realized how consumed he had become by the world of espionage and counter-intelligence; it was a small world, inhabited by few people. Seeing the vast naval operation at Alexandria, the huge training camp at Geneifa, and the countless bombers flying out over the sea or up the desert, had made him realize that, while the work done by SIME was vital, it was just one cog in a vast military machine. Now that he was preoccupied with his own mission, the import-ance of smashing the enemy circuit – Operation Cobra – had seemed to recede. As had his con-cerns over Tanja and his responsibility to Maunsell and the team at SIME. Getting away from claustrophobic Cairo was what he had needed; a little perspective went a long way. When he had thought of her, he had remembered her smile, her arms around his neck, making love to her, the curve of her body as she lay next to him. He was not prepared to throw all that away on a suspicion that seemed increasingly ridiculous with every day that passed.

He was looking forward to seeing her now. God only knew what lay in store over the next few weeks and, in any case, it seemed that Operation Cobra was dead and buried. Kirk had been right. In a couple of days' time, Vaughan's embryonic force would meet at Kabrit, where Stirling had arranged for them to train at the SAS camp, then go on to Alexandria for sea-training with Allenby. For now, though, a night with Tanja. That was something to be relished.

Away in the desert, along the southern end of the Alamein Line, A Company were patrolling in no man's land in front of the British minefields. Tanner had taken out two trucks and, having roamed around noisily for the best part of an hour, had decided to bring them in to the edge of the Munassib, out of sight, and watch for a while. The moon was high – and almost full – casting an immense glow over the desert. To the south the Himeimat Feature was silhouetted against the sky, and in their trucks they could see each other quite clearly.

'Quiet as the grave,' whispered Sykes.

'It is, Stan,' agreed Tanner. 'I don't understand it. I'd have thought they'd have blokes out clearing minefields by now.' He scratched his chin.

'Maybe we've had it wrong all along.' He sighed heavily. 'Beats me.'

'Sir,' said Brown, beside him. 'All right if I go for a crap, sir?'

'Bloody hell, Browner. Yes, all right. Off you go, but be quick about it.,

Brown clambered out, scurried up the escarpment and disappeared from view.

'Where the bloody hell has he gone?' muttered Tanner. 'Hardly any need to be shy around here.'

'It's quite a bright moon, though, sir,' said Sykes. 'Perhaps he's worried someone might see that white backside.'

The minutes passed, the desert silent. No guns fired, no aircraft flew overhead. The only sound was of the engines ticking as they cooled. Then, suddenly, there was Brown, scrambling down the slope towards them. 'Sir!' he said, reaching the edge of the truck. 'Jerry sappers, sir. They're lifting mines. I could hear them.'

'What? Over there?' said Tanner, indicating behind them.

'There's quite a clear run just back there,' said Brown.

'Right,' said Tanner. 'Let's have 'em.'

'Did you do your business, Browner?' asked Sykes.

'I was halfway through when I heard them. When I'd done I crawled on a bit and then I could see them. There's half a dozen at least.'

'Good work, Browner,' said Tanner, grabbing the flare pistol from beneath the seat. He went over to the other truck. 'You stay here and keep watching to the south. We'll be back in a minute.'

With Smailes carrying the Bren, they went up the escarpment and slowly crept forward until they could hear a soft *clink, clink* a short way ahead. The ground levelled, then Tanner could see that it dropped away in another fifteen-foot cliff. Beyond that there was a valley a couple of hundred yards wide, before the land rose again. Just forty yards below them a mine-clearing party was crouched on the ground, lifting mines with bayonets.

'What's the plan?' asked Sykes.

'Tell them to put their hands up and then we take them prisoner.' He turned to Smailes. 'Get that Bren ready, Smiler.'

Smailes nodded, shifted on his belly alongside them, then quietly pulled back the bolt.

Tanner squatted on his haunches, his MP40 ready and cocked. 'Oi, Jerries!' he shouted. *'Hände hoch!'*

The enemy sappers stopped and turned, but rather than put their hands in the air, one opened fire with a sub-machine gun.

'Jesus!' cursed Tanner, ducking as bullets zinged into the sandy rock in front of them. A split second later, Smailes opened fire, followed by an immediate fusillade of rifles from the others.

Tanner lifted his head. The enemy firing had stopped, and he saw all six men clearly prostrate and motionless. 'Bollocks,' he muttered. 'Why did they have to go and do that?'

From the Rifle Brigade positions somewhere up ahead, a flare was now fired into the sky, lighting up the desert even more, but it had come too late.

'Come on, let's get out of here,' said Tanner.

'What about their vehicle?' said Sykes. 'Worth a look? If we can turn ours round here, we could follow their tracks.'

Tanner thought a moment. 'All right, Stan. I'll tell Sergeant Braithwaite to get back and report what's happened, and we'll go and look for it.'

They found it more easily than Tanner had imagined. They soon found a route through the Munassib and into the *deir*, and half a mile beyond that they saw it, tucked into the escarpment. It was a four-wheel drive truck. 'A Phänomen Granit,' Brown told them, 'ton and a half, fifty horse-power.' He jumped out and wandered around it. 'Fitted with desert tyres too. Nice piece of kit, that.'

'Good,' said Tanner. 'Let's take it, then. We can find out what's in it when it gets light.'

'Know how to drive it, sir?' asked Brown.

'I'm sure I can work it out, Browner. They're like ours, aren't they? Once you've driven one, you've driven them all.' He felt in his pack for the set of reamers he kept there, then got into the driving seat. The ignition was on the dashboard. He thrust in one of the reamers and immediately a red light came on below what had to be the ignition button. He pressed it and the engine whirred into life. He glanced across at Brown, waved, and lurched forward.

A quarter of an hour later, they were back at Company Headquarters and Tanner was making a cursory inspection of their new acquisition.

'What do you think, Jack?' Peploe asked him. 'Anything worth notifying Battalion about now?'

'A few maps, but that's about it, I'm afraid.'

'Shame.'

'I think we saw all we needed to, though, sir,' said Tanner. 'It's a full moon tomorrow, and we've just caught some Jerry sappers red-handed lifting some of our mines.'

'Tomorrow night, then?'

'I'd put good money on it.'

'In that case, we'd better get some rest while we can. You get your head down, Jack. I'll go and see Battalion.'

'Thanks,' said Tanner. He felt exhausted. The adrenalin of earlier had worn off quickly. Having told the others to do likewise, he put on his greatcoat, wrapped himself in his ground sheet and lay down between the Bedford and the Phänomen Granit. For about three minutes, he thought about the battle to come, then his mind closed and he was fast asleep.

Tanner's prediction had been right. As the moon rose the following night, the battle would begin.

15

Sunday, 30 August, 11 a.m. Alex was working and, as there was a backlog of parcels, Tanja had been happy to go to the office to help Sophie and Ewa. She was grateful for the distraction and a bit of conversation.

'Oh,' said Sophie, as she sorted the mail that

had just arrived. 'A letter for you, Tanja.' She held it up. 'Who do you know in Tehran?'

Tanja took it, then stared at the handwriting with disbelieving eyes. Slowly, she sat down.

'Are you all right?' Sophie asked her.

Tanja opened the envelope and took out the thin, pale blue sheets of paper and began to read, one hand clasping her desk.

7 August, 1942

To Our Dearest Tanja,
We so hope and pray that this reaches you and that you are well and safe. My beloved girl, can it really be possible that you are alive and living in Cairo? It seems, after all this time, too much to hope for and yet it must be, because a friend of Stanislaw's received a parcel from you, signed by you from the Polish Red Cross. He knew we were in Tehran and so came to see us all the way from Iraq – imagine that! He handed us your letter personally, and we were holding the letter you had written. Your handwriting, your name at the end. I am afraid your poor mother fainted, but darling Tanja, this is such happy, wonderful news.

We had never given up hope. It is a terrible, terrible thing to lose a child, but at least we knew what had happened to Stanislaw, and have been able to grieve. With you, my darling Tanja, we feared the worst but dared not give up hope, and now it seems you are alive after all. It is a miracle and has given us so much strength.

We are as well as can be expected. After we were taken by the Russians we were put in Balyastok prison, where we were separated, and in February

320

1940 we were put on wagons and sent east, to collective farms in Siberia. We did not see each other again for almost a whole year, although we later discovered we were near each other but at different collectives. Somehow, we survived. It was bitterly cold at first and the Bolsheviks did not give us enough food or clothes, or rugs at night, but we both managed to keep our health, and in August 1941 – a whole year ago – we were released and, with a number of other Poles, told to make our way south.

Can you believe it? I saw your mother again at a railway station in Pechora, a God-forsaken town, somewhere in the Russian steppes. You can only imagine our reunion! Your mother was a lot thinner and her beautiful black hair had begun to grey, but she was still my Anna. She said I too had aged, but what can one expect? It was a small price to pay for being alive and together once more!

Together we made our way to Guzar in Uzbekistan, where your mother became gravely ill with typhus, but she is a strong woman, the doctor and nurses who tended her were good, and she made a full recovery. We had to wait for a passage to Persia – the young men were the priority, but eventually we got a boat and crossed the sea, finally off Soviet soil and into Persia, and on to Tehran. Three months later we are still here, slowly but surely building up our strength.

And now this wonderful news. My darling Tanja, you are alive! Our boy may have gone, our home may have gone, but we have survived and one day when this terrible war is over we can rebuild our lives. Hope has sustained us through these long months. That same hope will continue to sustain us.

We wonder when we will see you again. The thought

of looking at your beautiful face once more fills me with more joy than I can ever put into words. Write to us, Tanja, tell us your news. You must be doing wonderful work in Cairo, but we can only imagine the hardships you have had to face since we last saw you. We are proud of you, Tanja, so proud. The news that you are alive has made us very happy.

Your ever loving father,
Nikolai Zanowski

Tanja held the letter tightly, then reread it, silent tears running down her cheeks. She was scarcely able to believe what she was holding in her hands. *Sweet Papa!* She kissed the paper – paper he had touched with his own fingers. They were alive. *Alive!*

'Tanja?' said Sophie, a hand on her shoulder. 'Is it bad news?'

'No, no,' Tanja said, turning towards her. 'No, it is wonderful news. My parents – they're alive!' She laughed, and wiped her eyes. 'They're alive, Sophie! They're alive!'

Sophie held out her arms. 'I am so happy for you,' she said, embracing her.

Tanja showed her the letter.

'It's incredible how so many survived,' said Sophie, softly.

'Those Russian bastards,' said Tanja.

'Paddy Leigh-Fermor and Billy think they will win,' Sophie said.

'How do they know?' said Tanja, more sharply than she had intended.

She shrugged. 'We were talking about it last night. The Germans have been pushed back from

322

Moscow. They still haven't taken Leningrad and the Russians have counter-attacked again. It's September in two days' time. Winter comes quickly in Russia. If the Germans can't beat them now, they never will because the Russians are getting stronger all the time.'

Tanja felt quite light-headed. She gripped her chair to steady herself.

'And they also think we will beat Rommel now. The Americans are in the war. All those young men, all that money. If we beat Rommel and knock the Axis from North Africa, then Italy will probably collapse too. They think the tide has turned already.' She shrugged again. 'I do not know. I suppose it depends what happens when Rommel attacks. Billy thought it might even be today.'

Tanja sat down, her hand to her head. *We will beat Rommel.*

Sophie crouched beside her, and took her hand. 'This news. It is marvellous, but it is a shock, I know.'

'It is.' Tanja smiled.

'Go out for a bit. Or go home and lie down.'

'I think I'll ring Alex.'

Sophie squeezed her hand lightly and left her. Tanja put a call through and was connected first to the GHQ exchange and then, after a minute's wait, to MO4.

'Yes?' snapped a voice.

'Could I speak to Major Vaughan, please?' *Please be there.*

'Just a moment.' A clunk, muffled voices, footsteps, then Alex's voice.

'Hello?'

'Alex, it is me.'

'Tanja!'

'I need to see you, Alex. Can you get away?'

'Why? What's the matter? Is everything all right?'

'Yes, yes, quite all right. I will explain when I see you.'

'It's eleven thirty now,' he said. 'It's too hot to be outside, so let's meet at the Continental in, say, half an hour? Noon sound all right?'

'Thank you, Alex.'

'And you're sure you're all right?'

'Yes. I will tell you everything when I see you.'

She left immediately, her mind reeling. As she walked the short distance to the Continental, she was barely aware of the hordes of people, the mass of animals and vehicles, the blaring horns, the tram that rang its bell as it clattered past. The letter was such wonderful news – yet their pride in her now seemed so misplaced. She had got to Cairo by spying for the Germans. It was the Germans who had given her money, paid her passage, enabled her to rent her flat. She had spied for Germany for Tomas, for Stanislaw and for Poland, and because she believed the Russians had murdered her parents too. Anger and grief had driven her, but the anger was spent. A vision of a new life had emerged through the smoke of chaos and destruction.

Now it seemed the Germans would lose, not just a battle out here in the desert but the whole war. The war against the Soviet Union.

She sat alone, in the large bar of the Continental, with its high, curving arches and square columns, its whirring fans and potted palms. The usual mix of suits, khaki and patterned cotton were on display but she barely noticed them. And then Alex was standing before her, looking so handsome, concern etched on his face. Her heart leaped out to him, and she wondered whether the enormous lie that stood between them could ever be overcome.

'Tanja,' he said, and she stood up, wrapped her arms around his neck and held him tightly.

'Steady on.' He laughed. 'Now tell me, darling girl! Whatever is going on?'

The tears had begun again. I used to be so good at holding them back, but now... 'I had a letter this morning – from Tehran.'

'From Tehran?'

'From my parents, Alex! They're alive!'

He smiled and clasped her to him. 'Just when you think the war brings nothing but bad news,' he said, 'something wonderful happens.'

He sat her down, taking the chair next to her at the table, and keeping hold of her hands. 'I'm so happy for you, Tanja. Really I am. What will you do? Try to get to Tehran? Or bring them to Cairo?'

'Would that be possible?'

'I don't know. Iran's under British control. There are plenty of flights from Cairo to Tehran.'

She shook her head. 'It is still too much to take in. But, Alex,' she said, turning to him, 'I wanted to ask you. Do you think Germany can still win in Russia?'

Vaughan looked surprised. 'Why do you ask?'

'Sophie was talking about it. She has two

325

friends – Billy Moss and Paddy Leigh-Fermor.'

'I know Billy. A Coldstreamer like me. I didn't know he was in town.'

'They say that Russia will beat Germany now.'

'It's likely. The Red Army has lost vast numbers of men by all accounts but they have far greater resources than Germany, and now they've got American and British help as well. I think Billy's right. If Germany were going to defeat the Soviet Union, they needed to do so quickly. A couple of months ago, when we lost Tobruk, I'd have said it was all over. I honestly thought the Germans would take Leningrad, then push on against Moscow and probably take it too. I'm afraid I was thinking defeatist thoughts, because I was pretty certain Egypt would fall too. But it hasn't happened. If we survive the battle to come, we'll beat Rommel for good, I'm sure.'

'And in Russia, it'll soon be winter.'

'Yes. Even in this modern age, it's very hard to fight a war in snow and ice and temperatures well below freezing.'

'If Russia wins, what will become of Poland?'

'I'd like to think that we in the West will insist it's returned to the Polish Government in Exile and the Polish people.'

'But you do not think that will happen, do you?'

'I don't know, Tanja. I'm just a major in the British Army.'

A quick lunch, but then Vaughan had to leave her: there were no leisurely siestas for the men in the DMO's office. But Tanja's mind was still too full of conflicting thoughts for her to work so she walked back to her flat and lay in her dark bedroom, staring at the ceiling. Everything had changed with the arrival of her parents' letter. What had begun with growing doubt as, first, Rommel had been halted and then she had begun to fall in love with Alex, had now, with the letter from her mother and father, become an absolute conviction. Her betrayal of Britain and the Allies would not help Poland. She saw now what a catastrophic mistake she had made. And she wondered how on earth she could ever put right what she had done so terribly wrong. There was one way, and one way only.

On a day that had brought so much joy, Tanja now felt consumed with sorrow. Bringing her knees to her chest, she could not contain her tears. Lying there, crouched and broken, she wept as she had never wept before.

In the desert, the men along the southern end of the line had watched aircraft flying over much of the day – usually in small formations, high in the sky, dark dots that would glint as sunlight struck. And this time the enemy seemed to be responding to the probes, angrily engaging when a week before there had been little sight of the Axis air forces.

Speculation and anticipation had been mounting all day. Tanner had spent much time cleaning and recleaning his weapons, then, whenever an aircraft was spotted, clambering up on to the escarpment above their positions and watching what was going on.

There had been briefings too, around the battalion command truck and signals lorry. News of the massing enemy armour had reached Battalion Headquarters. Reconnaissance photographs suggested that as many as three thousand vehicles and at least a hundred tanks were concentrated behind the German minefields. Late in the afternoon, the ration wagon came up again, this time with compo packs – composite rations packed together in one box – which were handed out and stacked away in each of the vehicles.

At seven, Peploe called the company together for a briefing. It was still hot, flies buzzing incessantly. He stood in the back of his truck, Tanner beside him. 'Chaps, it looks like we're going to be in a battle in the next few hours,' he said, raising his voice so that he could be heard by the hundred and twenty men gathered around him. 'The enemy have massed most of their armour and vehicles some twenty miles to the west of here and we're expecting them to start moving towards us. Now, this will make a hell of a noise but don't be intimidated. They've only got a hundred or so tanks, and most of the rest are soft-skins – trucks, half-tracks and other lorries. Our job is to hold them up for as long as possible. We're not expected to stop them in their tracks but to delay them.' He paused.

Tanner gazed around at the men, bronzed faces glistening with sweat. This was the worst bit: the hanging around, waiting for it to start – nerves and nausea. Once it began, well, there was too much else to think about. Fear slipped away as adrenalin took over.

'Battles are very confusing and especially so in the desert,' Peploe continued. 'As well as the noise, there's a hell of a lot of dust and smoke and it can be damned hard to see what the hell is going on. The enemy will try to force a way through our minefields. The Rifle Brigade and the KRRC will be hammering at them with their six-pounders and we must support them. In A Company, we'll be towards the bottom end of the line, behind the KRRC. Once it's dark, we and B Company will move down to Himeimat, then lie up there until it's time to move out. When the enemy are at our minefields, keep moving, hammer them with the Brens and take pot shots where you can, particularly at their sappers. If and when they break through, keep harrying them, then fall back. We don't all have radio, so where possible, stay in your platoons, and if in doubt, get out of the way. We've got the Kiwis on Alam Nayil and then both 22nd and 8th Armoured Brigades, so let them do the bulk of the firing. And when we do fall back, it'll be eastwards, clear of Alam Halfa, not north between Halfa and Nayil. That way we can keep snapping at their heels.'

'It'll seem chaotic,' added Tanner, 'but keep your heads. Think calmly and clearly and you'll be all right.'

'Exactly,' said Peploe. 'And there's one other thing I should tell you. The Desert Air Force is primed and ready, and I hear her medium bomber squadrons are at full strength. The AOC has been deliberately holding them back and intends to give the enemy an absolute pasting. But what I would add is this: when our boys fly over, get out of the way. I don't want any of us to be hit by our own side.'

After his talk, the men were dismissed to eat their supper while they could. More planes buzzed overhead, but otherwise a strange calm seemed to have settled over the desert.

'When do we move out, sir?' asked Phyllis.

Tanner looked at his watch. 'In about an hour.'

Phyllis sighed. 'I wish we could go now. We've been waiting all day. I just want the bastards to get a move on.'

'They'll be waiting for it to get dark, Siff,' said Tanner, 'just as we are. Go and write a letter or play some cards or something. Have a kip.' That, he knew, was unfair. No one was in any mood to sleep. 'Look, nothing's going to happen for an hour or more yet.'

Phyllis wandered away from the truck to where Hepworth and Smailes were playing cards.

Sykes joined Tanner by the tailgate, lit two cigarettes and passed one to him.

Tanner glanced up from the map he'd been studying. 'Cheers, Stan,' he said, as he took it.

Sykes inhaled deeply, his cigarette held between finger and thumb. 'A few nerves?' he said.

'A few,' said Tanner. 'I'm with Siff. I just wish Jerry'd get a move on. How about you?'

'I've got through this war so far with barely a scratch – you've been bashed around a lot more than me. I'm worried my luck's about to run out.'

'Knock it off, Stan. It doesn't work like that and you know it. Fate, superstition – it's all bollocks. You'll be fine.'

'I hope so, mate.'

Guns had begun booming to the north soon after

dusk, but along the southern end of the line, no one was fooled into thinking that the sound of battle in the distance was anything other than a feint.

At around eight thirty, A and B Companies moved out, heading south towards the Himeimat Feature, two dark beacons on the horizon up ahead. Peploe led them behind it to where already considerable numbers of vehicles – mostly the KRRC's gun tractors, soft-skins and carriers – were sheltering.

'Now what?' said Phyllis.

'Try to listen, Siff,' said Sykes. 'What do you think?'

Phyllis shrugged. 'We sit and wait?'

'Exactly. So why ask?'

'In case I was wrong.'

'You usually are, Siff,' said Brown, 'but, amazingly, you got it right this time.'

'Time for a brew,' said Sykes.

It was not until around ten thirty that they heard them. A low rumble, far off in the distance, but then the night breeze dropped and it disappeared again, overshadowed by the fighting to the north. A little while later they heard it again. Half an hour later and there was no mistaking it: a constant deep drone.

'That's them coming, isn't it, sir?' said Phyllis, climbing into the truck.

'I reckon so,' Tanner replied, but after a further half-hour there was still no sign of them, and the rumble seemed only fractionally louder.

'Why are they taking so long?' Phyllis asked.

'Because they've got to get through their own minefields,' explained Tanner. 'They'll have cleared passages, but it's still a funnel through which they've got to get three thousand odd vehicles.'

'They're definitely getting closer, though,' said Sykes, who was brewing up a second round of char beside the truck. 'I can see the moon rippling in my water.'

Just then Tanner heard a faint squeak – the telltale sign of tanks on the move.

'What's surprising me,' added Sykes, 'is why they're not stonking us to hell already.'

'Maybe they're trying to surprise us.' Tanner grinned.

He had barely finished his sentence when the familiar rush of oncoming shells cut through the air. They all took cover, but most seemed to be falling a short way to the north and to the west of them. British guns retaliated. The ground shuddered, and in the gaps between the artillery fire, the squeak of tracks grinding their way across the desert became gradually more distinct.

Despite the shelling, Sykes handed round the tea.

'Good on you, Stan,' said Tanner, meaning it. It was what they all needed: something to do, and some hot, sweet liquid in their stomachs.

The squeaking and the rumble of engines now was growing steadily louder, while the artillery fire was now directed at their own minefields ahead. The scream of incoming shells was deafening, the ground trembling, but Tanner had heard worse. The front held by 7th Armoured Brigade was thirteen miles long, a wide stretch of mostly flat, open desert. The enemy were going to need more artillery laid down on the British minefields if they wanted an easy passage through. He glanced round at the men. Most wore woollen sweaters now or, like Tanner, their battledress jacket. Brown was sitting at the wheel, tapping it; Sykes was smoking another cigarette, as was Mudge. Smailes was biting a fingernail, while Phyllis had his Thompson across his lap and his hands over his ears.

Tanner jumped down and went to the back of the truck where he cuffed Phyllis lightly round the shoulder. 'I'm just going to talk to the boss,' he said, and strode over to Peploe's truck. The whole company was ready, waiting for the signal to move out, and despite the shelling, Tanner wondered whether perhaps the time had arrived.

'Any news from Old Man Vigar?' he said to Peploe.

'About five minutes ago. Stay put.'

'I really think we should get going,' said Tanner. 'It'll take time to get across our stretch of the front, and even more so for B Company. We want to be there ready when it all kicks off. I'm sensing they must be nearly through their minefields by now, then they've a quick dash across the desert and the lead units will be on us.'

'All right, hold on, Jack.' He turned to Bradshaw, the company signaller. 'Get me Battalion, will you?'

Bradshaw made the connection, then passed over his headphones and the transmitter from the number 19 set at his feet.

'Can you put me through to the colonel?' asked Peploe. He looked at Tanner. 'Sir, we're going to head out now. Can I give B Company the heads up too?' He flinched as a shell landed up ahead. 'Yes... Yes... Right, sir. Right away, sir. Thank you, sir.' He handed back the headset and transmitter, then turned to Tanner. 'We're going. Great minds clearly think alike, Jack.'

'Good,' said Tanner.

'Bradshaw,' said Peploe, 'tell B Company to move out, will you?'

Tanner held out his hand. 'Good luck, sir.'

Peploe shook it. 'And to you, Jack.'

Engines roared into life, throttles were revved, and they were moving, wheeling out of the protection of the Himeimat and heading in groups of three back towards the wide open gravel flats. They were moving westwards, towards the edge of their own minefields, where the King's Royal Rifle Corps were dug in, their six-pounders positioned in scrapes, rocks piled in front of them so that only the barrel peeked out. *And then us*, thought Tanner. He looked at his watch. *Twenty-five past twelve*. At that moment aircraft roared overhead, no more than a couple of thousand feet above them, half a dozen naval Albacores, relics now from the biplane age.

'Jesus, is that the might of the Desert Air Force?' said Phyllis. 'Six old biplanes?'

'I hope not, Siff,' said Sykes.

They drove on, leading the company alongside Captain Peploe. A minute later, they heard light anti-aircraft guns, and watched tracer dash into the night sky. Then parachute flares were

334

bursting into life, turning the desert orange. And below, caught in the bright lights drifting down towards them, was Rommel's strike force, emerging like tiny spectres through the dust.

'Christ, will you look at that?' said Sykes.

'Bloody hell!' whistled Brown, as the air above them was torn apart, not by more incoming shells but by the arrival of a squadron of Wellington bombers.

'Here they come!' called Sykes. More furious ack-ack was spurting into the air, vivid above the flares, but moments later bombs were falling among the mass of tanks and vehicles, and then the six-pounders opened up. Huge flashes of flame and mushrooms of smoke burst and billowed into the sky as more bombs fell. No sooner had the Wellingtons delivered their lethal loads than more flares descended, followed by another squadron of Wellingtons.

The enemy artillery shelling was more intermittent now as, ahead, a mass of German armour and vehicles hared across no man's land towards the British line.

Tanner yelled at Brown to move alongside the easternmost edge of their minefield, between two six-pounders that were already firing furiously.

'Hold it there,' he called, as another wave of Albacores flew overhead, 'but keep the engine running.' He put his binoculars to his eyes. Five miles away, tanks and vehicles were emerging from five lanes through the minefields and speeding towards them in a steady stream. Soft-skins led the way and now, only five hundred yards in front, the first were reaching the westernmost part of the

British minefield. He could see men jumping out of trucks, armed with mine detectors, then mortar crews, artillery and machine-gun teams.

'Right, boys,' he said. 'Time to start shooting. Smiler. Get that Bren going.'

'Sir,' said Smailes, standing on the body of the truck and leaning the barrel of the Bren on the roll-bar. He opened up, the sharp chatter ringing in Tanner's ears. He grabbed his rifle from its stand between the seats and brought it to his shoulder. He had already fixed his Aldis scope and zeroed it at five hundred yards.

'Where are you?' he muttered softly, then spotted a team of German sappers busily training their mine detectors. A moving target, but one that was heading slowly and almost perfectly straight towards him. He breathed in, held his breath, then pressed the trigger. The rifle cracked and he saw a man drop. Pull back the bolt, aim, hold breath, squeeze. The butt pressed into his shoulder and another man fell.

An enemy machine-gunner had opened up and had clearly seen their silhouette, as tracer now arced towards them. A burst of bullets zipped through the air above them.

'Move, Browner!' he yelled, and the truck lurched forward just as another burst of MG fire hissed behind them. More and more enemy vehicles were now hurrying across the open desert, and Smailes opened fire again with short, sharp bursts across the minefield. It was now almost impossible to see the westernmost edge beneath the thick dust and smoke. Tanner aimed again, this time at a series of dark figures, firing

336

one shot after another in quick succession until he needed to replace his magazine with two more five-round clips.

'They're bunching up beautifully, aren't they, sir?' shouted Sykes behind him.

'Not that we can see bugger all.'

'A big cloud of smoke makes a good target for the bombers, though.'

'Too right – especially with starlight shells over them. Let's hope they get over here fast.'

They did not have to wait long. More parachute flares were dropped, this time over the British minefields, lighting up the desert around them as though it were almost day. A strange luminous orange glow filled the sky, turning the desert white, and overhead they heard more bombers arriving, a thunderous drone between the shell- and small-arms fire. Moments later, bombs were whistling down, the whine clearly heard even over the din of the guns and the battle going on along the desert floor. Flashes of explosions pulsed through the smoke and then flames as a vehicle or tank was hit. Thick black smoke billowed upwards, swirling with the dust and the grey smoke of the shells and bombs, while arcs of tracer crisscrossed the sky.

Although they were only a few hundred yards away, Tanner felt like an observer, not a participant. Smailes had stopped firing; Tanner had laid down his rifle. All were dumbstruck by the carnage in front of them.

'I've got to say,' said Sykes, in Tanner's ear, 'that has got to be one of the most awe-inspiring sights I've seen. Thank Christ we're not German or

Italian right now.'

'It's hellfire, Stan!' Tanner agreed. 'Absolute bloody hellfire.'

Another wave of bombers came over, then another, so that all along the southern stretch of the line, bombs were crashing down on the enemy strike force. German and Italian guns were firing shells towards the higher ground where the British guns and armour were dug in, while more bombs whistled down from the RAF bombers overhead.

It was not until a little after two thirty that it seemed the enemy would soon force a passage through the minefields. A little to the right, and under cover of the smoke and dust, two anti-tank guns had pushed forward to within a hundred and fifty yards of the eastern edge of the mine-field, and suddenly opened fire, knocking out two six-pounders and a carrier.

'The bastards,' said Tanner, and while Smailes continued to fire short bursts with the Bren, he and the others took shots with their rifles. Over-head, the bombers kept up their attacks, wave after wave flying over, but the moment the enemy were free of the minefields and able to spread out, the attacks from the air would be less effective.

Tanner could see what was happening: the enemy anti-tank guns were providing a screen for the engineers behind. One of the enemy guns was soon knocked out by KRRC six-pounders, but machine-gun fire and mortars were now pouring towards them, tracer cutting across the desert.

'Keep moving, Browner!' shouted Tanner.

Other Rangers' trucks and carriers were speeding back and forth, firing into the mass, then wheeling around and heading away from the fray as enemy Spandaus and mortar teams got their bead. Tanner saw one Bedford hit – *A or B Company?* – and catch fire, figures jumping out and scampering towards a nearby carrier that rushed towards them.

Another passage through the minefields was developing away to their left, and Tanner guessed the same must be happening all along the line.

'We need to think about falling back, Stan,' he yelled to Sykes. 'Where's the skipper?' He turned to them all. 'Keep an eye open for Captain Peploe!'

'There, sir!' shouted Brown, pointing towards a Bedford firing to the left of a six-pounder. He drove towards it, then Peploe's truck suddenly reversed and began turning away. Brown followed as the Bedford fell back several hundred yards. Another wave of bombers roared overhead, distracting the enemy, as yet more starlight shells were dropped, the flares wafting down and casting a shroud of magnesium light over the battlefield. All at once, bombs whistled down, shells hurtled back and forth, and small arms chattered. The noise was deafening, the air thick with the stench of cordite.

Peploe saw them and came to a halt. Tanner jumped out and ran across.

'We're going to fall back soon,' shouted Peploe. He glanced at his watch. 'It's after three. Any moment now the six-pounders will start pulling back. We're going to cover them, then pull back too. We want to be clear of here before dawn.'

'Shall I tell any section we see?'

'Yes.'

While the bombers continued to shroud the enemy in smoke and dust, Tanner ordered Brown to run the course of their front, stopping by as many of their vehicles as they could. All still seemed to be in one piece. That was something. Out of the darkness, gun tractors and portees were now appearing and heading towards the six-pounders, which were still firing towards the enemy. Tanner ordered Brown up to where a battery of six-pounders was spread at the edge of the minefield. Once more he and the others opened fire, bursts of Bren and rifle shots aimed at any dark figure emerging through the smoke and dust.

Soon after, the first of the six-pounders was hitched up and pulling out, followed a few minutes after by another and then another. It wouldn't be long now, Tanner thought.

By four, the last of the guns had left, although Tanner saw several destroyed six-pounders left in their scrapes, their shields bent and barrels broken. Above them, the bombers had not let up. Just as soon as he thought they had called it a night, another wave appeared. Normally, out in the open, attacks against open formations of vehicles were of limited effectiveness, but as the mass of Rommel's strike force had been funnelled into the handful of lanes through the minefield, Tanner reckoned it must have been a slaughter.

The battlefield was still shrouded in smoke and dust. It was impossible to see what was going on,

340

but bursts of machine-gun fire continued to be aimed towards them and mortar shells rained down, but the aim was blind. Even so, thought Tanner, it only took one lucky shot.

Peploe drew up alongside, several other sections around him. 'Time to go, Jack,' he yelled.

Tanner nodded. 'I'll have a quick sweep. See if there are any others.'

Brown sped forward. A mortar shell burst forty yards away, but although a small amount of grit clattered around them, they were clear of the blast. Up ahead, another Bedford. Frantic arm waving – *Pullback! Pullback!* – but just then machine-gun tracer cut across the desert and peppered the truck as they neared it. A bang, a gush of smoke, and the Bedford ground to a halt. Smailes fired back into the smoke as, twenty yards ahead, men jumped out and ran towards them.

Tanner saw McAllister race to the front of the smoking vehicle and try to tug the driver clear – who was it in McAllister's section? *Parsons.* Tanner jumped out and ran over to help. Another burst of MG fire, this time well to their left, while behind him a mortar shell burst, a shower of grit pattering around him.

By the time Tanner had reached McAllister, Parsons was clear of the now burning truck.

'Here,' said Tanner, as McAllister tried to lift the man. 'You take one arm, I'll take the other.'

Parsons groaned. His right leg was sticky with blood, and, Tanner now saw, so was his side. *Damn it.* Brown was now alongside them, engine idling. Round to the back, and Mudge jumped down and together they hoisted Parsons into the

341

now crowded body of the truck. Scampering back to the front, Tanner leaped in as another burst of machine-gun fire fizzed nearby.

'All right, Browner,' he said. 'Time to go.'

As they sped away, Tanner glanced back and saw, emerging through the smoke and dust, the barrel of a panzer. *The Afrika Korps.* The enemy was through.

16

Peploe led them south, towards the edge of the Qattara Depression, and they continued east, along the Depression's edge. Dawn was breaking, the desert turning pink as the first sliver of sun rose above the horizon. Fifteen miles or so from the minefields, Peploe called a halt. Behind them and to the north, artillery fire continued to boom. A thick pall of smoke hung over the British minefields, so that the tip of Himeimat rose above it like a mountain peak bursting through cloud. Among the fog of smoke and dust they could see thin columns of black smoke rising, burning wrecks of enemy machines butchered by the Desert Air Force.

Time, though, for a head count, and to contact Battalion. And a much-needed brew.

A carrier from 2 Platoon was missing, as were two trucks from 3 Platoon. No one knew where they were but, equally, no one claimed to have seen them hit either. The only vehicle known to have been lost was Sergeant McAllister's; the rest of Lieutenant Shopland's 1 Platoon was still present and correct, as were the two trucks of Company Headquarters. They had also been joined by a six-pounder and gun tractor from KRRC.

I thought you was our mob,' said the sergeant. 'I was just following you and trying to get out of there.'

'Do you want to stick with us for the moment?' Peploe asked him. 'There's every chance we'll bump into the rest of your lot at some point.'

'Don't mind if we do, sir,' said the sergeant. 'It's Rakes, by the way. 5 Platoon, B Company.'

And apart from Rifleman Parsons, the company could report no further casualties. A miracle, but Parsons needed help quickly if he was to survive. He had been shot twice in the leg and once in his lower abdomen. Tanner had tied a tourniquet around the top of his thigh, but despite this and the mass of field dressings that had been pressed against his wounds, the lad was losing a lot of blood.

'Right, let's get him on to one of 1 Platoon's Bedfords,' said Peploe, 'and then to an RAP at Division HQ as quick as we can.'

Shopland picked one of his trucks and sent them on their way, speeding off.

While char was brewed, Tanner climbed on to the body of his truck with his binoculars and gazed back towards the stretch of desert through which Rommel's strike force was now pouring. He could see at least two main columns, clouds of dust following in their wake. He looked at his watch. *Nearly a quarter to five.* The nearest column

343

was some two or three thousand yards away, but he reckoned A Company needed to get a move on. If they were to fulfil their task, they had to get ahead of the enemy columns, then drive at them out of the sun, shoot up whatever was in front of them and scuttle away again. Harry and snap, Peploe had said.

He glanced around at the men. They all looked exhausted, faces smeared with oil and grime. Behind stretched the Depression, deep and hazy in the early-morning light. A faint breeze blew up, and Tanner wondered whether that was a portent of something stronger heading their way.

He jumped down, and Sykes thrust a mug of tea into his hand.

'Cheers,' said Tanner. 'You're still alive, then.'

Sykes grinned. 'So far. Some night, though.'

'Bloody impressive. Feels different this, doesn't it? Same old plan from Rommel, but this time we're better prepared. Everyone knows what they're doing. Christ knows how much of a pasting the Jerries got, but they've not even come up against our armour and artillery yet.'

Sykes smiled ruefully and lit a cigarette. 'I reckon there's a little way to go, though. We've been out here long enough to know it can go arse over tit at any point.'

'Nah,' said Tanner. 'We'll be all right this time.'

'Just so long as those cavalry boys stay put,' said Sykes.

Peploe came over to them. 'Sounds like the rest of the battalion got out all right,' he said. 'Bradshaw got through over the net. They're further east than us.'

'What about B Company?' asked Tanner.

'A bit spread to the four winds, but appearing in dribs and drabs.'

Tanner outlined his plan. 'We can make good use of the early-morning sun, I reckon.'

'Good idea,' agreed Peploe. 'Let's get on with it, then.' He turned and shouted, 'Right, let's move!'

Wearily, the men got back into their trucks and carriers. 'Everyone all right?' Tanner asked the men in his vehicle. Exhausted nods.

'Good. Iggery, then, Browner.'

Monday, 31 August. All morning the men of A Company sniped at the enemy column away to their left. To begin with, they had kept ahead of the southernmost column, but then, as it had wheeled north-east some twenty miles from the British minefields, they had turned north-east too, keeping a distance of around two thousand yards. In pairs, trucks and carriers would turn in, and, out of the sun, get within four or five hundred yards and pepper whatever vehicles they could with Bren and rifle fire. Most of the M/T they attacked had been trucks, half-tracks and even motorcycles – presumably, Tanner and Peploe guessed, the reconnaissance force of the Deutsches Afrika Korps.

The enemy had always returned fire, but by the time they got their aim and range, the A Company vehicles were already pulling away again, careering in a wide circle back out of danger. Just how much damage they had achieved it was hard to say: at least six vehicles and a brace of motor-

cycles, but maybe more. There was a further purpose, however. It would be unsettling the enemy,
getting on their nerves. Wearing them down.

The enemy columns began to halt some five
miles or so south of the Alam Halfa Ridge,
mustering their forces before any concentrated
and co-ordinated assault; the tail of their
columns was still trailing across the desert. For A
Company, another halt, and a chance to draw
breath.

Tanner jumped down, his legs stiff, and hurried
over to Peploe. 'What are you thinking, sir?' he
asked.

'We operate in platoons, taking it in turns to
harry the enemy. The rest pull back another
thousand yards and get something to eat. I don't
know about you, but I'm exhausted. I'm sure the
boys are too. And I'm bloody starving. Last
night's supper seems a long time ago.'

'Good idea, sir. Shopland's two sections down
so I'll take my truck and join 1 Platoon.'

'We both can.' He wiped his brow. Flurries of
sand were being whipped up by the breeze from
the south-west. 'That wind's getting up. Do you
think we're in for a sandstorm?'

'Maybe,' said Tanner. 'It's still bloody hot now
that we've stopped.'

They heard a low drone from the east. Tanner
turned, his hand shielding his eyes. They had not
seen the Desert Air Force for some hours, but the
enemy columns were massing once more and the
news had evidently been relayed to Air HQ.

'There they are,' said Tanner, pointing. A handful of black dots, gradually gaining shape. Then

they heard the faint sound of machine-guns, and a moment later a fighter was falling out of the sky in a wide arc. It disappeared from view far to the north.

'Ours or theirs?' said Peploe.

'God knows. Hopefully theirs.'

'Anyway,' said Peploe, 'let's get going.'

His truck moved off, pausing by each group of vehicles, which then began to pull back. Tanner moved up alongside Lieutenant Shopland's truck as the bombers began dropping their loads.

'The sixteen imperturbables,' said Shopland. 'Bloody marvellous sight, isn't it?'

'Too right,' agreed Tanner.

'I suppose we should hold on until they've done their stuff?'

'Sit back and watch the show.'

Bombs fell, whistling and exploding, the desert alive with the din of battle once more. The enemy were replying furiously, dark puffs of anti-aircraft fire bursting across the deep blue sky. On the ground, their formations once more disappeared in a fog of swirling dust and smoke. Something was on fire, flames visible through the haze – but then they saw the lead aircraft falter and the port engine catch fire, a trail of black smoke following.

In Tanner's truck no one said a word as they watched the plane, a Mitchell twin-engine bomber, bank in a wide arc towards them, losing height all the time. *He's trying to get behind our lines*, thought Tanner. The plane was only a few hundred feet off the ground, but it had completed its turn and now seemed to be heading almost directly towards them. Tracer and small puffs of ack-ack continued to rain towards it.

'The bastards,' muttered Brown. 'Can't they see it's coming down?'

'I don't suppose there's much sympathy after the twelve hours they've just had,' said Tanner.

The Mitchell wobbled and seemed to drop another fifty feet.

'Go on,' muttered Tanner, 'keep going.'

'He won't be able to, sir,' said Sykes. 'He's going to come down slap bang between us and Jerry.'

The Mitchell was now just fifty feet off the desert floor as small-arms fire continued to follow it. *Stan's right*, thought Tanner. *Where the hell is that six-pounder?*

'Jimmy!' he called to Shopland. 'Can you send one of your boys to get the six-pounder and iggery? Browner, turn the engine on ready!'

'Jack!' shouted Peploe. 'Get ready to move!'

'I've sent back for the six-pounder!' Tanner yelled.

Peploe raised his hand in acknowledgement as one of Shopland's trucks sped off. Just over a mile away, between them and the enemy concentrations, the Mitchell dipped a wing just feet from the ground.

Tanner glanced across to Peploe, saw the captain's truck move off, then said, 'Let's go, Browner!'

The Mitchell corrected itself at the last moment, seemed to hover inches from the ground, then hit the desert floor with a thunderous boom. Creaking and groaning, the bomber slid and yawed towards them, great clouds of dust and smoke from the port engine billowing in its wake, before finally coming to a halt. The Rangers sped across the desert towards it. With all the smoke and dust, it was impossible to tell whether the enemy were chasing after the aircraft as well, but Tanner knew that the smoke was protecting them as much it would the enemy. Just five hundred yards now. Ahead, the crew were clambering out of the aircraft, then huddling around the hatch. *A wounded man. Four hundred yards.* 'Come on, come on,' he muttered, grabbing his rifle from between the seats. He yelled at Smailes, 'Get ready, Smiler!' *Three hundred yards.* The crew were still huddled by the hatch, and then, through the thinning dust, he saw enemy vehicles speeding the other way – two motorcycles and sidecars with machine-guns, two half-tracks and an armoured car. Against five trucks.

'Damn, damn, damn!' Then, 'Go wide, Browner!' He stood up in his seat, clutching the roll-bar behind him and signalling wildly to Peploe. *You get the crew, we'll hold off the enemy.* He hoped Peploe understood. Yes: Peploe was heading straight for the stricken bomber, but the other side of the captain's truck, Shopland was pushing wider. *Two hundred yards.* An enemy machine-gun was firing – wildly, blindly, the tracer fizzing over their heads. Behind him, another of Shopland's section was following. *Good. Fifty yards.* Now they were racing around the edge of the Mitchell's broken wing, black smoke still pouring from the burning engine.

Tanner glanced around and saw Sykes hold up two sticks of HE No. 2, complete with short threads of fuse and detonators. *Good lad.*

'And I've got a packet of Nobel's ready too,' Sykes yelled. 'If I throw it, will you be able to hit it with the Schmeisser?'

'Yes!' Tanner shouted. Behind him, Smailes opened up with the Bren, then Brown swerved violently as MG fire streamed towards them and hit the nearside wing. Smailes cursed, but Tanner brought his rifle to his shoulder and aimed at one of the motorcyclists, whose sidekick was firing towards one of the other trucks. *A little bit of aim-off, squeeze the trigger.* The rifle cracked, the driver fell sideways on to his comrade, the motorcycle swerved, then rolled, both men flung clear.

'Good shot, sir!' said Brown.

Dust, bullets. It was hard to see what was what and who was who, but both sides had raced past each other and were now circling for another attack. Through the dust and smoke, Tanner saw one man being lifted from the Mitchell, while from the stationary Bedford the Bren gun was firing furiously. But magazines needed to be changed and that was the opportunity for the enemy machine-gunners. Through the haze Tanner suddenly saw one of the half-tracks pull to a halt and the machine-gunner swivel his weapon ready to fire.

'Three o'clock!' shouted Tanner. The half-track was only seventy yards away as Smailes opened fire. His aim was high but the machine-gunner had only fired a two-second burst when Smailes's bullets knocked him backwards and the men behind him ducked for cover. Tanner looked back at Sykes and nodded.

'Straight for it, Browner!' shouted Tanner. Then,

as they emerged from the dust just twenty yards from the German machine, he nodded again to Sykes, who hurled a stick of high explosive.

'Veer to the left!' Tanner called to Brown and, moments later, there was a deafening explosion followed immediately by a second. Tanner flinched, then looked back to see the half-track engulfed in flames.

One down. Tanner craned his neck. Two trucks appeared to be circling widely around the other half-track. *That's right. Take it in turns to fire, then nail him when he changes his magazine.* The German machine-guns were fine weapons, but he knew from experience that the barrels quickly overheated and lost all accuracy. And with the kind of mad firing that was going on, he reckoned they must be white hot already. But where the hell was the armoured car?

'There's a truck down!' shouted Sykes. It was about seventy yards from the burning wing of the Mitchell. The men were jumping out, and taking cover behind it.

'Five have got out!' yelled Sykes, but Tanner's attention was now on the armoured car, which had wheeled away to the right of the bomber and was firing its cannon towards it. Tanner saw two shells crash into the fuselage, but the crew were clear and running towards Peploe's truck. He saw Braithwaite lying on the ground next to the Bedford frantically trying to change magazines. *Come on, Ron.* He yelled at Brown to head straight for the armoured car. Another cannon shell hit the aircraft as Peploe and the crew threw themselves flat on the ground. Now the Spandau was firing too, and Tanner's heart sank as he saw Braithwaite's head drop.

He turned in his seat to Sykes. 'Got that jelly?'

Sykes held up the pack of Nobel's.

Tanner's heart was hammering. They were fifty, forty, thirty yards from the armoured car, but at any moment it would see them and turn its cannon and machine-gun on them – at point-blank range. They would all be dead. Tanner knew the same would be true if he took his time to hit Sykes's gelignite. And how easy would it be to hit it from a truck moving at twenty-five miles an hour? Not at all, and yet he knew he *had* to hit it immediately. *Only one thing for it.*

Twenty-five yards. 'Now!' he shouted to Sykes, who hurled the packet towards the armoured car. At the same time, Tanner threw himself from the truck. He yelled in pain as he landed hard on the gravelly ground, but clenching his teeth and gasping for breath he rolled over, brought his MP40 to his shoulder, and spotted the Nobel's just a yard from the side of the armoured car. He opened fire, a two-second burst. The gelignite exploded, the blast knocking the enemy vehicle off its wheels and hurling the turret from the chassis high into the air. Tanner flung himself flat, his hands over his helmet, as stones and metal shards hurtled over him.

Angry flames engulfed the remains of the armoured car, as Tanner stiffly got to his feet. There was blood on his right shoulder and he cursed to himself, then saw the Bedford speeding towards him. Brown braked hard, the truck ground to a halt, and Sykes yelled, 'Get in quick!

Look!' Tanner followed his outstretched arm and saw more enemy vehicles hurrying towards them.

'Christ alive,' muttered Tanner, barely in his seat before Brown was gunning the throttle and the truck was lurching forward. Frantically Tanner glanced towards the Mitchell, but there was no one there. The truck, the crew, Peploe – they had all gone. Then Tanner saw the dust trail of several trucks up ahead. Behind them machine-gun fire was chasing them, lines of tracer fizzing over their heads. Brown swerved, then righted himself as more tracer hissed wide. Ahead, a muzzle flash and Tanner felt a brief stab of panic.

'It's the six-pounder, sir!' shouted Sykes, behind him.

Tanner exhaled. 'Good on them,' he said. Another muzzle flash and the boom of the gun's report, then ten seconds later, yet another. They were firing well, those lads, Tanner thought. He leaned out of the truck and looked behind him to see that the dust cloud caused by the pursuing enemy had not come any closer. In fact, it had lessened. He grinned. The bastards had given up the chase.

'Are you all right, sir?' Brown asked, as they sped south-east across the desert. 'Your arm's bleeding.'

'Must have scraped it as I landed.' Actually, it hurt like hell, but he was sure it was nothing serious. Some hefty bruising maybe, but he could live with that. He was just grateful he'd not broken anything.

'That was mad, sir, what you did back there. Bloody brave, but mad.'

Following Peploe and the others, they soon reached the rest of the company. Tanner got out of the truck stiffly and walked round to the back. 'Everyone all right?' he asked.

Phyllis and Mudge were talking animatedly. 'Did you see that armoured car?' said Phyllis, eyes wide. 'Whoosh!' He made an expansive movement with his arms.

'I just can't believe we got out of there in one piece,' grinned Mudge.

Hepworth jumped down. 'I always knew you were a mad bastard, sir,' he said.

'He saved our necks,' said Sykes, grinning and slapping Tanner on the back, then turned to Smailes. 'Come on, Smiler.'

Smailes had remained sitting in the body of the truck, the Bren between his legs, his head bowed. 'Yeah,' he said.

'Are you all right, Smiler?' said Tanner.

Smailes sighed. 'I'll be fine. I just...' He trailed off. Slowly, he climbed down. Spent casings littered the floor. 'Sorry, sirs,' he said. 'I didn't think we'd get out of that one.'

Sykes put an arm around his shoulders. 'Listen, mate, have a brew and a fag and you'll be all right.'

Smailes nodded and wandered away from the truck.

'That's not like Smiler,' muttered Sykes.

'Leave him be for a bit,' said Tanner. 'It was pretty warm out there and he was the bloke on top cover with bullets flying everywhere. It gets to us all at times.'

'I suppose you're right.' He gave a wry grin. 'It

was a bit bleedin' hairy out there, Jack.'

Tanner took out his cigarettes, offered one to Sykes, then put one in his mouth and lit it. 'To be honest, I didn't think Jerry would bother with a downed bomber crew – not in the middle of a battle like that. When I saw those half-tracks and the armoured car coming towards us I did wonder for a moment how the hell we were going to play it.'

'They were probably thinking the same.'

Peploe hailed them and walked over with the pilot, whom Tanner recognized immediately.

'Jack, you remember Squadron Leader Archie Flynn?'

'Of course, good to see you again, sir,' he said, holding out his hand.

'I can't thank you enough,' said Flynn, as he shook it. 'That was some shooting.'

'I saw what you did with the armoured car, Jack,' added Peploe, 'you and Sykes. Well done.' He looked at the bloodstain on Tanner's sleeve. 'Are you all right?'

'A scratch. I'm fine. How's Braithwaite? Who did we lose?'

'We're patching him up. Shoulder wound – clean through. He should be all right if we can get him out of here. Otherwise we're just one truck and two men down. Parsons and Hooper, the 2 Section driver.'

'Dead?'

'I'm afraid so.'

'I'm sorry,' said Flynn. He had taken off his flying helmet, but still wore his Mae West life-jacket. His legs were bare – even his socks were rolled down. He was a big, broad-shouldered man and, Tanner guessed, in his mid-twenties, with long, dark hair, matted with sweat, swept back across his head. Like everyone else's, his skin was deeply tanned.

The wind stiffened and a blast of sand whipped across them.

'Jesus!' said Flynn. 'Where the hell did that come from?'

'It's been threatening all morning,' said Tanner. 'With all the dust that's been kicked up, we might have a bit of a sand storm brewing.'

'Not good news for us,' said Flynn. 'Can't bomb what you can't see.'

'And how's your crew, sir?' asked Sykes.

'I've got two wounded, one badly, but thanks to you blokes, we all got out of there. I'm sorry you lost good men in saving our arses, though.'

Tanner turned to Peploe. 'What now, sir? Have we got contact with Battalion?'

'They're about ten miles to the north-east. B Company's turned up too. They're missing a few vehicles, but confident they're temporarily rather than permanently lost.'

'The desert is certainly a hell of a lot bigger on the ground than it is from several thousand feet,' said Flynn.

'Old Man Vigar's told us to hold fire for the moment, but to be ready to move back to Divisional HQ, which has also fallen back about five miles, incidentally.'

'Good. I don't know about everyone else, but we could do with a resupply before long. We're low on ammo.'

'I know. They just want to see how things develop in the next hour or so, which is why we're to stay put for the time being.'

'And the wounded? Do you need me to arrange transport?'

'It's in hand. I'm sending a couple of trucks from 4 Platoon. They're going to take Squadron Leader Flynn and the other two from his crew as well.'

'There's time for a quick brew, though, isn't there, sir?' said Sykes, rubbing his hands together.

'A quick brew, Stan,' said Peploe.

'So, were you flying last night?' Tanner asked Flynn.

'We did a sortie at about four a.m., just before dawn. It was the Wimpeys of 205 Group that got the show going. Strictly speaking, they're not DAF, but under our command.'

'It was quite something. We've never had that kind of support before. It's like having an entire extra arm of firepower. I reckon those Jerries and Eyeties must have had the shock of their lives.'

'The Desert Air Force is a pretty slick outfit, these days. We've been watching the panzers massing for days.'

'Really? Christ, and there we were risking our backsides trying to capture prisoners every night.'

'Sorry, Cobber,' said Flynn. 'No, we've been trying to soften up Rommel for the past ten days or so. We must have hit Tobruk and Mersa half a dozen times and we've also been giving their landing grounds a fair pasting too.'

'I certainly haven't seen as many enemy planes about in the past couple of weeks.'

'I'd like to think we've played our part in that, but they're also low on fuel, I reckon. The long-range blokes have been giving Tripoli and Benghazi a good going-over. There's a whole load of Yanks flying Liberators now, you know.'

'I had no idea.' Tanner shook his head. 'Jesus,' he said, 'when I think what it was like when we were first out here. A handful of biplanes, half a dozen knackered Hurricanes and a couple of Blenheims. The enemy seemed to rule the sky. Every time you looked up there was a bloody Messerschmitt or a Macchi. I can't tell you what a difference it makes having air superiority.'

Flynn lit a cigarette and flapped at a fly. 'A lot of it's down to the AOC and his number two, Tommy Elmhirst. Mary Coningham's a bloody excellent commander. He knows what he's about, how to outsmart the enemy, and there's no bullshit. And Tommy Elmhirst is second to none with the admin side of things. They're a brilliant team. Everyone knows what they've got to do. As a CO, I don't have to worry about admin any more. We're part of a wing, each squadron at the same landing ground, and things like organizing ground crew, getting spares, new aircraft and all that bollocks has been taken off my hands and given to Wing to sort out. It means I can concentrate on flying and leading my squadron.'

That sounded like good sense to Tanner.

'And we've been at full strength for over a week now. I think the fighter squadrons are still a bit short, but we're in great shape. When I get back today or tomorrow, there'll be another kite waiting for me. And there's as much fuel as we need. I've been out here for five months, and I can tell you, the turn-around is incredible. Even over Gazala we were all pretty confident.'

'You blokes saved us,' said Tanner. 'If it wasn't for the Desert Air Force, I reckon we'd have lost the Middle East by now.' He took off his helmet and ran his hands through his hair. 'It's leadership we've been lacking out here. We've been flailing around, gad-arsing about the desert, making a bloody awful hash of things – and all because our commanders haven't really known what we needed to do. I just hope this new team's better. It feels like it is already.' He looked out towards the fog of dust that engulfed the enemy formations to the north. 'And now Rommel's strike force is lining up directly under our guns and armour. We ought to bloody murder them.'

'And there's still our blokes,' said Flynn, as Sykes passed him a mug of tea. 'We'll be back over as soon as we can.'

'But not until this wind has quietened?'

'No – well, look,' he said, pointing towards the dust clouds up ahead. 'Can't see bugger all. We don't want to be bombing our own blokes. Jeez,' he added, 'this sand's hurting my bloody legs.'

'It's one reason why we never wear shorts in this company.' Tanner grinned.

Peploe came back, his face turned away from the wind. 'Time to go, Archie.'

Flynn took a big swig of tea, gasped, then another, and wiped the back of his hand across his mouth. 'Well, look, fellers,' he said, 'I can't thank you blokes enough. And if you're ever in a tight spot – ever in a jam where I might be able

359

to help out – just put a call into 232 Wing. Good luck.'

'And to you,' said Tanner. He watched Flynn walk away with Peploe. Had they really turned a corner? He had been talking confidently since they'd got back to the front, but had never quite dared to believe that a sea-change really had occurred. Admittedly, from where they were standing now, it was hard to know what was going on, but it seemed to him that the battle was going well. The enemy had taken a hammering, and now – well, God only knew what Rommel was thinking, but Tanner knew it was much easier defending on higher ground, however slight, in dug-in positions, than it was to attack from the open. And, as Flynn had pointed out, there was also the RAF. *We've got to have him beat this time. We've just got to.*

It was around seven p.m. Despite the wind and the dust storm that continued to envelop the battlefield, the enemy had begun their attack against the ridges early that afternoon, just as A Company were arriving at Brigade and Divisional Headquarters. The battle had never entirely died all morning, with gunfire booming almost incessantly, but suddenly the desert had been torn apart by the noise.

The company had hastily taken on more ammunition, then, with the rest of the battalion, had joined those gun crews among the KRRC and Rifle Brigade battalions that had successfully fallen back. While the Afrika Korps had been launching an attack against Alam Halfa, the men

360

of 7th Motor Brigade had harassed them from the east and south.

Only as the sun began to lower did the gunfire lessen. Ten miles to the south, A Company had halted in the lee of a low ridge for some supper. The men were exhausted, their earlier elation long gone. A carrier had been destroyed, with three men killed, when they had been strafed by a flight of Italian Macchis, and two more had been wounded by enemy shelling. All were hot, filthy and sand-blasted. The dust storm had been no *khamseen*, but it had still made life uncomfortable. The sand got everywhere – in shoes, clothes, and particularly into ears and hair. It got into weapons too, sandpapering the metalwork and causing jams. It also found its way into food and tea, so that every sip and mouthful was accompanied by a grating of teeth. The only consolation was that the wind helped keep the flies at bay. But now, when at last they had stopped, the wind had died down. As tins were opened and supper prepared, the desert flies returned.

With Peploe and Sykes, Tanner walked to the summit of the ridge to see what was going on, glad to get away from the swarms buzzing around the food. As with most ridges in the desert, it was hardly a major incline. Rather, the horizon just appeared rather short, and suddenly they had reached the summit. Stretching away for more than ten miles they could see the shallow bowl of the gravel flats and beyond, marking the horizon, the fifty-foot rise of the Alam Halfa Ridge. The dusty pall that had hung over the desert for much of the day was now dispersing. As evening drew in, the landscape often sharpened in focus, as was the case now. Tanner sniffed. There were a number of low columns of dust several miles to the north, but it was only when he brought his binoculars to his eyes that he could see they were panzers – and not heading north towards the ridge, but south.

'They're falling back!' he said. 'They're bloody well falling back!'

'Hooray,' said Peploe. 'They've clearly hit a wall. Our chaps must have held their ground.'

'What d'you think they'll do now?' asked Sykes. 'Leaguer up or fall back?'

Tanner watched another formation of panzers four miles or so to the north. They appeared to be moving into a circular formation. 'The lot I'm looking at are leaguering,' he said. 'Here.' He passed the binoculars to Sykes. 'Have a dekko.'

'Which means their supply columns will be coming through the minefields again tonight,' said Peploe.

'We ought to make some mischief then, shouldn't we?'

'Indeed we should. That's certainly Old Man Vigar's intention. You think the men are up to it?'

'It's been hard going, that's for sure,' said Tanner, 'but for the most part I think they'll be all right.'

'I agree, but we're quite a few vehicles down now,' said Sykes, 'and one or two of the lads are done in. I'm worried about Smailes.'

'Me too,' said Tanner. 'I thought he just needed a bit of time to calm down, that with a bit of grub inside him and a beadie or two he'd be all right, but I'm not so sure.'

'We had to get Mudge on the Bren earlier,' added Sykes.

'Well, go easy on him, then. We're pulling back to Mena again after this show. Another day and we'll probably be out of the line. We can see how he is then.'

'Each man's only got so much courage,' said Tanner. 'I remember my old man telling me that about his time in the last war. A reservoir of courage, he called it. And once it's empty, it's empty. He said each man's reservoir was different.'

'I'd say your dad was spot on,' said Sykes. 'We've seen people lose their nerve. They don't mean to. It just happens.'

'You think that's happening to Smailes?' said Peploe.

'I'm not sure yet,' said Tanner. 'But maybe.'

The sun was setting, a huge semi-circular deep red orb, slipping beneath the western horizon. A faint drone could now be heard away to the east, rapidly getting louder. Tanner scanned the skies and spotted them: eighteen bombers, with fighter escorts above. 'Flynn said they'd be back as soon as the dust storm cleared.' From the west, they heard another drone: enemy fighters, swooping to intercept the bombers. He watched transfixed as a small air battle developed. Bombs were whistling down on the concentrations of enemy tanks and transports, the ground shuddering with the explosions, while machine-guns and cannons chattered and throbbed. A Boston bomber was plummeting, then another was struggling, long trails of smoke following. They watched four parachutes open and drift down as the stricken bomber disappeared to the west. A fighter was falling and then, in what seemed like no time at all, they had all vanished, the darkening skies clear once more. All that was left were columns of black smoke rising into the air.

Enemy tanks and vehicles burning.

17

Vaughan and Tanja had been finishing dinner at the Mohammed Ali Club when David Stirling had ambled over and invited them to his flat in Kasr El Doubara for drinks. There was a small crowd heading there now, he had told them. Why not join us?

Vaughan had initially demurred – the following day he was heading to Kabrit for the rest of the week – but Tanja had insisted. 'I want to meet the famous Phantom Major,' she had told him. 'Anyway, I have barely met any of your friends.' They had walked – it was only a short distance from the club and, other than first thing in the morning, it was the one time of day when the temperature dropped to a bearable level.

The flat was almost directly opposite the British Embassy, near the river. Here, the hubbub of central Cairo had melted away to the European grandeur of the government quarter, and they could hear the music coming from the flat long before they reached the front door.

Outside several jeeps and other cars were haphazardly parked. The door was open so they went in, following the music and the increasingly loud chatter. Outside, an officer in ragged desert uniform was dancing with a girl. Vaughan and Tanja squeezed past them into the hall. Letters were strewn across the long table, while a half-empty bottle of whisky stood beside a discarded Tommy gun.

'Alex! Come on in!' said David Stirling, walking towards them down the hall with a glass and a cigarette in one hand, a bottle in the other. 'And Tanja. Delightful.' They followed him into the sitting room, where there were at least twenty people, men and women, many of whom Vaughan knew, including Johnny Farrer.

'What can I get you?' Stirling asked. 'Scotch? Beer? Wine?' He raised an eyebrow and grinned. 'Champagne?'

'Champagne, please.' Tanja smiled.

'Scotch for me,' said Vaughan.

'Coming right up,' said Stirling, and disappeared into the kitchen.

It was a high-ceilinged room. Couples smooched on the shabby, stained sofas, the curtains were torn and the walls bare, save for pictures of the King and Queen, which had evidently been cut from a magazine.

'Tanja!' called a voice.

They turned to see Sophie Tarnowska weaving her way towards them, cigarette in hand and a long arc of ash about to fall – which it did as she kissed Tanja. 'And you must be Alex,' she said, to Vaughan. 'I've heard so much about you.'

'Hello, Billy,' said Vaughan, turning to her companion, a good-looking, dark-haired man in uniform. 'I heard you were in town.'

Stirling returned with the drinks. 'Of course,' he said, 'I forgot you all know each other.'

'Doesn't everyone?' said Vaughan.

'Tell me,' Tanja said, 'why have you stuck pictures of the King and Queen to the wall?'

'Because we're so patriotic. We love King George and his wonderful wife, Queen Elizabeth.'

'Don't listen to a word of it, Tanja,' said Vaughan. 'It's because he and Peter were doing pistol practice at the wall and the landlord decided to come around. They stuck those up to cover the bullet holes.'

Stirling put up his hands. 'Guilty, I'm afraid. But I'm a great patriot too.'

'So am I,' said Tanja.

'Of Poland or Britain? If you marry Alex, you'll be a British citizen, you know.'

Tanja felt her cheeks redden.

'Pay no attention to him, Tanja,' Vaughan said, laughing. 'He's a rude bugger who takes a peculiar pleasure from talking out of turn.'

The record finished and Stirling yelled, 'Lizzie!' at a man in a white suit with long hair that was falling over his eyes. He glanced up, cigarette between his lips. 'Put another record on!'

'Who's that?' Tanja asked.

'Lizzie Lezard. He used to be a barrister, but then became a gambler. He's a very funny man. I think he's living here at the moment.' They watched Lezard shuffle through a loose pile of records, grin to himself, then put one on the gramophone and wind it up. Noël Coward's reedy, clipped voice rang out. Lezard was singing along, and several others joined in:

> The natives grieve when the white men leave their
>   huts
> Because they're obviously, absolutely nuts.
> Mad dogs and Englishmen go out in the midday
>   sun.

A tall man in a pale suit walked in.

'Peter!' called Stirling. 'Where've you been?'

'Working. Some of us have to,' he said, in a slow, rather decadent voice. 'I need a drink. Got any champagne open?'

'Of course.' Stirling turned to Vaughan and Tanja. 'You've met my brother before, Alex, but, Tanja, you haven't.'

'Hello,' said Peter, one eyebrow raised. 'Charmed, I'm sure.' He turned to Vaughan. 'I'm assuming he's thrown this party to celebrate our success in the desert?'

Vaughan smiled. 'Perhaps. I heard about last night. Have you any more news?'

'I've just come from the embassy where everyone's in a very cheery frame of mind. It seems Rommel's strike force has been battering against a brick wall all afternoon. They were seen pulling back for the night and now the RAF is blasting them to buggery. Apparently they've dropped so many magnesium flares the whole place is lit up like daylight and Rommel's panzers are the proverbial sitting ducks.'

'That's marvellous,' said Vaughan. He won-

367

dered how his friends in the Yorks Rangers were faring.

'Yes,' said Peter. 'It seems we've turned a corner. All that fuss a month or so ago – incredible, really. There we were, thinking Armageddon was upon us – quite a turn-around.'

'We won't be beaten now. Not in North Africa,' said Vaughan. 'We've just got to make sure that when we go on the offensive, we do the job properly.'

'Absolutely. But I think we will this time. Alexander and Monty are cut from a different cloth. Alexander was staying at the embassy when he first got out here, you know, and he exuded calm. No wonder he's become Winston's go-to man in a crisis. Absolutely imperturbable – he's just what Middle East Command needs.' He turned to Tanja. 'Now, let me guess,' he said, finger to his lips. 'That accent. Not Balkan. No – northern European. Polish?'

'Bravo,' said Tanja. 'Yes, I am Polish.'

'It must be hard for you,' he said, 'with the Nazis on one side, the Soviets on the other. Does it worry you that the Russians are our allies?'

'I don't know who is worse – Hitler or Stalin.'

'I'll take that as a "yes" then.'

She looked him in the eye. 'I just want the war to be over and for Poland to be free again,' she said.

'Amen to that.'

The party showed no sign of breaking up with the onset of the curfew, but Tanja whispered, 'Can we go to your flat now?' She and Vaughan thanked the Stirling brothers and headed out into the quiet streets, walking quickly, hoping not to be spotted by the MPs or the Egyptian police. It wasn't far – five minutes or so – and the policeman they did see tapped his watch but otherwise left them alone. Vaughan talked most of the way. Rommel had been stopped. Now they could really start taking the fight to the enemy. They were on the path to victory.

Tanja half listened, clinging to his arm, her mind swimming with other thoughts. With the news from the front, and Alex going away, it was time to act. For two days she had racked her brain about how to do it, but now she knew. *You have to,* she told herself. *You have to.*

Tuesday, 1 September. At first light, the men of A Company were heading back eastwards along the southern edge of the battlefield towards Brigade Headquarters, driving slowly so as not to attract too much attention. Tanner, with his binoculars to his eyes, scanned the gravel flats to their left. A thin pall hung in the shallow bowl, but through the haze, Tanner could see the desert was littered with wrecks, some still burning, columns of black smoke rising into the sky. A sharp, acrid stench filled the air: smoke, cordite, and death – a familiar sickly sweet odour. *Christ, the flies are going to be even worse than usual.*

It had been a long night. They had sniped as much as they could, but the RAF had been relentless. Wave after wave of bombers had come over, dropping an endless supply of flares so that it had barely seemed like night at all. And while they kept up the bombardment, the artillery had

369

continued to rain down shells. The Afrika Korps, apparently stuck where they were, seemed helpless. Supply columns had tried to get through but had been bombed as well. A Company had had a prolonged fight with a convoy a few miles east of Himeimat. They had suffered another half-dozen casualties, with one more truck and carrier down, and eventually Peploe had decided they had done enough. That had been more than an hour ago.

'What can you see, sir?' said Brown, next to him.

'Lots of dead tanks and trucks.'

'D'you think that's it – that we've got him beat?'

'They'll attack again later, I'm sure, but they've had a night of hell-fire and they look pretty bloody stranded out there to me.'

Brown's head suddenly lolled forward, then lurched upright again.

'Keep going, Browner.'

'Sorry, sir. I'm fine. Really.'

'Looks like you're falling asleep at the wheel to me.'

'Just lost it for a moment there, but I'm all right now, sir.'

'Boiled sweet or beadie?' said Tanner, feeling for his pack.

'Wouldn't say no to both, sir.'

Tanner smiled, took out two cigarettes, lit them and passed one to Brown. 'You can have your sweet when you've finished that.'

He glanced behind him. The others were all asleep, including Smailes, despite the jolting of the truck over the rough ground and desultory gunfire to the north. *The lads need more than a catnap*. Damn it, he needed a rest himself. He'd not had more than half an hour's sleep for two days. Exhaustion swept over him like a dull weight. His eyes burned with fatigue but also because he'd let sand get into them the previous afternoon. He was thirsty, too, and hoarse from yelling over the din of battle. Grabbing his water bottle, he took a swig of the foul-tasting liquid, with its residue of petrol. That was one reason why they all drank so much tea: to hide the taste of the water. The old wound on his arm ached and the new cut on his other arm stung. Tanner sighed. Maybe they'd reach Brigade to be told they'd done enough. He hoped so.

However, when they got to Brigade HQ, some eight miles south-east of the Alam Halfa Ridge, they were told they had to patrol.

It was around ten a.m. when Tanner and the other A Company officers returned from their briefing with Colonel Vigar. Tanner found his men asleep, Brown with his head back and mouth open in the front of the truck, the others lying on the ground around it.

'Wakey, wakey,' said Tanner. Heads moved, hair thick and dirty, eyes half open. Even Sykes, normally so particular about his appearance and especially his hair, was dishevelled.

'Are we out of the line, then?' he asked.

''Fraid not. We've patrol work to do.'

Sykes sat up and scratched his head.

'What kind of patrol work?' asked Hepworth, getting stiffly to his feet.

'I'll tell you in a minute.' Tanner went to the

back of the truck, spread out his map and marked it with a pencil. 'Everyone awake and got their eyes open?' he asked. A few mumbled replies. 'Good, then gather round me here.' He glanced at Smailes, who was clutching the edge of the tailgate and staring into the far distance. 'Smiler?'

Smailes turned his head and Tanner saw that he was sweating – beads of moisture along his forehead and upper lip and running down the side of his face. *Bloody hell.* It was hot, but the heat was dry. No one else was sweating. Not having just woken up.

'First of all,' he said, 'a sitrep. And it's pretty good, as we thought. The enemy got nowhere yesterday and the line held all the way from the Kiwis to the eastern end of Alam Halfa.'

'Hooray,' said Hepworth.

'Say it like you mean it, Hep,' said Sykes.

'Most importantly, our armour didn't go careering after the enemy once they pulled back. They stayed where they were.'

'What were our losses like?' asked Sykes.

'Twenty-second Armoured Brigade took the brunt. We did lose a few tanks and guns yesterday but it seems the lads in the 1st Rifle Brigade did a bloody good job with their six-pounders.'

'Good on 'em,' said Sykes.

'Anyway,' Tanner continued, 'we've now identified the enemy units attacking the Ridge. It was the 21st Panzer Division in the scrap with 22nd Armoured Brigade yesterday, but so far there's been no sign of any movement from them. The intel is that they're now very low on fuel. However, 15th Panzer are already on the move,

372

and it looks like they're going to try and work themselves around to the east of 22nd Armoured Brigade.' He drew a few dashes on the map. 'So our old friends in 8th Armoured Brigade, who have so far done nothing and have been waiting a few miles to the south-east of the ridge, are being ordered forward to hit 15th Panzer's flank. Our job is to take over their positions and cover their arses.' He looked up. 'It's a cushy one. All we do is sit back and watch.'

'And hope the *Luftwaffe* don't come at us,' said Hepworth.

'You don't think, Hep, that they might have more pressing targets than us?' said Tanner. He turned to Smailes. 'Smiler, how are you feeling?'

'Fine,' said Smailes.

'You don't look it.'

'He needs to go to the MO, sir,' said Sykes.

'No,' said Smailes, angrily. 'I'm fine. I told you.'

Tanner put a hand on his shoulder. 'Listen, Smiler. You're not going to help the lads if they get your fever. So go to the MO and sit this one out, all right?'

Tanner could see Smailes's eyes filling with tears. 'It's all right, mate,' he said. 'You're a bloody good soldier. One of the best.' He gripped his shoulder. 'Now go to the MO, all right?'

Smailes nodded, tears running down his cheeks. 'Christ,' he said. 'This fucking war.'

They soon found 8th Armoured Brigade's former positions from the debris left strewn about the desert. On the map it was at trig point 87; on the ground, it was a patch of stony sand and desert

373

vetch littered with shell fossils, discarded fuel cans, food tins and ammunition boxes.

From their new vantage-point they could see the full scale of the carnage that had unfolded over the previous two days and nights. The desert was littered with wrecks, and, Tanner now saw through his binoculars, the dead. Both sides understood the importance of burying the dead right away, but there had been no time. The flies were having a feast, buzzing around the bodies, landing on arms and faces.

It was now around eleven in the morning as they watched the four tank regiments of the 8th Armoured Brigade push forwards. Four miles ahead, heavy tank and artillery fire was booming. One enemy tank was already on fire, thick black smoke pitching into the sky. Tanner now watched the two British tank regiments closest to them, the Rutland Yeomanry and the Sherwood Rangers. They were still at least two thousand yards away. *A bit further* – between a thousand and fifteen hundred yards. That would be about right, he reckoned. Then they needed to find a few dips in the desert, get themselves into half-decent hull-down positions, and pound the enemy flanks.

Suddenly the British tanks opened fire, a mixture of American Grants, with a short 75mm gun, and Crusaders with a mere two-pounder. They would hit nothing from that range. 'No!' said Tanner.

'What's the matter, sir?' asked Sykes, standing up in the truck.

'It's those bloody new boys,' said Tanner. 'Opening fire at two thousand yards. Don't they

374

teach them anything?' He passed his binoculars. 'Have a dekko.'

'Well, the enemy's not replying,' said Sykes.

Another salvo boomed but the tanks were now surging forward, trails of dust following.

'That should do it,' said Sykes, handing back the binoculars.

Tanner put them to his eyes once more. The tanks were still surging forward. 'Jesus,' he muttered. 'Bloody look at them. They're still going.'

'Huzzah, chaps!' said Sykes. 'Sabres forward!'

'You're not wrong, Stan,' said Tanner. 'They think it's a bloody cavalry charge.' They watched in silence as the Yeomanry tanks continued to surge towards the enemy. 'Damn it all,' muttered Tanner, 'when the hell are they going to stop?' Through the binoculars, it looked as though the British armour was now almost on top of the enemy.

Then they heard anti-tank fire, followed by several flashes of orange, visible through the smoke and dust.

'Oh, Jesus,' said Tanner. 'The stupid bloody idiots. Christ, Stan, how many times have we seen that?'

'Like insects to a light bulb,' said Sykes, 'so our tanks to Jerry's anti-tank screen.'

'What's happening, sir?' said Phyllis, now standing in the back of the truck next to Sykes.

'Our friends in the Yeomanry are getting torn to shreds, Siff, that's what.' More flashes of explosions. Through the haze Tanner counted at least eight tanks burning. Black smoke pitched into the air.

'I've seen enough,' he said, passing the binoculars back to Sykes, and sitting down. He took out a cigarette. 'Can someone make a brew? Mudge?'

'They're pulling back by the look of things,' said Sykes.

'What about Jerry? Is he pursuing?'

'Can't really tell. Don't think so.'

Overhead, another wave of bombers flew over and dropped their bombs on the mass of panzers and vehicles now dug in to the southwest of Alam Halfa.

'They're hitting 21st Panzer, I think,' said Sykes.

'And our suicidal cavalry?' asked Tanner.

'I can see twelve burning. The rest are still pulling back.'

Tanner shook his head. *What a bloody waste.*

Some time after midday, there were reports that 15th Panzer Division were pulling back and going on to the defensive, so 8th Armoured Brigade was pulled back too. At the same time, the Yorks Rangers were ordered to return to Brigade Headquarters, where they were told they were at last being withdrawn from the battle.

'It's over,' said Vigar, addressing the survivors from his command car. 'For us, at any rate. You've all done damned well. We can feel proud of ourselves.' They were to head back to Mena that afternoon, he told them.

But first another brew, some tiffin and the flies.

'Have we beaten Rommel, then?' said Phyllis, as he wafted the flies from his mess tin.

'Pretty much, Siff,' said Tanner. 'Put it this way, Rommel hasn't beaten us, and that's what he had to do.'

'So what next, sir?' asked Brown.

'We get ready to attack him.'

'When?'

Tanner shrugged. 'God knows. When Monty thinks we're strong enough, I suppose.'

'Just like that,' said Brown.

'Pretty much,' said Tanner. 'It's not complicated, you know.'

It was just after one when they got going again, rumbling back across the desert, heading northeast towards the coast road. They were filthy, all of them, and exhausted, but Tanner felt a strange sense of exultation. Gradually, the sound of guns faded, the air became fresher, and before long they could see the Mediterranean, twinkling iridescently to their left. The fighting was not yet over, but the battle had been won.

18

Wednesday, 2 September. It was just before seven o'clock in the evening that Tanner went up the stairs to Lucie's flat and knocked at the door. *Please be in.* To his relief, he heard footsteps approaching. A moment later, the door opened, and there she was, already out of her uniform, wearing a simple cotton dress. 'You look lovely,' he said.

Her face lit up and she flung her arms around his neck, kissed him and held him tightly. 'You made it back,' she said.

'I told you I would.'

She let go, the better to look at him, then ran a hand across his face. 'My darling Jack,' she laughed, 'you smell terrible.'

Tanner sniffed at his armpits. 'Why d'you think I'm here, Luce?' He grinned. 'I need a bath.' He held up his canvas haversack. 'Look, I've even brought fresh clothes.'

Holding his hand, she led him into the flat, made him sit on the bed and then went to run the bath. Tanner looked around. Everything was exactly the same. Even the copy of *Tess* was still on her chest of drawers, just as he had left it. It was as though the intervening fortnight had never happened.

'You're here sooner than I'd dared hope,' she said, coming back into the bedroom and sitting beside him.

'They reckoned we'd done our bit. Two nights and two days was enough, and we've got retraining to do. It was always the plan to bring us back.'

'Well, I'm glad. I've been thinking about you, wondering where you were. Whether you were still alive. The wounded have been pouring in today. We'd been bracing ourselves. I kept hoping you wouldn't be one of them.'

Tanner began to undress. 'I'm fine. Barely so much as a scratch.' He winced as he pulled his shirt over his head.

'Apart from the one on your shoulder.' Her brow knotted as she looked at the bloody bandage on his upper left arm. 'I'm going to take this rag off.' Tanner flinched. The gauze had stuck to the wound. Fresh blood trickled down his arm.

'Who dressed this?'

'Er, Stan. He's not much of a medic.'

'You can say that again. It needs a stitch or two, really. Do you want me to do that now?'

'Best get it over and done with.'

Collecting her bag and a bowl of warm water, she cleaned the wound, tutting about the amount of sand, then gave him a local anaesthetic and neatly put in three stitches. It took less than five minutes. 'There,' she said. 'You might keep your arm now.' She kissed his shoulder.

'Thanks, Luce.'

'How did you do it?'

'Fell out of a truck and landed a bit awkwardly.'

She looked at him sceptically. 'And now for part two of the clean-up operation.'

Ah, yes. Tanner sank into the warm, soapy water and ducked his head under. And then Lucie's hands were gently washing his back, neck and chest.

He grinned at her. 'I've been dreaming of this, you know.'

It was later that she told him about seeing Vaughan and Tanja. They were lying in bed, her head on his chest, an arm wrapped around him.

'It was last Sunday,' she said, 'in the bar of the Continental.'

'What were you doing there?'

'Meeting Susan.'

'Susan who?'

'Susan Travers. General König's lover.'

'Ah, yes – that Susan.'

'They're expecting to be sent up to the front

soon. She's wondering how she can go with them again. The general's told her she's got to stay here this time.'

'I thought he told her that before Bir Hacheim.' Lucie laughed. 'I suppose he did.'

'Will you go?'

'No. I'm staying here now. They need me at the hospital. I feel it's important, the work I'm doing there.'

'Of course it is. So you saw Vaughan and Tanja?'

'I suppose it was her. She was blonde, very striking. Beautiful, in fact.'

'Sounds like her.'

'I was going to say hello, but she seemed in quite a state. Not with him – he was rather tender towards her.'

'He's smitten. I can see why – she's a bloody cracker.'

'What about me?'

'Goes without saying.'

'You can say it, though.'

'All right. Lucie, you're a bloody cracker. So you haven't been tempted by some young cavalry officer with an estate in Scotland while I've been away?'

'I might have done if I'd had time.' She kissed him. 'No, of course not.' They were silent for a moment, and then she said, 'How was it out there? Was it terrible?'

'It was if you were a Jerry or an Eyetie. Jesus, they got a bloody pasting from the RAF. We lost a few good lads – none in my truck, thank God – but it's a hell of a lot easier getting through a battle when you're winning. Knackering,

380

though.' He sighed and stretched his legs. 'But this is bloody lovely, Luce.'

Saturday, 5 September, a little before ten a.m. An earlier than expected return to Cairo for Major Vaughan, but news had reached him that the Yorks Rangers were back at Mena Camp – reason enough for leaving Kabrit – and he had received a wire the previous evening from Maunsell, asking for an urgent meeting with Brigadier Bowlby. It wasn't ideal to leave the team, but Farrer was proving a more than capable deputy and the men were being kept busy by their SAS instructors. In any case, he needed Tanner and Sykes – and the support of Maunsell and Bowlby. Without them, C Detachment might prove the shortest-lived special-operations force ever created.

Operations Bigamy and Agreement were going ahead as originally planned. He had known that since before he had left for Kabrit three days earlier: Brigadier Davy was not to be budged. They had to think big and plan big, he had said, because anything less would never achieve the scale of destruction and disruption that would prove decisive. According to David Stirling, even John Haselden was now concerned that the operations had become overblown.

No matter. The raids were on, and the various forces due to hit Benghazi, Tobruk, and now the landing grounds at Barce, on the night of 13/14 September. Stirling was still in Cairo, but the rest of his men were already at Kufra Oasis, *en route* to Benghazi, as were Colonel Haselden and his Force B, in preparation for the landward attack

381

on Tobruk; Stirling would be flying down to join them any day now. The naval forces were preparing in Alexandria. His own C Detachment was due to be leaving on the tenth – in just five days' time.

But nothing Vaughan had seen or heard had made him feel any differently about it. He simply could not see how it could possibly work. The more detailed and convoluted the plans, the more sceptical he had become.

If he was right, and the raids failed, the plug would be pulled on C Detachment, the DMO would get his knuckles rapped, and Vaughan would be cut adrift. His lifeline was the SIS. He had met Brigadier Bowlby some ten days earlier, when they had discussed the possibilities of intelligence gathering on such missions, but without ever talking specifics. Now he had been summoned to another meeting – which Maunsell had said was 'urgent'. 'WILL BE IN CAIRO 0900 5/9/42' Vaughan had wired Maunsell. 'EXCELLENT. 1000 RED PILLARS' had been the swift reply.

And now here he was, stepping out of his jeep, striding past Abdu and climbing the stairs to Maunsell's office.

'Alex,' said Maunsell, as Vaughan entered, 'how good to see you! How the devil are you?'

'Very well, RJ, thank you. And you?'

'Couldn't be better.'

'What news on Cobra?'

Maunsell smiled. 'We haven't caught our mole, I'm afraid, but as a spy circuit, it's finished – in part because of our efforts, and also because the

situation in the desert has changed so remark-
ably.'

'Do you think we ever will catch the mole?'

Maunsell looked at him, a curious expression
on his face that Vaughan could not read. 'Oh, I
think so,' he said, then consulted his watch.
'Bowlby's expecting us at ten thirty at Grey
Pillars, so we should get going.'

They walked the short distance to their
meeting. The heat was so intense that even the
giant palms seemed to be sagging. The scent of
jasmine was heavy on the air, but breathing in
deeply seared Vaughan's nostrils.

Beside him, Maunsell seemed oblivious to it.
'So, crisis over, it would seem. Rommel stopped
in the desert and suddenly the ball's in the other
court.' He chuckled. 'He staked everything on
this last roll of the dice and it's failed. Apparently
he's back to where he started.'

'I heard. But minus quite a few tanks, vehicles
and men.'

'And fuel. The chaps from Malta sank that
tanker he was waiting for. Not one of those
Italian ships reached him in time.' He paused to
light his pipe. 'So now we've got to prepare for
the next ding-dong in the desert.'

'Which will hopefully be the last.'

'Has to be.'

They reached Grey Pillars and were taken to
Brigadier Cuthbert Bowlby's office. It was cool
and dimly lit, the shutters closed over the
windows and two fans whirring overhead. It was
also less spare than Maunsell's, with more
furniture, including a leather-topped desk, drinks

cabinet and low bookshelves on which stood an old globe. In the corner a hat-stand and an elephant-foot umbrella stand were empty. Pictures hung on the wall: the obligatory map of the Middle East and the Mediterranean, but also an oil landscape of somewhere in England. Yorkshire, perhaps? The room reminded Vaughan more of an office in Whitehall or even a London club than somewhere in the heart of the Middle East, to which the only concession was the mahogany-framed rattan chairs.

A secretary brought them iced lemonade and then Bowlby said, 'Right, let's get down to business, shall we? RJ, have you briefed Major Vaughan?'

'I thought I'd leave that to you.'

Bowlby leaned forward on his desk, hands clasped. 'When we last met, Vaughan, I mentioned to you the possibility of intelligence gathering – spying, for want of a better term.'

'Yes, sir,' said Vaughan. No first names at the ISLD.

'Well, we now want someone to act as a courier.'

'A courier? How do you mean, sir?'

Bowlby glanced at Maunsell. 'Look here, Vaughan, I know you've signed the Official Secrets Act, but we all know that there are plenty of loose tongues here in GHQ. What I am about to tell you really is of the utmost secrecy. Is that clear?'

'Of course, sir.'

'Good. We're about to send an agent into Mersa Matruh. A turned agent.'

'A German?' asked Vaughan.

Bowlby inclined his head. 'An agent, Vaughan.'

'May I ask who?'

'You may, but I'm not going to tell you. Now here's the nub. Mersa is a small place, as I'm sure you know. The moment our agent starts sending radio messages, they will be picked up by the enemy and so will our agent. But we still want our agent – let's say Agent X, for convenience's sake – in Mersa at this time. Getting Agent X into Mersa is straightforward – the Germans will do that for us.'

'But getting him out again isn't going to be so easy.'

'Exactly. Which is where you and C Detachment come in. I appreciate that you've got to do this raid on Tobruk, and I also know from RJ here that you think it a damn fool idea that's bound to fail.'

'I do rather, sir, yes.'

'I agree with you, as it happens. But be that as it may, I want you to get back from this raid and wait in Alexandria for a signal from us, then head back up the coast to Mersa and get Agent X. We will give you the details of where to meet and when, as well as two back-up meeting points, should either of you miss the first or, indeed, second liaison.'

'And bring him back.'

'Yes.'

'And what about sabotage?'

'I don't care what you do there so long as Agent X is delivered safely back to us. What did you have in mind? Time switches on harbour stores, and that kind of thing?'

'Something like that, yes.' Vaughan rubbed his

chin. 'And what about the DMO? I'm supposedly working for him in MO4.'

Bowlby waved a hand. 'Don't worry about that, Vaughan. RJ and I can handle it.'

'What about a date?'

'Around the eighteenth of September. But that may change in the next day or so. We'll let you know as soon as the details have been confirmed.'

There was a pause while Vaughan digested this news.

'Take a small squad only, Vaughan. I cannot stress to you enough the vital importance of bringing Agent X back alive.'

'I understand.'

'You think you can do it?'

'Absolutely. It's why I suggested setting up small squads of coastal raiding parties in the first place. But such an operation carries a fair degree of risk. It *might* go wrong. You must be prepared for that.'

Bowlby nodded thoughtfully. 'I understand.'

Vaughan turned to Maunsell. 'And do you mind me asking what your role is in this, RJ?'

Maunsell beamed genially. 'Let's just say Cuthbert and I both have vested interests in Agent X.' The rattan chair creaked as he leaned back and shifted in his seat. 'I said to you earlier, Alex, that we had to prepare to beat Rommel once and for all.'

'Absolutely.'

'If we can pull this off, we'll be making a significant step towards ensuring that happens. The tables may have turned, but we still need to beat Rommel and his Panzer Army decisively. To 'achieve that, intelligence still has a vital role.'

'And you have a vital role, Major Vaughan,' added Bowlby. He stood up, the meeting over. 'A vital role.'

Vaughan had left GHQ and driven out to Mena Camp. It was nearly midday and the heat was at its worst. Flies and other insects buzzed about – a number were crawling over the outside of Colonel Vigar's tent as Vaughan was shown in.

The colonel was not in the best of moods. 'Letters,' he muttered. 'The worst kind.' He shuffled some papers on his desk and dabbed his brow. 'So, what can I do for you?'

Vaughan explained. 'You may recall, sir,' he added, 'that it was with Tanner and Sykes that we were able to wreak so much havoc at Heraklion.'

'Strewth,' said Vigar. 'I lose Tanner for the best part of two months and finally get him back only to be expected to give him up again. And now you want one of my CSMs as well. Don't you think I need them here?'

'I understand you're retraining, sir. On six-pounders. With the greatest respect, Tanner and Sykes know perfectly well how to fire almost any artillery piece that we have – German too, for that matter.'

Vigar grunted. 'And what if something happens to them? I'm going to need them in the battle to come.'

'These two missions are of vital importance for the battle to come, sir.'

'Do I have any choice in the matter, Vaughan?'

'I wouldn't want to take them away without

your blessing, sir.'

Vigar snorted. 'In other words, no.' He scratched his head. 'And how long will this be for?'

'About ten days. Two weeks at the most.'

Vigar sighed. 'Damn it all,' he said. 'I don't see that I've got much say in the matter, but as a courtesy, you need to clear it with Peploe first. He's their immediate OC. Just make sure you bring them back in one piece.'

Peploe, however, was not as easily persuaded as Colonel Vigar, taking Vaughan aside and arguing vehemently against such a move. Tanner and Sykes were his two best men, he explained, and Tanner had only just returned. 'I can't tell you the effect he has on the company. He gives everyone confidence. He's so bloody imperturbable. Do you know what he did out there? It was extraordinary. We were being pegged back by an enemy armoured car, so Tanner gets his driver to head towards its blind side, then Sykes throws a packet of gelignite towards it. Tanner knows that if he opens fire but misses, the armoured car will have them at point-blank range, so he jumps out of the moving truck and, when it's out of the way, takes careful aim and shoots the gelignite and blows up the armoured car. An incredible feat.'

'It's for precisely that kind of nerve and cool-headedness that I need him, John,' argued Vaughan. 'This isn't any old job. I wish I could tell you more, but you have to trust me on this.'

Peploe tugged an earlobe. 'You're asking me to lose my 2i/c and CSM at a time of crucial retraining, Alex – and for an operation which is no doubt fraught with danger. I understand you can't tell me about it, but it doesn't take much to work out that it's something behind enemy lines and of high risk. I need them when we next go into battle, Alex – not dead or in hospital somewhere.'

'Look, John. Think about it this afternoon. Talk to Tanner and Sykes. It's only ten days I'm asking for, and you know what they're like. They're far too smart to get themselves killed. Jack even helped me draw up the plans for this.'

'He did?' Peploe was taken aback.

'Yes. It really won't be for long and I'd put very good money on absolutely nothing happening to them whatsoever.'

'Careful, Alex. You can't know that at all.' He kicked at the ground.

Vaughan was surprised by Peploe's reaction. He had hardly expected him to be pleased, but had thought he would concede readily enough. Nor did he want a kind of *rapprochement* with Peploe. They had been through much together on Crete – and he both liked and admired him. 'Look, let's forget about this for the moment,' he said. 'It'd be good to see you, John, in more–' he waved an arm '–salubrious surroundings. Why don't you, Jack, and I meet for a drink or dinner tonight? Could you get away?'

'Not sure about tonight,' he replied. 'But maybe now. As you can see, there's not a lot going on at the minute.'

Vaughan looked at his watch. 'All right,' he said. 'Where were you thinking of? Mena House?'

'No. I want some greenery. How about the Sporting Club?'

'Have you got time?'

'I'm giving myself time. Jack, too.'

'And you'll think about letting me second them?'

'I'm not happy, Alex, but, yes, I'll think about it.'

They had a convivial lunch in the cool and sedate surroundings of the Gezira Sporting Club, the topic of Tanner and Sykes's secondment to C Detachment carefully avoided. Afterwards, as they ambled outside under the shade of ilex and gum trees, Peploe said, 'It's incredible to think we were in the middle of a battle just a few days ago, isn't it, Jack? Look at this place. I know there are plenty of uniforms, but it's so calm and quiet. You'd be forgiven for thinking the war wasn't going on at all.'

'It reminds me of some of those hill stations in India. Simla was a bit like this – lots of green and people sitting out on terraces. White buildings and the like.'

The clatter of hoofs behind them made them start and they turned to see four men on horseback. They were dressed for polo. One of the mounts was skittish, its rider clearly frustrated.

'Come on, behave!' said the man, pulling hard on the reins. The pony's eyes widened, its teeth bared. 'Damn you!' said the man, much to the amusement of his friends. He yanked the reins again, but the animal scampered towards the three men standing in front of them. Peploe and Vaughan hurried out of the way, but Tanner remained where he was, held out his arms, said, 'Easy now, feller,' reached up and took hold of the bridle. The pony snorted and lowered its head. Tanner stroked its cheek. 'There you go,' he said. 'Just got a bit frightened, didn't you, boy?'

He looked up at the officer, and smiled. 'Mr Rhodes-Morton, well, well.'

'Tanner – what the bloody hell do you think you're doing?'

'Saving you from a nasty accident.' He stroked the pony's nose again. 'You want to be a bit easier on him. He doesn't like being yanked hard like that.'

'And what the bloody hell do you know about it? I don't suppose you've ever been on a horse in your life.'

The three other horsemen now joined their friend, separating Tanner from Peploe and Vaughan.

'Who are you?' said another man.

Tanner stared at him. 'I wouldn't talk to me like that if I were you.'

'Good God,' said another, 'this man's an officer. Is he an imposter?'

'No, he's not,' said Peploe, behind them. 'How dare you?'

'It's all right, John,' said Tanner. 'Leave this to me.' He turned and glowered at the four men.

'He's a farm hand who's been given a jump up,' said Rhodes-Morton. 'We've met before. He might be wearing the pips of an officer but he's certainly not a gentleman.'

'Come on,' said one of the others, 'let's go. There's no need for this.'

'You should listen to your friend, Harry,' said Tanner. 'I'm not going to warn you again. Who the hell do you think you are, lording it over me like this? You need to earn your bloody spurs before you talk down to me, son.'

'We have, as it happens,' said one of the others. 'We took on the 15th Panzer Division.'

'No, you didn't,' said Tanner. 'You opened fire at two thousand yards, then charged their anti-tank screen. I was watching. It was the single most idiotic thing I saw on our side the whole battle.'

'Take that back!' shouted Rhodes-Morton. 'Good men were killed in that action.'

'Good men killed pointlessly.'

'Jack – enough!' said Peploe.

'You take that back!' said Rhodes-Morton.

'No. It's true, and you, mate, need to learn some manners.'

'I'm not going to be talked to like that by a peasant,' sputtered Rhodes-Morton.

Tanner's anger boiled over. *How dare this bastard humiliate me?* Tanner reached up, grabbed Rhodes-Morton, pulled him off the pony and drove his right fist into the lieutenant's head. Rhodes-Morton fell backwards, unconscious.

For a split second the others looked at him, incredulous, then Tanner whacked the rumps of their ponies in turn.

'What the devil?' said one, as they cantered off.

Tanner stood over the prostrate Rhodes-Morton.

'Jack,' said Peploe, behind him. 'What have you done?'

'They were being rude. I warned him, but he wouldn't listen.'

Vaughan was trying not to laugh. 'Jack, that, er, might not have been very sensible, you know.'

'I don't give a damn,' said Tanner, as he watched two of the men wheel their ponies and trot back towards them. 'Sometimes a man's pride is more important than decorum.'

Rhodes-Morton groaned, then began to sit up, a hand clutched to his head. His eyes widened as he saw Tanner still standing over him. 'You hit me!' he muttered.

'I warned you,' said Tanner, 'and I warned you before as well. Now get up and get your pony and get out of my sight.'

Rhodes-Morton got to his feet, faltered and clutched his head.

'You're a bloody disgrace,' said one of his friends, keeping a good ten yards from Tanner. 'You've not heard the end of this. I'm going to report you.'

'Look here,' said Peploe, moving between them. 'I heard the entire thing. You surrounded him and insulted him. You behaved with arrogance unbecoming of the gentlemen you suppose you are. If you report this man, I will report you in turn. Your friend will have a sore head for a few hours but no real harm has been done.'

'He struck an officer,' said the man on horse-back.

'Which was wrong,' said Vaughan, 'but not entirely undeserved. Now have your game of polo and let's forget it.'

'No,' said Tanner. 'I'm not forgetting it.'

'Jack!' said Vaughan.

'I've been insulted. Until these men apologize,

I won't forget it.'

'You and your damned pride, Jack,' muttered Peploe.

'I'm not apologizing to you,' sneered the man.

'Then I'd watch yourself in future,' said Tanner. 'I won't forget this.'

'Now he resorts to ugly threats,' laughed the man. 'Come on, Harry,' he said, passing the reins of Rhodes-Morton's pony.

For a moment, the three stood in silence, watching the cavalrymen trot away. Then Peploe said, 'Come on, let's get out of here,' and strode off in the direction of Vaughan's jeep.

'Jesus, Jack,' he said, as Tanner got in, 'what the hell were you thinking?'

Tanner said nothing.

'You can't behave like that. Brawling with fellow officers – and at the Gezira Club of all places – it's just not on.'

'You saw what they did,' said Tanner. 'They were having a go at me three weeks back at Shepheard's. Then they surround me with their nags, trying to intimidate me, and looking down their noses at me. And for what? Because I stopped his bloody horse throwing him and because I haven't got a plum up my arse.' He sighed. 'I'm sorry, *sir*, if I embarrassed you – I willingly apologize for that – but those bastards deserved it. I warned them. You say it's my pride, well, it damn well is. It's a matter of honour.'

Peploe rubbed his forehead. 'There are other ways of going about these things. Knocking fellow officers out cold is not on.'

They continued in silence, and only when they

arrived back at camp did Peploe turn to Tanner and say, 'Just leave me for a moment, Jack. I need to talk to Major Vaughan.'

Tanner nodded, saluted, thanked Vaughan for lunch, then headed off.

Peploe wandered away from A Company's tents and vehicles. 'Of course, this will get around Cairo in no time,' he said.

'Only because people will enjoy the story. If you weren't involved, you'd be thinking it hilarious.'

'Listen, Alex, I don't give a damn about decorum. But I care about my men and this regiment. Colonel Vigar had to fight hard to get Tanner his commission, you know. Of course, it's more than deserved, but it takes time to change views that are well entrenched. People might enjoy this little escapade, but there are many who will take a very dim view of it and will say that that is why men should not be commissioned from the ranks. Surely you can see that.'

'You're worrying too much,' said Vaughan. 'The Yorks Rangers have a fine reputation, and so does Tanner. Most people will see this for what it was: a highly experienced soldier putting a few young pups in their place.'

'You think I'm being too hard on him?'

'No. He needs to know that he can't start throwing his weight around. But he *does* know that, doesn't he? His behaviour is normally second to none. When he was seconded to SIME with me, he never put a foot wrong, but then SIME is not like the rest of the army. No one there batted an eyelid that here was an officer with a Wiltshire burr. No, John, he only sees red when he feels humiliated or if he feels he's been wronged. Remember Alopex in Crete?'

Peploe smiled. 'Yes, and I remember having to give Tanner both barrels then.' Away to their left, the Pyramids loomed, shimmering in the afternoon heat. Peploe squinted in the brightness. 'But maybe it would be no bad thing for him to keep a low profile for a little while.'

Vaughan's face brightened.

'Ten days you said?'

'Two weeks at the most.'

Peploe looked back towards A Company's camp. 'All right, Alex. I expect I can manage without them for a bit. But I want them back, d'you hear?'

Vaughan grinned. 'Loud and clear.'

19

It had been a simple message, once more translated into code with the help of *Hausboot Muschepusche: Get me out of Cairo,* Tanja had signalled in numbers. *Have important information to deliver. Need to speak with Cobra urgently. Marlin.*

The reply had come a few minutes later. *Received and understood. Be waiting for reply tomorrow, 0600, 7.9.42.*

That had been nearly twenty-four hours earlier – twenty-four long hours; a day of waiting anxiously to see how Cobra would respond. Alex had gone again – 'I'll be back in a day or two' –

although he had not told her where he was going or what he was doing. It was probably just as well that he was away: she didn't have to pretend that all was well, that nothing was troubling her.

But one part of the plan appeared to be working. Orca had always seemed to know whenever she sent or received a message, and he had since been in touch, just as she had hoped he would be. He had rung at the flat, his voice as charming and cheery as ever. A meeting tomorrow at eleven. Not in their old meeting place – not any more – but in the Moski, at the address in Khan El Khalili. *Of course, how lovely – I'll be there!* Would he smell a rat? It was not the first time she had contacted Cobra independently, but it was the first for a while. *Maybe*, but she had her answer ready.

At five fifty a.m. on Monday, 7 September, she pulled the battered case from her wardrobe, took out the radio set, attached the battery, hung the aerial from the curtain rail, then put the headset over her ears and switched it on. The minutes ticked by. At six, a glance at her watch. *One minute past. Two minutes past.* Tanja tapped her fingers on the table. She hated having the radio set out. Sitting there waiting, the headset over her ears, she could hear her heart beating, rapid pulses. *Come on, come on.*

A crackle of static, then a series of bleeps, as numbers in Morse sounded in her ears. Quickly, she noted them down. The signaller was good: he always took his time, never rushing. Then silence. She waited and, satisfied the signal was complete, opened her German novel and began to translate. 'TAKE – TRAIN – TO – EL –

TEIRIEH – AND – AIRCRAFT – WILL – PICK – YOU – UP – 1930 – 8942.' Her breathing had quickened. Tomorrow night. *My God.* She tapped a reply. *Received and understood.* With trembling fingers she took down the aerial, packed away the radio and returned it to the wardrobe, then sat down again. *My God.*

It was eight a.m., and at Mena Camp, Peploe had forgiven Tanner – although, as he had suspected, word of the contretemps had spread. Vigar had not been at all amused and had agreed with Peploe that it might not be such a bad idea if Tanner was out of the way for ten days. There had been a warning too: *You're an officer now. Behave like one.* Tanner had apologized to Vigar for any embarrassment he might have caused the OC, but had been otherwise unrepentant. That morning, as they had left Mena Camp, Peploe had shaken him and Sykes by the hand and wished them luck. 'Make sure you both come back in one piece.'

Tanner and Sykes had been given twenty-four hours' leave – they were due to meet Vaughan later that evening and head together up to Alexandria the following day – and Lucie had been due a day off, so they had arranged to meet at her flat at nine that morning. Sykes had initially been reluctant. 'You don't want me hangin' around, getting in the way,' he had told Tanner. 'I know what you love-birds are like.'

'Give over, Stan. It's not like that. You know Lucie well enough – she wants you to come along and so do I. Anyway, what else are you going to do?'

Sykes had shrugged. 'Dunno. See a film. Go to one of the clubs.'

'Bollocks to that. Come with us.'

From Battalion Headquarters, they had made straight for the CQM's stores, where there was a staff sergeant Sykes had befriended. They loaded up with a few supplies: extra 9mm ammunition for Tanner's Schmeisser, plus explosives, time pencils and other devices.

'They'll have all this in Alexandria, Stan,' Tanner reminded him.

'You'd have thought so, but I'd rather play safe and get a few bits and pieces now, while I've got the chance.'

Staff Sergeant Coombes had given him half a dozen one-pound slabs of American TNT, then had wandered off, returning a short while later with a cardboard box. ''Ere,' he said, 'you might like some of these. They're Aussie.' He took one out and showed it to Sykes.

'It's a switch,' said Sykes.

'That's it,' said Coombes. 'But you can use it as a pressure switch, a pull switch or a release switch.'

'Clever.' Sykes nodded.

'It gets better,' grinned Coombes, ''cos it uses a .303 cartridge as a fuse lighter. You take the bullet out, put your fuse in, stick the end of the cartridge on to the end of the switch and, bang, there you go. The Murray Switch, they call it. Here, take a box.'

'Much obliged,' said Sykes.

'Any clothing you need?'

'You haven't got any denim battledress, have

you?' asked Tanner.

'Might have,' he replied. 'Follow me.' He led them to a different storehouse, where boxes of uniforms were stacked high, mostly khaki drill. Eventually, however, he found what he was looking for.

'I only need the trousers,' said Tanner. 'I had a pair before but they fell to pieces.'

'Not denim,' said Coombes, pulling out a box, 'but cotton. Made in India.'

'Even better,' said Tanner. 'I like having the pockets.'

'Tell you what, though. Here's something good that came in the other day. They're for Special Ops apparently and came here by mistake, but I reckon they should be general issue.' He pulled out another large box. 'Literally – they come in just the end of last week.' He held up a thick cotton smock jacket, camouflaged in green.

Tanner grinned. 'Just the job. Look at those pockets, Stan. Can you spare them?'

'I shouldn't really, but if anyone asks, I'll just say the box came two short.'

'He's a good bloke, is Coombesy,' said Sykes, back outside.

'How do you do it, Stan?' Tanner asked, as they walked from the camp towards the tram stop outside Mena House.

'Do what?'

'Get fellows like Coombes to give us all that stuff. He could get in real trouble if they find out he's been handing out new Special Ops jackets to the likes of us.'

'I'm nice to 'im.'

'Come on, there's more to it than that.'

Sykes grinned. 'Coombesy's a bit of a hoarder. He hasn't seen much front-line stuff, but he likes getting his hands on German and Eyetie kit. German especially. So I get him stuff. Got him a Luger in July. I can't see the fuss myself, but blokes go mad for them. A few Iron Crosses, that sort of thing. He's got a real good collection of clobber that he's going to take home with him.'

'And in return he gives you Murray Switches.'

'And windproof smocks. So you've me to thank for all this.' He paused and lit a cigarette. 'I still don't know what I'm doing, but at least I've got some good clobber.'

As luck would have it, a tram pulled up almost immediately, and twenty minutes later they had reached Midan Ismailia, just five minutes' walk from Lucie's flat.

As they crossed the busy square, Tanner said, 'Still all right about doing this?'

'What – spending a day with you and Lucie?'

'Joining C Detachment.'

'Someone's got to hold your hand, Jack.'

Tanner grinned.

'I mean,' added Sykes, 'we wouldn't want you thumping any more cavalry officers, would we? Not even from the Yeomanry.'

Tanner laughed. 'What about Jerries?'

'That's allowed. Positively encouraged, in fact.' He hoisted his pack. 'Nah, I'm quite excited about it, actually. I'm looking forward to a trip on an MTB. I've always fancied that. And doing something different. I know you and I are happier in the desert than a lot of blokes, but it does

401

get to you a bit, don't it?'

'Too right.'

At Lucie's flat, Sykes received an affectionate embrace.

'See?' said Tanner. 'I told you she liked you, Stan.'

'Did you think I didn't?' Lucie asked Sykes.

'It's not that,' said Sykes, his shoulders hunched. 'I just didn't think you'd want me getting in the way.'

'Nonsense,' she said. 'So what are we going to do today?'

'Don't know. It's not as hot,' said Tanner. 'Jesus, it was bloody terrible here in August, Stan.' He'd noticed while they were walking from Midan Ismailia that the shimmering, all-pervasive heat of three weeks before had gone. Less than a hundred degrees, definitely; a sure sign that autumn was on its way.

'What about some sightseeing?' suggested Sykes. 'I've been into Cairo loads of times but I'm always with you or the lads and we always get drunk. I haven't seen half the sights.'

'It's a thought,' said Tanner.

'Let's do that,' said Lucie. 'We'll start with a drink in Groppi's Garden. I've got a guide book. We can have a look at it in Groppi's, then decide. Perhaps we could visit a bazaar.'

'Good idea,' said Tanner. 'You never know what you might see.'

As usual, Artus was waiting. *Artus*, Tanja thought. *Eslem Mustafa.*

'Good morning, Mademoiselle,' he said, getting up from the cushions on the floor. A single oil lamp, with a brass shade, hung from the centre of the ceiling, and incense burned on a low table.

'Artus,' she said. 'I am glad Orca made contact. It's ridiculous having no way of contacting him.'

'We were alarmed,' he said, his gaze holding hers. 'Why did you signal to Cobra?'

'For instructions. Rommel has lost the battle in the desert.' She narrowed her eyes. 'Why? What reason did you think I had contacted him?'

Artus smiled. 'We have been concerned about your commitment, Marlin, you know that.'

'There is nothing wrong with my commitment,' she retorted, 'only my faith in Orca's judgement. The two things are not the same at all.'

Artus bowed his head. 'And what have you to tell me? What news from Cobra?'

'This.' She showed him her handwritten transcript of the message. 'A summons. I also have details of an operation in which Major Vaughan is involved.'

'As do I.'

Tanja looked at him. *Oh, really?*

'The British are planning a joint raid on Benghazi, Fort Jalo and Tobruk.'

'Orca knows of this?'

'And half of Cairo. The British have hardly been discreet.'

'I have details of these operations. I will be giving them to Cobra tomorrow.'

'From Major Vaughan?'

'Yes, from Major Vaughan – just as Orca instructed me. Not the originals, of course, but

403

notes of the details. Numbers involved, timings, objectives.'

'Good,' said Artus. 'I will accompany you.'

'That won't be necessary.'

'Really? I think it will. That way I will know for sure whether you are telling the truth.' He took a step closer. 'Because, Mademoiselle, I do hope you are not double-crossing us.'

Tanja held his stare. 'More threats. Then accompany me if you want, but let me warn you. The British Secret Service knows all about you. They know you are part of the Cobra operation.'

Artus looked alarmed.

'And I know who you are too – Eslem Mustafa.'

'How? How do you know?'

'Because I saw a dossier on you in Vaughan's briefcase.'

Artus put his hand to his head and stepped away a few paces.

'Cobra is finished, Artus. We have provided Germany with some vitally important intelligence, but our usefulness is over. That is why I suggested we lie low for a while. Disappear until it is safe to run Cobra again.'

He nodded. 'Yes,' he said. 'You are right. But I will still accompany you tomorrow, I and some of my men. Not directly, of course, but discreetly.'

'As you wish.'

'Will you take the radio?'

'No. The risk is too great.'

'What will you do with it?'

'Get rid of it.'

Artus bowed his head. 'It is probably better that way. And what train are you planning to catch?'

'It leaves at seven minutes past five and arrives at El Teirieh at ten minutes past seven.'

'We will be on the train.' He eyed her carefully. 'I hope I am right to trust you, Marlin.'

'Why should I double-cross you?' said Tanja, her voice low and calmer than she felt. 'Why do you do this, Artus? Why do you risk so much? Because you want the British out of Egypt. Why do I? Because I want the Soviet Union to be finished for what it did to my home and family and because I am married to Germany.'

He looked at her quizzically.

'Because, Artus,' she said, 'my husband was German.'

At the bazaar of Khan El Khalili, Cairo seemed to have closed in on itself. The tight, narrow lanes were shaded by the awnings and canopies of the shops and stalls at either side, while people and animals thronged beneath, an ever-shifting crowd of Arabs, Turks, Africans and, of course, servicemen from around the British Empire. Turbaned, bearded men gesticulated and bargained over fine carpets and pieces of jewellery, while donkeys and mules plodded through the crowds, shackled to carts and gharries carrying European women with wide hats and sunglasses, and self-conscious young troops on leave. The smell was exotic too: incense and spices blending with animal dung.

'I always think of this place as being like something out of *Arabian Nights*,' said Lucie, as they wandered along one of the lanes.

'There's a lot of colour, isn't there?' said Sykes.

'The clothes, the spices and carpets and everything. You get used to everything being khaki and now this.'

Tanner paused by a stall that sold elaborate curved daggers. He picked one up and pulled the blade stiffly from its sheath.

'You like, sir?' said the vendor, who had a long beard and a hooked nose.

Tanner glanced at him.

'I give you very good price. Ten piastres.'

Tanner laughed, then noticed Lucie frowning down the narrow street. 'Isn't that Tanja Zanowski?'

Tanner followed her gaze and saw Tanja standing by the edge of the road, looking to either side of her, then walking away from them.

'Yes, it is,' he said. 'Come on, let's catch up.' No sooner had he said this, however, than a man appeared where Tanja had just stood.

'Mustafa,' muttered Tanner. 'My God, that's bloody Eslem Mustafa.'

'He came out of the same shop as Tanja,' said Lucie. 'I saw her.'

Tanner grabbed Lucie's hand. 'Come on,' he said. 'Stan, quick!'

'What's going on, Jack?' Lucie cried, as they hurried along the street, pushing past people as they went.

'I'll explain in a minute.' He could still see them both. Mustafa thirty yards ahead, Tanja perhaps fifty.

'Jack!' cried Lucie. 'Tell me!' They had reached the shop from which Tanja and Mustafa had emerged. Half glancing ahead and half at Sykes and Lucie, Tanner said quickly, 'Luce, sweet-heart, stay here, all right? Don't move an inch. Stan and I have got to go after them.' He held out his hands – *please stay* – then turned to Sykes. 'Stan – come on!'

'Jack!' called Lucie.

'Stay there!' Tanner shouted back, as he pushed on through the mass of people, Sykes right behind him. He could still see them both, but then Tanja turned left.

'Damn!' he muttered. Mustafa was still walking ahead.

'Keep your eye on that bloke with the tarboosh, Stan,' said Tanner, as they reached the lane where Tanja had turned. He could not see her. *Do I follow her? No, Mustafa is more important.* He hurried back, saw Sykes ten yards ahead and Mustafa thirty yards further on. He caught up with Sykes.

'Right, Stan,' he said, 'let's get him.'

They quickened their pace, and still Mustafa had not looked around. A surge of a few yards, and then a cart or the weight of people held them back.

'Come on, come on,' muttered Tanner. 'Get out of my way!'

Ten yards separated them now, and then Mustafa glanced around. Had he seen them? Tanner couldn't tell, but it was unquestionably the man they had been looking for in vain at SIME. The elusive Eslem Mustafa in person, just ten yards ahead. A gap appeared in the throng, and Tanner hurried forward, Sykes beside him – but a gharry drove out of a lane, coming between him and his quarry. Tanner deftly squeezed past but Sykes was momentarily trapped. Tanner glanced back and saw his friend surrounded by children demanding *baksheesh*, but Mustafa was just ahead, still walking calmly. *Five yards now.* A group of Egyptians in his way. Tanner side-stepped, pulled out his pistol, took three quick paces and grabbed Mustafa's shoulder.

Mustafa turned, stared at him, noticed the pistol, and let his shoulders drop. *You've got me.*

'Eslem Mustafa—'

With lightning speed the Egyptian drove his knee hard into Tanner's crotch. Tanner gasped, doubled up in pain, and Mustafa was away, shoving through the crowds. Tanner fell to his knees and then his side, vaguely conscious of footsteps running past him and people closing in around him.

20

He cursed himself. Christ, it was the oldest trick in the book and he'd fallen for it. How could he have been so stupid?

A hand was held out to him. Tanner looked up and saw Sykes grinning at him.

'Ouch!' he said. 'Come on, up you get.'

'I don't know why you're laughing. Bastard got away.'

'I wouldn't be so sure about that,' said Sykes, as Tanner slowly got to his feet.

'What do you mean? Cut out the smart-alec

stuff, Stan.'

'I sent those kids after him. They know these streets better than we ever will. 'E spoke pretty good English, their ring-leader, so I offered him generous terms to tail him.'

Tanner leaned forward, hands on knees. 'Good work, Stan.'

'I gave him twenty piastres there and then, and told him to follow him, and to come to Lucie's flat with details of where he went, but for one of them to keep watching him all the time. I offered him five quid if he did a good job.'

'Good money for a nipper.'

'That's what I thought.' He patted Tanner on the back. 'Fancy you falling for that one.'

'I can't believe it. And it bloody well hurt.' He straightened up, winced, then said, 'Let's get back to Lucie. Poor girl'll be wondering what the hell's going on.'

'Me an' all, Jack.' He took out his cigarettes, offered one to Tanner, then lit both. 'What *is* going on?' he said, exhaling.

'I'll tell you what I can when we reach Lucie. It's big, though. Even bigger now.' He thought of Vaughan and Tanja. 'Jesus,' he said.

She was waiting where they had left her. 'What on earth was all that about?' she said.

'I'm sorry,' said Tanner. 'Really I am.'

'And an explanation?'

'I can't give you much of one, I'm afraid. But I will tell you this. In that week before I returned to the battalion, I was working with Vaughan on an intelligence job. That man is a dangerous anti-British subversive they've been trying to catch for bloody ages. So I had to go after him.'

'Blimey, Jack,' said Sykes.

'You obviously didn't catch him, though.'

'I did,' said Tanner, 'but he kneed me in the bollocks.'

'Sorry, Lucie,' said Sykes, 'but he might not be on best form tonight.'

Lucie smirked. 'Jack, you fool. So what was Tanja doing coming out of this place with him?'

'I'm wondering the same thing.'

'So what now?' asked Lucie.

'I'm afraid Stan and I are going to have to go into this shop, arrest the owner, then take him to Field Security HQ in Garden City. I'm sorry.'

'And Tanja?'

'I don't know, quite. But it doesn't look good.'

'She knew him, Jack,' said Lucie. 'I saw her say something to him as she left.'

Tanner kicked at the ground. 'Damn it all,' he said, then turned to Sykes. 'Come on, Stan. Let's get on with it.'

Tanja had hurried away from Artus and the bazaar. Outside the Mosque el-Azhar, she hired a gharry to take her back to her flat. As she rumbled through the Moski towards Ezbekiyeh, she felt relieved, sensing that Mustafa had believed her. More than that, he seemed to accept her questioning of Orca.

Relieved, but fearful too. Hiding behind her polarized sunglasses, she picked at her fingers. She was a good actress, she knew; she always had been, even as a little girl, when she had discovered it could be useful to hide emotions or to portray a mood quite different from how she was feeling inside. But acting was just that: an act. She had shown a degree of steeliness to Artus that she had not felt inside. God only knew what would happen tomorrow, but if she ever made it to Mersa, how would she control her fear? What if her hands wouldn't stop shaking? Or if she panicked? It had been hard enough here, in a city of millions, but in Mersa, a tiny coastal town seething with the general staff of the Panzer Army Africa, she knew she would have to be on her guard constantly. The mask could never drop, not for one moment. She closed her eyes. *How did I get to this?* She had never wanted any of it. She bit her lip, anger and grief searing her.

And then there was Alex. She had never expected to fall in love again, and yet she had. In a world without war, they could have had a future, but now she was about to leave him. She knew that the course she had taken had been the only one open to her, but she also knew that he would never forgive her. The truth would out, and with it, whatever love he had for her would die. She felt her eyes moisten. *No, you cannot cry.* And yet already she had begun to mourn him, and sadness overwhelmed her, bearing down upon her like a leaden shroud.

She got down from the gharry at Opera Square, but instead of heading straight back to the Polish Red Cross, she made for her flat. She wanted to compose herself before she had to put on yet another act of normality in front of Sophie and the girls.

Five minutes later, she reached the apartment

block, where she was accosted by Mohammed, the *bawaeb*.

'*Sitt* Tanja,' he said, 'there is *askari* to see you. He wait by you door.'

'A soldier?' she said.

'Yes, *Sitt* Tanja.'

Tanja took the stairs and saw Alex. 'Hello,' he said, smiling, and she ran to him, crouched before he could get up, put her arms around him and kissed him. 'I've missed you,' she said. 'Alex, I love you. Whatever happens, I want you to know that.'

He tucked a strand of hair behind her ear. 'I'm rather keen on you too.' A hand on her face, his eyes searching hers. *He's so close to me now*, she thought, *and then he'll be gone*.

He kissed her again. 'Shall we go inside?'

There had been a bit of a scene in the shop. The man had protested his innocence, his wife had spat at Tanner and scratched his face, and then they had emerged, Tanner frogmarching the man, Sykes pointing his revolver at the captive. And all in front of Lucie, too. It was hardly the enjoyable, convivial day she would have imagined.

They had tied the Egyptian's hands behind his back with Tanner's handkerchief, and, back on the main Moski road that led to Ezbekiyeh and Opera Square, Tanner had hailed a taxi.

'I'm so sorry, sweetheart,' he said to Lucie. 'Let me get this bloke to Garden City and I'll come straight back.'

'It's all right, Jack,' she said, her arms folded across her chest.

'Stan – look after Lucie, all right?'

'Can't I take this joker to Field Security?' he said.

'No – I know them. I won't be long. Where shall I find you?'

'At Chanti's, in Ezbekiyeh Gardens,' said Lucie.

Tanner shoved the Egyptian through the open door of the car, then followed, sitting beside him in the back seat.

'Tolombat Street,' he said to the driver, who glanced at him anxiously. 'Garden City.' He put his pistol away. What could the man do, after all? He was unarmed, and Tanner was twice his size. The shopkeeper began talking animatedly to the driver in Arabic, who turned, gesticulating wildly.

'Shut up, the pair of you,' said Tanner, then added to the shopkeeper, 'You've already ruined my day. Don't make it worse.'

They quietened down, the shopkeeper burying his head in his hands and sobbing. The man was frightened – of course he was – but for the moment he had nothing to fear. SIME's interrogation techniques were soft: a prisoner was offered tea, cigarettes, then given a bath or shower and a hot meal. Having been terrified, expecting torture, he was disarmed, and usually easily persuaded as to the reasonableness of the British.

But it was not this man that Tanner was worried about. It was Vaughan. *Jesus, what a bloody mess.* How was Vaughan going to take it? He knew how smitten his friend was. And just before this operation on Tobruk too. *Ah, damn it all to hell.* If only Lucie hadn't seen her. If only *he* hadn't seen her. But he had, and he had to tell SIME, no

413

matter how much he valued Vaughan as a friend. *Perhaps it was nothing.* But, no, that was wishful thinking. He knew what he'd seen.

Despite the heavy traffic on the roads, it did not take long to reach Red Pillars. Pulling the Egyptian out of the taxi, and pushing him up the steps, Tanner was greeted cheerily by Abdu, then took the lift to the third floor. To his relief, Sansom was there.

'Jack,' said Sansom, 'this is a surprise, and you come bearing gifts too.'

'Don't take this the wrong way, but I'd like to be out of here as quickly as possible. I'm supposed to be on twenty-four hours' leave.' He gripped the Egyptian's shoulders. 'This man is a shopkeeper in Khan El Khalili and has been allowing meetings between Eslem Mustafa and a Polish girl called Tanja Zanowski.'

Sansom frowned. 'I see.' He called over one of his men. 'Mackenzie, take this man to the interrogation centre and wait there with him.'

'Yes, sir.'

'Jack,' continued Sansom, 'come into my office a moment, will you?'

They went in and Tanner took a chair. Sansom sat at his desk, lit one of his fat Turkish cigarettes, and said, 'Tell me all.'

Tanner did so, although he skirted around what had happened to Mustafa. 'I lost him, unfortunately.' He couldn't bring himself to admit that he'd been kneed in the groin.

'Have you told RJ?'

'No, I came straight here.'

'We should go downstairs,' said Sansom, 'see if

414

he's there.'

'It gets worse,' said Tanner. 'Do you know who Tanja Zanowski is?'

'No. Who?'

'Alex Vaughan's girlfriend.'

'Oh, Christ,' said Sansom, his brow creased. 'We definitely need to find RJ. Do you know where the girl lives?'

'No, but she works at the Polish Red Cross.'

Sansom pressed the intercom on his desk. 'Bones,' he said, 'I'll explain everything in a minute, but can you get a section on standby to carry out an immediate house raid, and can you find out the address of Miss Tanja Zanowski, a Pole who works for the Polish Red Cross?' A pause. 'Good man. Just heading downstairs. Back shortly.' He looked up at Tanner. 'Right,' he said. 'Let's go and find RJ.'

But Maunsell was out, not due back until later that afternoon. Of the 'deputies' only Kirk was in.

'We should act right away, sir,' Sansom told him. 'I've got Astley getting an address for Miss Zanowski. I suggest we carry out an immediate search of her flat and pull her in as soon as possible.'

'I agree,' said Kirk. 'I'll try and get a call through to RJ.'

Sansom cleared his throat. 'There is a complication, though, sir.'

'Oh, yes?'

'Miss Zanowski is Vaughan's girlfriend.'

'Bugger.' Kirk put his hands together and tapped his mouth. 'Where is Alex? Do we know?'

'He's due back in Cairo today,' said Tanner.

415

'He's been in Alexandria.'

'The bloody idiot,' said Kirk. 'How long's this been going on? Is he our mole?'

'No,' said Tanner, a touch of anger in his voice. 'That's out of the question. They've only been together a month. I was with him when they first met. It was at Shepheard's.'

'All right, but this isn't going to look good for Alex. If she's part of Cobra and he's been bloody sleeping with her, he's allowed himself to be horribly compromised.' He sat back and rubbed his forehead. 'All right, Sammy. Get someone round to his flat. We're going to have to pull him in as well.'

'Hold on, George,' said Tanner. 'You can't think Alex would have told her anything? I've never met a more honourable man.'

'That's as may be, Jack, but if he's been sleeping with a spy, we're going to have to question him.'

'But we're due to head out on operations tomorrow,' said Tanner.

'That might be out of the question now. If Tanja Zanowski is who we think she is, Alex Vaughan won't be going anywhere.'

'Don't be ridiculous!' said Tanner, his temper rising.

'Jack – calm down. You can't sleep with a traitor and assume it never happened. Now, thank you for all you've done, but let us deal with this from now on, all right?'

Tanner put his hands to his face. 'God damn it!' he said.

'Jack,' said Kirk, 'this is not helping.'

'Come on, Jack,' said Sansom. 'He's right. We

all like Alex, and we all wish it could be otherwise.'

'If Vaughan's good name is dragged through the
mud,' snarled Tanner, 'I'll—'

'You'll what, Jack?' said Kirk.

'Just show him some bloody respect.' He left
them.

Vaughan was lying on the bed with Tanja en-
folded in his arms, a hand stroking her head,
thinking he would gladly stay there for ever when
there was loud, urgent knocking on the door.

'Open up!' an English voice shouted.

'What the devil?' said Vaughan. He felt Tanja
physically recoil.

'My God,' she said.

More knocking. 'Open up, I say!'

'All right, all right!' Vaughan shouted, putting
on his underwear. He glanced at Tanja, saw the
fear in her eyes. 'It's all right, darling.' He hurried
to the bathroom and handed her her dressing-
gown. 'Better get this on. Just in case.' He smiled,
hoping to reassure her.

More banging on the door. 'I'm coming!'
Vaughan shouted.

As he opened the door, Sansom brushed past
him, followed by one of his Field Security
sections, all armed with pistols and Tommy guns.

'Sammy?' said Vaughan. 'What the bloody hell's
going on? What d'you think you're doing, man?'

'I'm sorry, Alex,' he said, and pushed past.
Already the men were spreading through the flat.

Vaughan grabbed Sansom's shoulder. 'Sammy!'
he said. 'How bloody dare you? Explain what the

hell you think you're doing!'

Sansom shot him a glance. *Pity? Contempt?* Vaughan couldn't tell. Then he marched into the bedroom. Tanya was compressed against the back wall as though she had physically shrunk.

'Tanja Zanowski?' said Sansom.

Tanja nodded.

'Tanja Zanowski,' he said, 'I am arresting you on suspicion of espionage.'

Vaughan looked at Tanja, saw her pleading eyes and, in that moment, the terrible, unthinkable truth.

'You do not have to say anything,' Sansom continued, 'but it may harm your defence if you do not mention when questioned something which you later rely on in court. Anything you do say may be given in evidence.'

'No,' said Vaughan, quietly. 'No.' For a moment he stood there, dumbfounded. It wasn't possible – it couldn't be. Men were moving about the flat. The wardrobe was opened, a case brought out and shoved on to the bed. One of the men said, 'Sir!' and took out a small aluminium transmitter.

'Good work,' said Sansom. 'Put it back in the case and take it out.'

He turned to Tanja. 'Better get some clothes on.'

'Can I go into the bathroom?' she asked, her voice quiet.

'No. Get dressed here, please.'

She glanced at Vaughan – *help me* – but he could not bear to look at her. He turned away, hardly able to take in what was happening. *Why?* And then he remembered the conversation at the Union. *Of course* – her hatred of the Soviets. What a fool he had been! What a bloody stupid fool! An FS man brushed past him but he barely noticed. The world around him seemed to have become silent, as though he was now merely an observer in something too terrible to comprehend. *The mission*, he thought. *What about the mission?* And he wondered what would happen to him, and the disgrace that surely awaited him. He leaned against a wall and closed his eyes. Minutes earlier, he had thought himself in love, happier than he had ever been. How could he have been so cruelly betrayed? Tanja passed him now and touched his arm.

'Sorry,' she said quietly. 'I'm sorry, Alex.'

Vaughan recoiled.

Tuesday, 8 September, a little after seven a.m. Tanner drove Vaughan's jeep back through the curving, shaded streets of Garden City. There were a few other vehicles on the road, General Staff men and women heading to work, but it was as quiet and sedate as ever. Tanner had always been struck by the marked contrast between this area and the rest of the city. Here, it really was a little corner of Britain: calm, ordered and tidy.

His head throbbed, which he knew was entirely his fault – he had drunk far too much the previous evening – or, rather, the previous afternoon. He had found Lucie and Sykes easily enough, but had still been in a foul mood when he reached them. Angry about Vaughan, he was also resentful that what had promised to be a relaxing and enjoyable

419

day, not just for him but for Sykes and particularly Lucie, had been first interrupted and then tarnished. He had been determined the rest of the day should not be ruined and had, he now recognized, over-compensated. A late lunch at Chanti's had continued into the evening, and by that stage none of them cared a damn about errant Egyptian subversives, least of all Tanner. From Chanti's they had gone on to Madame Badia's, so that when they had finally reached Lucie's flat some short while after curfew, all they could do was collapse into bed or, in Sykes's case, on to Lucie's sofa.

There had been a note waiting for him, however, which he had drunkenly read and had vaguely remembered when Lucie woke to get ready for work at five thirty that morning.

'How's the head?' she had asked him.

'Painful,' Tanner had replied. 'How about you?'

'I've felt better but I don't think I drank as much as you and Stan.' Soon after, she had gone – another farewell – having passed Vaughan's note to Tanner. After he had dunked his head in cold water and swallowed a couple of Alka-Seltzer tablets, fizzing in water, he had reread the handwritten note.

7.9.42

Dear Jack,
Apologies for missing our rendezvous this evening, and now you're not here. No matter. I have a few things to attend to tomorrow, so I will meet you and Sykes in Alex. Take my jeep. It's at GHQ, and should still have plenty of fuel. Ask for MO4 and someone will give you the key and show you where it is. When

you reach Alex, go to the Naval Dockyard and ask for the 15th MTB Flotilla and Lt-Com Jim Allenby. I'll be there by evening.
Yours,
Alex Vaughan

Tanner had read it twice. No mention of Tanja, or of being questioned, or any suggestion that his part in C Detachment had come to a premature end. That was good, Tanner thought. But strange. And at GHQ, there had been no hint that anything was amiss. At MO4, they had been expecting him, the key to the jeep handed over without any fuss.

'Have you seen Major Vaughan this morning?' Tanner asked the young subaltern who took him to the jeep.

'He was in briefly, but he left about—' a glance at his watch '—about a quarter of an hour ago.'

'And he seemed all right, did he?'

'Yes,' said the lieutenant. 'Why do you ask?'

'Oh, nothing.' *Curious.*

Reaching Lucie's apartment block, Tanner jumped out, kites circling high overhead, and went up to the flat, where he found Sykes up, shaved and dressed, his hair freshly oiled and combed, with company: a young boy of perhaps ten or twelve years old.

'This is Hanif,' said Sykes. 'We've been waiting for you. Hanif is the lad I paid yesterday to tail that Mustafa bloke when you got kneed by him in the nuts.'

'All right, Stan, don't rub it in.'

'And I don't know whether you remember this,

Jack, but we decided even before we left Chanti's that there wasn't a chance in hell that Hanif and his mates would ever be seen again and that I'd lost twenty piastres and that was that.'

'I do as you say,' chirped Hanif now. 'I come here yesterday once in the afternoon and then in evening, but you not here, Captain sir.'

'It's lieutenant, Hanif,' said Tanner.

'And then curfew,' continued Hanif, 'so I come this morning. We go now. *Yallah! Yallah!*'

'Just hold your horses a moment,' said Tanner. 'I need an explanation here.'

'They know where this Mustafa joker is but they think he's moving soon,' said Sykes. 'He's with two other blokes and one of them went to the railway station yesterday afternoon and bought tickets for the Alex train, not the express, though, the stopping one.'

'So he leave any moment, Lieutenant sir,' added Hanif.

'All right, then,' said Tanner. '*Yallah*, Hanif.'

'What about our clobber?' asked Sykes.

'Leave it here for the moment.' He picked up his MP40, a few magazines and spare rounds, which he put in his gas-mask case and slung over his shoulder. 'Right,' he said. 'Let's go.'

'I'm sniffing trouble,' said Sykes, grabbing his Thompson. 'Do you really think we should just go straight to where this bloke's hiding?'

'Don't you?' said Tanner.

'No, I don't. We should go to your mates in Field Security and hand it over to them.'

Tanner paused, then asked. 'Hanif, where is Mustafa?'

'Near the El Mouayad Mosque.'

'That's east of here,' said Tanner, 'and the Field Security offices are to the south. I thought we were in a hurry. We can be there in ten minutes or so. By the time we get to Sansom and he gets a section together it could be another hour.' He opened the door to the flat, and waved Hanif and Sykes on to the dark landing.

'I just don't see that it's our problem, Jack,' said Sykes, as they hurried down the stairs. 'Haven't we got other things to think about today? Such as making sure we get to Alex in one piece?'

They stepped outside into the bright morning air, and Tanner felt his head throb once more. 'Get in,' he said to Hanif, who skipped into the narrow rear seat of the jeep, his face lit with delight.

As Tanner started the engine and pulled away, he was conscious that Sykes had not said another word. 'Look,' said Tanner, 'if they're still there, we'll stake it out and one of us can go and get the FS lads, or we can send Hanif here. How about that?'

'You're the boss,' said Sykes. 'At least we won't be conspicuous, driving round the Islamic city in a jeep.'

'No more conspicuous than the FS boys.'

'Maybe, but it's their job, isn't it?'

'Listen, Stan, I thought time was of the essence here. I spent a week trying to catch Mustafa, and Vaughan and the boys at SIME have been after him for weeks. He's important – a big fish. If we go via Red Pillars, valuable time really will be lost.'

'Fine,' said Sykes, 'as long as it's got nothing to

do with you trying to get one over on a bloke who got the better of you yesterday.'

Tanner said nothing. *We don't have time to get Field Security involved*, he told himself, but Sykes's comment rankled. Perhaps he did want to catch Mustafa himself, but time was forcing his hand, not bloody-mindedness.

They reached the enormous gateway of Bab Zuweila at the south-eastern corner of the mosque. 'Drive through the gate, Lieutenant sir,' said Hanif, squatting on his haunches between the two front seats.

Tanner did so, the sound of the engine reverberating loudly through the huge stone archway. The towers and minarets built above the stone arches loomed high into the cloudless sky.

'Nearly there,' said Hanif. They drove on another hundred yards or so and then, as they pulled into a small square, Hanif asked them to stop.

Tanner parked beside an Egyptian policeman. 'Here,' he said, handing him a five-piastre coin, 'keep an eye on this, will you?'

The policeman took the coin and positioned himself on the bonnet.

'Follow me, sirs,' said Hanif, nimbly climbing out of the jeep. Traffic and people thronged the street, but almost immediately he led them left down a dark, narrow side-street, and then, thirty yards further on, down another lane to the right. The buildings seemed to close around them, casting the alley in shadow. A shrouded woman watched them from a doorway, as a cat skulked past. Refuse and excrement lay in the gutters that ran either side. Forty yards ahead, a lone car – an old Austin – stood parked in the street.

Hanif stopped and gave a low whistle. Immediately, a head appeared over the top of the building beside them, grinned, then disappeared.

'He come down,' said Hanif.

'Where are they, then?' whispered Sykes.

'In that building by the car, sir,' said Hanif.

Hanif's friend popped out of an alleyway across the street and scurried over to them. He began jabbering at Hanif.

'Ahmed say they moving about the house. *Arba'a* men.' He held up three fingers.

Ahmed was talking again. Hanif translated, 'Another man come this morning in car. An *afrangi*.'

'A white man?' said Tanner. 'A European?'

'Yes, Lieutenant sir.'

Tanner's mind raced. *The mole?* 'Is he still there?'

'No, Lieutenant sir. He go. Ahmed think they ready to leave soon.'

Sykes turned to Tanner. 'So what now, boss?'

Tanner thought a moment. 'Can we get up on that roof too?' he asked Hanif.

'Yes, Lieutenant sir,' he said.

'Good. Stan, you go up and give me cover, and then I'll go to the house and arrest the bastards.'

'Just like that?'

'Unless you've got a better plan?'

Sykes shook his head. 'All right – but if you get yourself shot, don't blame me.'

'I won't, Stan, I promise.' He patted Sykes on the shoulder and watched him hurry across the road with Ahmed.

Suddenly, there was movement ahead.

'Lieutenant sir!' hissed Hanif, his eyes wide.

425

'They coming!'

Tanner cursed. A man emerged from the building, walking around the car to the driver's side, then Mustafa, his red tarboosh still firmly on his head, but his face now clean shaven. Glancing down the street, he immediately saw Tanner standing in a doorway and shouted some urgent commands.

'Damn it!' muttered Tanner. *What to do?* He looked up, but there was still no sign of Sykes. Ahead, the car engine turned over, fired, and now a third and fourth man were hurrying from the house. Tanner cursed again, then ran forward, cocking his Schmeisser.

'Stop!' he shouted. 'Stop there!' He heard the driver put the car into gear, and then a submachine gun was pointing from the window, bullets spitting wildly around him, zinging as they ricocheted off the stone, and Tanner was diving on to the ground. When he looked up again, the car was speeding away.

'Stan!' he shouted. 'Get back down here quick!' Then he turned and saw Hanif cowering in a doorway. 'You all right?' he asked.

'Yes, Lieutenant sir, but I need extra cash for being shot at.'

In spite of himself, Tanner laughed. 'All right – and I'll give you another ten piastres if you can get us to the railway station in time.'

'Yes, Lieutenant sir,' said Hanif. 'No problem. The bad men have very narrow roads to get through first.'

'Stan!' shouted Tanner again.

'All right, all right!' Sykes appeared, breathless,

426

on the road.

Tanner started running back towards the jeep, Hanif, Ahmed and Sykes following. At the end of the road, several men had gathered, peering down it anxiously, alarmed by the gunfire. Tanner ignored them and ran on, back to the main road and to the little square where he was relieved to see the policeman still guarding the jeep.

'Cheers, mate,' he said, hoisting himself into the driver's seat, as Hanif and Ahmed scrambled in behind him.

'I knew this was going to be a bloody cock-up,' said Sykes.

'Stop grumbling, Stan,' said Tanner, as the jeep roared into life.

'*Dughri*, Lieutenant sir,' said Hanif. *Straight on.*

'You could have got Hanif killed,' said Sykes.

'Give over, Stan,' said Tanner, gunning the throttle and forcing pedestrians to hurry out of their way. 'Anyway, if we'd gone to get the FS boys as you suggested, we'd have missed them altogether.'

A loaded cart held them up but Tanner yelled and revved the engine, then raced past and soon they were turning left on to the wider Sikket El Gedida, accelerating towards Ezbekiyeh Gardens.

'Keep your eyes peeled!' Tanner called.

Heavy traffic clogged the road, and Hanif said, '*Ruh alyeminak*, Lieutenant sir!' urgently pointing to the right.

Tanner took the turning, narrowly avoiding an oncoming bus, and immediately found himself in the calmer back-streets of the Rosetti Quarter. He drove past elegant French-built town houses,

427

lush gardens, then into a square and eventually into a narrow winding lane, which ended in a marketplace. They were briefly held up by a number of camels and a raging argument between the drivers of two carts, but Tanner nudged one of the carts, which stopped the argument dead. The anxious-looking driver skittered out of the way. At last they were turning on to Sharia Clot Bey, which led them straight to the central station.

'Where the hell are they?' muttered Tanner.

'There, Lieutenant sir!' shouted Hanif.

Tanner strained his eyes and saw, before it disappeared behind a passing tram, the Austin.

'Good work, Hanif!' said Sykes.

'More *baksheesh*, sir?' Hanif asked.

'If we get 'em, yes, mate.'

'I thought you weren't interested,' said Tanner.

'Well, there's no point in chasing something if you never get a chance to catch it, is there?'

Tanner speeded up again, weaving through the traffic and slowly gaining on the Austin, which was now about a hundred yards ahead.

'What happens when we catch up with them?' said Sykes.

'I don't know, Stan,' said Tanner. 'We jump out and nobble them. We'll think of something.'

'Here,' said Sykes, handing some notes to the boys. 'Thanks – you've been really helpful, lads.'

'*Tank* you, sir!' Hanif grinned.

'I gave 'em five quid,' said Sykes. 'That's good money for urchins like them.'

As they neared Midan Bab El Hadid, the large interchange outside the railway terminus, they saw the Austin just ahead, but as two trams converged, it sped forward, narrowly passing between them, and was then immediately blocked from view.

'Bollocks!' shouted Tanner, but then the trams moved off and they saw the Austin again, this time pulling over between the gharries and taxis at the front of the station. Three of the men got out and hurried towards the station entrance. Tanner pulled over behind a taxi and leaped out with Sykes.

'Boys, stay here,' said Tanner, and held up another coin as Mustafa's red tarboosh disappeared from view. Then, with Sykes in tow, he ran.

They entered the station concourse, Tanner scanning the mass of people and platforms. Plenty of khaki, plenty of turbans, but too many tarbooshes. An announcement was broadcast in Arabic, then in English, the voice crackling and reverberating around the concourse. 'The eight thirty-five stopping service to Alexandria is about to depart.'

Frantically, Tanner glanced at the platform numbers, then spotted an arrow towards Platform 1. At the same moment, he saw Mustafa hurrying across the far end of the concourse, out of the main atrium.

'There!' he cried, and was already running, but a train had just arrived on Platform 4 and hordes of people were rushing towards the concourse and blocking their way.

'Please!' called Tanner. 'Out of my way!' He and Sykes forced their way through, then tore across the rest of the concourse and back out of the main station hallway to an outside platform. Even before they reached it, Tanner could hear the great puffs as the engine began to move out. Amid clouds of steam, the last of the five carriages was slowly clacking past him.

'Bugger it!' said Sykes.

'I can make a dash for it!' said Tanner, sprinting forward. He was gaining on it, and reached out his hand towards the rear carriage but the train was gathering speed and stretching away from him. Tanner gave up, gasping, his hands on his knees. He glanced up, and saw Eslem Mustafa wave at him from an open carriage window.

'Damn him!'

'Listen, mate,' said Sykes, coming towards him, 'we gave it our best shot.'

'That's the second time he's got away from me,' growled Tanner. 'I swear the bastard's not going to do it again.'

21

Tanner brushed past Sykes. 'Come on,' he said, 'we need to get a move on.'

'Why?' said Sykes. 'We haven't got to be in Alexandria until this evening.'

'Because we're going after that train, that's why.'

'What?' said Sykes. 'Tell me you're joking.'

'I've seen it before. It's bloody slow *and* it's a stopping train. If we're a bit jaldi about it, then I reckon we'll soon catch it up.' He was running again, back through the concourse. Passing a bookstand he picked up a folded timetable, left a one-piastre coin on the counter, and gave it to Sykes. 'Here,' he said. 'Look through this while I drive us back to the flat.'

The boys were still beside the jeep.

'You no get the bad men, Lieutenant sir?' asked Hanif, jumping down.

'Not yet,' said Tanner, passing him another five piastres, 'but we will.' He started the engine. '*Shukran*, boys,' he said. With Sykes beside him, he put the vehicle into gear and sped away.

He drove straight down the Sharia Abbas, the widest thoroughfare in central Cairo, past the Egyptian Museum and Kasr El Nil Barracks, and around Midan Ismailia. In five minutes flat they had reached Lucie's apartment. Three minutes to collect their kit and then they were on their way, back up Sharia Abbas, over the Bulaq Bridge alongside the railway, and speeding through Embabah, a town on the far side of the river and the first of the train's stops.

Logic suggested Mustafa would not have alighted there. 'He's got to be heading some distance,' said Sykes, the open timetable flapping in the wind, 'otherwise why get on the train in the first place?'

'I agree,' said Tanner, 'but let's think about this. He can't be going all the way to Alexandria either, or he'd have got on an express.'

'There's a map of the rail network here,' said Sykes. 'It looks like it joins the main line again at a place called Tel El Baroud.'

'Where in God's name is that?'

'Give me a moment,' said Sykes, as he made a rough measurement. 'I'd say about seventy miles south-east of Alex. The last stop before it joins the main line is a place called Waked.'

'Then somewhere between here and Waked,' said Tanner.

They reckoned they were twenty minutes behind when they left Lucie's flat, but the journey to Alexandria took nearly seven hours, which meant the train was travelling at an average of less than thirty miles per hour. The jeep could do forty-five at a push, but thirty-five comfortably, even on the rough desert roads – barely more than tracks in the sand – that ran alongside the railway line. The train's second stop was at Station Aoussin, but the third was at El Manachi, some twenty-two miles north-west of Cairo.

'It's due to get into El Manachi at nine seventeen,' said Sykes, 'and if we keep this speed up, we'll be there about the same time. It'll be nip and tuck, Jack.'

'But even if we don't get there quite on time, those lads won't be going anywhere without us being able to see them. There's not much around, after all.'

It was true. The railway line ran almost exactly along the edge of the Nile Valley. On their left the desert stretched endlessly away from them, while on the right the palm-lined river wended its way towards the coast. They passed a few mud-hut villages, the occasional flat-roofed white house, and once in a while saw children playing, or men and women working in the fields.

When they reached El Manachi, at just after twenty past nine, there was no sign of the train, but past a dense grove of date palms they saw it, steam and soot puffing from the funnel, the five carriages trundling along the line.

'How much further to the next stop, Stan?' asked Tanner. 'Another twenty miles. It's due in at nine fifty-nine.'

'Good,' said Tanner, making sure he held back. The jeep was kicking up a fair amount of dust and he didn't want anyone on the train to see them.

He yawned and blinked.

'You all right?' said Sykes.

'Fine. My hangover's gone at last.'

'Mine too.'

'I do feel a bit done in, though, after all that racing around this morning. And I'd forgotten how tiring driving is. You're constantly fighting the steering out on these tracks, and there's the endless gear-changing and double-declutching.'

'Where's Browner when you need him?'

'Firing a bloody six-pounder. We should have brought him with us. Anyway, you're going to have to take the wheel soon.'

'You're going to jump on the train, are you?'

'Yes. It's the only way I can think of that we're ever going to take him alive. If we wait until they get off we're only going to end up shooting at each other.'

'We could kill the others and hit him in the leg.'

Tanner screwed up his face, weighing the options. 'Maybe, but the beauty of having a crack at them on the train is that we're all in a confined space. There's no easy escape.'

'But it'll be three against one.'

'They've only got pistols and knives at the most, though,' said Tanner. He tapped his Schmeisser and grinned. 'It'll be fine.'

The railway left the green Nile Valley and cut through a low escarpment into the desert. Tanner continued to keep his distance but then, just before ten o'clock, the train began to slow.

'We must be there,' he said. Ahead he saw a single stone building. 'Look,' he said, 'the stop's on the right. People will be getting off that side.'

He slowed with the train and stopped as the train stopped, some fifty yards behind, still on the left-hand side of the track.

'All right, I'm off,' he said, grabbing his MP40 and jumping out of the jeep.

'Good luck, mate,' said Sykes, moving into his seat.

Tanner ran forward. The line was elevated several feet above the road. Keeping it on his right, he saw several people getting off and on. There was a door at the rear of the last carriage. An open carriage, he thought. *Good – third class.* Mustafa was urbane, educated, a former officer in the Egyptian Air Force. Not a man who would readily sit in third class with the peasants. Class snobbery was even greater in places like Egypt and India than it was in England. Mustafa would not be in that carriage. *Unless.*

Steam blew from the train and wafted slowly down its length. Tanner climbed on to the line, ran along the last ten yards of track, and at the rear of the train, he stopped to peer underneath. A few pairs of feet, but none that belonged to the men he was after. Getting on to the train, he realized, was going to be potentially the riskiest thing he had to do, because at some point he would have to open a door blind. If he *had* been spotted, there was a chance Mustafa and his men were waiting – and then he would be a dead man. He had intended to open the rear door and hope for the best, but now he changed his mind. Others getting on to the train could provide useful cover. Walking around the side of the carriage, he waited until two men were mounting the steps on to the train, then scurried low along the carriage towards the steam-gushing locomotive. He was pleased to note the guard looking the other way. With his pistol cocked in his trouser pocket, Tanner quickly jumped up behind the two elderly men. One looked at him strangely– *Where did you come from?* Then he saw the sub-machine gun and shuffled into the carriage.

It was, as he had guessed, open plan, wooden benches in rows. Worried Egyptians stared at him, several clasping boxes of chickens. At the far end, a young girl clutched a goat, which now bleated pitifully. The train chuffed, the carriage lurched forward, and steam billowed past the open window so that Tanner got a waft of soot. A shrill whistle blast, and slowly the train moved off, the carriage clacking as it rolled along the rickety track. Beside him, a door led into the next carriage. Would the men be in there? He had been cavalier in the jeep, almost looking forward to getting his own back on Mustafa. Now, however, with a quickening heart and uncertainty gripping him, his clammy hand on his pistol, he

435

closed his eyes briefly, counted to three, then opened the door into the next carriage.

Third class again. Quick eyes scanned its length. He was looking for suited men, but there were no suits here. Slowly, calmly, he walked down the middle, eyes watching the door ahead. A young child looked up at him, eyes wide. Tanner winked, and strode on steadily towards the door at the end.

He reached it, carefully turned the handle, opened the door and passed over the swaying plate that linked the carriages. Ahead of him there was the wall of a compartment, the corridor running to the left. Tanner stepped forward, saw a man directly in front of him by the window. When he turned, Tanner recognized him immediately – he was one of Mustafa's men. The man gave himself away with the shock that registered on his face. He reached for the inside pocket of his jacket, but Tanner was too quick for him. At lightning speed he swung a short, sharp, powerful jab to the man's right temple. He crumpled to the floor. *One down.*

He stepped backwards as the door of the first compartment opened. *Mustafa?* He would be armed, of course, but the door was now open, which gave Tanner an idea. With his pistol in his hand, he looped his arms under the unconscious man, and quickly stepped towards the still open door. He saw Mustafa, saw the look of alarm and the pistol raised and fired. *Too quick* – the aim was wild.

Tanner ducked behind the man's back, heard the bullet hit something, then kicked the door wide and shoved the unconscious man as hard as he could at Mustafa, who fell backwards. Tanner crashed in, saw Mustafa try to aim again but this time the shot hit the ceiling. Now Tanner was on top of both men on the floor, Mustafa gasping as the wind was knocked from his lungs. Tanner grabbed his wrist, beating his hand against the floor so that he cried out in pain and dropped the pistol. Tanner now put one hand around Mustafa's neck and firmly squeezed, while with the other, he rolled the unconscious man clear. Mustafa was choking, flailing with his right hand trying to reach something. *A knife, a pistol?*

Tanner got to his feet, his grip on Mustafa's neck never loosening, and pulled the Egyptian up with him, then drove his knee hard into his groin. Mustafa doubled up in pain, collapsing on the seat as Tanner whipped out his pistol and pressed it to the Egyptian's kidney. He was about to feel Mustafa's pockets when he heard a noise behind him. The third man stepped into the doorway. His eyes went to the prostrate Mustafa. Tanner moved his pistol arm clear and fired a fraction earlier than the man in the doorway, whose shot thumped into the plush seating as he fell dead into the corridor.

But it was now Tanner's turn to lose his pistol. In that moment, Mustafa struck out, smashing Tanner's right arm into the window so that he dropped the Sauer and staggered backwards. Mustafa leaped at him, his hands clenching round Tanner's neck, long nails digging into the skin. Tanner gurgled, starved of air. He was shocked, too, by how strong Mustafa's grip was. He swung his right arm but missed. Mustafa's grip tightened, thumbs pressing hard against Tanner's voicebox. A moment of panic. *No – no panic*, he told himself. *Think*. To release the grip he just needed to loosen one arm, so he now used both his arms on Mustafa's weaker left. His vision was blurring but, summoning his last remaining strength, he yanked down hard, and suddenly felt the Egyptian's hands slacken. Tanner gasped, rammed his forehead into Mustafa's nose and, at the same time, raised his right leg and kicked hard, sending his opponent staggering backwards against the door. He coughed as Mustafa recovered his balance, producing a knife from his pocket that, with a flick of a catch, sprang open to reveal a thin, pointed, gleaming blade.

For a moment, Mustafa stood there, crouched, eyes wild. Tanner could see his pistol on the floor beside him. Did he have enough time to grab it and fire? He couldn't be sure. Mustafa took a step towards him, while Tanner, still struggling to breathe, watched him carefully. He reckoned he was taller than Mustafa by several inches – several inches that could be a crucial advantage. He stepped towards Mustafa so that they were now just a few feet apart. A feint – that was what he needed. Quickly, he moved forward a further inch, dipping his left shoulder as he did so and, as he'd hoped, Mustafa lunged, the blade flashing towards his neck, but Tanner flicked his head and shoulders to his left and drove a short, sharp right hook into his opponent's jaw. Mustafa staggered backwards again, out into the corridor, but recovering his balance saw, as Tanner did, that the dead man's pistol was lying within easy reach.

Tanner cursed – his own was now behind him, and in a race to grab their pieces, he would lose.

A split-second decision. Tanner hurled himself at Mustafa, who had grabbed the pistol. A third shot fired harmlessly into the carriage ceiling. Tanner smashed Mustafa's hand again, the pistol dropped a second time, but Mustafa's other hand was on Tanner's face, yanking his head backwards and then punching him in the side. Pain coursed through him, as Mustafa rolled him over and again closed his hands around his neck. Tanner was vaguely conscious of someone shouting at the far end of the corridor, but his vision was blurring, his strength deserting him. Desperately, he fought to get his own hands around Mustafa's neck, but it was no good.

One last chance, he thought, as Mustafa's grimacing face closed to just inches from his own. *One, two, three.* He let his body relax, and felt Mustafa's grip loosen just a fraction. With all the strength he could summon, he jerked his head up, his forehead crashing into Mustafa's nose. The Egyptian cried out, put his hands to his face, and Tanner pushed himself backwards, trying to get clear. But Mustafa lunged at him again, blood streaming across his face. *No*, thought Tanner, *I haven't the strength*, but suddenly Mustafa's head jerked forward, his eyes closed and his body went limp, dropping bloodily on to Tanner's chest.

Tanner gasped. The same lady he had seen just a day before in the bazaar at Khan El Khalili was standing over him, holding a pistol. He had thought she was still in the custody of Secret Intelligence Middle East. Tanja Zanowski.

22

Around fifty miles away as the crow flies, Alex Vaughan sat in a Lockheed Hudson as it thundered down the runway at Heliopolis. The aircraft had been designed as a twin-engine medium bomber but when they had been allocated to 216 Transport Squadron a couple of months earlier, they had been hastily converted. While they were definitely an improvement on the ageing Bristol Bombays, they were hardly a relaxing or comfortable mode of transport.

Not that Vaughan cared. As the Hudson left the ground and rapidly climbed, he looked out of the window at the vast burnished desert. As the plane banked, he saw the verdant Nile Valley and the spread of Cairo, sun-baked and creamy in the mid-morning haze, but with patches of green marking the city's many gardens. Down there, Tanja was locked in the cells of the interrogation centre at Kasr El Nil Barracks.

The war had revealed many horrors. He had seen many people bloodied, burned and mutilated; he had killed and nearly been killed; he had lost friends in the carnage. He had witnessed the destructiveness of modern war, and the terrible suffering of the civilian population caught up in it. Yet no matter how shocking some of those images had been, nothing had prepared him for the gut-wrenching, heartbreaking humiliation and loss of the previous afternoon. To be in the arms of the woman he loved, and then to be so starkly betrayed, had hurt him as much as any bayonet twisted into his guts. And the betrayal had been so public – Sammy Sansom, for God's sake, with an FS section Vaughan knew as well as any under Sansom's command. Caught with his trousers down. Caught with a spy! *A spy! Tanya was a fucking spy!* He closed his eyes again and banged his head against the Perspex window.

At least he had not had to sit with her on the way to the interrogation centre. At least he had not been arrested. They'd spared him that. Lieutenant Knightly had not said a word as they'd driven to Kasr El Nil. A brief glimpse of Tanja being ushered out of the car and that had been it – his last sight of her. He hoped he would never see her again.

He had been interrogated by Sammy Sansom and George Kirk – all very friendly, a cup of tea and a fag. Nothing too formal – a bit of casual questioning. Sansom had apologized repeatedly. 'I know this must be difficult, Alex,' and 'Believe me, I wish it could be otherwise.' *Yes, well, believe me, so do I.* He had known that co-operation was the only way, but it had been hard recounting conversations, telling them of her views on Stalin and Soviet Russia, when his heart was breaking.

Kirk and Sansom had been called away and had returned, looking slightly shaken, to tell him he was free to go.

'Is that it?' Vaughan had asked. 'Am I going to be court-martialled?'

'No, you're not,' said Kirk. 'Go home. Get a drink.'

He'd done just that. Half an hour later, when he was on his second Scotch, there had been a knock on the door. When he had opened it Maunsell had been standing outside.

RJ had apologized. It should never have happened – if only he had been in the office at the time, he would have ensured that the flat had been properly watched first and that Vaughan had been nowhere near.

'But I've been sleeping with a spy,' said Vaughan, a renewed stab of despair surging through him.

'Did you ever tell her anything?'

'No, of course not. I didn't even tell her what my job was. Nor did she ever push the point.'

'And what about papers? Could she have stolen any?'

'I never took any state secrets out of the office. If she'd looked through my case she wouldn't have found very much. I certainly wasn't aware of her doing so.'

Maunsell had smiled and clapped his hands together. 'Then you have nothing to worry about. I trust you implicitly, Alex. Rest assured about that.'

'But there is something I haven't told you,' said Vaughan. He looked straight at Maunsell.

Maunsell cocked his head slightly. *Yes?*

'I followed her – about two weeks ago. She went into the Islamic Quarter and I saw her emerge from a shop. Half a minute later a man came out – he looked like Mustafa. I couldn't say one hundred per cent that it was him, but I'm pretty sure. She said she had wanted to buy Turkish Delight but the shop hadn't had any. I checked later – it didn't. I began to think I was being paranoid. Seeing a sinister situation when the simple explanation was the right one.'

'A common enough occurrence. It's something I've warned all our operatives about.' He leaned forward and gripped Vaughan's knee. 'I'm sure you're upset, but you've nothing to worry about as far as I'm concerned. We've instituted a news blackout on this. Sammy, George and the FS section involved have all been informed and there will be no stain on your exceptional record whatsoever. We need you, Alex, heading up C Detachment. When you next go to GHQ, no one will be any the wiser. On that, you have my word.'

'Thank you, RJ. Really.'

Maunsell held up a hand. 'Say no more.'

'And was she Marlin?'

'Yes. The radio operator in the circuit. We've lost track of Mustafa again, but at least we know for sure who we're looking for. Or perhaps I should call him Artus.'

'And Orca?'

'Still in the dark on that one.'

Vaughan was quiet a moment, then said, 'I know it was Jack who reported her.'

'He fought tooth and nail to spare you. He had to report what he'd seen, Alex.'

'I know – it's all right. I don't blame him.'

'Good. We want you two to work together on the Mersa operation.'

'You don't have anything to worry about in that regard – honestly, RJ.'

443

'Good man.'

'And Tanja?' Vaughan asked.

'Under lock and key and facing a considerable amount of interrogation. We have the radio and the codebook.'

'Really?'

'Yes – it's rather curious. A German comic novel. Something of a contradiction in terms – I never knew such things existed.'

'What will happen to her?'

Maunsell smiled again. 'I wouldn't worry yourself about that. Just make sure you get in and out of Tobruk safely, and then we can get you to Mersa.'

When Maunsell had left, Vaughan thought about getting blind drunk, decided against it and headed to GHQ. As RJ had promised, no one gave him so much as a strange glance. It was as though nothing had ever happened.

And yet it had. The Hudson droned on. In less than an hour he would be at Alexandria. For Vaughan, rejoining the men could not come soon enough. Distraction, that was what he needed. *Christ*, but he would miss her.

The train was approaching the next stop, El Khatatba, from where a small-gauge line ran to the Wadi Natroun on the ancient desert road that cut across to the coast. Tanner leaned out of the window and waved to Sykes, who accelerated, then eased the jeep over the track. Once the train had halted, he jumped down and ran over. 'D'you get 'em, then?'

'Yes. Are you all right to keep driving to the

next stop?'

'El Teirieh? Course. It's only about twenty-five miles. What's going on?'

'I'll tell you later.'

'Your neck – ouch, mate, that looks painful. Your voice don't sound too clever either.'

'Let's just say the bastard's got sharp nails.'

'Want some water?' He passed a bottle. 'Take it.'

'Cheers, Stan.' Tanner patted Sykes on the back and ran back to the train. The guard and an Egyptian policeman at the El Khatatba halt were still overseeing the removal of the two dead men. Tanner had their wallets safely tucked away in his gas-mask case, and watched as the bodies were taken to the station building. He wondered what would happen to them – buried somewhere out in the desert, he supposed, shallow graves that would soon be picked apart by scavenging birds and animals. In a few weeks they'd be nothing but bones. He shook his head, and went back to the compartment where Tanja still sat opposite the unconscious Eslem Mustafa.

He could still barely believe she was there. And to think she'd pistol-whipped Mustafa! The man who'd refused to lie down had been finally knocked cold by a woman. He couldn't help admiring her for that. His mouth creased into a smile.

'What?' she said. 'What is so funny?'

'Nothing – I'm sorry.' Good God, but she'd been angry, though. And what the bloody hell was she doing there?

The guard had appeared – he'd obviously been

skulking out of harm's way – and people from the other carriages had begun pushing into the corridor to see what all the noise and fuss were about.

'Get these people out of here,' Tanner had told the guard, who had immediately started yelling at the passengers with officious self-importance. It had done the trick: they had scuttled back until the carriage had been clear once more. Tanner had undone Mustafa's tie and used it to bind the Egyptian's hands behind his back. Then, having collected his Sauer and MP40 – not to mention Mustafa's pistol and flick-knife – he had ordered the guard to help him drag the still unconscious Mustafa into the nearest compartment, and the two bodies to the carriage door, ready to be taken off at the next stop.

'Tanja,' he had asked, 'would you mind guarding Mustafa a moment?'

'If I must,' Tanja had replied.

Soon after that, they had reached El Khatatba. Now they were on their way again, the train gathering speed, the next stop, El Teirieh, due around twenty minutes before midday.

'So,' he said, 'what are you doing here? Why aren't you in prison?'

Her cheeks flushed, but not because of the heat. 'You're the one who reported me!' she said angrily.

'I saw you with bloody Mustafa,' he replied.

'When? I've never seen him before in my life.'

'Tanja, I saw you talking to him yesterday in Khan El Khalili. I know what I ruddy well saw!'

She peered down at him. 'He's covered with

blood. It's hard to see who he is.'

It was true. Mustafa's face looked a mess. 'You were coming out of a shop,' said Tanner. 'I saw you talking to him.'

'I cannot remember that. Maybe I was asking him for the time. I go to Khan El Khalili a lot,' she told him. She glared at him. 'This is what I told those stupid Field Security men. Those bastards ransacked my flat and what do they find? Nothing. Nothing at all!'

'Then if you're so innocent, what are you doing on a train with Eslem Mustafa?'

'I'm not on a train with him, as far as I am concerned. I know nothing about this man. I had no idea I was on a train with someone who wants to kill you. Why was he trying to kill you, by the way?'

'Jesus,' Tanner muttered, shaking his head. He took a swig from his water bottle, then offered it to her.

'No – thank you,' she said. 'Look, if I'm some kind of spy why would I be trying to save you from this madman?'

'I don't know.'

'For which you have yet to thank me, by the way. And why would I have been so quickly released again?'

Tanner felt his sore neck, then leaned his head back and briefly closed his eyes. 'Thank you,' he said, opening them again and looking straight at her. 'Thank you for saving my life. Now, can you put the gun away?' It looked like a Sauer. Or was it a Walther?

She put it into her satchel.

'Hold on a moment,' he said. 'May I see it?'

She sighed, then delved into her bag and passed it to him. He looked at it. Yes, it was a Walther. A Walther PPK, very similar to the Sauer, also 7.65mm calibre. 'It's a German pistol.'

'So what? So is yours. Does that make you a spy too?'

'Where did you get it?'

'It belonged to my husband.'

'Your husband?'

'Yes, Jack Tanner, my husband. We did have German makes of pistol in Poland, you know, and before you ask, he was killed before the war. By the Russians.'

'I'm sorry.'

'So am I.' She glanced out of the window, then back at Tanner. 'Is the interrogation over?'

'Just tell me one thing. What the bloody hell are you doing on this train?'

'I am going to Alexandria for a few days' leave. I was hoping to get away from Cairo and forget about what happened yesterday.'

'But why not take the express?'

'I just wanted to get out. It was the first train available. I do not care how long it takes.'

Beside him, Mustafa groaned.

'Can I go now?' she asked, her eyes still cold with anger. 'I'd like to continue my journey alone, if you don't mind.'

Tanner nodded. 'I'm sorry,' he said. 'And thank you again – for saving my life.'

Without another word, she stood up and left.

Tanner got up and took her seat. From the window, he saw Sykes driving alongside the train, leaving thick clouds of sandy dust in his wake. He took another glug from the water bottle. It seemed so unlikely that she could be on the same train as Mustafa without knowing it, and yet in all other regards her story had seemed plausible. Mustafa groaned and rolled his head. He was almost unrecognizable, with his broken nose, blood-stained face and swollen cheek. And he had shaved off his moustache since the previous afternoon too. Maybe he and Lucie really had just seen a chance conversation in the bazaar. Maunsell had told him to resist looking for sinister reasons when usually the reality was far more mundane. And if she was lying, what the hell was she doing out of prison? He yawned. He had always liked to think he was a reasonable judge of character and that he could sense a liar when he came across one. But with Tanja Zanowski – he clicked his tongue against his teeth – well, he couldn't tell.

Soon after, Mustafa came round, eyes searching in confusion until he spotted Tanner and regained his focus.

'Nice kip?' said Tanner.

Mustafa winced.

'I've a good mind to cut your nails. Vicious bastard, aren't you?'

'I'll kill you,' Mustafa hissed.

'I don't think so, chum,' said Tanner. 'What I'd like to know, though, is what you're doing on this train?'

Mustafa glared at him.

'Anything to do with Tanja Zanowski, by any chance?'

Mustafa's expression did not change.

'What about your friend Orca?' A flicker of Mustafa's eyes. *Ah!* 'Seen at your hideout this morning. Are you going to tell me about him?' Mustafa remained silent. 'No, I thought not. Well, you're not really my problem any more. As soon as we get to Alexandria, you'll be handed over, sent back to Cairo, interrogated until you're blue in the face and then – well, God knows.'

'You British tyrants will go to hell where you will be given pus to drink,' muttered Mustafa.

'What a bloody thought,' said Tanner.

'As Allah is my God, you will be driven from Egypt. If I am to die then I do so for a noble cause. But I warn you, I am not dead yet, and while there is still breath in my body you should be very careful, Lieutenant. If we should meet again, I *will* kill you. I curse you,' Mustafa continued, 'a curse upon you and your children. May Allah–'

Tanner punched him again in the side of the head. 'Put a bloody sock in it, will you?' Mustafa lost consciousness. Tanner sat back and pulled out his cigarettes. 'Jesus,' he muttered. 'What a load of old bollocks.'

Soon after, the train began to slow once more. *Good*, thought Tanner. He planned to take Mustafa off here, but he felt inclined to leave Tanja on the train. She was free, after all – it wasn't his place to arrest her or start telling her what to do. And she *had* saved his life.

Hoisting Mustafa over his shoulders, he carried him out into the corridor and then, as the train halted, opened the door, clambered out and

450

dumped him unceremoniously in the back of the jeep.

'Dead?' said Sykes.

'Sadly, no,' said Tanner. 'He needs a good grilling first.' He hurried back to the train and walked down the corridor but saw no sign of Tanja. Where the hell was she? The guard's whistle. *Damn it*. He hurried off the train to Sykes.

'All right?' said Sykes.

'Just hold on a moment,' said Tanner. 'Wait until the train leaves.'

A burst of steam, and then the wheels turned, the carriages jerking and chinking forward, and the train was on its way, gradually building speed until the station was empty once more.

But not entirely empty. Alone with her suitcase stood Tanja Zanowski.

'What the devil?' muttered Tanner. He called to her and waved, but she just stared at him. Then, from around the stone station house, several men emerged, Europeans, wearing suits. Tanner recognized Colonel Maunsell walking towards him.

'What's going on, Jack?' said Sykes.

'Your guess is as good as mine, mate.'

'Jack,' said Maunsell, stepping over the track. 'What on earth are you doing here?'

'I could ask you the same, sir. We've been following Mustafa and his men.'

Maunsell looked at the prostrate figure in the back of the jeep, then glanced at his watch.

'Don't worry, sir,' added Tanner. 'He's alive.'

'Why didn't you call for help?'

'There wasn't time. We only tracked him down this morning and then we nearly lost him.'

'And the others?'

'Two of them. They're dead. We offloaded them at the last stop.' He delved into his gas-mask case and took out their wallets. 'Here.'

'Good work, Jack, but I need you to get out of the way now, and very quickly too.' He glanced at his watch, then to either side of him. 'No,' he said, 'it's too late to have you drive off. You'll have to take the vehicle behind the station house and lie up in the date grove.'

Tanner nodded. 'Get going then, CSM.'

Sykes did so. Some hundred yards away was the edge of the Nile Valley. As ever, the transition from green zone to desert was a single stride. They drove deep into the date grove, the palms towering above them and switched off the engine. Almost immediately they heard a faint whirr somewhere to the south.

'What the hell's going on, Jack?' said Sykes.

Tanner did not answer him, but instead got out of the jeep and walked forward through the palms a few yards. He was beginning to understand – no wonder Maunsell wanted them out of the way. *Jesus.* RJ must have had the shock of his life when he suddenly saw them. The sound of aircraft was much louder now and Tanner strained his eyes to see, but the strong sun was high above them and the sky blindingly bright. He hurried back to the jeep, grabbed his binoculars and saw, high above, two German fighter planes – Messerschmitts – circling. And then, breathtakingly near, he saw a twin-engine Junkers 88 roar into his field of vision, coming in to land. A few moments later, it touched down, rumbled onwards, then turned, its engines whipping up clouds of dust and sand. And there was Tanja, running across the desert towards it. A hatch opened, and a member of the crew jumped out, beckoning her. She ran on, the engines of the bomber still a noisy whirr. The man grabbed her hand and helped her in. Then the engines opened up to a thunderous roar, and the Junkers was rolling forward, speeding across the desert until suddenly there was a dark shadow on the ground and an ever widening gap of sky between the underside of the bomber and the ground.

Some five minutes later, they drove back to the station house, Maunsell emerging to greet them.

'That went off all right, I think,' he said.

'It explains a lot, sir,' said Tanner.

'How successful it will prove is another matter.' Maunsell glanced at the now stirring Mustafa. He called over two of the men with him, neither of whom Tanner recognized. 'Take him,' he said.

They hoisted Mustafa clear.

'I'm glad to be shot of him,' said Tanner. 'Watch him, sir. He's a slippery bastard.' He rubbed his neck.

'Don't worry, we will. You've done well, Jack – he's quite a catch, and thankfully, I don't think your sudden arrival spoiled the party. Nip and tuck, but all right in the end.'

'Actually, sir,' said Tanner, 'we have Sykes, here, to thank for that. He managed to get the tail on him yesterday.'

Maunsell bowed his head. 'Much obliged to you, Sykes.'

'Pleasure, sir. Can't say as I knew why I was

doing it, but I'm glad it worked out.'

Maunsell took out his pipe. 'Jack, two things. One: make sure you get back safely from Tobruk because I'm going to need you and C Detachment very soon. Two: never mention this to anyone. Either of you. Do you understand? Not to anyone – not Vaughan, not anyone at all. Forget you were ever here.'

'Of course,' said Tanner. 'You have my word.'

'And your friend?'

'Yes, sir,' said Sykes. 'Mine too, sir.'

'Good man.'

'Vaughan, sir,' said Tanner. 'He's all right, isn't he?'

'Humiliated and wounded, but no stain on his record. He doesn't blame you, either.'

That's something. 'Sir, just one last thing,' he added. 'Tanja Zanowski. Was she always working for you?'

Maunsell lit his pipe. 'Is she now? That is the question.' He patted Tanner on the shoulder. 'One day I'll explain everything, but for now – skedaddle.'

Tanner saluted, then Sykes opened the clutch and they drove away, following the railway as before.

'You know,' said Sykes, 'it's still all pretty hazy to me. To be honest, I don't even know why we were chasing those blokes on the train, and then we get here and some Englishman in a suit appears, there's that Polish bint standing by the tracks, and a few minutes later the *Luftwaffe* shows up and whisks her away.'

Tanner lit a cigarette. He wasn't quite sure what

he should tell Sykes, if anything. So far, he'd barely said a word, except that Mustafa was a much wanted subversive. Yet since that chase through the bazaar the previous afternoon, Sykes had seen a great deal. He'd also given a pledge of secrecy to Maunsell, so surely it wouldn't do any harm to give him the bare bones. And it wasn't over yet – whatever Vaughan was planning for after the Tobruk raid clearly had Maunsell's involvement too. *Sod it.* His neck hurt, his body felt battered and he was tired. All this cloak-and-dagger stuff – he was fed up with it. 'All right,' he said. 'I'll tell you a little bit. But, like the colonel said, don't bloody breathe a word, Stan, all right?'

'Course,' said Sykes. 'Goes without saying, mate.'

'The bloke in the suit,' Tanner began, 'is Colonel Maunsell, head of Secret Intelligence Middle East. The Egyptians we were chasing were part of an anti-British movement called the Ring of Iron, or they might be the Muslim Brotherhood. I'm not too sure, but Eslem Mustafa–'

'The bloke you knocked out but didn't kill?'

'Right. Well, he's not only a highly connected subversive and agitator, he's also been part of a spy cell called Operation Cobra.'

Sykes whistled. 'Christ alive! I had no idea.'

'Before I rejoined the battalion, I was working with Major Vaughan and Maunsell at SIME, trying to break the cell.'

'So he really is a big catch, then?'

'Yes – that was why I was so pissed off when he got away yesterday. He was heavily involved with rousing anti-British sentiment last year, working

455

with an Egyptian general called El Masri.'

'I remember something about that.'

'Then he disappeared, and it seems that during that time he was helping to set up Cobra in Cairo.'

'And the bint?'

'She was part of the cell, and sleeping with Vaughan at the same time. But I only realized that yesterday. Now I'm not so sure.'

'Bloody hell! And the major knows about this now?'

'Oh, yes. I imagine he's a bit cut up about it because he'd fallen for her in a big way.'

'Poor bastard.'

'I know. Deserves better. Anyway, it looks like she's a double agent. At least, that's what I'm guessing. All I'll say is this: on that train old Mustafa was about to have me beat when she comes along behind him and pistol-whips him.'

Sykes laughed. 'Good for her. So she can't be all bad, then?'

'Maybe not. So now you know.'

'Christ,' said Sykes. 'Makes you bloody think, don't it? There's us fighting our arses off at the front and all the while there's this kind of malarkey going on behind the scenes. I bet you're glad you're out of it now, aren't you?'

'That's just it, Stan,' said Tanner. 'I don't think we're out of it at all. I think we're just about to get ourselves in even deeper.'

23

Monday, 14 September, around 1.30 a.m. It was a dark night, with no moon, but from the prow of MTB 270, Tanner could see with uncomfortable clarity as tracer cut across the sea and flares lit up the sky almost as bright as day. A short distance up the coast, at the mouth of the long, narrow harbour into Tobruk, another MTB burned, with silhouettes of men jumping overboard, while beyond, on the far side of the harbour entrance, two destroyers were standing offshore, their guns blazing. Men were struggling down netting draped over the side, whalers bobbing on the surface below, several more already rowing towards land. The flare died and the destroyers were once more shrouded in darkness. Then a shell hit one of the ships near its stern, causing another flash. More shells landed around them, huge plumes of water erupting into the sky. From the inner harbour, a searchlight had been lowered, sweeping back and forth across the mouth of the harbour, then occasionally catching a vessel in its beam.

'Jesus,' muttered Tanner, from his position at the port twin Browning machine-guns. Behind him, at the bridge, stood Vaughan, alongside the helmsman and Lieutenant Commander Jim Allenby. The Elco boat was idling in the water, some eight hundred yards out to sea and to the east of the town. Spaced out in an arrowhead formation some hundred yards apart, the other three MTBs were in their formation of four.

The raid was already proving a fiasco. The plan had been for forces attacking from the landward side of Tobruk to infiltrate the town and spike the guns, enabling the seaward forces to land largely unimpeded. Clearly that had not happened, because as the first wave of MTBs had approached the inlet of Mersa Sciausc, they had been heavily fired upon, not only from the inner harbour but also from positions further along the coast. One MTB had managed to land its men, but had then run aground and had been abandoned, while another had been shot up and sunk.

In the second wave, Allenby had led the group of four towards the inlet but they had come under even more intense fire from MG teams on the shore. One of Allenby's gunners, Leading Seaman Holmes, had been shot, and the MTB had received a line of bullets across its side. Tanner had volunteered to take over from Holmes, but he had barely had a chance to fire a single bullet, even when they had closed towards the inlet a second time. Another frantic retreat had followed, and another MTB had been hit and caught fire. From his position at the Brownings, Tanner had watched the men and crew leaping into the water, some already aflame. Allenby had ordered his four vessels to turn around and a nerve-racking rescue operation had hastily been launched, the MTBs circling the stricken vessel and picking up as many survivors as they could under heavy fire. Tanner had helped haul two aboard – they had picked up six in all – but with tracer hurtling towards them and flak guns firing straight out to sea, rather than into the air, Allenby had not stayed long, returning to their current position where they had become little more than spectators in the unfolding carnage.

Tanner looked again towards the headland, where the attempted landing by the destroyers *Zulu* and *Sikh* appeared to be going every bit as badly as the MTBs' landings to the east of the town. He faced the bridge. 'How long do we stay here?' he asked Allenby.

'I'm not sure – hopefully not much longer. The position's hopeless. There's no chance of us getting into Mersa Sciausc now.'

'You don't think we should try again to get ashore on the headland and have a crack at spiking those guns up there?'

'The men from the destroyers are trying to do that,' said Vaughan.

'And in those whalers – they're not getting very far.' A pall of smoke hung over the sea, the flash of guns and tracer filtered by the haze. One of the destroyers let off another salvo, but the return fire was just as heavy. A shell whistled over from the inner harbour, exploding a hundred yards in front of them, the blast rocking the Elco.

'Jack, if we can't land here,' said Vaughan, 'how the hell are we going to get to the headland?'

More shells exploded around the two destroyers. *Bloody hell. We're going to lose those bloody ships in a minute.* Tanner felt so helpless, bobbing about on the sea, offering a target for the gunners in Tobruk.

'I know you're right,' he said at length, 'but it's

bloody torture watching those lads flailing about in those whalers. At least we've got some speed. We could maybe go around the destroyers and get a little further along the headland.'

'I agree it's a possibility,' said Allenby, 'but we've got to follow Commander Blackburn's lead, and at the moment he seems to think it's the better part of valour to hang back here.'

'I'm more interested in getting out of here in one piece,' said Vaughan. 'It's bloody uncomfortable watching good men getting slaughtered, but we need to make sure we can fight another day. This was always a cock-eyed plan and we've known that all along, so let's just hope an order comes through telling us to get the hell out of here.'

The burning MTB was still billowing smoke, but then it started to sink, the stern slipping below the surface. Moments later, its prow tilted upwards and it was gone.

'A good man, the skipper of 269,' said Allenby. 'I hope he got picked up.'

'How many down are we now?' asked Farrer.

'Three,' said Allenby. He leaned down to the hatch. 'Barclay,' he yelled, 'any news?'

A moment later, Barclay's head appeared from the cabin. '*Zulu* has managed to get three whalers ashore,' he replied. Allenby crouched and called down to the W/T operator, whose radio room was just below the bridge on the starboard side. 'Got anything for me?'

'No, Cap'n sir,' Barclay replied.

Another shell hurtled towards them, landing even closer and sending a fountain of water high into the sky. Tanner ducked, gripping the rail of the pilothouse as the boat rocked and spray lashed over them. He could taste salt on his lips, and smell smoke and cordite blended with the petrol and oil fumes from the boat.

'They're getting a bit close again,' said Allenby. 'Time to move, I think.' As if on cue MTB 260, Commander Blackburn's vessel, now sped away, further out of range. 'All right, Wiggans,' said Allenby, to his coxswain, 'let's follow.'

'Aye-aye, Cap'n sir,' said Wiggans, opening the throttle of the three Packard engines and turning them back out to sea.

Cutting the throttle, they circled slowly, as further out from the headland another surface vessel began blasting the coast.

'Reinforcements?' said Vaughan.

Allenby looked through his binoculars. The shape of the ship was briefly revealed as its guns fired a salvo. 'Looks like a cruiser. Must be *Coventry*.'

'Not much good to us over here, though,' said Farrer. 'Those guns from the harbour aren't slowing up at all.'

Tanner glanced at the spectral image of the ships a couple of miles away in the smoke haze, then gripped the twin Browning machine-guns. Next to him, his fellow mid-gunner manned another pair of Brownings, while in front of the bridge at the prow there was a further twin pair of Lewis machine-guns, and at the stern, a single 20mm Oerlikon cannon. Either side there were also two torpedo tubes. *All this firepower and we're not doing a bloody thing.* Nothing – except being shelled at and watching the unravelling disaster

461

around them. Vaughan was right – he knew that. Even if they managed to get on to the headland, there would be little chance of them knocking out more than a couple of the guns on the headland, and none in the town. He looked at his watch. Two a.m. It would be dawn before they achieved anything, and by then it would be over, their chance gone.

More shells burst over the headland, the destroyers lit up like ghost-ships in the smoky pall. A flash from the guns of one of the ships, while the first, smoking from its stern, was pulling back.

From one of the MTBs, a blue box lamp now flashed. 'Sparker!' shouted Allenby. 'Get your arse up here. I need you.'

Barclay scrambled up the steps, joining Allenby on the bridge.

'Orders to retire,' said Allenby. 'Can you confirm?'

The signal was repeated. 'Yes, Cap'n sir,' said Barclay. 'All MTBs return to Alexandria. No stopping.'

'Is that Blackburn?'

'It's certainly 260, sir. That's definitely Smithy signalling.'

'How can you tell?' asked Vaughan.

Barclay grinned. 'Oh, you get used to the way people signal, sir. Everyone has a slightly different style.'

'At any rate,' said Allenby, 'the fun's over. Time to go home.'

'About time,' said Vaughan.

'But we'll need to keep a bloody sharp look-out,' Allenby added. 'Three hours until dawn and then we'll be fair game to any marauding Messerschmitts and Macchis.'

They left the battle behind, although even twenty miles along the coast, the distant boom of guns and occasional orange flash could be seen and heard. Relieved from gunnery duty, Tanner went below for a kip, taking one of the cots in the officers' cabin near the prow. He was amazed by how smooth the vessel was, even at forty knots – that was nearly fifty miles per hour, a good speed by any reckoning – and in no time at all he was fast asleep.

When he awoke, dawn was approaching. Vaughan and Allenby were asleep in their narrow cots, as were a number of the crew and those rescued earlier. Carefully, he stepped over the bodies sprawled out in the low trunk cabin and scaled the steps to the bridge out of the fetid smell of damp and petrol. Coxswain Wiggans was still at the helm, alongside Lieutenant Charteris, Allenby's number one, and Captain Farrer. Above, the canopy of stars still twinkled, while the boat's wake showed a strange phosphorescence that seemed to colour the foaming water: rather than being white, it was silvery and glowing, almost charged with little pinpricks of electric light.

'Peculiar, isn't it?' said Charteris. He was a Scot, in his early twenties, with a soft voice and gentle brogue.

'It is. Does it always happen?' asked Tanner.

'Along the Mediterranean coast, it seems to. I don't know why. It'll be dawn soon, though, and then it'll look as white as it usually does.'

'White against blue,' said Tanner. 'Twelve or so MTBs will make a pretty obvious target.'

'Unfortunately, yes,' said Charteris. 'We've got a few uncomfortable hours ahead, I'm afraid.'

'At least we're travelling at a good lick,' said Farrer.

'We're a pretty small target,' added Charteris, '*and* our firepower isn't bad, actually. Even so, coming under air attack is never pleasant. I'd rather be travelling by night, I must say, and lying up by day like we did yesterday.'

'Why are we heading straight back, then?' asked Tanner.

Charteris shrugged. 'I don't know. Maybe they just decided they wanted us back to base as quickly as possible. The raid has obviously failed. Let's get it over and done with – that sort of attitude.'

Dawn broke, the horizon ahead of them gradually lightening, and then the golden tip of the sun burst over the horizon, light spreading in a swathe across the sea and over the coast. Tanner moved back to the stern and sat on a locker in front of the Oerlikon, his legs hanging over the edge, his arms on the rail. The speed, he thought, really was incredible, the brilliant white wake streaming behind them for hundreds of yards. Either side of them, spaced well apart, were the other three MTBs in their formation, their own vessel, MTB 270, leading the arrowhead. There was a kind of feline power to these vessels: just seventy foot long, but sleek, fast and deadly.

Presently he was joined by Vaughan and Sykes, the latter handing him a mug of tea as they sat down beside him.

'This is the life, eh?' said Sykes. 'I'd pay good money to go on one of these beauties, and yet His Majesty's actually paying me to sit here.'

'As well as to get shot at and bombed by Jerries and Eyeties,' said Tanner.

'Not at the moment,' said Sykes. 'I can be grateful to His Majesty for that.'

'We managed to get out of that hell,' said Vaughan, 'but it angers me that good men had to die in such an ill-conceived and poorly planned operation.'

'I didn't tell you this, sir, but even my barber in Alexandria knew about it,' said Sykes. 'He said, "I hope you have a pleasant trip to Tobruk, sir," and I said, "What you talking about?" and he said, "Ah, yes, very good, sir. Top-secret, ha, ha, ha."'

'I'm horrified, of course,' said Vaughan, 'but not the slightest bit surprised. About two and a half thousand people have been involved in these raids. No wonder half the damned world knew about them beforehand. And no wonder those guns weren't spiked. I imagine that as soon as our landward forces turned up, Jerry put them straight in the bag.'

'Or had them shot,' said Tanner. 'Most of the saboteurs were German Jews from Palestine, weren't they?'

'Yes – and you're probably right. My God, it makes me sick to think of it.'

Tanner said nothing. There had definitely been a change in his friend. Vaughan had always been so good-humoured. A real gent, Tanner had always thought, someone who liked to see the

465

best in any person and any situation. But now a deep anger was boiling within him. Tanner didn't blame him – the bloke was heartbroken, which had made the futility of this operation seem even worse than it was. Vaughan had had such high hopes, such good intentions for C Detachment, yet this trip had been nothing but folly. *Poor bugger.* He wished he could tell him what he'd seen at El Teirieh, and what he knew about Tanja. But he'd vowed not to. When he gave someone his word, he meant it. It was a matter of honour. Perhaps the truth would eventually come out, and perhaps one day Vaughan would get over it and return to his old self.

Tuesday, 15 September. There was a final briefing with Oberleutnant Berendt and Major von Mellenthin in the intelligence office. At one end of the room, half a dozen clerks tapped away on typewriters and answered telephones, while at the other, sitting on folding chairs at a wooden trestle table, Tanja Zanowski and Hauptmann Becker raised chipped shot glasses with von Mellenthin and Berendt.

'Down the hatch,' said von Mellenthin, 'as the English like to say.' He smiled, but there was no hiding the weariness in his face. Both men looked exhausted – dark rings around their eyes, patchily shaved and gaunt, their green desert denim uniforms faded and filthy. Beads of sweat pricked their brows, and Tanja now felt a trickle of moisture run down the side of her face. She was hardly a picture of health and cleanliness herself, and she had only been in Mersa a week. These men had been in this subterranean headquarters for nearly ten weeks, living with the sandflies and scorpions, breathing in fetid air that stank of sweat and urine and stale smoke, living off insufficient and monotonous rations that were barely enough to keep a small child from hunger. An enforced troglodyte existence in the one place that was safe from the daily bombing by the RAF. No wonder they looked so rough. No wonder Rommel himself was struggling with increasingly poor health. It was enough to make anyone ill.

'I fear the conditions in Tobruk will hardly be much better, Fräulein,' said von Mellenthin. 'As I'm sure you're aware, Tobruk has found itself in the firing line, pummelled by us one moment and the British the next. I don't suppose there can be more than half a dozen buildings in the entire town that are still unscathed.'

'It's all right,' said Tanja. 'I've been spoiled living in Cairo so long. It does me good to see how you soldiers are faring.'

'And at least in Tobruk you won't be living underground,' added Berendt. 'In Navy House I hear there is even hot water still.'

Becker looked at his watch. 'We should get going.'

'Yes,' smiled von Mellenthin, 'you should. I shall miss your good humour, Becker, and, Fräulein Zanowski, your charm and beauty.' He bowed his head. 'We are somewhat starved of female company out here.'

'Certainly one can hardly call the Arab and Italian whores women,' laughed Becker.

'No, indeed,' agreed von Mellenthin. 'It has

467

been good for us to be reminded that we fight so that we might enjoy such company as yours again in more peaceful times.'

'Thank you, Major,' said Tanja. 'I shall miss you both too. You have been perfect gentlemen.'

'Then let me hope you will continue to think so by allowing me to escort you out.'

They finished the schnapps, and Tanja followed the three men out through the long, rock-hewn corridor and up several steps to the bunker's entrance. Outside, dusk was falling. On the track below the entrance, the *Kübelwagen* was waiting. Seeing his passengers, the driver stepped out and opened the passenger door.

'Good luck, Fräulein,' said Berendt, from the bunker entrance, but von Mellenthin walked down the steps with her to the car, took her hand and kissed it lightly.

'Goodbye, Tanja,' he said. 'And good luck. You too, Becker.'

'Thank you, Major,' said Tanja. 'Good luck to you too.'

Through the fading light, they drove the length of the spit, past the harbour, now empty apart from a few lighters lashed together, and out of the ruins of the village towards the camp beneath the escarpment, several miles to the south. She had been told she would be going to Tobruk the moment her debriefing had finished the day after her arrival at Mersa. It was her lack of knowledge of the planned Allied raids on Tobruk and Benghazi that Becker had returned to again and again in her interviews. 'But I did not hear from Orca,' she had told him. 'The lack

468

of communication from him and the knowledge that the British were on the trail of Artus was why I contacted you and suggested the circuit be closed.' She had stuck to her story and, it seemed, had been believed. Now the raids had taken place – and been successfully repulsed – it was safe for her to move to Tobruk, a bigger town with a bigger port. A place from which false information might be more convincingly fed back to the British Secret Intelligence Service.

They reached the camp as the last light was slipping away, and immediately boarded a truck, one in a convoy heading back along the coast road to Tobruk, some hundred and fifty miles away. Von Mellenthin had been most apologetic, but fuel was too precious, he had explained, even for a beautiful woman like her. It had required Rommel's special authority just to pick her up from El Teirieh. Some blankets and two sleeping-bags had been put in the back of the truck – a thoughtful gesture – and Tanja took the hand the driver offered and sprang on to the wooden body.

'Will you be all right, Fräulein?' he asked, passing up her case.

'I will be fine,' Tanja told him.

Becker opted to sit in the cab with the driver. Tanja was glad. There was something about him she disliked intensely – something that reminded her of Orca; perhaps it was the oily smoothness. Perhaps it was just that she disliked spies. Von Mellenthin and Berendt – they were soldiers first, intelligence officers on Rommel's staff, courteous

469

and charming, despite the terrible privations they suffered. Becker, on the other hand, was an *Abwehr* man, an intelligence agent, codename Cobra – the man who had masterminded the Cairo circuit, and who was now to be her handler as she became a double-agent for them. It was his job to be sly, cunning and mistrustful; she understood that, but found his presence oppressive and menacing, just as she had Orca's. He was a reminder of the fragility of her existence.

Now, though, a few hours of escape lay ahead. She would be alone in the back of an Opel truck. A hard wooden floor, a canvas covering, and a powerful stench of petrol from the cargo it had brought to the front, but Tanja did not mind. The luxury of Cairo – the decadence even – seemed to belong to a different life, and in many ways she supposed that was so. But at least the back was open to the elements. She could smell the fresh, cool desert air, and watch the incredible canopy of stars. She had blankets, a few cigarettes, a little water. And most of all, for a few precious hours, she could be herself.

Alexandria, Thursday, 17 September. A breeze was blowing across the sea and small eddies of sand were skittering across the road, while overhead the brittle leaves of the palms rustled against one another noisily. As in Cairo, the traffic in the city was constant during the day, and now, at eight in the morning, in full swing, gharries and taxis competing with the trams. Vaughan slipped nimbly between two trams, crossed the square, and went over to the Cecil Hotel. In the foyer, the concertina gate was shut, the lift rising sedately, huge coils dropping as it disappeared from view. He took the stairs two at a time. On the second floor, he turned left and left again, until he found himself outside Room 223. He knocked and waited.

The door was opened by Colonel Maunsell.

'Ah, Alex, my dear fellow, good to see you.' Maunsell pumped his hand, his face creased in a broad smile.

'How are you, RJ?'

'All the better for seeing you alive and well. I'm glad you survived the débâcle of Tobruk.'

'Yes,' said Vaughan. 'We survived both Tobruk and the journey back.' He now saw that Maunsell was not alone: Colonel Bowlby was standing by the window next to an armchair and table. 'How are you, sir?' he said, stepping forward and offering his hand.

'Well, thank you, Vaughan. Have a seat.' Vaughan glanced around the room. There was no bed, but half of the space was dominated by a large, rectangular table surrounded by straight-backed chairs, while the other had a low rattan coffee-table and four wing-backed armchairs. Three french windows led on to small, narrow balconies overlooking the square, the Corniche and the sea.

A tray lay on the coffee-table.

'Would you like a cup, Vaughan?' said Bowlby, leaning down and pouring before Vaughan had answered. 'It's still pretty fresh.'

'Thank you, sir.' Then a cigarette was offered, which Vaughan took – Turkish, an expensive brand, from an expensive gold case. What was

471

coming, he wondered, that required such service beforehand?

'I'd like to echo what RJ just said, Vaughan,' said Bowlby. 'I'm relieved to see you safe and sound. You've heard, no doubt, about the rest of the fiasco?'

'Yes, sir.'

'*Zulu* sunk, *Sikh* and *Coventry* badly damaged, our German Jews gone, Haselden killed, five MTBs lost and some hundred and fifty men taken prisoner. And that's just Agreement. Bigamy was every bit as much of a balls-up. Stirling's mob rumbled as they reached Benghazi, and the SDF failed to take Jalo. A lot of men and equipment lost for absolutely no gain whatsoever.' He paused. 'Or, rather, almost no gain whatsoever.' He glanced at Maunsell. *Your turn.*

'We do now,' said Maunsell, 'have a better picture of the defences at Tobruk.'

'I suppose so,' said Vaughan. 'But if so, it's come at one hell of a cost.'

'Of course, but what's done is done. We must now look forward, and take what we can from the situation. And as it happens there has been one positive result from this.'

'Oh, yes?'

'Yes,' said Bowlby, taking the reins once more. 'One of our agents has now been sent to Tobruk.' He shuffled to the edge of his chair and leaned forward conspiratorially. 'And as we speak that agent is gathering all sorts of intelligence for us. Intelligence that will be damned useful in the coming battle.'

'I see,' said Vaughan.

'Unfortunately, though,' continued Bowlby, 'we have no way of getting that intelligence.'

'I don't understand, sir.'

Maunsell smiled again. 'Apollo – that's the agent's codename – is a double-agent, Alex. The *Abwehr* think Apollo is one of theirs, but Apollo in fact is one of ours.'

'Apollo is signalling messages being fed by the *Abwehr* who think we are swallowing every word,' said Bowlby.

'I see,' said Vaughan, 'and he can't signal any intelligence to you without them knowing about it.'

'Exactly,' said Bowlby. 'Apollo's cover would be blown in a trice.'

Maunsell cleared his throat. 'When we first broached the idea of you fetching one of our agents, Alex, we were deliberately vague. We weren't quite sure how things would pan out. To be honest, we weren't quite sure where our agent would end up. For the past week, Apollo has been at Rommel's headquarters in Mersa Matruh, but last night was moved to Tobruk.'

'How do you know for sure? I thought it was impossible to be that precise.'

'It is when you're tracking from radio waves only. But part of the double-bluff is that Apollo reveals that kind of detail. The *Abwehr* think it adds to the verisimilitude.' A knowing smile. He took out a typed message from his pocket and passed it to Vaughan. *Have been sent to Tobruk. Saw vast fuel store beneath escarpment two miles south-west of town. Another German division is being landed at Benghazi in two days' time.*

'That's all rot, of course,' said Maunsell. 'No

doubt several large tents have been erected and, of course, we'll go over and bomb it. I wouldn't be surprised if they detonate some explosives too, just to add to the sense of authenticity.'

'And the division?'

'Completely bogus. It's all part of a plan to make us think they're stronger than they really are. A delaying trick. They want us to hold off attacking for as long as possible.'

'But we want Apollo back,' said Bowlby, 'and quickly.'

'So you can find out more about Rommel's headquarters?'

'Yes. We have a pretty good picture, but nothing like the complete picture Apollo can provide.'

'And presumably he can offer some useful intelligence on Tobruk as well,' said Vaughan.

'Quite,' said Bowlby.

'So you want C Detachment to go and get him.'

Maunsell smiled. 'Yes, Alex, we do. And as soon as possible, before Apollo gets moved again.'

'And what about sabotage?' Vaughan asked. 'We could blow up real fuel dumps, not bogus ones. Spike guns. I can't imagine Tobruk's held by the best troops the Axis have over here.'

'First and foremost, your job is to get Apollo out of there. If the chance offers itself, then, yes, any sabotage is to be welcomed.'

'But Apollo is our number-one priority, Vaughan,' said Bowlby.

Vaughan nodded. 'I understand. And how will I find him?'

'Apollo is billeted at the hospital in one of the staff buildings.'

'I know – single-storey villas across the road from the main hospital.'

'You've been there, then?' said Maunsell.

'Yes, I was taken to the hospital when I was wounded earlier in the year.'

'Then as you know, Vaughan,' continued Bowlby, 'the hospital is perched on the hill overlooking the harbour, slightly away from the centre of the town. Less bombed than the rest of it.'

'Which villa? There were a lot, running down one side of the road. And how am I going to find him? I don't know what Apollo looks like.'

'There will be a black stone by the foot of the door.'

'It seems a bit vague, if you don't mind me saying so.'

'I'm sorry, Alex,' said Maunsell, 'but it's the best we can do. If Apollo starts being too specific the Germans are going to smell a rat.'

'And when do we go?'

'No time like the present,' said Maunsell. 'Allenby is pretty familiar with that coastline by now, I should hope. Get close tonight, lie up during tomorrow, then get Apollo out tomorrow night. We'll make sure the RAF gives you a clear steer.'

'It's a big thing to ask, I know,' said Bowlby, 'but I hope you can see why it's so important, Vaughan.'

'Of course, sir. Should I tell my men?'

'Only as much as is necessary: that you are going to Tobruk and that you're there to pick up an agent. You have German uniforms, I believe?'

'Yes, sir.'

'Good.' He stood up, signalling that the interview was now over. 'Risk,' he said. 'It's always a question of weighing up the odds, and wondering whether the benefits outweigh the potential cost of failure. In the case of the recent operations, I think we're all agreed that it was not. In this instance, however, it most certainly is.'

Maunsell got to his feet. 'Good luck, Alex. And here's hoping that we shall be seeing each other again in just a few days' time, with your mission a glorious success.'

'There's one thing troubling me,' said Vaughan. 'I appreciate that you don't want to tell me Apollo's name, but do you have a photograph? Something at least?'

He saw Maunsell glance at Bowlby, who gave a barely perceptible shake of the head.

'I'm sorry, Alex. We're keenly aware that this is a highly hazardous operation. If you're captured, it's better you don't know Apollo.'

'What I will say is this,' added Bowlby. 'That Apollo will recognize you.'

Half a minute later, Vaughan was retracing his steps along the empty corridor, his mind whirring. The mission was all that he had hoped for when he had first been given command of C Detachment, and yet there was a leaden feeling in his stomach. Over the past week, he had often wondered whether he really cared whether he lived or died, but now he knew the answer: he wanted to live.

By the lift, he lit a cigarette and discovered his hands were shaking. Memories of the intense enemy fire two nights before swarmed into his mind as the enormity of the task before him sank in. One thing was certain: there was no middle road. Either they would get Apollo out or they would die in the attempt.

24

Friday, 18 September, dusk. The desert was transforming from biscuit to pink. The eight-man team scrambled up the low, rocky cliffs and, at the top, paused. On the western horizon, the sun was dipping out of sight, and the desert, that strange chameleon, was changing again, from pink to darkening orange, then russet.

'Come on,' said Vaughan, 'let's go.'

The men were in German uniform – dusty green denim field tunics, matching trousers, rubber-soled boots, and on their heads, the distinctive peaked field caps that the Germans seemed to wear far more than their tin helmets. Their cover had been agreed in Alexandria: that they were from 1 Company, 63rd Combat Engineer Battalion, or Pionere Abteilung as the Germans called their sappers, part of the 90th Light Division. They were in Tobruk to help rebuild defences after the British raid of a few days earlier. To complete the authenticity, each man had been issued with German aluminium oval dog-tags, a *Soldbuch* – the German soldier's pay and identity book – and various other papers and letters. Tanner had a sweetheart in Hameln, Sykes a wife in Dresden. It had amused them greatly, but while the attention to detail had been impressive, Tanner felt it was a wasted effort. He fancied it would all be over before anyone read his love letter from Gretl.

So far, though, so good. The journey back up the coast the previous night had been uneventful. In an MTB, it was just under nine hours from Alexandria to Tobruk, but with autumn drawing on and the equinox just a few days away, there were now ten hours of darkness, which had enabled them to take a wide berth around Tobruk, then cut back in and lie up in a narrow cove some three miles west of the town on the headland. They had covered the MTB with camouflage netting and had waited all day, taking turns to keep watch on the shallow cliffs above. For much of the time it had been quiet. A few planes had buzzed high above them, and a number of transport planes had landed and taken off to the south of the town, some five miles away, but there had been nothing to suggest they had been spotted. Then, at around four, they had noticed increased air activity, flights of fighters heading out to sea, and this had been followed by the appearance on the horizon of two ships, which, over the next two hours, had grown in size as they had neared the coast. Just before six, they had slipped past the headland a few miles to the east and entered Tobruk harbour. A good omen, Tanner had thought. After all, the arrival of ships made the appearance of new troops in town more likely. And then there was the small matter of sabotage – a secondary aim of the mission, Vaughan had explained: there was no denying that the ships would provide an opportunity at the very least...

At this time of year, the light faded rapidly with only around half an hour between sunset and darkness. With that in mind, they had decided to use the last of the light to walk a mile and a half along the coast to where a narrow wadi ran from the sea to a track that went roughly west–east into the town.

They reached the wadi a little before half past seven, the horizon lined with thin streaks of cloud silhouetted against the last fading light of day, while above, the fathomless sky prickled with glittering stars. The air was still and cool, with barely a breath of wind, so that even in their rubber-soled boots each step they took and each chink of equipment seemed horribly loud.

They heard nothing and met no one. Half an hour later, daylight gone, they reached the track. From the town they heard engines and, lying on the ground among the salt-bush, they waited as a convoy of trucks approached. What was in the back? Tanner wondered. It looked like fuel barrels, but he could not be sure. 'Boom,' he said softly to himself.

When the last lorry had passed, they got to their feet, made their way to the track and began walking down it until, silhouetted against the sky, they saw the outline of buildings. The faint sound of voices to their left made them stop. Tanner strained his ears. Nothing distinct – and then he saw two glowing pinpricks. *Cigarettes.*

'Gun emplacement,' he whispered, to Vaughan and Farrer.

Vaughan nodded and, as quietly as possible, led

them back into the open desert of the headland.

A couple of hundred yards from the hospital, they paused in a little rocky hollow in the ground. Vetch and salt-bush surrounded them, offering ideal cover. A little way to the south there was another gun emplacement, its great barrel pointing skywards, while in front, the dark shape of the hospital loomed. It was a large stone building, originally built by the Italians in grand neo-classical style. Bungalow villas and block-houses, normally white and sand-coloured during daylight, stood around it and down the hill. In the harbour, they could hardly see the ships, but lorries were rumbling back and forth in a near constant stream, as the newly arrived cargo was unloaded and whisked away.

Tanner watched, his spirits rising. Anything that kept the enemy busy was all right by him.

'Right,' said Vaughan. 'Time to find out where Apollo is.' The plan had caused considerable debate. Captain Farrer had suggested they split into two groups, and that the first, including Sykes, would create a diversion at the harbour; they had all thought the arrival of the two ships propitious. In the mayhem that would result, the second group would hurry to find Apollo. Meanwhile, Farrer and Tanner's group would prepare a number of other explosive devices. There was, however, a major flaw in the plan: if Apollo was not in any of the villas, finding the agent within the town and wider garrison, which would be on full alert, might prove extremely difficult, if not impossible. The alternative was to forgo the diversion and simply try to get Apollo out without being discovered – they should not allow the arrival of the ships to cloud their judgement. In the end, Vaughan had said they would make the decision when they reached the edge of the town, as they now had.

A further complication for Tanner and Sykes was that they suspected Apollo was not a male agent but the woman they had seen boarding the Junkers ten days earlier. They had speculated about it during the journey up the coast, Sykes increasingly convinced as the rescue mission drew closer.

'You've got to tell Vaughany,' Sykes had urged earlier, as they had sat on watch at the top of the cliff.

'We gave our word, Stan,' Tanner had replied. 'If they'd wanted him to know, they'd have told him.'

'But it's affecting our chances of pulling off this mission,' Sykes had argued.

Tanner knew he had a point, but what if they were wrong? What if Apollo was not Tanja Zanowski? He would then have revealed a secret he had been honour-bound to keep. They had been sworn to secrecy and there had to be a reason for that. He was not a man to break his word.

'Sir,' he now said in Vaughan's ear, 'why don't you and I carry out a quick recce on our own first? It'll be easier for two of us to scamper about than all eight. We could give ourselves until, say, nine o'clock, and if we're not back then, the rest can set up the diversion.'

'Good idea,' said Farrer. 'It seems pretty quiet after all.'

Vaughan thought for a moment. All day he had been worrying that there were so many variables. It was impossible to know whether or not he would be making the right decision. Now he realized he would have to rely on his gut instinct and hope for the best. He was commander of this operation, and he had to lead. 'All right,' he said. 'Yes.' Instinct told him that Tanner's suggestion was the least flawed of the ideas they had come up with so far. It occurred to him then that finding the others again might be difficult, so he said, 'But we'll all move up to the villas before the hospital. You can stay close by, while Tanner and I make our recce.'

They crept out, crouching the last few hundred yards until, on the crest of the ridge overlooking the town and with the last of the villas just forty yards ahead, they paused. A rough road ran down the hill to the main part of the town and the harbour. On the side nearest to them were the bungalows, and on the other, the main hospital building, faint lights visible between the shutters. One end of the building had been hit, as had several of the villas, but for the most part, the hospital and its accompanying buildings appeared to have been spared the worst of the Allied bombing.

Vaughan looked at the men, dark faces in the thin light from the stars, then turned to Farrer. 'Twenty-one hundred, then. Back here.'

'Good luck, sir,' said Farrer.

They scrambled out of the hollow and set off towards the nearest villa. Dim light showed from several of the windows to the building's rear, and as they drew closer, they could discern a passageway between the first villa and the next.

'Let's go between them and on to the road,' suggested Vaughan.

Tanner nodded. A dog barked a little way off and now, as they reached the passageway between the two villas, they heard the faint hum of a radio and then laughter. *At least someone's got something to laugh about*, thought Vaughan. They sidled along one wall until they reached the road, opposite the balcony of the main hospital's ground floor, but it seemed empty and quiet, as did the road itself.

Vaughan whispered to Tanner, 'Ready?'

Tanner had his MP40 loose over one shoulder, his Sauer in his trouser pocket and a Walther 9mm fitted with a silencer in a canvas holster. Attached to his leather belt were six spare magazines for the Schmeisser, as well as some explosives in a pack on his back. Loosening the clasp on the holster, he felt the Walther's grip, then said, 'Yes. Let's go.'

Together, they stepped out into the road, glanced to either side, then turned left, beside a long, single-storey building. It contained half a dozen apartments, each with a stone balustrade outside and dark-painted doors and shutters, which he recalled had been green. In the first, there was no sign of life, but a light glowed from behind the shutters of the second. They peered at the doorstep, but there was no obvious black stone. Nor was there one at the next, or at the door after that.

A voice hailed them. Tanner felt his body go

taut. Turning, he saw a man on the main steps leading into the hospital across the road. Christ, but he hoped Vaughan could still pass himself off as a convincing German.

'I'm going to talk to him,' whispered Vaughan, as though reading his thoughts, and walked towards the man.

A doctor, he guessed. 'Good evening,' Vaughan said, in the very correct German he had perfected before the war.

'What are you doing?' asked the man.

Vaughan walked right up to him, climbed the first two steps, and saw that the man wore the rank of major on his shirt. 'I beg your pardon, good evening, Herr Major,' he added hastily, saluting.

The man waved a hand at him. *Oh, don't worry about that.* 'It's quiet tonight,' he said, as though he had forgotten his earlier question.

Just wants to talk. Vaughan tried to think clearly. *Act naturally*, he told himself. 'Yes, it is. Where are the Tommies tonight – with a convoy in too?'

'Staying away so far, thank God,' said the man. 'It's not easy trying to operate with bombs falling all around.'

'No, I can imagine not,' replied Vaughan, taking out a cigarette. The major moved towards him, pulling out his lighter, and lit it for him. Briefly, Vaughan saw his face. Middle-aged, a two-day growth of beard, deep lines running from his nose to his mouth. 'Thanks,' he said.

Tanner, watching this but understanding little of what was being said, stood silently on the road. *Jesus*, he thought. *Get a move on.* He

484

glanced down the hill towards the town. Another truck was passing through – he could see the dim slits of the lights and heard the change of gear.

'Fuel,' the major said, looking down towards the harbour, 'but not enough medical supplies.'

'There's never enough,' said Vaughan, 'but that's always the soldier's lot.'

'The doctor's too.'

From across the road, they heard a radio playing 'Lili Marlene'.

'I hate that song,' said the major.

Vaughan chuckled. 'I know what you mean. Have you been in Tobruk long?'

'Since the end of June. It was calming down a bit, but we had a lot more in after the Tommies attacked the other night.'

'We must have taken a lot more of them, though. A victory of sorts.'

'I suppose so.' They smoked in silence for a moment, then the doctor flicked his butt away. 'I must get back inside.'

'Here's hoping our quiet night continues,' said Vaughan.

'That would be most welcome,' said the doctor. 'By the way, what are you doing here?'

'Oh, looking for someone. An old friend.'

'A doctor?'

'No. But it doesn't matter. It was only on the off-chance.'

'They're doctors and medical staff in those villas, with just a few others – it is safer up here than down by the harbour. Anyway, I must be running along. I hope you find your friend.' He turned and went back inside.

Vaughan breathed a sigh of relief. Thank God the doctor hadn't pressed him.

'You took your time,' whispered Tanner.

'We're still alive, aren't we? Come on, let's find this bloody stone.'

While Vaughan had been conversing with the doctor, Tanner had been watching the road and wondering again whether he should mention Tanja Zanowski. How might Vaughan react if they found her? He now cursed himself: he should have suggested Farrer and he carried out the recce instead. *Well, it's too late now.* The next block down the road revealed no black stone either, but then, at the first door of the next villa, there it was: a round black stone as big as a fist on the doorstep.

'This is it,' he whispered to Vaughan, his heart quickening.

Vaughan breathed in deeply and glanced to either side of him once more. Then, satisfied that the coast was clear, he stood before the door, Tanner just behind him. They could hear talking and laughter from within.

Just knock, thought Tanner. *Let's get it over and done with.* He reached into his holster, pulled out the Walther, cocked it and flicked off the safety catch.

Footsteps, then the door opened, and a young woman, in a nurse's uniform, was standing in front of them.

Bollocks! thought Tanner.

'*Ja?*' she said.

'Ask for Tanja,' hissed Tanner, in Vaughan's ear.

He felt Vaughan flinch, but to his relief, Vaughan said, *'Ich bin für Tanja suchen. Ist sie hier?'*

The girl looked at him warily, then said, *'Ja. Kommen Sie in,'* and opened the door. *'Tanja, es gibt einige Leute hie für Sie.'*

Vaughan stepped forward, Tanner close behind him, his fingers curled around the grip and trigger of the Walther. For a moment no one said anything. There, sitting at a simple table in the-front room of the apartment, sat Tanja Zanowski, another nurse, and three men, all in uniform.

Christ, thought Tanner, and shut the door behind him.

'Tanja,' said Vaughan.

'My God,' said Tanja, in English. The light was dim – an oil lamp on the table the only illumination – but Tanner saw the shock on her face, and so did the man next to her: he glanced at her, then back at Vaughan, frowning.

'Was ist das?' he said now, getting to his feet. There was a pistol at his side and, seeing his hand instinctively reach for it, Tanner pushed past Vaughan and raised his weapon.

'No one say a word,' he said quietly. 'Sir, tell them.'

'Schweigen Sie alle!' said Vaughan.

Tanner's eyes slid over the ensemble before him. One of the men – blond hair, small chin – was unarmed, but the other two, the thickset man, and another with glasses, had pistols at their waists.

'Tell the girls not to scream,' Tanner said to Vaughan, 'or I will kill them all.'

Vaughan repeated the order, then said in

English, 'Tanja, come here now.'

With wide, frightened eyes, Tanja carefully pushed back her chair and stood up. As she did so, the man next to her lunged, dragging her in front of him so that Tanner could not get a clear shot. In the same moment, he had whipped out his pistol and now pressed it into her side. Tanja let out a muffled cry, but Tanner kept his arm outstretched, pointing at the man.

'What are you doing, Becker?' said Tanja.

'It's over,' he said in English. 'Put your weapon down, or I will shoot her.'

'No!' said Vaughan. 'Don't!'

'Then order your man to lower his pistol!'

Vaughan said nothing, but Becker moved his head clear. 'Now!' he said again, and in that moment, Tanner made a split-second decision. The shot hissed from the Walther, hitting Becker just above the right eye. He fell backwards, part of his skull and brain splattering against the wall behind. One of the girls let out a small scream. The man in the glasses reached for his pistol and Tanner shot him too.

'Shut up!' he said. 'All of you!' He nudged Vaughan. 'Tell them to stand up and face the back wall.'

Like an automaton, Vaughan repeated the order, as Tanner pushed the third man and the two girls roughly around the table. 'Sir,' he said, 'find a sheet. Tanja, grab any papers from Becker.'

Tanja did as she was told, but Vaughan just stood there, mute with disbelief.

Damn it all, thought Tanner. The man was whimpering and, Tanner now saw, had soiled himself. 'Bloody hell,' he muttered. 'We haven't got time for this.' He turned the man around, said, 'Sorry, chum,' then gave him a short, sharp jab on the left temple. He crumpled to the floor. Tanner pulled out Mustafa's flick-knife, ripped the German's shirt and tore it into strips, which he then used to gag and bind the hands of the two girls. They glared at him – and at Tanja.

'Right,' he said. 'Let's get them into one of the bedrooms.' A corridor led from the room, and Tanja now hurried ahead to open one of the doors.

'Tell them to lie face down on the floor,' he told her.

Tanja did so, the two girls obeying immediately.

Tanner stood over them and tore the last of the shirt into two. 'Here,' he said, handing a strip to Tanja. 'You tie her legs and I'll do the other's. Then let's get the hell out of here. Do you need anything?'

'Just my satchel,' she replied.

'Then get it, quickly.'

The girl who had initially answered the door began to writhe, and Tanner sighed. He hated having to act like this towards women. 'Sorry, ladies,' he said, standing up and shutting the door behind him. Tanja was now beside him too.

'All right?' he said.

She nodded. 'You killed Becker,' she said, a look of incredulity on her face.

'Who's Becker?'

'Cobra, Jack. Becker was Cobra.'

'He looked like a bloody snake to me,' Tanner muttered. 'Come on, let's go.'

He brushed past Vaughan and, without another

glance at the carnage within, opened the front door, checked that the road was clear, then ushered out Tanja and Vaughan. Calmly, steadily, they walked back up the road, then turned down the narrow passageway between the two villas through which they had come just fifteen minutes earlier. No one spoke as they carefully stepped across the sand and salt-bush to where the others were waiting.

'Evening, miss,' whispered Sykes.

'Right,' hissed Vaughan, suddenly returning to his senses. 'Let's keep moving.'

Four hundred yards on, they found another small hollow in the ground and paused. The town seemed as quiet as ever; barely anything stirring.

'I always said this was the way to do it,' said Vaughan. 'Infiltration of just a handful of troops. Anyway, we should get back to the MTB. We've done what we came for. We've got Apollo.'

'What about sabotage?' said Farrer.

Tanner turned to Tanja. 'Where are they taking all the fuel that's just come in?'

'It is divided into different dumps, but the biggest is just below the escarpment in an old quarry. It is perhaps a kilometre from Fort Solaro, just to the north of one of the landing grounds.'

'So that's about two miles south of here. Four miles from the coast, another mile or so to Allenby. That's the best part of six miles to cover.'

'Yes, but we got Tanja out far quicker than we'd imagined,' said Tanner. 'Look, sir, we've got a load of explosives, and if we can get that fuel dump it'll be a hell of a good job done. We all know that fuel is the one thing Rommel needs above all.'

'Why don't we get ourselves on one of those lorries?' suggested Farrer. 'Then we'll get a ride straight to the dump.'

'We could use time pencils,' said Sykes. 'Set them for a couple of hours hence, which would give us plenty of time to get away.'

Vaughan thought a moment. 'Farrer, you take Tanner, de Villiers, Sykes, McInnes and Ferguson. The rest of us will get back to the MTB.' He looked at his watch. 'It's a quarter to nine. Let's say an hour to reach the dump, half an hour to set the HE, then two and a half hours to get back. That's four hours, so one o'clock – that'll give us five hours of darkness, which means we should be beyond Mersa by then. Make sure you're back by one o'clock. Understood?'

They reached the town without incident, making their way quietly and carefully down the hill, away from the hospital, the villas and block-houses and towards the gentle curve at the end of the harbour. It was no wonder, Tanner thought, that Stirling's men, the LRDG and others had been having such successes. The desert was so vast and the enemy could not be everywhere all the time. Tobruk was three hundred miles behind the front line. Of course, as an important port, it needed to be well defended with guns, but anti-aircraft gunners were hardly expected to be the trained elite of the German and Italian armies, and in any case, most were positioned on the headland above the town or atop the escarpment, half a mile to the south of the town. Nor was the town throbbing with troops. They were needed at

491

the front. Most of those around the ships were B Echelon – the support troops who unloaded ships, took supplies to the front and protected the airfields. In any case, they wouldn't be billeted here, in this Godforsaken spot where they could be bombed and blasted to hell.

Tobruk had almost ceased to be a town at all, its buildings mostly reduced to rubble. The old British garrison had extended in a wide arc some ten miles from the sea, surrounded by wire, a minefield and gun positions. The town was small – Tanner imagined it had been little more than a sleepy fishing village before the Italians had arrived and built the hospital, the church and the military buildings around the harbour.

They picked their way over the rubble, dodging a light ack-ack gun and a searchlight manned by Italians, then making their way along the remains of a ruined street, past smashed and twisted cars and other vehicles. They clambered on to the rubble-strewn rise overlooking the quayside to watch the unloading.

The two ships were moored toe to tail. The men were operating almost entirely in darkness, although flashlights were flickering and a few dim oil lamps lined the quayside. Men were calling out to one another, the sounds distinct on the still night air.

A convoy of trucks now drove towards the port from the south, eventually coming to a halt so that they faced back the way they had come, with the increasingly large numbers of fuel barrels to one side of them. The derricks along the harbour's edge continued to delve into the ships' holds, then swing large pallets on to the quayside. Now that more trucks had arrived, swarms of men descended on the stocks building at the harbour's edge. Planks were laid from the tailgate to the ground, and the barrels rolled on to ropes. From the body of the trucks, several men pulled on the ropes while others pushed from behind until each barrel was safely on board and moved into position.

It was a laborious, time-consuming business, and Tanner was conscious that precious minutes were passing. Already it was twenty to ten.

'We need to get a move on,' whispered Sykes next to him.

'Just wait a minute, Stan,' said Tanner, who was rolling a plan of action in his mind. A few minutes later, loading of the lead vehicle was finished and he saw the driver edge it forward along the quay and stop. *Good lad.* Turning to Farrer, he said, 'I've an idea.'

Having made their way down to the western end of the harbour, they waited in the shadows as the loaded trucks came forward and halted in turn. They could hear the drivers getting down and talking to one another. Cigarettes were lit. Occasional laughter and a throaty guffaw. Unlike the men loading the barrels, the drivers seemed to be German, rather than Italians. *Even better.*

'Sir,' whispered Sykes, in Tanner's ear. 'What about causing a bit of mayhem around here?'

'Good idea.'

'I could set the time pencils on green.'

'How long's that?'

'Five hours.'

Farrer agreed. 'But you need to move quickly,' he said. 'They're loading the fifth truck now.'

Sykes disappeared.

'Will he be all right on his own?' Farrer whispered.

'He'll be fine. He's very light on his feet, is Sykes.'

It was half an hour later that Sykes reappeared, just as the eighth truck finished loading and moved forward. 'That was easy enough,' he said. 'They're all making such a racket down there it was easy to move about. I put a packet on one of the derricks and another next to the ack-ack gun at the end of the quay. Should cause a few headaches.'

Tanner patted him on the shoulder. 'Good work, mate.'

Eleven o'clock. *Two hours left.* There were ten trucks in all and as the ninth trundled forward the chatting drivers broke up their conversation and began returning to their vehicles.

'Now!' hissed Tanner. He, Sykes and Farrar scuttled across from their hiding place at the far edge of the quay towards the second truck, while de Villiers, McInnes and Ferguson hurried, crouching, towards the third in the line. Leaving Sykes and Farrer crouched at the passenger side of the lorry, Tanner moved round the back and crept towards the driver's door. He and Ferguson had had some discussion about the best way to make their attack, but eventually they had agreed to try to reach the driver's door undetected, then open it, jump up and stab the man in the kidney. Certainly, a blade in either kidney was the most effective way to kill a man silently: the pain was so intense, it caused the body to shut down instantly. The risk would be the time it took to jump up and the difficulty of hitting their mark. However, as Ferguson had pointed out, an assault was the last thing the driver would be expecting and the human brain always took a second or two to react to shock. As long as they made their moves swiftly and decisively, they had every reason to feel confident of success.

Tanner crouched low by the truck's cab. Above him, he heard the driver strike a match, then smelt cigarette smoke. The man sighed, then began humming to himself. Tanner took out the flick-knife, holding it, blade still folded in his palm. A change of plan... *One, two.* He heard the catch of the door on the truck behind him – *Ferguson. Three.* He stood and opened the door.

'*Was?*' said the driver, startled. Tanner punched him hard in the side of the head. The man gasped, rolled over, and Tanner opened the passenger door for Sykes and Farrer.

'Is he dead?' asked Sykes.

'I just knocked him out – cleaner and easier. No point killing a bloke for the sake of it.'

'It's just a bit of a squash with him here too.'

'Stop complaining, Stan. It's only a couple of miles.'

The lead truck's engine started, slits of lights came on, and Tanner saw another man run back past him.

'I forgot to ask,' said Farrer, 'you do know how

to drive this thing, don't you?'

Tanner laughed. 'An Opel Blitz? Oh, I think so. With or without an ignition key.' He felt the dashboard. 'Good.' Turning it, he saw the red light and pressed the starter button – *no need for choke*. A couple of turns and then the engine sputtered into life. Seeing the truck ahead move forward, he thrust the Opel into gear, released the handbrake, and rolled forward. The wing mirrors had been left in place and he saw the headlamp slits behind them.

'I think that's de Villiers at the rear,' he said, as they drove around the harbour's end.

'Good,' said Farrer. 'I'm sure we'd have heard something if there'd been a problem.'

They headed south, the barrels clanging together as they drove over a rock or a rough part of the track, then climbed a short, sharp incline and turned on to the edge of a landing ground where a number of aircraft were lined up, dark shapes in the starlight.

Sykes whistled. 'Look at all those lovely planes! Let's hope this fuel dump's nearby.'

It was. At the far end of the landing ground, they drove down the escarpment and turned into an old quarry where a large number of barrels had already been stacked. Following the truck in front, they pulled to a halt behind it.

'I'll stay with the truck,' said Farrer.

'Stan, you ready?' said Tanner.

'Yes – but what about matey here?'

'Leave him to me,' said Farrer. 'Go now.'

Tanner and Sykes jumped down as a number of men hurried towards the truck. By the time they had walked to the back, German troops were already climbing on to the body and laying two planks from the tailgate to the ground.

Someone spoke to them but they didn't reply and walked to the Opel behind. At the driver's door, Tanner said to de Villiers, 'Stay with the truck. Where's Ferguson?'

'Beside me,' de Villiers replied.

'Tell him to get down here.'

Flickering torches and barked orders. Barrels of fuel were being rolled out of the truck like beer into a cellar. Tanner and Sykes ducked round to meet Ferguson, then Tanner whispered, 'Come on, let's get going.'

Someone bumped into him, muttered something and walked on, but in the darkness they were able to use the shadows and slip clear of the work parties now swarming over the trucks.

'It's not going to need much,' said Sykes, as they crouched at the edge of the quarry. He had already prepared his devices: five-pound packets of Nobel's 808 cartridges, detonators already fixed, with a strip of safety fuse running from each detonator to the time pencil.

'I'm setting these on white,' said Sykes. 'An hour and a half.'

'Perfect,' said Tanner. 'They should blow at about one in the morning.'

Sykes laid the first between two of the barrels, then added a second. 'One more as a precaution,' he said, 'but that should be it.'

Footsteps made them start. A German walked towards them, asking something, his tone harsh, angry, even.

Damn it, thought Tanner – but Ferguson now stepped forward. A flash of a blade in the starlight, and the German crumpled. Ferguson caught him and dragged him into the shadows.

'Good work,' said Tanner, impressed.

'As you know, sir,' said Ferguson, 'speed and decisiveness are everything in close combat.'

'The dark helps.'

'Yes.' Ferguson chuckled. 'Just a little bit. Don't think he saw me coming.'

Calmly they made their way, unchallenged, to the far end of the quarry, set another device, then returned to their trucks. Tanner and Sykes got in beside Farrer.

'All done,' said Tanner, then noticed the driver on the floor. 'He's not woken up yet, then?'

'He did, I'm afraid. I pistol-whipped him. A little too hard, unfortunately.'

'Poor bugger,' said Tanner. 'Just not his night. Anyone spoken to you?'

'Not really. They're too busy unloading.'

'Looks like they're nearly done,' said Sykes. 'What about those aircraft?'

'Let's not push our luck,' said Farrer.

'But it's not every day you find yourself within touching distance of a line of Jerry and Eyetie planes,' said Tanner.

'No,' said Farrer, firmly. 'Let's rejoin the others and get the hell out of here.'

'Maybe you're right,' said Tanner.

'I know I am,' said Farrer. 'In any case, we don't have time. It's nearly midnight.'

A few minutes later, the truck in front started up and they were on the move again, driving away from the quarry and climbing the escarpment back up to the landing ground.

'Breaks your heart,' said Sykes, staring at the aircraft.

'If that fuel dump blows, they won't be going very far anyway,' said Farrer. 'Console yourself with that thought.'

'All right, sir,' said Sykes. 'I'll try.'

They reached the harbour around ten minutes later, and climbed out once more, but as they got down and approached de Villiers's truck, they saw the other three being challenged by several men.

'Damn!' whispered Farrer. 'They're being asked about the other driver.'

'We need to be ready to run, then,' said Tanner, cocking his MP40.

As they approached de Villiers and Ferguson, they saw the German asking the questions pull out a torch and shine it in their faces. He was looking at them carefully, then asking for something. De Villiers felt in his breast pocket for his *Soldbuch* and handed it over. The German had begun looking at it when he saw Farrer, Tanner and Sykes nearing and shone the torch on them instead. *'Und wer sind Sie?'* he said. Tanner squinted, but was conscious of the driver of the lead vehicle now approaching too. *Damn it.*

'Wir wurden gebeten,' said Farrer, *'diese Fahrzeuge fahren hier.'*

'Sie,' said the man, calling over the driver of the lead truck, *'ist das wahr?'*

Before he could answer, a cry came from de Villiers's truck where the bloody corpse of the

499

driver had been discovered. Without waiting a moment longer, Ferguson stepped forward, stabbed the man with the torch, while Tanner, pulling out his Walther, shot the other three. Despite the silencer, though, it was too late. Men were shouting; the alarm had been raised.

'Stick to me!' called out Farrer, as a shot rang out.

They ran across the quayside towards the rubble of a ruined building, more shots following them. Crouching beside the remains of a wall, Farrer did a quick head count. 'We stick together,' he said. 'We'll head into the town – the rubble will give us cover.'

'And don't fire,' hissed Tanner. 'It'll give us away.' He turned to Sykes. 'Now's the time for a diversion.'

Torches were being shone, orders barked. A sub-machine gun opened fire, bullets pinging and ricocheting nearby.

'We need to move,' said Farrer.

'Sykes and I'll catch you up, sir,' said Tanner.

'We stick together.'

'We need to create a diversion. Go, sir – we won't be far behind.'

Farrer clasped Tanner's shoulder, then crouching, set off, the others following.

Another burst of sub-machine-gun fire rattled out, and Tanner ducked instinctively, but this time it was further to their right.

'Here – quick,' said Sykes, passing a packet of TNT to Tanner. 'It's got a detonator in.' With a pair of cutters he snipped the safety fuse so that it was just a quarter of an inch long, then struck a match and lit the end. Footsteps were approaching, and another burst of submachine-gun fire rang out, closer again this time, the bullets pinging nearby. 'Now!' said Sykes, and Tanner stood up and hurled the packet towards the trucks.

Shouts of alarm, a furious volley of bullets towards them, but then the TNT blew. Crouching by the wall, head down, Tanner felt the explosion and the blast of heat just forty yards away. Then there was a second, louder explosion and he peeped up to see three trucks engulfed in flames and a fireball rising behind them. Debris showered down, and then Tanner was getting to his feet and yelling at Sykes to follow. Frantically, they scrambled up the rubble-strewn rise above the quayside. Where the hell were the others? Tanner glanced back, saw the trucks still engulfed in flames and thick smoke pitching into the sky. The survivors would be getting to their feet again soon, so he hurried on, Sykes close behind him.

'Here!' called a voice, and following it, Tanner hauled himself over another pile of rubble and into the remains of a street, where dark figures now stepped towards them.

'Some explosion,' said Farrer. 'We're one down. McInnes.'

'Damn,' said Tanner. 'He was a good bloke.'

'Yes, but we need to hurry,' said Farrer. 'We've got forty minutes to get back.'

They moved off again, picking their way along empty, rubble-filled streets. From the harbour, the glow of the flames flickered, and as they crested the headland above the town, they saw vehicles moving back along the road towards the town and heard motorcycles. From the end of the harbour, a searchlight made sweeps down the length of the water and the shores either side.

The hunt is on, thought Tanner, as they stole back towards the track on which they had first entered the town. Where was that gun position? Almost immediately he saw the barrel pointing skywards, no more than sixty yards away. They kept going, Tanner wincing at the sound of every step on the still night air, convinced they would be heard at any moment. Then vehicles were heading towards them, and Farrer led them south of the track.

''Ere, sir,' Sykes whispered to Tanner, as the others crept on. 'You remember those Murray Switches?'

'Can you set one up before that M/T reaches us?'

Sykes glanced up the track. 'A quarter of a mile? I reckon so.'

'Come on, then.' Cutting back to the track, they found a couple of big stones. Sykes tied one end of some fuse around the larger one, then ran it across the track to the other side, where he set the switch to its pressure mode. Checking the tension in the fuse, now some four inches off the surface of the track, and content that it was tight enough, they ran, the vehicles now no more than seventy yards away.

They were well clear when the device blew, the explosion sending a pulse through the ground and ripping the first of the vehicles into fragments. The second, too close behind, was also engulfed in the blast. Tanner watched the Krupp truck momentarily framed in the light of the explosion before it was enveloped in flames. Burning men tumbled out on to the ground, some screaming, others already dead.

Tanner felt a wave of nausea, then said, 'Come on, Stan, iggery,' and dashed away.

They caught up with the others as they were crossing the track beside the mouth of the narrow gully that led to the sea.

'We've got just twenty minutes,' said Farrer.

'Then let's go straight across the headland to the coast,' said Tanner. 'No need to head down the gully now.'

They ran, more intent on covering the ground as quickly as they could than worrying about making a sound. In any case, the watch they had carried out earlier in the day had not revealed any gun positions along this stretch.

12.50. Tanner could sense the open sea not far ahead, could smell it on the light breeze wafting over the headland. His legs ached, his lungs ached, and now he stumbled and tripped. Cursing, he got to his feet once more, heard Sykes say, 'You all right, sir?' grunted in reply that he was, and then ran on. *12.55.* They reached the coast and paused to get their bearings. Damn it, where was the cove? Had they run past it? Then de Villiers said he recognized the curve of the rocks below – they were almost there, just another hundred yards or so. *12.57.* The cove was now in view, and they were scrambling down the shallow cliff towards the sea. *Where's the sodding MTB?* thought Tanner, his heart sinking. *Please – please don't let it have gone.*

At that moment, the three Packard engines

roared into life and there, bobbing on the water, was MTB 270. A minute later, the four men were running up the narrow gangplank from the shore.

'That everyone?' said Charteris's familiar voice.

'Yes,' said Farrer, 'all but McInnes. I'm afraid he bought it.'

'I'm sorry,' said Charteris, pulling in the gang-plank. 'You cut it bloody fine, though. We'd have given you one more minute. Sounded like quite a party.'

'Where's Vaughan?' asked Tanner.

'Down below,' said Charteris. 'Guarding our agent.'

Tanner breathed a sigh of relief. 'Thank God,' he said. 'We got her out all right.'

'Maybe, but we've still got to get back to Alexandria,' said Charteris, as they slipped out of the little cove and headed out to sea. 'This mission isn't over yet, you know. Not by any means.'

25

There had been some discussion as to whether the enemy would have found the explosives down at the fuel dump in light of what had followed, but a little before one thirty, when they were some ten miles east of Tobruk, they heard a low, distant explosion.

'That's got to be worth all the effort,' grinned Farrer, as they sat below in the galley.

'It will be if we get back all right,' muttered Vaughan.

Tanja was sitting apart from the others. She looked exhausted, Vaughan thought, and, frankly, *dirty*, her hair unwashed, her dress dusty and stained. The glamour she had exuded during those heady days in Cairo had gone, yet there was no doubting her beauty. Unkempt hair and clothes in need of washing could not hide it.

He had been stunned to see her. *Stunned. Dumbfounded.* Literally – he'd frozen, unable to think clearly, so much so that he'd nearly bungled the entire operation. It had not occurred to him for one minute that she could be anywhere other than in captivity in Cairo. But she had been released, sent back into the clutches of the enemy, a double-agent. Or was she? He hardly knew what to think now. Not just Tanja, but Maunsell, Bowlby – all of bloody SIME, for all he knew – had been using him, lying to him. He felt so let down, so betrayed. So humiliated. Now she caught his eye. A look of real sadness, of regret – except he doubted it now. *All a bloody act.* He looked away. He could hardly bear to see her, let alone talk to her. What was there to say, after all? He'd thought everything of her, but now there was nothing.

And everyone bloody well knew it, too. He looked at Tanner, out of German uniform now, arms resting on his knees, staring into space, lost in thought. Christ, he'd not even spoken to Tanner yet. Barely a word had passed between them since he'd heard him whisper, 'Ask for Tanja.' Tanner looked at him now, as though sensing Vaughan's eyes on him, and gave an almost imperceptible nod.

'Fancy some air?' Vaughan asked him.

Wordlessly, Tanner followed him out of the hatch at the stern of the MTB and on to the unmanned rear deck, where they sat down on the low cabin roof. Tanner took out a packet of cigarettes, offered one to Vaughan, then lit his and offered the glowing end to light Vaughan's. Behind them, the wake glittered and sparkled with its strange phosphorescence.

'I'm sorry,' said Tanner, eventually.

'You knew,' said Vaughan.

'I guessed.'

'How, Jack? How could you possibly have guessed?'

Tanner told him of seeing Mustafa, of following him, first through the bazaar and then on the train north to Alexandria. He told him of his fight with the man they had been hunting so long, of finding Tanja on the train and of seeing the Junkers coming to get her, of finding Maunsell at El Teirieh and the oath of silence the intelligence chief had made him and Sykes swear.

'Stan was all for us telling you yesterday,' he confessed, 'but I reckoned there had to be a reason why they'd not told you. And I suspected it would be her, but I couldn't say for sure.' He turned to Vaughan. 'I was wrong on the first point, I see that now, and wrong on the second.'

'I suppose they were worried I'd not carry out the task if I knew Apollo was Tanja.'

'Then they don't know you very well, do they? I gave my word, Alex, and until this evening, I've felt obliged to keep it. I'm not even sure I'm allowed to tell you now, but they've treated you badly, and as far as I'm concerned I'm not honour-bound to RJ any more. I live my life by my own code, and I believe a man should look out for his mates, stand by them. It pains me to think I've helped make life worse for you.'

Vaughan sighed. 'Thanks, Jack.' He inhaled deeply. 'Anyway, we did what we were asked to do. We got her out.'

'And killed Cobra.'

'Cobra?'

'Yes. That bloke Becker – the one who put the pistol to Tanja. He was the one running the Cairo circuit.'

Vaughan was silent for a moment, then added, 'A fuel dump blown up too. A good night's work.'

'Yes,' said Tanner. 'I reckon we must have pissed off a fair few of them tonight.'

'I still wonder, though, whether we shouldn't have gone straight back to the MTB and got out of there sooner.'

'We got away with it last time.'

'But we weren't very successful then. The hornets' nest wasn't quite so thoroughly stirred up.'

It was six a.m. They heard the Macchis long before they spotted them, Barclay calling up to the bridge from his W/T station.

'I'm getting lots of Eyetie chatter, Cap'n sir,' he said. 'I'm pretty certain they're pilots.'

Tanner had again offered to man the port side Brownings so had been at action stations, facing west, and had begun to sweep the sky with his binoculars, when the Lewis gunner up front

507

yelled a warning, followed almost immediately by a further shout of recognition from the bridge.

'Bandits, one o'clock!' yelled Allenby.

Tanner turned, swinging his Brownings as he did so, and spotted them, as they closed rapidly towards them out of the sun. Fighters, single engine, four of them and, yes, Macchi 202s.

Allenby gave instructions for the helmsman to zigzag the boat, the vessel lurching to port as the Macchis opened fire. *Way off*. Tanner held his fire, then aimed at the flight leader, lower and further ahead of the other three. At the front, the Lewis guns were opening up and tracer was pumping out, the sky torn apart by bullets and cannon shells. Allowing plenty of aim-off, he opened fire at around two hundred yards as a stream of bullets scythed across the sea to their starboard. A couple of seconds later, the lead Macchi was past, its pale belly streaking low overhead no more than two hundred feet above them, followed by the others in turn.

Tanner swung the Brownings around. The MTB was now speeding straight ahead again as he watched the Macchis climb and bank, preparing for another run. They turned in line astern, one following the other, unthreatening dark insects until they were rapidly growing again and bearing down upon them. Machine-guns and cannon opened up as the Macchis swooped down, their guns spitting bullets and cannon shells. Tanner fired again, the twin machine-guns juddering. One of the Macchis was flying straight towards them, orange stabs from the gun ports, bullets spitting a line of little fountains across the sea that seemed to be heading straight for them. Tanner grimaced, tensing, but then the MTB lurched to starboard, Tanner almost losing his balance as the deck tilted, and the Macchi was hurtling past, Tanner swinging his Browning. Bullets raked across the fighter's fuselage – *mine?* It hardly mattered. As another flew over, bullets clattered across the stern of the boat and the gunner on the cannon staggered backwards and fell.

Tanner fired again as the final pair swept over them, swinging his twin MGs round in a high arc. Wiggans, the coxswain, was hurrying to the stern and Allenby had taken over the helm as the Macchis flew on and began to climb. But now there was a catch in one of the Italians' engines, and Tanner saw a belch of smoke. The other three were still climbing in a wide arc, as the stricken aircraft stuttered again. The Italian pilot was trying to gain crucial height, but there was a loud bang from the engine, another puff of smoke and then the Macchi plunged towards the sea a few hundred feet below. A wing sheared as it hit the water, and then it was gone.

The other Macchis were turning south, back towards the thin strip of land several miles away. *Thank God they've gone*, thought Tanner.

Wiggans looked back towards the bridge, Smithson, the gunner, at his feet. 'He's gone, Cap'n sir,' he called back.

'Damn it!' cursed Allenby. He shouted below, 'Get some men aft and help Wiggans.'

Tanner watched two men emerge through the hatch, then saw Wiggans hurrying back to the bridge. 'We've got a problem, sir,' he said to

Allenby. 'Fuel tanks have been hit, both of 'em. It's gushing out the back.'

'Shit!' said Allenby, banging his hand on the instrument panel in front of him. 'And Smithson gone too. All right, Coxswain, you take over the helm.' He called below, 'Number One!'

Charteris hurried forward. 'Yes, sir?'

'I need our position. Where are we?'

'Ten miles off the coast and about forty miles east of Mersa.'

'Call Major Vaughan, will you? Then both of you come up to the bridge.' He turned to Tanner. 'Could do with your opinion too.'

Climbing down from the gun turret, Tanner asked Sykes to take over, then went forward up to the bridge.

'I'm sorry, gentlemen,' said Allenby, 'but we've got a big problem. That attack ruptured the fuel tanks. God knows how long we've got left, but it won't get us back to Alexandria.'

'Bugger it!' said Vaughan. 'I'm sorry, Jim. It's my fault. I should have ordered everyone to return to the MTB as soon as we'd picked up Apollo.'

Allenby raised a hand. 'Blaming anyone isn't going to help. The point is, what are we going to do? We can try to keep going and we might make it past the Alamein Line. On the other hand, it's a quiet stretch of shore, forty miles east of Mersa where the coast road is some ten miles further south. We could pull in there, hole up for the day and radio for help tonight.'

Vaughan rubbed his chin. 'But the enemy are likely to intercept any radio signal, aren't they?'

'Yes, but they'd have to send troops down to

find us. It wouldn't be easy. There's still no moon.'

'Where's the nearest enemy landing ground?' asked Tanner.

'That would have to be Fuka,' said Vaughan.

'For what it's worth,' said Allenby, 'I'd say heading for the coast now is our best bet.'

'There is one other alternative,' said Tanner. Allenby and Vaughan looked at him. *Yes?* 'We radio now and ask to be picked up by air.'

'By air?' said Allenby, incredulous.

'Yes,' said Tanner. 'In the battle a few weeks back, we rescued the CO of 649 Squadron, a Kiwi called Archie Flynn. He said if we were ever in trouble to call him and he'd help. He and his men are based near Burg El Arab now. That's less than two hundred miles away. They could be at the coast in an hour. I can't see the enemy getting troops there from Mersa in that time.'

'But they could send aircraft.'

'They're going to send aircraft whatever we decide.'

Allenby cleared his throat.

'If we signal now,' said Tanner, 'Naval HQ could tell Air HQ and Flynn or someone else can be airborne in under ten minutes. Does Naval HQ know about this mission?'

'Of course,' said Allenby.

'Then they know the importance of getting Apollo back safely.'

Allenby looked at Vaughan. 'I'm sorry,' he said, 'it's one of those decisions where we'll only know which is the right one later. I think we should send the signal now. It's the option that gives us the quickest chance of getting back to Alexandria.'

'All right.'

'Helmsman, head for the coast,' said Allenby.

'Yes, Cap'n sir,' replied Wiggans, rolling the wheel so that a great arc of white foam followed them as they turned south.

'I'm going down to talk to Sparker,' said Allenby.

The others followed, standing anxiously between Barclay's radio and Charteris looking at the chart.

'All right, Sparker,' said Allenby, 'send this. "From MTB 270, urgent air rescue needed from coast forty miles east of Mersa Matruh. Apollo on board. Ask for Squadron Leader Archie Flynn, 649 Squadron. Precise co-ordinates to follow. Repeat urgent."'

Barclay tapped out the message, paused, sent it a second time, then glanced up at Allenby, who was biting one of his nails. 'It's gone, sir.'

Allenby looked at the roof of the galley, breathed out heavily, then said, 'Start praying, chaps.'

A minute passed, then a signal came through, Barclay hastily scribbling in pencil. '"Received and understood", Cap'n sir,' he said. Another minute passed, then five more. The MTB was still surging towards the coast, as Wiggans shouted from the bridge, 'Enemy aircraft ahead!'

No sooner had he said this than Barclay was scribbling again. 'Flynn on way with fighter escort,' he read out. 'Send co-ordinates. Urgent.'

'Thank God,' said Vaughan.

Allenby had already hurried back up to the bridge. Tanner made his way aft to the stern hatch, and climbed out, scanning the sky. He heard the chatter of machine-guns and the *pom-pom-pom of* the cannons almost immediately. Then their own guns opened up, the sound deafening. A moment later two Messerschmitt 109s roared overhead, just a hundred feet above the sea. Tanner watched them fly on, climb and bank, then turn back for another run. More furious gunfire. The MTB lurched to port and Tanner slid across the deck, but again the Messerschmitts' fire was wide. A third run was just as unsuccessful; Allenby, Tanner realized, was skilled at manoeuvring the vessel out of the line of fire at just the right moment. The Messerschmitts flew off, presumably low on fuel, and ammunition spent. *Two attacks already*, thought Tanner, *and still not half past six*.

The engines were coughing and spluttering as, shortly after, they reached the coastline. Directly ahead lay a long beach of white sand, but to the west the coast dropped south, and Tanner saw they were tucking the MTB in there. Moving along the deck towards the bridge, he watched Wiggans manoeuvre the vessel. The end of the beach was squared off, almost at right angles, and the MTB was able to run alongside and moor right at the water's edge.

'Bloody good spot, this,' he said to Allenby. Beyond, there was nothing, just flat, featureless desert. He couldn't see so much as a single shack anywhere.

'They've got a low draught, these Elcos,' Allenby replied, 'but actually, the water's quite deep here – look.' Tanner leaned over the rail and peered into the clear water, which twinkled a deep blue in the early-morning sun.

'What are our co-ordinates, Number One?'

Allenby yelled down to the galley. Charteris called them out. 'Got those, Sparker?'

'Yes, Cap'n sir – just sending them now.'

'With a description.' He peered through his binoculars. 'And say that the ground will make an ideal landing strip.'

'Yes, Cap'n sir,' Barclay replied.

'Keep at action stations!' Allenby shouted, as several of the crew jumped ashore with ropes and began tethering the vessel. At the same time, camouflage nets were laid over the boat, two poles hammered into the ground to keep the netting clear.

'Right,' said Allenby. 'We watch and wait.' He glanced at his watch. 'Forty minutes or so.'

Tanner went below and found Tanja lying on a bunk in the officers' cabin. 'Are you all right?' he asked.

She smiled weakly. 'My God,' she said, 'what a mess. Do you think we will ever get out of here?'

'I don't know. I'd like to think so. The netting will make us hard to spot from the air to anyone more than a few hundred feet up, and in any case, we've quite a lot of firepower.'

'And what will happen to me if we do get back?'

'I honestly don't know, Tanja.'

'Damned either way.'

Tanner was about to say something, then changed his mind. What was there to say? *Damned either way*. He reckoned she was about right.

It was forty minutes since the first signal had been sent when they spotted the next enemy air-craft, four fighters buzzing over at two thousand feet. Tanner stood on the steps of the pilothouse leading up to the bridge as Barclay picked up pilot radio chatter.

'What are they saying?' asked Vaughan, standing behind him.

'I can't understand, sir,' Barclay replied.

'Here,' said Vaughan. 'Let me have a listen.' He put the headset on and looked at Tanner. 'Two of them are going to dive lower,' he said. 'They've been told where we are but they're complaining they can't see a damn thing.'

Tanner saw them now, two Messerschmitt 109s peeling off and diving.

'Don't fire until fired upon!' called Allenby.

The aircraft thundered past at just a thousand feet.

'They still can't see anything,' relayed Vaughan. 'They're trying further along the coast.'

Five minutes later they hurtled past again.

'He's spotted us,' said Vaughan. 'They're coming down for one pass each, then heading for home.'

'Get ready, everyone!' called Allenby. Machine-guns and cannons rattled loudly as the first 109 hurtled towards them, but it was met by a volley of return fire, which forced it to bank and, in so doing, lose its aim.

Tanner climbed up beside Allenby, feeling impotent. 'Our boys need to open fire a fraction earlier,' he said. 'We need to put them off their aim.'

Allenby nodded, as the second 109 swooped in low towards them, but on this occasion overshot. Now the third approached.

515

'Plenty of aim-off!' shouted Tanner, then yelled, 'Fire!' A hail of bullets and cannon shells met the enemy fighter as it flew straight into their line of fire. As it screamed over, Tanner saw that the wings and underside were peppered with holes. A moment later there was a small explosion, flames fled backwards from the cowling and the 109 careered on to the beach and exploded. The men cheered, but already the fourth Messerschmitt was upon them and this time a line of bullets scythed across the prow.

'Tanja!' muttered Tanner to himself, hurrying down below. Bullets had torn through the cabin, hitting two of the men. One of the crew lay crumpled on the floor, a rapidly expanding pool of blood beneath him. Ferguson, too, lay slumped, groaning, as blood spread from his stomach. Tanja was bent over him, calling for bandages, but Tanner could see that water was beginning to pour in. Grabbing his pack, he pulled out a handful of field dressings, ripping open the thin cotton packaging and passing one bandage after another to Tanja and Farrer.

'This man needs morphine,' said Tanja. 'Quickly.'

Ferguson groaned, as one of the crew hurried forward with the first-aid kit, ripping open the box and producing a phial and syringe. 'Here,' he said, pushing forward and thrusting the needle into Ferguson's arm. But it was no use. Ferguson had been hit three times, once in the leg, and twice across his stomach and chest. He spluttered, blood spilling from his mouth, looked at Tanja with frightened eyes, gripped her arm, and then, with a spasm, died. Tanja released his hand gently, and turned away.

Tanner looked down. Already an inch of water was swilling at their feet. He went halfway up the steps. 'Water's coming in fast,' he said to Allenby. 'I'd say there are too many holes to try and fill them.'

Allenby came down and was confronted by the wreck of his cabin. 'Bloody hell,' he said. 'Carter now too – and Ferguson.' He wiped a hand across his mouth. 'Get all essential kit on to the shore. Sparker – stay at your station for the moment. Everyone else, get out of there.'

'Yes, Cap'n sir,' called back Barclay, then shouted, 'It's them! It's bloody well them!'

Tanner stood on the shore, listening, as Allenby jumped down beside him with a Very pistol in his hand. 'Come on, you buggers!' he said. Then one of the men pointed and Tanner brought his binoculars to his eyes. He saw the plane, a Mitchell bomber, low over the water, just below the sun.

Allenby fired the flare, but as it soared into the air, they heard distant machine-gun chatter and saw the glint of the sun on Perspex as a fighter rolled high in the sky above. The dogfight rapidly moved forward, Macchis and Messerschmitts battling with a squadron of Kittyhawks, bursts of fire flashing across the sky.

A Macchi broke away and dived down towards them, but the gunners on the MTB opened fire again, the Italian pilot banking as a Kittyhawk raced after it, hugging its tail. The Mitchell was now almost over them, its engines a deep roar as it turned over the shore, banked in a wide arc to

517

the south, then slowly came into land. Tanner watched, scarcely daring to breathe, as the wheels touched down and the great beast lumbered towards them, jolting over the rough sandy surface.

'It's going to overrun,' muttered Farrer beside him, as the Mitchell continued to run forward.

'No,' said Tanner. 'He'll be fine.'

The bomber pulled up yards before the edge of the beach, then turned and halted, its propellers still whirring. A hatch opened, and they were all running towards it, the gunners jumping down from the MTB and sprinting over the desert scrub.

A roar of engines overhead and the tell-tale chatter of machine-guns made Tanner turn. A 109 was bearing down on them but two Kitty-hawks were on its tail and as the Messerschmitt opened fire with a one-second burst that clattered over the Mitchell's fuselage, the British pilots hammered it so that it hurtled over the Mitchell and ploughed straight into the desert beyond.

Come on, come on. A bottleneck at the hatch as they frantically jumped aboard. Overhead, the Kittyhawks managed to steer the enemy fighters clear of the Mitchell. Another explosion, this time a grenade thrown into the sinking MTB, the *coup de grâce* to prevent the enemy getting their hands on it, and Allenby was running towards them.

'Go on, Jack,' said Vaughan. Tanner leaped up, felt arms grab him and pull him clear, then Vaughan and finally Allenby tumbled on board. The hatch was closed and now the Mitchell was rolling forward, gathering speed. More machine-

gun fire, so close that Tanner ducked instinctively, but still the Mitchell was surging forward
until, miraculously, the terrible jolting eased and
the bomber was airborne.

Tanner glanced at Tanja, her face and dress
stained with Ferguson's blood, then went
forward, past the radio operator and navigator, to
the cockpit. Behind, the tail gunner was still
firing, but the battle was dying away as the
Mitchell sped out over the Mediterranean,
weaving low over the surface of the sea.

'That's those little bastards gone,' muttered the
pilot, his oxygen mask dangling free.

'Archie,' said Tanner.

Squadron Leader Flynn grinned. 'Jack bloody
Tanner as I live and breathe!'

Tanner laughed. 'Thanks for the rescue,' he
said. 'I honestly don't think I've ever been more
glad to see someone in my life.'

26

Sunday, 20 September. It was still early in the
morning, although for Tanja it already seemed
one of the longest days of her life. The sailors,
Allenby and his crew, had already left by truck
for Alexandria, but she and the rest of C
Detachment were waiting at Burg El Arab for an
onward flight to Heliopolis.

Burg El Arab. It was here, she realized, that
General Gott had boarded his fatal flight. She

still bitterly regretted her part in that. Twelve o'clock, she'd been told by Orca. Noon. She had known what it had meant, and had changed it to two o'clock. If either Cobra or Orca challenged her, she would have pretended an oversight had made her miss the '1' of '12'. She had signalled two p.m., not twelve. Her well-intentioned ploy had backfired. As Bowlby had explained during her initial interrogation, Gott had been delayed not once but twice. Fate had played a cruel hand that day.

She sat apart from the others. Exhaustion swept over her. She desperately wanted to talk to Alex, but he had steadfastly refused to speak to her, avoiding her as much as possible. Such hatred in his eyes! It was more than she could bear. Tanja stood up and wandered outside. It was warm, but not overwhelmingly so – not yet at any rate. The heat of the day rose later, in the third week of September.

'I'm sorry,' said a familiar voice behind her, 'but I need to take you back inside the tent. Where we can see you.'

'And where exactly am I going to run to?' she asked, conscious of the catch in her voice and the tears threatening to flow from her eyes. 'Alex,' she said, taking a step towards him. 'Please. There's so much I want to explain to you.'

'Why?' said Vaughan. 'What's the point when I know it will all be lies?'

'It is not all lies.'

'But how can you expect me to believe you? After what you did?'

'Alex, please,' she said. 'Come over here. Away

from the others.'

He glanced back at the tent, then took a few steps towards her. 'All right,' he said. 'I'm listening. Tell me, Tanja.'

She closed her eyes for a moment. *Where to begin?*

'Get your story straight first,' he said.

A tear ran down her cheek. 'I love you, Alex,' she said. 'When I told you that, I was telling you the truth.'

He swallowed, and breathed in deeply, then whisked away a fly from his face.

'I never thought I would ever love again after Tomas died.'

'Tomas?'

'Yes, Alex – my husband. He was a German. Not a Nazi, but an educated German, in the diplomatic service, working in Warsaw. I met him in 1936, we married six months later, and within a year he had been murdered – by the NKVD.'

'The Russian secret service.'

'Yes. And the Russians also killed my brother, destroyed my home, ransacked the village, raped a number of the women and murdered anyone who tried to defy them. I managed to flee, having abandoned my parents. I was completely alone, running and running, south through Poland, into Romania, then to Yugoslavia. I was in Belgrade when the government there collapsed. Suddenly there were the Germans and I was being offered a chance – a chance for survival but also a chance for revenge. By spying for the Germans, I thought I could help bring the downfall of Stalin and Communist Russia.'

521

'By spying against the British? Oh, Tanja, please, spare me.'

'No, Alex, this world – this war – it is not black and white. You remember when I got so angry at the Union Club? It was because I have heard this so often. That the only enemy is the Nazis and that the British cause is the moral one. It is not as simple as that. I was married to a German – a good man – and my family and home were destroyed by the Soviets. If you had had your home and family – your life – ripped to pieces, you would see things very differently. I was angry, so very, very angry. And I was guilty, too. I had survived. I needed to do something – something to help *my* people.'

'And in so doing sent countless people to their deaths.'

'We're all doing that, Alex!' she said, exasperation and despair in her voice. 'God knows, you must have killed enough people in your time, and what about Flynn and his crew? What about your men last night? Do you think it right that innocent supply troops and dock workers should be killed? Do you think it fair that thousands of innocent civilians should die at the hands of Allied bombers? You British do not have the moral right to judge everyone and everything by your own standards. Of course I regret every life lost, but I did what I did for my country, however misguided that might have been. And I also did what I could to ensure as few people lost their lives as possible because of what I was signalling to Cobra. Even Gott I tried to save.'

'Gott? How?'

She told him. 'It was then,' she said, 'that I began to realize that what I was doing was not helping Poland in any way. I had thought that if Britain could be defeated here then the forces freed up might tip the balance on the Eastern Front, but now I realized that the chance for a German and Italian victory had gone. And, Alex, I met you. I fell in love with you. All the anger, the lust for revenge I had felt – it began to melt away. And then a miracle – I learned my mother and father are alive and with the Poles who are training to fight alongside the British. I knew then that I had to stop, that I could spy for Germany no longer. At David Stirling's party, I met his brother. The next day, I went to the embassy and confessed everything. It was the hardest thing I have ever done because I knew then that you would learn the truth and that we would not be together for much longer. I knew it would destroy what we had, and that broke my heart again.'

'And Peter contacted Bowlby?'

'Yes, and Maunsell. I was interrogated over and over. I gave them my codebook, deciphered all the messages that had been intercepted, and they told me they wanted me to become a double-agent and spy for them instead. They said I had no choice. I was to contact Cobra, tell him that the circuit was finished in exchange for their help in getting me out. None of Maunsell's colleagues knew. None of them. It was all arranged, but then Jack saw me with Artus – Mustafa – at the bazaar and told SIME. Maunsell was not there that afternoon, or else he would have stopped it.'

'So Sammy raided your flat and we were caught

like peas in a pod,' said Vaughan, unable to hide the bitterness in his voice.

'Yes. Maunsell released me a short while later. He pretended to interrogate me and then announced that I was innocent. That I could not be Marlin.'

'Jack said that Mustafa was visited by Orca the morning you left.'

'I had to tell Mustafa I was being picked up by Cobra. He insisted on escorting me – I think because he wanted proof that what I had told him was true.'

'So Orca believed you had slipped through the net – that you really had been freed?'

'He must have done. I expect he still does.'

'And then Jack turns up. He told me you saved his life.'

'Mustafa is a very dangerous man. I always hated him. I hated Orca too, and Cobra, although I liked Rommel's intelligence chiefs. They were kind to me.'

'You know Orca, then?'

Tanja shook her head. 'No. I saw him once, but not his face. I would recognize his voice anywhere, though.' She searched his eyes. 'So, now I have told you, and I will tell Maunsell and Bowlby that I have told you. It has been a terrible nightmare these past ten days. I miss you so much, Alex. I miss what we had.'

'But don't you see, Tanja?' he said. 'We were living a lie.'

'No, we were not. What we felt for each other was real. You never told me about your work, I never told you about mine, but I know you loved me too.'

Vaughan stood there, head bowed, as a Hudson approached the landing ground, arriving low out of the desert. 'I'm exhausted,' he said. 'I can't think straight any more. I want to believe you, Tanja, I really do, but I can't just turn back the clock, pretend that none of this happened. Perhaps you did have reasons for doing what you did, but you were still a spy for Germany. I can't just put that to one side.'

The Hudson touched down in a cloud of dust and sand.

He turned, but she caught his hand. 'Alex,' she said, 'please. I am frightened. I cannot do this any more. If Orca finds out about me, he will kill me.'

Vaughan let her hand drop. 'I'm sorry, Tanja. But I can't do this any more either. You're a beautiful, clever woman. Find someone else to save you.'

For a moment she stood there, watching him walk back to the mess tent to collect his kit. She felt crushed. The Hudson stood before her, large and menacing, the propellers still whirring. It would be so easy, she thought, to run into them, and end it there. At least she would have some control over that. But returning to Cairo was to venture once more into an unknown and uncertain future. *It is what we do not know that we fear.*

Vaughan had promised Captain Peploe that he would need Tanner and Sykes for two weeks at the most. For Sykes, it was thirteen days: after they had reached Cairo safely, he was given one more night, then sent back to Mena Camp. For Tanner, however, the return to the city had been marked by a series of debriefings – first with SIME and ISLD, and then, the following morning, at GHQ with the DMI and his team.

Slaps on the back, and enthusiastic praise: everyone had been delighted with the mission's success, which had gone some way to rectifying the disaster of a few days before. Maunsell had been positively cock-a-hoop, his gamble on sending Tanja Zanowski into the lion's den more than justified, even if Cobra had been killed, rather than captured.

'A shame he couldn't have been brought back alive,' Maunsell had said.

'Sorry about that, RJ,' Tanner replied, 'but I'm afraid it was him or Tanja.'

Maunsell had beamed. 'Of course, of course! You did absolutely the right thing. Anyway, can't have everything, eh?'

But Mustafa was dead. He had, Maunsell told Tanner, killed himself in his cell. 'With a small piece of glass in his suit pocket. Can you believe it? He cut his own throat and bled to death. He wasn't found until it was too late.'

'He didn't spill the beans on Orca, then?'

'No. Didn't say a word. He's the only person we've failed to break. Of all the people who have been through the interrogation centre, he's the only one. Incredible.'

'I can't say I'm sorry,' said Tanner. 'He was a right bastard. Nearly had the better of me. Tanja saved me.'

'Ah, yes, Tanja. What a gold mine she has proved.

The GS are absolutely over the moon with her information about Panzer Army Headquarters. They're all ill, apparently. Rommel's sick as a dog. I think we knew that they were struggling to get enough supplies but it's the state of his forces that's been such an eye-opener. Honestly, you chaps in Eighth Army don't know how lucky you are – rations galore, ammo aplenty, and the flesh-pots of Cairo on your doorstep. What do our enemy have? Bread like rock and twice daily renditions of "Lili Marlene"!'

'That's good to hear,' Tanner had said, but then had returned to Tanja. 'She saved my life, you know.'

'I didn't.'

'She pistol-whipped Mustafa. Another moment, and I'd have been a croaker.'

'Brave girl.'

'At El Teirieh,' he said, 'you promised to explain everything. Just who is Tanja? Was she Marlin?'

Maunsell had smiled enigmatically. 'One day I *will* tell you everything. But maybe not just now.'

'I only know what I saw,' said Tanner. 'Neither Vaughan nor Tanja told me anything.'

'She's a double-agent, Jack. That's all you need to know.'

'What will happen to her?'

Maunsell had smiled affably. 'Don't you worry about her. We have plans for Miss Zanowski.'

'And what about her safety? What if Orca discovers who she is? Or Mustafa's friends?'

'Jack,' Maunsell had said, putting an arm on his shoulders, 'we'll look after Tanja Zanowski, don't you worry. When do you rejoin your battalion?'

'Tuesday morning.'

'Well, when you get back to your men, if I were you, I'd put her, Orca and Mustafa right out of your mind and focus your energies on the battle to come.' Maunsell had been as tactful and charming as ever, but the message could not have been clearer: *this doesn't concern you any more.*

The debrief with the DMI had been more straightforward and had been conducted not one to one but with the other officers of C Detachment: Vaughan, Farrer and de Villiers. Brigadier Williams and the GS(I) boys were more interested in their descriptions of Tobruk, of what they'd seen of the port and the town. Apparently, Rommel was seething at the amount of fuel that had been lost. Enemy air forces had barely flown since. 'You've done bloody well,' Brigadier Bill had told them. 'Bloody well. Far more effective than that other fiasco.'

Tanner spent the afternoon with Lucie – and this time they had gone nowhere, barely venturing from her bedroom. It was like the old days, when he'd been recuperating. They made love, slept, talked, and Tanner felt himself relax in a way he had not been able to do for one moment since he'd left Cairo days before.

'The battle's coming, isn't it?' Lucie said to him later, as she lay with her head on his chest.

'Yes,' said Tanner.

'When?'

He shrugged. 'I doubt it'll be this month now. Probably October. When there's a moon. Maybe even November.'

She held him more tightly. 'All I ever seem to do is say goodbye to you. I'm worried that one day it'll be for the last time.'

'Well, don't,' said Tanner. 'I know how to look after myself.'

'You don't have to see as many torn and wounded men as I do.'

'I reckon I see enough. Listen, Luce, this will be the last big one for a bit. I'm sure of it. Rommel's finished this time. We'll have the battle, get him beat, and I'll be back again before you know it.'

She kissed him. 'Make sure you are.' She sighed. 'One day it's got to come to an end, hasn't it?'

'The war? I suppose so, yes. One day, but not just yet.'

Lucie was on nights, so Tanner had agreed with Johnny Farrer's suggestion that they all meet at Shepheard's. He liked Farrer, de Villiers too. In any case, it was his final night before he returned to the Rangers; very likely it would be his last time in Cairo before the battle. He was also glad that Vaughan had said he would join them. He reckoned a night on the town would do his friend some good. Might stop him brooding.

The terrace was as busy as ever, but by the time Tanner arrived a little after six, Farrer and de Villiers had already found them a table next to one of the giant ferns at the top of the steps. 'Ah, this is the bloody life,' said de Villiers, taking a large draught of his Stella.

'And nice to see men in uniform without sweat stains on their shirts,' added Farrer. 'This is my kind of temperature.' It was warm still, but the intense heat of August had gone.

'Here's to an autumn night in Cairo,' said Tanner, raising his glass.

Vaughan arrived soon after, looking exhausted. He sat down, lit a cigarette and ordered a beer.

'We'd begun to give up on you,' said Farrer.

'Sorry. The debriefings and meetings have gone on, rather. C Detachment is being put on hold, though.'

'Really? Why?' said de Villiers.

'Haven't we just had the most stupendous success?' added Farrer.

'Yes, but there's no obvious mission for the moment. Tobruk has been hit, Mersa's not big enough, Benghazi and Tripoli are too far, and Malta is proving ever more successful again as an anti-shipping base. From now on, C Detachment will come and go. Re-formed when required.'

'What will you do now?' asked Tanner.

'Freddie de Guingand's asked me to be one of his ADCs at Monty's HQ for the coming battle.'

'Congratulations,' said Tanner.

'It's an opportunity, certainly. And, to be honest, I'm sick to the back teeth with intelligence work. I'm looking forward to getting into the desert again.'

Farrer looked at de Villiers. 'We need to get a posting, old cock, and fast.'

'Back to your battalions?' said Tanner.

'I'd like to try for Stirling's lot,' said de Villiers.

'Hmm, that's a thought,' said Farrer.

'I'll give you a reference if that would help,' said Vaughan.

'Thanks,' said de Villiers. 'It would.'

They had talked on, one beer following another, until, as darkness fell, they had begun to wonder whether perhaps they shouldn't get something to eat.

'What do you think, Alex?' asked de Villiers. 'Shall we stay here?'

But Vaughan was no longer listening. Instead he was staring towards the steps.

Tanner followed his gaze. Tanja was standing there, no longer filthy and covered with blood but in an elegant evening dress, her hair combed and lips painted red. *Dazzling*.

'Tanja,' he said, pushing back his chair and getting up. De Villiers and Farrer were also on their feet.

'Oh, Jack,' she said, noticing him. 'I am sorry to interrupt.' She looked at Vaughan. 'Alex,' she said. 'Please. I need to talk to you.'

Vaughan sighed. 'Excuse me a moment, chaps.' He led her away, towards the hotel entrance.

'Bloody hell!' said Farrer. 'I always knew she was a pretty lass, but she looks incredible.' He whistled.

'She's a stunner,' agreed Tanner.

'What's going on?' asked de Villiers.

Tanner shrugged. It wasn't his place to tell them about those two.

A few minutes later, Vaughan walked back to them, Tanja in tow. 'Look,' he said, brow creased, 'I think I'm going to call it a night.'

'Really?' said Farrer. 'What about dinner?'

'Sorry, chaps,' he said. 'I'm done in. I just need a good night's kip, if I'm honest.'

He turned and left them, hurrying down the

531

steps, but Tanja remained where she was, her hand to her mouth, looking – what? *Looking scared*, thought Tanner. 'I'm going to bring her over,' said Tanner. 'You don't mind?'

'Mind?' said Farrer. 'Are you joking?'

'Tanja!' Tanner hurried over to her. 'Come and join us. Please.'

'I am sorry. I have ruined your evening.'

'No, you haven't.' He led her to the table, and Farrer held her chair for her.

'Tanja's worried she's spoiled the evening,' said Tanner.

'Nonsense,' grinned Farrer. 'You've improved it. Alex wasn't exactly in the best of spirits anyway.'

'If you are sure...' Her eyes were flitting from one table to another. *What is she so nervous about?* Maunsell had told him to forget about her, to leave her handling to SIME, but Tanner could see her fear was real enough. Whatever Maunsell had put in place for her protection, clearly she did not think it was enough. She'd saved his life: he couldn't forget that. And he was intrigued, too. Since he had cleared the air with Vaughan on the MTB, his friend had said no more on the matter, and Maunsell wasn't telling, and yet he was sure Tanja was connected with the Cobra circuit – she'd almost admitted as much in Tobruk. Perhaps she *was* Marlin. Marlin and Apollo – a double-agent, Maunsell had admitted. *Poacher turned gamekeeper.* She wouldn't be the first. The Russians had done it, after all.

It was almost ten o'clock, and the curfew was upon them. Farrer and de Villiers were drunk, but Tanner had deliberately held back. *Perhaps just a little bit tight.* And Tanja? It was hard to tell, but she was certainly agitated again, glancing at her watch and looking around.

'I'll walk you back,' he said.

Her face visibly relaxed. 'Thank you, Jack.'

'I owe you that, at least, I reckon.' He turned to Farrer and de Villiers. 'Time to go.'

'Ah,' said Farrer, waving a finger, 'not for us. We're staying at this fine establishment.'

'Well, we're not and it's almost ten,' said Tanner. 'Cheers, lads. And good luck.' He patted them on the shoulder.

'Don't let him take advantage of you, Tanja,' said de Villiers.

She kissed them both. 'I won't,' she promised.

When they were clear of the hotel, Tanner said, 'What are you so nervous about?'

Tanja stopped. 'Oh, Jack,' she said, 'I'm so frightened.' She felt in her bag. 'Here,' she said, passing him a note. Tanner unfolded it. *Watch out. You know what happens to pigs that squeal.*

'It was put under my door this afternoon. I opened the door and saw a boy running down the stairs. The *bawaeb* said he had never seen him before.'

'And who is it from? Orca?'

'I think so.'

'Tanja, I want to help you, but I don't know what the bloody hell is going on any more. Are you Marlin as well as Apollo?'

'Yes,' she said quietly.

'I think you'd better tell me everything,' said Tanner.

'All right.'

Ah, so that's it, thought Tanner, as the entire story emerged.

'I told this to Alex,' she said, 'at Burg El Arab. I hoped he would understand. I do love him very much, you see.'

'Maybe he does understand,' said Tanner. 'But understanding and forgiveness are two different things, aren't they? He's broken-hearted, that's obvious to any bloke, but his pride's hurt too. He's been humiliated by this, Tanja. And you *were* our enemy. You spied for Germany. I'm not going to judge you, but you're expecting a lot if you think Alex can just put that to one side.'

As they crossed to her street, the city seemed suddenly very quiet. It was after ten now, and all traffic had gone. Cairo was still once more, yet Tanner couldn't help feeling they were being followed. Twice he looked back, but there was no one. Not even a cat. He chided himself – Tanja's fears were making him paranoid, and yet the note was sinister.

'I don't,' she said. 'But I had hoped that if he knew my life was in danger then perhaps he would help protect me. I hoped he would not wish to see me dead.'

'Did you tell Maunsell and Bowlby about your fears?'

'Of course, and they've put a guard outside my apartment block. One Field Security officer.'

Tanner thought a moment. 'All right. Look, I'll stay with you tonight, then tomorrow we'll both go and see Maunsell. He told me he had plans for you. Maybe he can speed those up. Get you away from here. Or maybe we can just bloody well find out who Orca is and nobble the bastard.'

Tanja took his hand. 'Thank you, Jack.'

'You saved my life,' he said, 'so I'll try and make sure you keep yours.'

They passed the FS guard, who sat in the entrance hall of the apartment block, reading a book, and went up to her flat, where she poured them both a Scotch.

Tanner sat her table, wondering if she had sent all those signals to Cobra from it. What was it she had said as they'd walked back to her flat? *Plenty of people have been killed in this war who did not deserve to die.* She had mentioned the other officer Tanner had killed when he had shot Becker. *Did Ganz deserve to die? Or all those you killed blowing up the fuel dump?* Tanner did not take any pleasure in killing people, but his job was to help win the war. If people got killed in the process, then so be it. But perhaps she had a point. It all depended on which side you were on. If he'd been born a German – or if he had experienced what Tanja had experienced – then perhaps he, too, would have been fighting on the side of the enemy. *But the Germans support the Nazis, and they're evil.* Yet she had told him, as they'd walked to her apartment, that the Stalinist regime was every bit as bad as the Nazis, and the British were now its allies. Tanner ran his hands through his hair. He'd told her he would not judge her. Nor would he.

'Thank you, Jack,' she said again, sitting down opposite him. 'Really. I can see why Alex thinks so highly of you. You are a good man.'

535

'I don't know about that. I just don't like seeing a lady in distress.' He lit a cigarette, then leaned forward, elbows on the table. 'It must be possible to find Orca. Who the hell is he? I mean, he seems to know almost your every move, except that he didn't know your real identity had been discovered when you boarded that train.'

'If he had, Artus would have killed me.'

'But who did Maunsell and Bowlby spin that story to? Who interrogated you when Sansom raided your flat?'

'Sansom, to begin with. Then Maunsell arrived. He apologized. Told me it had been a mistake, then explained that only he, Bowlby and Peter Stirling knew who I was and that I was now working for the British. He told me that, however embarrassing and unfortunate, his men had acted quite correctly following a tip-off.'

'A tip-off from me. But for Orca to know that you'd been released without charge, he must have known you'd been arrested in the first place. How many people knew that?'

Tanja shrugged. 'I do not know.'

'Not many. Those involved in the raid. A few people at the interrogation centre. Some of the SIME operatives. No one at GHQ. Why would anyone there need to know?'

Tanja shrugged again.

Tanner slammed his palm on the table, making Tanja start. 'Sorry,' he said, 'but, Tanja, Orca *has* to be someone at Red Pillars. *Has* to be. I'd put good money on it. Jesus,' he said, suddenly realizing the enormity of what he was saying. 'That's why they've known everything all along.'

'But who?' she said.

'I don't know.' He looked up at her. 'You've seen him once, you say.'

'In a car, yes, but I did not see his face. I tried to, but it was dark. He was wearing a hat pulled low over his eyes.'

'Did you see anything? Anything at all? A ring? A distinctive watch?'

'He had a signet ring.'

'Coloured in any way?'

'I am not sure. I did not notice.'

'A moustache? Beard?'

She put her hand to her head. 'I could not see.'

'Is there anything, Tanja? Anything at all?'

'I have asked myself that question a thousand times, but no, there is nothing. Nothing but his voice.'

'His voice?'

'That was how he made contact. He would call and pretend to be my lover. "Hello, darling, will you meet me today? At the usual place? I cannot wait to see you." That sort of thing. I always thought it a hateful voice.'

'Why?'

'I don't know. It was a soft voice. English. Perfectly normal in many ways. But there was something in the way he always said "darling" that made my skin crawl. But if I heard it again, I would know it. I would know it anywhere.'

Tanner smiled. All he had to do was take her to Red Pillars. Abdu would let him pass. He could take her to Maunsell and get her introduced to the others working at SIME. *So simple.* If he was right, as soon as the mole opened his mouth,

Tanja would know who Orca was.

'Why do you smile?'

'A voice,' he said, 'might be enough.'

Vaughan had returned to his flat, poured himself a large glass of whisky, then sat on his bed and smoked. If he was honest, he had not been in the mood to spend an evening with Tanner, Farrer and de Villiers. He had gone because he had hoped they might take his mind off things, that with a few drinks inside him and some bon-homie, he might forget about Tanja for a while. But then there she was, imploring him to protect her, gazing at him with those beseeching eyes, and he had been overcome with a renewed wave of despair. He hated this. It was purgatory, a torment worse than any time he had been under fire. Yes, he had been scared – frightened witless, even – on occasion, but nothing had been as bad as the oppressive shroud of misery he now felt.

And the damnable thing was that he wasn't just mourning the end of their affair, he was still madly in love with her. Good God, she had looked stunning tonight, and he had remembered every curve of her body, and how, for a brief moment, his life had been so very nearly perfect.

He poured another Scotch, picked up a book and tried to read, but it didn't work. He couldn't stop thinking about her. His feelings – they were such a conflicting mixture. He loved her still, yet the knowledge of what she had been was repugnant to him. It would, he thought, have been better to discover she had been a whore. Anything but this. For three years he had been fighting a war to rid the world of the Nazis, to help protect his mother and father, his younger sister and his friends, his home, his country. But by sleeping with Tanja he felt as though he had betrayed them all.

Another whisky, and another after that, and then, exhausted and not a little drunk, he had fallen asleep.

Some time later – several hours, he supposed – he awoke, fully clothed, the light still on in his room. He looked at his watch – nearly one in the morning – then sat up, intending to take a shower. An image of Tanja's face – her anguished, imploring face – came to him, and it suddenly occurred to him that it was himself he was loathing; he felt self-disgust because he still loved her so deeply, while the ideals and values by which he lived told him this was profoundly wrong.

It was what she had done, what she had been, that had offended his sensibilities so greatly, yet perhaps he had placed too great an emphasis on his ideals. Perhaps she had been right all along. Perhaps it was both priggish and pompous to take the moral high ground. Whose hands could ever really be clean in a time of war? And what had given him the right to judge her? He had not lost his home and family, for whom he had believed he was fighting. He had not lost a wife, as she had a husband. He had not been forced to trek, alone, across half of Europe with little more than the clothes he stood in.

And perhaps she *had* told the truth. Perhaps she had risked all, in part, for him, for the person who had offered her a chance of happiness. She had told him she understood how he felt, that she had accepted their affair was over, but fear, real fear, had compelled her to find him and ask for his help. Those imploring eyes had been searching for a sign of compassion, and he had turned her away, consumed by self-loathing.

'I've been such a bloody fool,' he said out loud. He stood up, put on his cap, belt and pistol, left the flat and went out into the cool, deserted street. He would go to her now, ignoring the curfew, show her the compassion he should have given her earlier, and plead for her forgiveness. Vaughan quickened his pace. Having made this decision, he wanted to be with her now, not waste a minute walking the empty streets of Cairo. And with every step, his spirits began to rise.

A strange scuffling sound woke him. Tanner opened his eyes, struggled to focus, and cursed his stupidity for sharing more than half a bottle of whisky with Tanja. He sat up on the sofa, grabbed his Sauer and listened, but there was nothing. Switching on the light, he paused by the door to Tanja's bedroom, heard her breathing, then tiptoed into the hallway, and paused. Was that something? Yes – more scuffling. He switched on the hall light, walked slowly to the front door and listened again. Nothing. A cat perhaps, or maybe even a rat. Or a lizard. He was about to turn, when he heard it again, outside the door. He shook his head, cocked the pistol, unbolted the door and turned the handle.

The movement was so quick, he had no time to react or see what was coming: a dark shape, pushing open the door, a gloved hand reaching out and, with lightning speed, smashing him in the side of the head. Tanner staggered backwards, his vision greyed. Then something hard cracked the top of his head, the light went out and he was falling, falling... And then nothing.

Vaughan knew, with a sickening, quickening heart, that something was wrong when he saw the front door of the apartment block was open and no sign of the *bawaeb* or the FS guard. Hurriedly climbing the stairs, he reached the corridor only to see the light in Tanja's flat on and the door ajar. *No – please, no.* A mounting sense of dread accompanied every step he took towards the door. Swinging it open, he saw Tanner lying on the floor. Bending down, he felt his friend's neck. *A pulse.* That was something. He straightened and hurried along the hallway to Tanja's bedroom.

He knew the worst before he switched on the light, but he had not been prepared for what he saw. Tanja lay on her bed, eyes open, with a deep, vicious gash across her throat.

'No!' he said. 'No, no, no!' He ran to her, and saw her blink. She lifted a hand and touched his face.

'Tanja, no!' he cried. 'Please. Please don't die.'

She blinked again, a faint smile on her face.

'No,' he said again. 'Tanja, I'm so sorry. Please, please, don't leave me.'

But it was too late. She had gone.

ALAMEIN

October and November 1942

27

Friday, 23 October. A never-ending day. The men of A Company, the Yorks Rangers, were edgy, fidgety. Tanner had smoked almost incessantly, while the brew can seemed to be almost constantly on the boil. Waiting in their assembly area some fifteen miles to the east of the front line, the Rangers found themselves surrounded by the massed vehicles of 1st Armoured Division. There was constant activity. Jeeps and trucks tore back and forth, while a little way off, clusters of tanks and lorries huddled together.

Tanner felt uneasy to see so many vehicles and troops jammed into one area. He had become used to operating freely in the desert, for the company – or his own truck – to have the space to move at will in the vastness. This was more like a military pageant. He kept scanning the skies, expecting to see enemy aircraft at any moment. At least they were well prepared, he thought. Every man knew what he had to do, which in itself was something new. He was not sure what to make of Montgomery. The general had visited them four weeks earlier when they had been training near Burg El Arab. A small man, with a reedy, nasal voice, who couldn't pronounce his Rs properly but who had spoken with authority, with enthusiasm, with self-belief. Rommel had been dismissed as unimaginative, a man with an unenterprising and repetitive battle strategy. Eighth Army's old habits were to be consigned to the dustbin: no more defended boxes as there had been at Gazala and when they'd first reached the Alamein Line; they had been defensive in concept, which had inhibited flexibility and balance.

Well, Tanner had agreed with that, all right. He'd always thought defensive boxes were a hopeless tactic. Neither would there be any more operating in penny packets. From now on, Montgomery had told them, they would make the most of their superior strength in arms and armour and operate in force. Again, Tanner agreed wholeheartedly. From now on, there would also be greater understanding between the armour and the anti-tank guns, for which the Rangers had been training. Ill-disciplined tank charges across the desert were also a thing of the past. And Montgomery wanted the men to be fit, and to be ready for a gruelling and hard-fought battle.

The Rangers and the rest of the 7th Motor Brigade had been moved, after two years, from the 7th Armoured Division to the 1st Armoured, part of X Corps, specifically created by Montgomery to be his main battle strike force, what he termed the *corps de chasse*. It had meant changing the jerboa emblem of the Desert Rats to a new logo, a rhinoceros, and had caused much grumbling among the men, who were proud of the jerboa and what it stood for. Yet this aside, most felt, as Tanner did, that at last they had a strong commander who seemed to have a clear and sensible idea of what was needed.

The training had been intense. All through those first weeks of October, they had operated together as a division, practising minefield penetration, clearing gaps, marking passages, how to emerge and disperse once through to the other side. The tanks – new Shermans, as well as Grants and Crusaders – gave demonstrations of using new armour-piercing and high-explosive rounds. Tanner had been impressed. Around them, signallers had continued to lay thousands of miles of wire, while at night, a near constant stream of supplies had headed past them towards the front. Tanner had never seen anything like it.

He and Sykes had finally been sent on a five-day six-pounder gun course, like everyone else. Not every platoon in the company had been converted to six-pounders; some remained as rifle platoons in their trucks and carriers, but everyone had been taught gunnery. No six-pounder in the 2nd Battalion would ever stop firing for lack of men who knew what to do. And when Tanner and Sykes had rejoined the company, they had travelled up to the front through concentrations of dummy lorries, tanks and guns – wooden boxes painted and camou-flaged. They had been amazed. The attention to detail, the sheer logistical effort, had been impressive. The Rangers had even been given ropes to drag from their trucks, then sent down to the southern end of the line, stirring up huge clouds of dust and sand as they went, simulating the build-up of forces to the south, rather than the north.

Whether all this bluff and effort had fooled the enemy, Tanner had no idea, but he had watched the growing confidence of the men. The mere thought of pulling the wool over German and Italian eyes had given them a lift.

It was now just after five in the afternoon. *Three hours to go.* He had stripped and cleaned his weapons three times already; he could not do so again. The boys were quiet and withdrawn. It had been good, he thought, to have had more than a month back with the company. That fortnight with C Detachment had seemed longer than it had been, and when he'd returned there had been a few new faces. Smailes had been posted home, his replacement at Company HQ a young lad from Manchester, called Peck. Tanner had also been conscious that he had left to join Vaughan under something of a cloud, yet on his return there had been no further mention of his dust-up with the Rutland Yeomanry. All had seemingly been forgotten. Perhaps it had been just as well that Sykes had rejoined the battalion a couple of days before him. By the time Tanner had arrived, the news of their achievements in Tobruk had gone round not only A Company but the entire battalion. He was not a man to brag, but on this occasion, his friend's big mouth had done him a favour.

Tanner now looked around the company, the men sitting on or standing beside their vehicles. The Bedfords and carriers had been joined by Austin gun portees, the six-pounders already positioned on the backs. Tanner patted his kit, then decided to go for a wander. *Check the men.*

Some were writing letters, others standing around brew cans, smoking. He spotted McAllister.

'How are you, Mac?'

'All right, sir. Just wish we could get on with it now. It feels big this time, don't it?'

'Does a bit.'

'I don't mind admitting I'm nervy.'

'We'll be fine. Those Jerries and Eyeties won't know what's hit them.'

They both looked up at a jeep speeding towards them. As it got nearer, it seemed to be heading straight for A Company.

'Well, blow me,' muttered Tanner, stepping towards it.

As it drew up, Alex Vaughan said, 'Evening, Jack. Everything all right here?'

'Everyone's a bit twitchy but, yes, I think so,' he said. 'How are you, Alex?'

'All right. Busy, as you can imagine.' They had only seen each other a few times since Tanja's murder. Tanner had been fortunate. He had suffered concussion and a gash on his head, but after a few stitches and an extra day's leave, he had returned to the desert. Vaughan had been posted immediately to Eighth Army Headquarters.

Vaughan stepped out of the jeep and took the cigarette Tanner offered. 'I never thought I'd say this,' he remarked, 'but this battle has been a Godsend. A bloody selfish thing to admit, I know, but I've barely had a moment to think since I got back out here. It's been good for me. Taken my mind off things.'

'I can't tell you how many times I've run that evening over in my mind,' Tanner told him. 'I've

549

really tried to remember, but all I can see in my mind's eye is that gloved fist and a dark shape, nothing more. I can't believe that bastard's still out there.'

'I don't know that he'll ever be caught now. People have other things to think about.' He glanced at Tanner. 'You and I have other things on our minds.'

Tanner nodded thoughtfully. 'How's the chief?'

'Very chipper. Exuding plenty of confidence. He thinks it'll be a tough fight, but I don't think he has any doubt whatsoever about the outcome.'

Tanner smiled wryly. 'I should bloody well hope not, with the build of forces we've got. But how many of us are left at the end of it – well, that's another matter.'

'I know. The tension is extraordinary. I've been visiting units all day and everyone's nerves are taut as hell.' Vaughan flicked away his cigarette. 'I must dash.' He held out his hand. 'Good luck, Jack. And when this is all over, let's try and get that evil bastard. I can't think of it out here, but I'm certain there's something – some clue – that can help us nail him.'

'All right,' agreed Tanner. 'We both owe her that.'

Vaughan sped off again and Tanner went to Peploe's truck. He found the captain looking again at his marked-up map, an enlarged sheet of the northern part of the line. They had all known for some days what the battle plan was and their own role in it. Montgomery had personally briefed every officer down to lieutenant colonel, which had included Colonel Vigar. He had briefed his own officers in the mess tent, complete with swagger stick as his pointer and a large map hung at one end.

Montgomery, he assured them, was certainly not 'shilly-shallying' about. 'His message to us was crystal clear,' he told them. 'That we stand here and fight until we have won. The Army Commander is of the view that the only way to win the war is by killing Germans. He didn't mention Italians, but I'm sure he meant them too.' There had been a ripple of laughter at that. 'In any case, I agree with him entirely. He says the battle will be hard fought, believes it will last about a week, but that our tails are up, and that he fully expects us to hit Rommel for six, right out of Africa.'

Vigar had cleared his throat. 'So: to the plan,' he had said. 'We're going to make two big punches, one in the south, which will effectively be a feint, and one in the north – here.' He prodded the Miteiriya Ridge with his stick. It was a long, low feature that ran diagonally north-westwards five miles to the west of the El Alamein railway stop. 'The problem, as you well know, is that we've both been laying staggering numbers of mines. The Hun and Eyetie minefields are marshes of the bloody things, as much as three miles thick in places. It's no problem for the infantry because there's hardly an anti-personnel mine out there, but it's a bugger for our armour. So here's what we're going to do. XXX Corps is going to make the initial punch. Four infantry divisions – the Aussies, the new boys, the 51st Highland, then the Kiwis and the Boks – will attack along a ten-mile front, with the aim of reaching an imaginary objective just beyond the enemy minefields, which he's calling "Oxalic" here.' He ran his stick along a line marked in red on the map. 'Within this ten-mile front, the sappers are going to clear two corridors, here and here.' Two more taps on the map: the first corridor cut across the Miteiriya Ridge; the other lay a couple of miles further north.

'These,' he continued, 'will each contain three eight-yard-wide lanes, which the sappers will clear and through which our armour in X Corps will pass to debouch behind the enemy's main front line. Now, I realize that's barely going to be wide enough to swing a cat, but for obvious reasons, our sappers need to work under the cover of darkness. We cannot expect them to clear more than that in one night. The plan is then to widen them each to sixteen yards. I should also add that the operation through the minefields will be preceded by a barrage from nearly a thousand guns and a sustained, concentrated assault from our air forces that will begin tomorrow, the twenty-first of October. Everyone clear so far?' A few nods and yes-sirs.

'Good, because here's where we come in. We are, as you know, now part of 1st Armoured Division, the exploitation or strike force. Along with our cousins in 2nd Rifle Brigade, we are to be the Minefield Task Force. And what does that mean? It means we are to protect the sappers during their mine-lifting operations. They will be leading the clearance of the lanes through the enemy minefields and we will be with them, at the very van of the advance.'

There had been a few groans.

'It's an honour,' Vigar had continued, raising his hands to silence the dissenters. 'We are to clear any pockets of resistance bypassed or left behind by the advancing infantry, in our case the Jocks in 51st Highland.' He now drew three lanes on a blackboard that stood beside the map. 'The three lanes in the northern corridor are to be codenamed Sun, Moon and Star, and these will be indicated by posts into which will be put a flimsy-can lightshade, with the relevant shape of each lane stamped in the tin.' Vigar then told them the other codewords, which were to be given when the lanes had reached the required width and various levels of penetration. 'If the Minefield Task Force becomes engaged by the enemy during this process and progress is halted, the codeword "Sanctimonious" should be issued. This will mean, "Brigade engaged by enemy – cannot push on". I know it's a lot to take in, but in the next few days, I need you all to study the plans in detail. Mark up your maps, make a note of the codewords and learn 'em so that you know it all like clockwork.'

Soon after, they had been dismissed.

'A bit bloody optimistic, isn't it?' Tanner had said to Peploe, as they'd walked back to the company. 'I mean, how many bloody vehicles are they trying to put through just twenty-four yards?'

'Barely more than a cricket pitch,' Peploe had replied. 'Perhaps you should take it up with Monty. He seems to like his cricket analogies.'

Since then, Peploe, Tanner and the other

officers in the company had worked hard to drum the plan and its details into every single man. The attack was coming, everyone knew it, but no one could say for certain when it would take place. Not until the previous evening, Thursday, 22 October, had the order of the day been issued. Late in the afternoon, Peploe had been summoned to see Vigar.

'D'you reckon this is it?' Sykes had asked Tanner, as Peploe had hurried to the battalion commander's tent.

'Odds on,' said Tanner. 'Moon's full enough.'

Peploe had reappeared a short while later and had then called the entire company around him. Speaking from the body of his truck, he had told them that tomorrow evening, 23 October, the battle would commence.

'I'm going to read out the order of the day from the Army Commander,' he had said. 'It won't take long. He says: "One. Our mandate is to destroy Rommel. Two. We are ready now. Three. Every officer and man should enter battle to see it through – to fight, to kill, to win. Four. The sooner we win this battle, the sooner we will get back home. Five. Let no man surrender as long as he is unwounded and can fight."' Peploe had folded away the thin piece of paper. 'That's it. We'll be moving up to our start positions at twenty hundred. Those in carriers will remain in their vehicles, the rest of us, I'm afraid, will be on foot.' A collective groan. 'Chaps, I know you're all brave men, and I know you'll all do me, Old Man Vigar and this fine regiment of ours proud. It's a privilege to be your company commander, and I know this will soon be one of the finest victories in our long history. Good luck to all of you. Let's fight together, for one another and for all those back home. These are great days, and years from now we'll look back and be proud we played such a key part in one of the finest victories in Britain's long, noble history.'

The men had spontaneously raised their arms and cheered, and Tanner had been surprised by how moved he felt.

'Well done, sir,' he had said to Peploe.

'Didn't think it was overly Churchillian? I got a bit carried away.'

Tanner had laughed. 'No, I liked it. So did the boys.'

Twenty-four very long hours had passed since then, and now, as Tanner joined Peploe by the bonnet of the truck, he looked down at the lines and markings on the map, then back up at the mass of vehicles and the vast expanse of desert ahead of them. Up there was the battlefield, and for all the talk, for all the confidence, for all the carefully prepared lines on a map, he'd been fighting in the desert long enough to know that, in a few hours' time, it would be mayhem out there. Absolute bloody mayhem.

At long last they were on the move. The RAF had been flying over all day, hammering the enemy positions, and they continued to do so now. Dull explosions flashed, the glow already filtered by the haze and smoke of earlier bombing. Ordered out of the transport, they had been led towards the Sun track, already marked, a dotted, rather mesmeric trail through their own minefield, which had been cleared by the sappers over the previous evenings. To his amazement, Tanner saw that every ten yards or so, there was a post at either side of the eight-yard gap from which shone an oil lamp. And cut into every single shade was a circle, denoting the sun, while below, stretching across the vetch and sand, there ran a strip of white tape.

'Who the hell did all this?' asked Sykes, as they walked forward beside the carriers. 'It goes on for bleedin' ever.'

The desert here was about as flat as could be, and the twin lines of lights appeared to mark an infinite avenue into the unknown. 'God knows, Stan,' said Tanner, 'but there must be thousands of them. The wonders of the British Army, eh?'

At just before nine o'clock, they reached no man's land. Directly ahead of them, the sappers moved forward in their trucks and jeeps, still at walking pace as they hammered more posts along the white tape left as a trail by the advancing infantry. Here, on the southern side of the northern corridor, no man's land was a little over two miles wide.

Already men were coughing and spluttering at the dust. The noise of hammering and the rumble and squeak of tracks was continuous, but there was an absence of small-arms fire.

'Sir,' said Phyllis, having recovered from a coughing fit. 'I don't feel that scared any more.'

'Glad to hear it, Siff.'

'I think it was all the hanging around. But now we've started it's not so bad, is it?'

'We're doing all right at the moment,' Tanner replied.

'Just you wait, Siff,' said Hepworth. 'When we hit their minefields that's when the fun and games'll begin.'

Tanner glanced at his watch. He could just see the luminous dials. *Twenty to ten.* No sooner had he done so than a flash of what seemed like sheet lightning streaked across the sky behind them, and then, a moment later, there was a deafening eruption of noise as more than nine hundred and fifty guns opened fire all along the line. Shockwaves pulsed through the ground as hundreds of shells screamed and hurtled over them, exploding in a series of dull-orange waves a few miles ahead.

Amid this numbing din, the Rangers continued forward, following the sappers as they began clearing the lanes at the beginning of the enemy minefield. Tracer ahead, soundless above the racket of the barrage, as the enemy machine-gunners opened fire and the Highlanders returned their own. Flares were being sent into the sky and now Tanner could see the Highlanders pressing forward, spread out, silhouetted like spectres.

As the gunners' loading rhythm changed, the sky became a kaleidoscope of flickering colour. A quarter of an hour later, there was a sudden pause. Now the small-arms fire ahead could be heard. Flashes of light, tracer zipping across the open battlefield, yet so far the Rangers had been kept clear of the fight. Tanner felt strangely untouchable as he walked slowly beside one of the carriers.

Counter-battery fire was screaming over their heads, but a few minutes later, their own began again as the artillery switched to a rolling barrage before the advancing infantry. Again, the ground trembled beneath them, while between the scream of shells, they heard the RAF once more, the imperturbables taking over the role of bombarding the enemy's gun positions.

Something seemed to have gone wrong. Progress had ground to a halt. In the lanes at the edge of no man's land, the sappers' vehicles had stopped.

'What's going on, sir?' Tanner shouted up to Peploe, in one of the carriers.

'Haven't a clue. Bradshaw's been told nothing over the R/T. Will you go and have a dekko?'

Tanner hurried forward, following the line of lamps, but the sappers could say only that they'd been told to hold firm for the moment.

'Were you given a reason?' he asked.

'Not really,' replied a captain. 'Only that there's been a problem with the Star lane and all the traffic going through there has had to be diverted down Moon and then cross over.' He glanced towards it, but they could see nothing in the haze, only hear the low rumble of tanks and the squeak of tracks through the din of the bombardment.

'Well, that doesn't stop us pressing forward, does it?' Tanner asked.

'It shouldn't do, but orders are orders.'

'For God's sake!' said Tanner. 'This is madness. It's already a stiff enough task as it is without any sodding delays.'

The captain shrugged. "'Ours not to reason why, ours but to do or die.'"

As Tanner headed back, cursing, he saw one of the carriers, losing patience, venture out of the lane and promptly hit a mine. There was a flash, the vehicle seemed to jolt into the air, then landed again, its right track blasted apart and useless. The men seemed to be all right, but Tanner hurried over and yelled at them. 'You bloody idiots! Stay on the sodding lane!'

For the best part of an hour, they remained where they were on the edge of the German minefield until, at around eleven o'clock, they began to get moving again. Immediately, the dust was swirling thickly. It soon became almost impossible to see more than a few lamps ahead, as the fog of war thickened. Smoke was drifting across the battlefield, but directly behind them, the division's armour inched forward. As it drove over the fine sand that covered the northern part of the desert, the tracks of the thirty-ton tanks ground the sand to powder and whipped it into the air. Tanner could feel it cloying his mouth and nostrils, catching in his eyes. Men were coughing and spluttering, but now the enemy was stonking them too, and although most of the shells were landing wide, Tanner found himself frequently taking cover. Smoke from the shells added to the misery, and as the fog thickened, the armour, densely packed into that narrow lane, began to flounder and crash into one another.

'Jesus, sir,' said Sykes, beside him, 'this is a strange kind of hell, innit?'

'It's a sodding joke, Stan, that's what it is, only

I'm not finding it very funny.'

Amid the flash of explosions and umbrella of light from flares, Tanner watched the crouching signals men and sappers, bent double under the weight of their loads, barely recognizable under the increasingly thick coating of sweat and dust, struggling to lay wire, the vital link that would maintain contact between the forward troops and those following behind.

A hand fell on to his shoulder, and Tanner turned. Peploe was leaning out over the edge of his carrier. 'Jack?' he said. 'Oh, good, it is you. It all looked so clean on the map.'

'It's horrendous,' Tanner replied. 'I don't remember anyone mentioning the dust in any of the bloody briefings.'

Peploe began coughing, then pulled out a handkerchief, dampened it from his water bottle and wrapped it around his face. 'My God,' he said, 'how the hell are we ever going to get through these minefields? It'll be dawn before we know it, and then what?'

'I don't know,' said Tanner. 'I really don't bloody know.'

28

Before the battle began, General Montgomery had established a small Tactical Headquarters on the coast a couple of miles north of El Alamein, while his chief of staff, General de Guingand, had remained with the main Eighth Army Headquarters at Burg El Arab. A caravan for the Army Commander, a map lorry, a few tents, all draped with camouflage nets – that was all, but it enabled Montgomery to be near to the front, and for his ADCs to be his eyes and ears.

Alex Vaughan had been glad of the move, and the chance it had offered to be near the thick of things. In the days running up to the battle, he had got to know the entire Alamein position as well as anyone. He had been one of three ADCs to ferry the chief about, but had also been sent off on his own, relaying messages or observing preparations. Certainly, the preparations had been thorough, and the visits to the enormous supply dumps and various Field Maintenance depots had reinforced the belief that now, at long last, the British Army would not be found wanting when it came to kit and ammunition. Everywhere he had looked, there had also been lines of wire linking one unit to another. Back in France, in the early days of the war, it had been lack of communication, Vaughan believed, that had been the key instrument of defeat.

The men, too, seemed to know what they had to do, the plan drummed into them by Montgomery in a way no other general had ever done before a battle. New words and phrases that could be easily understood and absorbed had been added to the military dictionary. The initial battle to get through the enemy minefields was the 'break-in', and the operation by the infantry was to be 'crumbling' – which, as it implied, meant they were to chip away at the enemy defences, breaking solid, in-depth infantry positions until the armour could burst through, fan out and deal with the enemy armour by force of numbers. Once through the minefields, the next operation was to be the 'break-out', the 'dogfight'. Simple phrases, a simple plan, and everyone singing from the same hymn sheet. There was no room in Montgomery's army for what he called 'bellyachers'.

Vaughan had found himself falling under the chief's spell. His energy, his force of character had been something to behold. His talks too – Vaughan had watched him addressing a battalion or an armoured regiment and had seen how quickly he'd had them eating out of his hand; his confidence was infectious. Evenings in the mess tent had been entertaining. Most of the staff at Tac HQ were young officers like himself and dinner was always marked by a series of provocative comments from the chief. Only once had Montgomery gone too far: the chief had goaded Vaughan to reveal all about his sex life in Cairo. Vaughan had answered noncommittally, saying he'd been too busy for such things since the war had begun.

'That's not what I heard,' the chief had said, eyes twinkling. 'I heard you had a stunning Polish spy as a lover. I can hardly imagine a more scintillating sex life than that.'

Vaughan had said nothing, but Montgomery had not finished. 'Whatever happened to her, Vaughan?'

'She was murdered, sir. Had her throat slit.'

'Well, that was rather careless of you, wasn't it?'

Later, John Poston, the senior ADC, had taken him aside. 'Don't mind too much what the chief said. You know what he's like. Always trying to stir it up.'

'It's all right. It's, er, still a bit raw, that's all.'

And to give Montgomery his due, he had apologized. The next day, driving down to see 7th Armoured Division, he had said, 'I was out of line last night, Vaughan. Wrong of me. I'm sorry.'

'That's all right, sir.'

'Good. Say no more about it, then.' Nor had he.

Vaughan was certainly of the opinion that Montgomery was far and away the best commander Eighth Army had had, but two aspects of the chief's plan troubled him; as a mere major and ADC, though, he felt unable to mention them. The first was the location of the main thrust. Vaughan had seen enough of the line to know that in the north the going was very soft indeed. Salt-bush and vetch mottled the ground, but in between it was sand – sand that would turn to powder once the weight of British armour went over it. Dust clouds might act as a smoke-screen, but might equally make a once-simple plan very confusing indeed.

Around the centre of the line, however, at the Ruweisat Ridge, it was stony and firmer for the heavy British armour. Furthermore, he had seen the intelligence reports and knew that the bulk of the enemy's own tanks were in the south. It struck him as more sensible to launch a heavy infantry attack in the north, on a narrow front and supported by plenty of artillery, and then, when the enemy was distracted with it, to force

563

the bulk of the armour through the line at Ruweisat and take on the panzers. He realized that this was only an opinion, and he hoped the chief would be proved right, but he could not dispel the nagging doubts he had about so much infantry and armour bludgeoning its way together on such thin, sandy ground.

His other concern was the fire plan. He had watched the opening barrage the previous evening, standing with the other ADCs outside the chief's caravan, clutching his ears and feeling the ground trembling beneath his feet. It had been an impressive display, no question about it, but he could not understand why the chief had put less than half of his nine hundred field guns in support of the main attack. Why hadn't there been more like seven hundred behind that ten-mile attack line? He had also realized that each gun was effectively firing straight ahead. By his calculations, that meant there was one gun for every forty-five yards of the ten-mile attacking front. And that didn't seem quite so impressive. He couldn't understand why a mass of guns had not been directed to pour fire in concentration on to one target at a time.

He had brought this up with the chief, but had received only a patronizing smile. 'Perhaps I should make you my CRA, Vaughan,' he had said.

'But it seems like the old fire plans of the last war, sir,' Vaughan had replied, 'and they never really worked.'

'That's enough, Vaughan,' Montgomery had snapped. 'Don't you think that if you were right our fire plan would be as you suggest?' *Ah, well.*

Perhaps there had been something in what the chief had said. Time would tell soon enough.

The chief had gone to bed at ten, as was his usual way. It was, Montgomery had told them, important that he slept well and that his mind was always sufficiently rested. Barrage or no barrage, he had correctly surmised that there was little more he could do that night. Vaughan had followed soon after, wrapping himself up in his sleeping-bag, with a tarpaulin to protect him from the dew, and settling down in the sand beside the chief's caravan.

It was around five thirty a.m. that Tanner watched two squadrons of Crusaders and Grants from 2nd Armoured Brigade veer clear of the Moon track and, bypassing the Rangers and the sappers ahead of them, surge forward across the uncleared minefield.

'What are they playing at?' said Tanner, as he sat beside Peploe in the company command carrier.

'They've been ordered to, sir,' said Bradshaw, who was tuning into Brigade's net. 'Orders from General Briggs to push on.'

'No wonder they call him the Black Pirate,' said Tanner.

Flares and explosions ahead continued to show fleeting glimpses of the tanks as they pressed forward, but it was not long before fierce firing could be heard and in moments several tanks had been knocked out, burning brightly in the darkness.

'I can't believe what I'm hearing, sir,' Bradshaw said to Peploe. 'They've lost four tanks just like that.'

'May I?' said Peploe, and Bradshaw offered his headset. 'I see what you mean. There's a chap who's just said, "I'm having trouble with my horse's insides. I think I urgently need a vet." I'm sure that's not standard radio code.'

'Who the bloody hell are this bunch?' asked Tanner.

'I'm not entirely sure, sir,' said Bradshaw.

'Someone's now lost a shoe and says he needs a farrier,' said Peploe. 'Oh, hang on a minute. This is more serious. This one sounds really bloody scared. He's been hit and he's baling out but doesn't know how they're going to get back.' He looked at Tanner. 'I wonder whether we ought to go and help. Look,' he said, pointing back towards the east, 'it's getting light. They'll be sitting ducks before long. If we send a carrier, then at least we can help pick up some of the crews.'

'And have a quick dekko while we're about it,' said Tanner. He was already jumping out of the back and hurrying to the vehicle in front of them. Bell, 3 Platoon's sergeant, was in the passenger seat beside his driver, Rifleman Upton.

'Tinker, we've got a little errand to run,' said Tanner.

'I don't like the sound of that, sir.'

Tanner clambered into the back, ordered four of Bell's men out, but told Greening, the Bren gunner, to remain. 'We're following those tanks that went forward a little while back.'

'Bloody hell, sir, do we have to?' said Bell.

'Yes, so let's get a move on.'

It did not take long and, following the tracks, they passed through the minefield without trouble. Five tanks were now burning, and in the thin light of dawn, Tanner could see an enemy tank screen some five hundred yards ahead. Italians, he reckoned, 75s, arcs of stones built up around each one. Closer by, several Grants were firing, but from static positions. The creeping light revealed the dead that now littered the desert floor, Italians and Highlanders, the bodies already thick with flies.

'No wonder they're getting hit,' said Tanner. 'Upton, make sure you bloody well keep moving. Don't stop, all right?' He now spotted three tank crew lying behind a large bush of desert vetch and a further crew hiding behind a trackless Crusader. He watched one of the men poke his head from around the side of the tank only to be met by a burst of machine-gun fire. *Ah, so that's the problem.* But where was it coming from? Then, as they hurried forward, a burst of fire greeted them, too. Swiftly bringing his binoculars to his eyes, he scanned the open desert. *Got you.* A few hundred yards away: a two-man Italian MG crew dug in beside some vetch.

'Pull back a moment, Upton,' he called. He wanted to be clear of the enemy machine-gunners while he took out his Aldis sight and fixed it to his rifle. 'All right,' he said, once he had done it. 'Upton, I want you to move forward again, then briefly stop. Greening, I want you to fire a good burst at eleven o'clock and at a range of five hundred yards. Got it?'

A nod from Upton and Greening.

'Right,' said Tanner. 'Let's go.'

The carrier sped forward, lurching and creaking, the tracks squeaking.

'Stop!' called Tanner. Beside him, the Bren chattered loudly, and Tanner brought his rifle to his shoulder, resting the barrel on the carrier's high side, and found his quarry immediately. He could see the machine-gunner, who was firing at one of the Grants but now changed his aim towards the carrier.

Too late, mate. Tanner breathed in and squeezed the trigger. Through the scope he saw the Italian jerk backwards and his crewman lean over to help. A moment later, Tanner fired a second time and he slumped forward too.

A shell landed nearby and Tanner shouted, 'Move! Head for those three on the ground.' The carrier sped forward and as they neared the three cowering tankmen, Tanner yelled, 'Come on! Run!' beckoning them with his arm. They looked around nervously, then crouching, hurried towards the carrier. Upton paused to let them jump into the back, then on Tanner's command, lurched forward again, halting only once in the lee of the knocked-out Crusader.

'Come on!' bellowed Tanner, jumping clear and pushing them into the back of the open carrier. Machine-gun fire spat out again, from away to their right, as Upton reversed, turned, then sped back the way they had come.

'Good work, Upton,' said Tanner. He sat down, breathed out and looked at the seven men they had picked up. 'Well, well, well,' he said, to the lieutenant now sitting opposite him. 'My old mate Harry Rhodes-Morton.'

'Tanner,' said Rhodes-Morton. 'Good God. I

didn't recognize you at first.'

'Nor me you. I didn't realize it was your mob set off on that suicide mission.'

'You know this man, Harry?' said one of the others.

'Er, yes,' said Rhodes-Morton. He rubbed his face, which was filthy with oil and sweat. 'Look here, Tanner,' he said, 'I've got to admit I'm jolly glad to see you. Didn't think I'd ever say that, but, er, really I am.'

'War,' said Tanner, 'is a great leveller.'

'Yes,' said Rhodes-Morton at length. 'Yes, it is. You and your men very probably saved our lives back there. Thank you.'

Tanner took out a packet of cigarettes and offered one to him.

'Thanks,' said Rhodes-Morton.

'Don't mention it,' Tanner replied.

'Christ,' said Rhodes-Morton. 'That was bloody terrifying.'

'We saw the brew-ups,' said Tanner. 'Did anyone get out?'

Rhodes-Morton shook his head. 'One of them was a good friend of mine. An old friend – I knew him from home.'

'Charlie?' said the other officer.

Rhodes-Morton nodded. 'I can't believe he's gone. Just like that.' He clicked his fingers.

A short while later, Tanner dropped them back with the rest of their regiment, most of which was still toe to tail behind the Minefield Task Force. As he got out, Rhodes-Morton faced Tanner. 'I owe you an apology. I was arrogant and rude. I'm sorry.' He held out his hand.

Tanner shook it. 'Forget it,' he said. 'But just tell me one thing.'

'Yes?'

'Who worked out your radio code?'

'Ah, yes,' said Rhodes-Morton, looking embarrassed. 'I'm afraid we've been struggling a bit on that so we decided to use our own.'

'Based on horses and cricket,' grinned Tanner.

'Er, mostly, yes,' Rhodes-Morton admitted.

'Well, it's entertaining, I'll give you that.' He slapped him on the back, then jumped into the carrier.

'This battle,' said Rhodes-Morton, 'it's going to be tougher than we thought, isn't it?'

Tanner shrugged. 'Fighting in the desert's always bloody confusing. No one ever knows what's going on. Keep your head down and shoot when you see the enemy. Oh, and don't go charging after them. Stick to those basic rules and you'll be fine.'

The carrier lurched forward again and Tanner sat down. He'd tried to sound confident to Rhodes-Morton, but he had been surprised by the depth of the enemy defences: there would be no easy fight once they broke clear of the minefield. No wonder Monty had said it would take a week. This battle was going to be a hard slog, no mistake, and bloody treacherous for those in the van, like the Yorks Rangers. With the sun beginning to rise behind them, and now stuck in the middle of the enemy's minefields, Tanner wondered how they would last the day, let alone a week.

Vaughan and the other ADCs had been up since

dawn, and had headed out in their jeeps to report on the night's progress from the various parts of the battlefield. Vaughan had been sent to report on the 51st Highlands' sector and that of 1st Armoured Division. The Highlanders had lost a lot of men – Vaughan had seen reams of ambulances beetling back and forth as well as all too many bodies – but General Wimberley had reported that both his infantry brigades were now well forward of the enemy minefields, even if not at the imaginary Oxalic objective line.

Vaughan had then motored on to 1st Armoured Headquarters, where General Briggs had painted a horror picture of dust, smoke, confusion and appalling congestion, but despite his armour being nose to tail halfway across the enemy mine-fields in the three lanes of the northern corridor, the onset of daylight had not caused them to suffer as much as he had feared. The dense fog covering the minefields had helped but, as Briggs had pointed out, 'Jerry's lying doggo.'

Vaughan had decided he had better take a look for himself, so had managed to make his way through their own minefield, across no man's land, and then decided to risk driving outside the marked lanes. Speeding up the edge of Moon, dodging past a number of ambulances and other supply vehicles, he stopped by a column of Shermans and Crusaders from 2nd Armoured Brigade and learned that two squadrons of the Rutland Yeomanry had been all but destroyed as they had tried to force their way out of the enemy minefields. Shells and mortars were whistling over with some regularity, eruptions of sand, dust and grit bursting into the air, while shells from their own artillery and the drone of bombers overhead added to the din and the yellow cloud of smoke and dust.

Pressing on, he reached the Minefield Task Force, which had ground to a halt. Sappers were widening the existing lanes, but a major, yelling at him over the din, told him that pushing on through the minefield would be impossible until darkness fell once more. He had then seen men from the Yorks Rangers and, having been directed towards A Company, had found Peploe and Tanner. Seeing him driving slowly forward, they had waved and called him over.

He had not recognized them at first, so covered were they with dust. It was as though a sack of flour had been flung over them. Their voices were hoarse, too.

'Amazing thing about vetch.' Peploe had grinned. 'It's only a scraggy bush but it makes you feel a hell of a lot safer when you're behind it.'

'Shelling's not too bad,' said Tanner. 'We keep telling ourselves that the desert's a bloody big place and there's still lots of space.'

'Any casualties?' Vaughan asked.

'A few,' admitted Peploe. 'Ones and twos. But they'll soon mount up. What's the news?'

'Not entirely sure, to be honest,' Vaughan told him. 'That's why I've come up to see you – to find out. Broadly speaking, the infantry seems to have got through the minefields all right, but not the armour.'

'Jack went up ahead earlier,' said Peploe. 'You're worried the enemy is in greater depth than we thought, aren't you?'

'Too bloody right,' said Tanner. 'Once we finally get through these minefields, there's still plenty of infantry well dug in, as well as anti-tank screens. And they're Eyeties up ahead, not Jerries, and fighting hard, I'd say.'

'Well, it's good to see you chaps still in one piece,' said Vaughan.

'Yes – thank God the enemy hasn't counter-attacked,' said Peploe.

'Maybe the fog of war has something to do with it,' suggested Vaughan. He had been glad to leave the front line and return to Tac HQ.

It was four p.m. and reports from the ADCs and the various units in the field had been reaching Tac HQ throughout the day and painted a fairly consistent picture. It seemed the infantry were between one and two thousand yards short of the Oxalic objective, but had crossed the enemy minefields. The armour had had less success – not a single lane had been completely cleared, and what small amount of armour had got clear of the minefields had been badly mauled. The southern thrust – the secondary attack – had been even less successful. Despite this, and rather to Vaughan's surprise, Montgomery seemed reasonably pleased.

'I said it was going to be a tough fight,' he observed, 'and so it is proving.' However, with the enemy apparently showing no stomach for a counter-attack, he saw no reason why a renewed assault should not begin right away. There was, after all, enough fog over the battlefield to cover their advance.

For Tanner and the Yorks Rangers, it had been a frustrating day. Smoke and dust had hung on the windless air. Above them, aircraft could be heard roaring over, followed by the whistle and boom of bombs, while shelling from both sides continued incessantly. Occasionally small arms chattered ahead, and brief glimpses of the battlefield could be seen as the haze thinned. Stretcher-bearers picked their way through the minefields, collecting the dead and wounded.

At four thirty Peploe had gone to Battalion HQ to confer with Colonel Vigar, and Sykes had joined Tanner. The men were spread out either side of the Sun track, their carriers, for the time being, abandoned. Their positions had been fortified with sandbags. Each man had been given ten sacks each, which they could fill whenever they were stationary and place around themselves. It wasn't much, but better than nothing.

'If only we could bloody see the enemy,' said Tanner. 'We're sat here in the middle of the sodding battle, but there's sod all for us to have a go at.'

'At least we're still alive,' said Sykes.

'That's true,' admitted Tanner. 'I wasn't convinced I would be twelve hours ago.' He caught a whiff of food on the air. 'Christ, I'm hungry,' he said. He realized he'd not eaten anything since the battle began.

'I'm hungry and parched,' said Sykes. 'Not a single bleedin' brew-up all day.'

Tanner felt in his pack. A small tin of bully

beef, hard-tack biscuits and some chocolate. He opened the tin with his clasp knife. A waft of processed meat drifted up to his nose. 'I'm not sure I'm that hungry after all,' he said. He took a mouthful, but it tasted strange.

'You've swallowed too much dust, mate,' said Sykes.

Peploe reappeared.

'We're about to attack again,' he said, squatting beside them.

'In broad daylight?' said Tanner.

'Yes. The orders are for 2nd Armoured Brigade to push forward regardless. There are enough tracks now for them to follow. There's a low feature a thousand yards beyond the edge of the minefields that's been christened Kidney Ridge. That's their new objective.'

'And what about us?'

'We keep sticking to the sappers like glue. They're to get going again behind the advance.'

Soon after, the mass of tanks and armour roared into life. Belching fumes, the tanks began trundling and squeaking away. Either side of them, fresh companies of Highlanders were also moving forward. And then a piper struck up, the reedy sound clearly heard over the din of battle.

'Look at them,' said Sykes. 'Calm as you bloody well like.'

They reminded Tanner of the figures in a film he had seen as a boy of the Tommies walking across no man's land at the Somme, clutching their bayoneted rifles, distinctive helmets on their heads. *Twenty-six years on, and we're doing the same thing.*

They continued to watch as the Highlanders pressed forward. Occasionally a man would drop, but the infantrymen kept going, finally disappearing into the smoke and haze. Even after they had vanished from view, the haunting dirge from the pipes could still be heard.

Vaughan had sensed that trouble might be brewing. Earlier in the day, Briggs had been complaining about the suicidal nature of the task facing his tanks, and later General Gatehouse, commanding 10th Armoured Division in the southern corridor, had told him that he feared Montgomery was expecting too much. A conversation with General Freyberg a short while later confirmed his impression that tensions were mounting between the armour and the infantry.

'I'm not sure about the tankmen's offensive spirit, I'm afraid,' the New Zealand commander had told him. 'Gatehouse is a bit of an old woman. A couple of Shermans brew up and he pulls 'em back.'

Vaughan had reported this to the chief and to General de Guingand, but Montgomery had seemed unfazed. Despite the renewed battle raging both in the north and the south, he had retired to bed at his normal time, just before ten o'clock.

De Guingand, however, had not been quite so unperturbed, and had remained at Tac HQ rather than heading back to Burg El Arab. In and around the map lorry, as reports began to arrive, the ADCs smoked incessantly. De Guingand was pacing back and forth. Every time a new message arrived, everyone sat up expectantly, watching de Guingand as he snatched the slip of paper from one of the signals clerks and read the missive. They could hear the battle – aircraft, small arms, the whistle of shells, explosions – just beyond their encampment. Vaughan had watched it unfolding from the entrance of the tent: dull flashes flickering and pulsing across the horizon. He could smell it too, smoke, fumes and cordite drifting from the west.

A picture soon began to emerge, and it was hardly encouraging. It seemed that, in the northern corridor, the 2nd Armoured Brigade had hit a number of mines and was still struggling to reach Oxalic. In the southern corridor, 8th Armoured Brigade had been forced to pull back across the Miteiriya Ridge and had then been hammered by Stukas, which had destroyed much of their fuel and ammunition, and had left twenty trucks blazing. Not only was progress limited but the congestion was getting worse. Just after midnight, Vaughan read a signal from 10th Armoured Division: *Complete chaos. Southern corridor is like a badly organized car park at an immense race meeting held in a dust bowl.*

At two thirty a.m. de Guingand took a call from Lumsden, X Corps commander.

'Damn it all,' he said, once the call had finished. 'Bloody Gatehouse! He wants to call off 10th Armoured Division's attack for the night. Lumsden wanted to check before giving him the authority.'

'What did you tell him, sir?' asked Poston, the senior ADC.

'Told him to keep going for the moment. Apparently, they're losing lots of tanks and Gatehouse thinks he should pull them all back behind the Miteiriya Ridge.'

De Guingand stood in the doorway at the back of the map lorry, chewing his lip and thinking hard. Eventually he said, 'I think we need to wake the chief. Vaughan, go and get Leese. Poston, put a call through to X Corps HQ and get Lumsden. I'm calling a conference for three thirty a.m.'

Vaughan hurried the five hundred yards along the coast to the neighbouring encampment where XXX Corps had their headquarters. Like Montgomery, General Leese had gone to bed and now had to be woken. He was not pleased.

'Bloody armour,' he muttered, when he emerged, wearing trousers, a pullover and a sheepskin jacket. 'It's all right for the infantry to get themselves killed but as soon as a few tanks start brewing up, the armour wants to pull back.' He looked at Vaughan. 'Come on, Major, let's go and have this show-down.'

The Army Commander was already up and dressed by the time they reached Tac HQ, at around three twenty. Sitting on a stool in the map lorry he greeted Leese cheerfully enough.

'Oliver,' he said, 'sorry to have to wake you, but Freddie's done absolutely the right thing. We need to nip this in the bud, and I'm the only man who can do it.'

Lumsden arrived soon after, looking exhausted, and was immediately taken to the map lorry. With John Poston and two of the other ADCs, Vaughan waited outside on the sand, listening to snippets of the discussion: Lumsden describing the terrible congestion, the hulks of burning Shermans, the lack of space to manoeuvre, and Leese snorting with derision– 'But you've got the whole bloody desert.'

'No, we haven't, Oliver, we've got six lanes eight yards wide and I've lost more than forty tanks already.'

'And how many tanks does Eighth Army boast?' said Montgomery. 'Hm?'

'That's hardly the point, sir,' said Lumsden.

'It *is* the point, Herbert. At least a thousand. I never said this would be easy. Victories cannot be won without loss of life and equipment. The reason I have waited until now to attack is because I wanted to be sure of overwhelming superiority in numbers. Now, I know what I saw when I first came out here: a beaten army that had become far too used to throwing in the towel and falling back at the first sign of trouble. It was commanded by men who were frightened of building up too much of a butcher's bill. I told you then that it was an attitude that had to be stopped in its tracks. No more retreats, I told you, and no more bellyaching.'

'But, sir–' interjected Lumsden.

'No buts, Herbert,' said Montgomery. 'These are my orders: you will tell Gatehouse to keep pressing forwards. We need our armour out of the minefields and into the open. The more you keep moving, the less of a problem there will be with congestion. I want to hear no more bellyaching from you or Gatehouse or any of your commanders, d'you understand? If you haven't got

579

the steel to drive your men forward, tell me now and I'll have you replaced without delay with someone who has. Clear?'

Crystal, Vaughan thought.

29

By the morning of 26 October – the third since the battle began – the Yorks Rangers' role as part of the Minefield Task Force was over, and the battalion had at last been pulled back to the comparative safety of what had been no man's land. A Company's casualties had been light – just sixteen dead and wounded – but the men were all exhausted and filthy and in need of a decent feed. Tanner reckoned he'd had less than two hours' sleep since it had begun; for the past two nights and the previous day, they had been involved in traffic control, helping to feed the flow of armour that was now being funnelled through the ever-widening gaps. Tanner had hated it. Fighting a battle when you could shoot back was one thing; standing amid the dust and mayhem directing tanks while being shelled and mortared was quite another.

Still, as Sykes had again reminded him, they were still alive and the battle did seem to be going in the right direction, even if more slowly than perhaps they would have liked. By the afternoon, Tanner's mood had improved considerably. He'd had a nap and, despite the flies, had managed to eat some hot food and drink several cups of tea, scrounged some more cigarettes and even managed to wash his face with the water brought up by the B Echelon trucks.

Peploe had been called to see Colonel Vigar, but the rest of Headquarters Company were now beside the company command carrier, cleaning weapons and preparing yet another brew. To the north, they could hear heavy fighting, but it had been impossible to tell what was happening. Reams of bombers had been over, pummelling some kind of enemy formation or position, Tanner guessed, but he was conscious that the others barely seemed to notice. It was amazing, he thought, how quickly they had come to rely on the Desert Air Force, but they were an integral part of their firepower. He wondered how Flynn and his squadron were getting on. The RAF really had been magnificent, even in the days leading up to the battle.

'What do you think we'll be doing now, sir?' asked Phyllis.

'God knows.'

'What about that attack we thought we'd be doing last night?' said Brown.

'It was cancelled, Browner, remember?' said Hepworth.

'Maybe they'll want us to do it tonight instead,' said Phyllis.

'I'd put good money on it,' said Sykes.

'Then it's bound to happen,' said Tanner. 'Stan never bets unless he knows his money's safe.'

'It might, it might not,' said Hepworth. 'Generals can never make up their bloody minds.

I've noticed that. The plans are always changing.'

'That's because nothing ever goes to plan in the first place, Hep,' said Sykes.

'You're telling me,' muttered Hepworth. 'All battles are chaos and confusion.'

'I'm confused,' said Phyllis. 'To be honest, I haven't really got the faintest idea what's going on. I suppose we must be winning, but all I know is that I've been shelled for three days and three nights and I've still not fired a single shot.'

Peploe was heading towards them with Vaughan.

'Here's a man who can put you in the picture.' Tanner stood up. 'Hello, sir. How's the Army Commander?'

'Quite chipper,' said Vaughan.

'Phyllis here is feeling confused,' said Tanner. 'He thinks we're winning but he's worried because so far he hasn't fired his rifle.'

'*I* think we're winning,' said Vaughan. 'Slowly but surely.'

'I told him you might be able to put us in the picture, sir.'

'Well, first of all, you'll be using your rifle soon enough, Phyllis,' said Vaughan.

'We're putting in an attack tonight,' said Peploe.

'Bloody brilliant,' said Hepworth, smacking the ground in disappointment.

'You were right, then,' Brown said to Sykes.

'Told you,' said Tanner. 'As before?'

'Yes,' said Vaughan. 'There's a low feature up ahead called Kidney Ridge. There's a shallow hollow to the north we're calling Woodcock, and two to the south, Snipe and Grouse. The KRRC are to take Woodcock, 2nd RB Snipe.'

'And we're to take Grouse,' added Peploe. 'And then hold it with our screen of six-pounders while the armour pours through tomorrow at dawn.'

'Good,' said Tanner. 'It's about time we got to have a go at Jerry.'

'Is it, sir?' said Hepworth. 'Wouldn't it be more fun to be taken out of the line?'

'Hep, you know you don't mean that.' Tanner grinned.

'I bloody do, sir.'

Tanner cuffed the back of his head. 'Anyway, sir,' he said, turning to Vaughan, 'what is the latest situation?'

'The Aussies are doing really well,' he said. 'They've captured Point Twenty-nine to the north of here and we're hoping they'll press on towards the coast.'

'There's been a lot of fighting up there this afternoon,' said Sykes.

'The RAF have certainly been giving someone a hammering,' added Tanner.

'It's been quite a big counter-attack by the panzers,' said Vaughan. 'Fortunately they haven't got very far, though. The Aussies still had Point Twenty-nine a short while ago.'

'What about in the south?' asked Tanner.

'That's been called off,' said Vaughan. 'Thirteen Corps are containing and nothing more at the moment. In the southern corridor, they're making small gains, but orders have just been issued to pull some units out of that part of the line.'

'Some blokes get all the luck,' said Hepworth.

'Pulled back for the final stage of the battle,' added Vaughan. 'The Kiwis, 10th Armoured and your old mob, 7th Armoured. They're going to spearhead the attack.'

'Not quite so cushy, Hep,' said Sykes.

'So it's you chaps and the Aussies who are leading the main drive at the moment,' said Vaughan. 'Or, rather, you will be as of tonight.'

'Talking of which,' said Peploe, 'we're supposed to be at the start line at nine p.m., so we'd better be getting ready.'

'Feeling a bit clearer now, Phyllis?' asked Vaughan.

'Yes, thank you, sir.'

'Excellent. Well, good luck.' He made to leave, but then stopped. 'This operation tonight,' he said. 'It's a key one. If we can take and hold those positions, it'll give us crucial ground and help us achieve the break-out we need. If 7th Motor Brigade can take and consolidate those features, and secure the Kidney Ridge, I can't see there being any way back for Rommel. We'll have him all but on the run.'

The men looked at him in silence. Then Hepworth said, 'No pressure then, sir.'

'You can handle it, Hepworth. Good luck, chaps.'

Around midnight, A Company were leading the rest of the battalion out to the ground south of Kidney Ridge. In the lead carrier, Peploe now stopped, jumped out and ran to Tanner, who had earlier collected his truck and brought it forward to the head of the column.

'Do you think this is it?' Peploe muttered.

The moon was now up and although there was still some smoke and haze, it did seem as though they were in a two-hundred-yard-wide shallow bowl. 'It can't be Snipe, can it?' said Tanner.

'No, they're to the north of us, I'm sure.'

'Well, even if it isn't Grouse, it looks like as good a position as we can hope for, don't you think?'

Peploe breathed in deeply. 'All right.'

Tanner watched him return to his carrier. If they were in the wrong place, it would be in keeping with the way the operation was going so far. The truth was, they had not been given much time to get themselves organized and in formation. During the period of retraining, D Company had been redesignated X Company and given sixteen six-pounders. These guns had been left behind during their stint with the Minefield Task Force and had had to be brought up from Brigade HQ, near their original start positions, along with their portees and ammunition. A number of the trucks – Tanner's included – had also had to be collected, as had the larger supply trucks of the rear link. Then the battalion had had to form up, but already precious time had been lost and by the time all their guns and trucks had arrived, and the detachment of sixteen sappers and a battery of six-pounders had found them, it was getting dark.

The colonel had allocated two columns, led by A Company on the left with two platoons of X Company, and C Company on the right, with two six-pounder platoons. Behind them were Battalion Headquarters, plus a troop of 240th Battery with four six-pounders, and B Company – the battalion reserve – with the remainder of 240th Battery.

If it had been getting dark as they had begun forming up, it was completely so by the time they had managed it. The moon was not yet up and, with no forward lights on the vehicles, it had been difficult to find the start of the Moon track, which, after three days of battle, looked very different from how it had on the opening night. Now, the sand had been driven over countless times, furrows of fine powder dug along its length. Fuel cans and battle detritus littered either side. To make matters worse, the enemy had been shelling – not heavily, but enough to stir up more dust and smoke. Only occasional flares or the flashes of guns gave them any illumination at all. Eventually they had made it to the start of Moon track, not by 2100, as had been agreed, but nearly two hours later.

The plan had been to leave B Company and the supply trucks at the start line until Grouse had been found and secured. Then the signal would be given for them to move up too, but the two lead columns of carriers, trucks, jeeps, gun portees and walking rifle platoons had got under way shortly after eleven, by which time the moon was casting a faint light over the desert. A barrage had been laid on to cover their advance, and to begin with all went well. But as they reached the end of the minefield, they began to struggle in the increasingly rutted ground. Two portees had driven into each other and could go no further. That had held them up for ten minutes, and a further fifteen minutes had been wasted when Colonel Vigar's jeep, hurrying forward to lead the column towards their objective, had driven straight into an old enemy slit trench and had had to be pulled out by a carrier. The colonel, shaken by this humiliation, had handed leadership of the column back to Peploe. On they had pressed, Tanner increasingly uncertain as to whether they were even remotely close to where they should be. He had been looking at his compass but it was the distance that was so hard to judge. Some enemy troops had opened fire with rifles and machine-guns, tracer suddenly spitting across the open desert. They had replied with heavy Bren gunfire, and a number of troops had been seen running away, dark figures melting into the night, just as renewed enemy shelling opened up. Fortunately, it was inaccurate and dropping over their heads so they had moved on.

And now, at long last, they were at Grouse. Or were they?

As Peploe clambered back into his carrier, Vigar's jeep struggled forward and pulled up alongside. Seeing this, Tanner nimbly stepped down and hurried over to join them.

'Is this it?' asked Vigar.

'We think so, sir,' said Peploe. 'There's part of me worrying that we're driving into the middle of an enemy strongpoint, but this is certainly a hollow like the description of Grouse and I'm pretty sure it's on the right bearing.'

'Sod it,' said Vigar. 'That's good enough for me.'

'Sure, sir?'

'Absolutely. Tanner, you take your truck and the carriers and reconnoitre forward. Peploe, you can help me consolidate and allot company sectors. We need to get ourselves into position as soon as poss. Now send up those Very lights and let's get a bloody move on. We've wasted enough time fannying about this evening as it is.'

Tanner led the six carriers across the bowl in a south-westerly direction. The moon was high, the smoke and haze thinning. Enemy troops, in twos and threes, stood up and, arms aloft, surrendered. On each occasion, the carriers stopped, stripped the men of weapons, then bundled them into the back of the vehicles. They were all German.

'Not exactly heavily defended, this sector, is it?' said Sykes.

'Not so far, Stan,' said Tanner.

'Sir?' said Phyllis. 'Why aren't these Jerries putting up a fight?'

'Why do you think, Siff?' Tanner replied.

'I dunno, sir.'

'If you were sitting in a slit trench with your mate and you saw half a dozen fully armed Bren carriers coming towards you, how would you rate your chances of survival?'

'Oh,' said Phyllis. 'I see your point, sir.'

They had gone about a thousand yards or so when they met some entanglements of wire.

'A minefield, sir?' asked Brown.

'Doubt it,' said Tanner. He led them south a short way until they found a gap. 'Come on,' he said to Brown, 'let's go through. It'll be all right.'

A few hundred yards further on they saw a

huddle of men and trucks and, quickly telling the carriers to fan out, Tanner ordered a warning shot to be fired above their heads. Immediately the men put up their arms.

'Blimey, sir,' said Sykes, 'if only it was always this easy. Must be a hundred here at least.'

'At least,' said Tanner, 'plus a few trucks. What do you think? Jerry sappers?'

'Probably. We should send one of the carriers back to get some help. We can't manage this lot ourselves.'

'Good idea.'

Having done so, Tanner sped up and down the huddle of Germans shouting, *'Hände hoch! Hände hoch!'* but as they were circling around the back of them, Sykes said, 'I don't want to worry you, sir, but I can see a bloody great panzer leaguer up ahead.'

Tanner now saw them too: a few hundred yards to the south-west, the unmistakable hulks and gun barrels of tanks silhouetted in the moonlight.

'Ah,' said Tanner, and at that moment, they heard shouts and orders. Several tanks roared into life. 'Time to pull back, I think, Browner.'

A tank shot rang out, ripping apart the night, and was closely followed by a second and a third. Suddenly, one of the German sappers' trucks was hit, and burst into flames. Now the desert was alight. Bren guns from the carriers pounded and then tank and Spandau fire were cutting across the open desert. The men caught in the middle began to shout and cry out, but many were cut to ribbons, scythed down by their own side.

'Pull back! Pull back!' Tanner ordered, as the

panzers continued firing, more accurately now that the carriers were silhouetted in the light of the burning truck. One of the carriers was hit – *whose?* – the dying men lit up briefly as the fuel tanks exploded, arms outstretched before they were engulfed by flames.

As they scurried back, hurrying towards the gap in the wire, Tanner remembered what Tanja had said: *How many people have been killed who did not deserve to be killed?* A whole load more now, he thought.

First light began to glimmer across the desert at about six a.m., and the Riflemen could finally see the lie of the land. A Company Headquarters had found a patch of scrub on the western edge of the hollow. Tanner and the rest of the carriers had made it back to Grouse a few hours earlier, the panzers not following. B Company and the soft-skins had arrived soon after, although some of the six-pounders from 240th Battery had apparently lost their way because now Tanner could count only twenty-one of their anti-tank guns arranged around the bowl. That was five short.

In the hollow, which was barely eight feet lower than the surrounding desert, stood the carriers, portees and other remaining vehicles. The ground was sandy, littered with thick, brittle vetch and salt-bush, providing decent cover for the men and guns that were now positioned around the southern, northern and mainly western edge of the oval bowl. Wooden boxes of ammunition were now stacked ready behind each gun.

A good position, Tanner thought, but as he

brought his binoculars to his eyes, he saw just how far they had pushed into enemy territory. The leaguer they had run into the previous evening was closer than he had realized – about eight hundred yards to the south-west – and Italian. But a thousand yards to the north there was an even larger leaguer of German panzers, nearly all Mark IIIs and IVs. If they were at Grouse, where they were supposed to be, he reckoned Snipe should be a mile or so to the north-east.

Beside him, Peploe was also looking through his binoculars. 'I'm developing a rather unpleasant sensation of nausea,' he said. 'We seem to have inadvertently put ourselves bang in the middle of Rommel's panzers.'

'What have we done, sir?' said Hepworth. 'We're never going to get out of this one!'

'Course we will,' said Tanner, hoping he sounded more reassuring than he felt. Yes, the position was good, but there was a limit to how long twenty-one guns could hold out against more than two hundred panzers.

Sykes, having brewed them all tea, came over to the lip of the bowl alongside Peploe and Tanner. 'If only we had a few more six-pounders,' he said. 'We all know how to use the bloody things, but most of us are going to be doing little more than taking cover for much of the time. I just hope the OP arrives. Otherwise we're up the creek.'

'Hold on,' said Peploe, still glued to his binoculars. 'They're on the move.'

Engines were now starting up, belches of exhaust fumes clear even from where they were lying at the edge of the bowl. In minutes, the entire Italian leaguer was heading north. Moments later, the six-pounders opened fire, the guns rocking back with the recoil.

'Good shot!' said Peploe, as one of the tanks was hit and began burning. Then another was hit and another. The Italians were firing back now, shells hurtling towards their position. One of the six-pounders was hit, the crew flung backwards, and another became stuck in the sand because of the violence of the recoil, but the rest kept firing. A shell landed just in front of A Company's position, kicking up a shower of sand and grit. Tanner ducked, felt the patter of sand on his helmet and down his back, but then he felt for his scope and fixed it to his rifle.

The six-pounders continued firing, more Italian tanks losing tracks. Several were now burning ferociously, thick smoke pitching and rolling into the sky. Smoke from their own guns was wafting over the hollow, cordite sharp against the back of their throats. Firing could also be heard to the north – Snipe? Now Tanner saw that the northern leaguer of panzers was on the move too, turning south-westwards and across their position.

'What the hell are they doing?' he said aloud. 'Can't they see they're walking straight into our line of fire?'

'It's bloody marvellous, though, isn't it?' grinned Sykes. 'I mean, how many times have we watched our own armour get crucified by well-positioned Jerry anti-tank guns?'

'I think they might have clocked us now, Stan,' said Peploe, and a split second later, a flurry of tank shells exploded on the eastern edge of the bowl. Still the gunners kept firing and after more than an hour, Tanner counted sixteen panzers hit.

'I just wish they'd get a bit closer,' he said to Peploe. 'The range is too great at the moment for the rifle.'

Suddenly a shell hurtled over from behind them, exploding just forward of their position. Another burst to their left.

'For God's sake!' shouted Tanner. He could see them now – Shermans cresting a ridge a couple of thousand yards to the east, behind them.

'That's all we bloody need!' shouted Peploe. 'Jack, go and find out from the colonel what the hell is going on, will you?'

Tanner sprinted across the bowl to Vigar's command post, set up near the middle of the western lip of the bowl.

Vigar was yelling into a wireless set. 'Get those bloody idiots to stop firing at us!' he shouted. 'Yes – now!' He passed back the mouthpiece and kicked the ground in frustration as tank shells from both sides rained down around their position. One of the carriers was hit and began to burn.

'What do you want, Tanner?' Vigar snapped, seeing him.

'Shall I drive over and get them to stop, sir?'

Vigar thought a moment. 'Yes, all right. Think you can make it?'

'With a bit of luck, sir.' He sprinted to his truck, clambered into the driver's seat, started it up and carefully drove out of the hollow – only for a shell to land some twenty yards ahead of him.

Cursing, he drove on through the fountain of sand, weaving his way across the open desert towards the Shermans. A rattle of small arms opened up, then stopped, and several more shells landed nearby, but by keeping moving, and zigzagging back and forth, he soon reached the southern formation of Shermans, who had now stopped firing as he frantically waved one arm above his head.

Spotting the pennant of the command tank, he pulled up alongside.

'Where have you come from?' the major shouted down.

'That hollow two thousand yards ahead,' he yelled back. 'We're the Yorks Rangers – an anti-tank gun position. Stop bloody well shelling us, will you, sir?'

'Cripes!' said the major. 'Awfully sorry. We thought you were Huns.'

'Well, we're bloody well not! Can you get on your net, sir, and tell everyone to stop? Those Jerry and Eyetie tanks need your shells, not us.'

'Yes, of course,' said the major. 'I'm so sorry. Apologies to all your chaps.'

Tanner put the truck into gear and sped off again. As he neared the Grouse position, he could see that, ahead, the German panzers that had been moving from the northern leaguer were now forming up hull-down behind a slight ridge some thousand yards away. The six-pounders were still firing furiously as he hurried back into the centre of the bowl, jumped out and sprinted back to the colonel.

'They promised to stop, sir,' he told Vigar.

'Seems to have done the trick too,' said the colonel. 'Good work, Tanner.'

He ran back to A Company Headquarters, where Peploe said, 'Well done, Jack. Looks like our armour's moving up.'

Tanner glanced back and saw the Shermans rolling forward, clouds of dust in their wake. Loud cheering made him turn towards the enemy. Around twenty-five long-barrelled 75mm Mark IV panzers were now hull-down on the ridge, and what seemed to be half a dozen 88mm anti-tank guns, but, despite the Germans' good position and the range, the six-pounders hit two panzers in quick succession.

The Shermans were now reaching the open ground between Grouse and Snipe to the north and the enemy guns turned their attention to them. Smoke shells were fired and Tanner watched with fascination as the German panzers fired smoke canisters at the Shermans, most of which fell within twenty yards of their target, and acted as a marker for the 88s. Round after round slammed towards them, the fearsome velocity of the guns making light work of the British tanks.

Poor bastards, thought Tanner. In minutes, seven Shermans were alight, crewmen trying frantically to leap clear, some already on fire. Soon after, the British tanks began to withdraw.

'Looks like we're going to be on our own again,' said Peploe.

'What we need,' said Tanner, 'is an artillery OP who knows what the hell he's doing. We've got our binoculars, but it's not quite the same thing. If we had a gunner down here directing our field guns further back, we could hammer those panzers.'

'And where's the RAF?' said Sykes. 'I know they've been hard at it, but we really could do with 'em now.'

'Let me go and talk to Vigar,' said Peploe.

It was now after nine a.m. and, for a brief while, there was a slight lull. Smoke lingered in the base of the bowl and hung in threads over the desert. To their immediate north, and away on the ridge ahead, columns of smoke continued to billow into the sky. The smell of gunpowder, smoke, burning oil and rubber hung heavy on the air. Tanner's mouth was as dry as chalk, but there was no time to brew any tea. Petrol-flavoured warm water would have to suffice. Tanner drank greedily, then took off his sweater and battle blouse; it had been cold in the night but was warm enough now. The guns continued to boom. Another six-pounder had become stuck and was hurriedly towed out by the portee and re-positioned. Only three of the guns had been knocked out or damaged – small losses, considering the ferocity of the past two hours. Empty shell cases littered the ground.

Peploe arrived back. 'Vigar's called for an OP and apparently an FOO is on his way.'

'Good,' said Tanner. 'That'll help. Any idea when he might be here?'

'No. The colonel's also about to send some carriers to pick up some more ammo, get the casualties out and bring us a medical officer.'

'How many have we lost?'

'Twelve wounded and three dead so far.'

By the time the B Company carriers trundled off, it was clear that the enemy armour was on the move as well. While the 88s remained on the ridge line, more than thirty German tanks now moved after the retreating Shermans, while another column of enemy tanks had appeared from the north-west.

'We're in the wrong place,' said Tanner. 'This lot are going to cut across our north flank.'

'Then let's move,' said Peploe.

Quickly they ran along the southern rim of the bowl, telling the riflemen to change position. Furious gunfire ripped through the air. Smoke and dust engulfed the position. Shells were hurtling towards them, and two more carriers were hit. Through the smoke and haze, Tanner saw one of B Company's carriers hit as it hurried back across the open desert. The men got out but were gunned down. Crouching low, Tanner ran, his men with him, eventually reaching the northern lip of the Grouse position. Finding some cover among the vetch, he brought his rifle to his shoulder. Tanks were moving across their front now, just five hundred yards away. Some were firing ahead towards the retreating Shermans, others, turrets swivelling, towards the Rangers' positions. To the north, around Snipe, an equally fierce battle seemed to be taking place.

Two Panzer IIIs were hit, while a little further away he spotted an Italian M13 shed a track and grind to a halt. But Tanner was searching for tank commanders to hit. A German now stuck his head from the turret of a Mark IV. *Yes*. Four hundred yards. *Perfect*. A little bit of aim-off, breathe in, squeeze the trigger... The butt pressed into his shoulder and he saw the tank commander jerk backwards. Then, as another tank was hit and shed a track, men began to clamber out. *Aim, breathe in, fire. Aim, breathe in, fire.* Three more men dead. Beside him, Mudge was firing the Bren, casings littering the ground. A few yards away, a six-pounder rolled backwards. Smoke was billowing from the burning carriers, dust, smoke and haze covering the ground ahead so that at one moment there were targets but at the next they disappeared. Tanner wiped his brow as a tank shell scored a direct hit on another six-pounder just twenty yards away. One man was obliterated, another lost an arm and a third was flung backwards ten yards.

'Bloody hell,' muttered Tanner, then saw Phyllis blanch and vomit.

'Sorry, sir,' he mumbled, wiping a filthy hand across his chin.

Men hurried over to the dead and wounded, but Tanner saw that one of the X Company six-pounders attached to A Company was now being brought over from the southern side of the bowl. A carrier was pulling it with rope, the gun tilting horribly in the sand. At last it righted itself and the carrier sped forward. It was halfway across the bowl when a burst of machine-gun fire raked them, killing the driver and the men behind.

'Damn it!' cursed Tanner. 'Stan, Browner, come with me!' Sprinting into the bowl, Tanner pulled the dead driver out, jumped in and drove the carrier forward while, behind, Sykes fired the Bren, bullet casings clattering on to the metal body. A tank shell whistled over them, but now smoke offered a screen of protection. Crouching and grimacing, Tanner took the carrier forward, then swung it around beneath the northern lip, and waved at the men to help manually bring the gun into position. A dozen were soon around it, pulling and heaving, sweat glistening on brows and forearms.

'Someone grab the ammo!' shouted Tanner, as they swivelled the gun so that it faced the enemy. Several men hurried forward with ammunition boxes and the gunners opened fire. Tanner saw two more tanks hit, but it was enemy MG fire that was causing the most casualties. As another flurry of tank shells pounded their position, a Spandau from a Mark IV raked the top of the lip and Tanner heard Mudge cry out.

'Oh, no!' said Tanner, but as he reached him, Mudge slipped back into the sand. Quickly turning him over, Tanner saw that a bullet had hit him in the neck. Blood was pumping from the wound, Mudge's eyes searching wildly, his face draining of colour.

'Come on, mate,' said Phyllis, now beside him and frantically tearing open a field dressing. 'Come on, Mudgy.'

Tanner opened another packet, pressing the gauze against the wound but Mudge's lips had stopped moving, and his eyes, although still wide open, were lifeless.

'Damn – damn!' Tanner punched the ground, then closed Mudge's eyes.

'I can't believe it,' said Phyllis. 'Not Mudgy.'

The enemy tanks were now being engaged by

599

the British armour hull-down a mile or so to the east of Grouse, and with more panzers knocked out and burning, they began to fall back.

'Thank God for that,' said Peploe, wiping his brow.

Tanner took another glug of water. 'Poor old Mudgy,' he said. 'A good lad.'

'And a good cook,' said Sykes. He patted Phyllis's shoulder.

Tanner's mouth was too dry to smoke, but he put a cigarette between his lips all the same, and glanced around their position. A scene of chaos: burning vehicles, upturned ammo boxes, empty casings, mounting numbers of dead and wounded. And just fourteen guns left.

Christ. This is not good.

Enemy shelling continued relentlessly, but for a while, the enemy tank formations held back. Then, at around one o'clock, a dozen Panzer Mark IIIs appeared and directly attacked the northern lip of the bowl. The four six-pounders there opened fire at long range, but with no sign of either the promised FOO or more ammunition, within minutes only one was still firing; the rest had run out of shells.

Two of the tanks had already been hit, but the remaining ten were getting ever closer and firing with both their main guns and their Spandaus.

'We need more ammo!' shouted Lieutenant Carver, the troop commander. 'We've got to get some more bloody ammo!'

'I'll get some,' said Peploe. 'There's got to be some spare on the southern lip.'

'I'll come with you,' said Tanner. 'We can take my truck.'

A nod of agreement, and then they were sprinting, a burst of MG fire hissing over their heads. The smoke had lessened – the knocked-out carriers smouldering now – but as they reached the still intact truck and sped off, a tank shell exploded just behind them.

'Here, Jack!' They drew up alongside one of the knocked-out guns. Boxes of unused ammunition still stood beside it, so they leaped out, heaved the boxes on to the back of the truck, then set off again. Another shell whammed into the sand nearby, then another burst of MG fire, bullets spitting up the ground as Tanner swerved.

'Christ alive!' yelled Tanner, but they were nearing the northern lip again now. The six-pounder rolled back in recoil but more machine-gun bullets spat towards them and raked one side of the Bedford, hitting the fuel tank and setting it on fire.

'This way!' said Tanner, pulling Peploe over to the driver's side, then staggering to the back and dragging the ammunition clear. Their men were around them now, grabbing the boxes and taking them to the waiting six-pounders.

Tanner hurried over with a box, dropped it on the ground, prised open the top, then lay down beside the gun and looked out ahead. The panzers were now only six hundred yards away, but the six-pounder crews were firing again and, in moments, four more panzers had been hit. Several shells thumped nearby but then another landed right in front of the gun, knocking it back

601

on its wheels. The blast sent the crew flying backwards. As the sand and grit settled, Tanner lifted his head. The crew were spreadeagled: two appeared to be dead and the other two badly wounded.

Tanner cursed, yelled for help, then grabbed a shell, hurried to the gun and, crouching to the left of the breech, one knee on the trail, pushed the cocking handle down, then loaded the shell. The breech closed automatically. He peered through the sights, picked out one of the leading panzers, to the right of the others, pressed his shoulder against the pad on the left of the breech and pushed against it slightly until the barrel had traversed sufficiently. With the panzer now perfectly in his sights, at less than four hundred yards, he was about to jump up and move to the other side of the breech to fire, when Sykes scrambled up beside him.

'Stan, get over the side and get ready to fire!'

'Sir!' said Sykes, crouching to the right of the breech.

Tanner peered through the sight again, then said, 'Fire!'

Sykes pulled the operating lever, the gun fired with a resounding crack, the breech flying thirty inches backwards. Tanner remained watching ahead of him. To his relief, the six-pound shell smacked between the turret and the hull at precisely where they had been aiming. But although sparks flew off the metal, there was no explosion.

Quickly he pulled down the cocking handle again. The empty casing flew backwards and

Sykes rammed in another. A glance through the sight, a turn of the elevating handle, and Tanner shouted, 'Fire!' again. Another crack, the gun rocked backwards and this time the entire turret was flung into the air followed by an explosion inside the belly of the tank as the ammunition caught fire. Bullets and shells crackled and spat as angry flames and smoke gushed from the open hole.

Another panzer had also ground to a halt, the crew shot by a burst of Bren fire as they tried to escape, but the remaining three were now only two hundred yards away, still firing furiously towards them. Several shells landed nearby, and Tanner saw men fall backwards – *who?* He couldn't say, but the gun on their right had stopped firing. Two guns against two tanks. A clatter of MG fire against the sixpounder's shield as Tanner aimed again. The nearest panzer was not heading directly for them but slightly at an angle and Tanner now turned the elevating gear and aimed for its tracks.

'Fire!' he shouted to Sykes again. The breech rocked back and they saw the shell smack into the side of the panzer, a track snapping forward like a crack of a whip and several wheels spinning off wildly.

'And another, sir!' cried Sykes, pulling down the cocking lever and pushing in another shell.

The stricken panzer was now a sitting duck, halted in the open at what was effectively point-blank range. A cheer went up as the last panzer burst into flames, but Tanner was now in no mood for mercy. Another turn of the elevating gear and, with the Mark III locked in his sights, he shouted, 'Fire!' once more. The shell hit just above the wheels and immediately a burst of flame hurtled upwards through the hatch, as fuel and ammunition inside exploded.

'Got you,' said Tanner.

Another lull, but just before five, British armour appeared to the north-east, shelling them.

'For God's sake!' shouted Peploe. 'Not again!'

The colonel's jeep was hit, but the remaining twelve guns were spared. In any case, the appearance of the British armour drew forward more enemy panzers and soon the Shermans and Grants were firing towards them instead.

From what Tanner could see, the enemy tanks, all German panzers, were moving forward in two formations of about forty each. To his amazement, they appeared not to have seen the Rangers' position in the Grouse bowl and cut across their northern flank, presenting as good a target as any they had had all day.

Manning the six-pounder again, this time with Hepworth and Brown to help and with another box of salvaged ammunition, he began firing at the vulnerable tracks of the exposed panzers. A target moving across their sights was not, Tanner discovered, quite as easy to aim at as one heading directly for them, but they still hit two, tracks snapping off and the beasts grinding to a halt. Ammunition was now so low that they decided not to waste a second shot. Bren and rifle fire would do for the crew if they tried to escape.

Two more six-pounders were knocked out, but

604

a further ten panzers had been left halted and burning, and by half past five the enemy began to withdraw once more. At this, Sykes rolled over on the sand and put his hand across his eyes. 'No more,' he said, 'please, no more.'

But now Peploe was hurrying towards them. 'There's another attack developing from the south-east, I'm afraid, and we've taken all the ammunition from the guns there.'

'All right,' said Tanner. 'So we need the boys round there with what we've got.'

'Yes, but the good news is that the colonel's had a signal that we're to be relieved. If we're still alive by then, of course.'

Tanner held out a hand to Sykes. 'Come on, mate. Let's get it done. Iggery, all right?'

With two men to a box and others carrying loose shells in their arms, they ran, crouched, to the southern side of the bowl where they had begun that morning. Shells and machine-gun fire were already pouring towards the position as they reached the four guns. Each now had just six rounds and the troop commander ordered no one to fire until the panzers were within two hundred yards.

'Come on,' muttered Tanner, his rifle ready as he lay beside some vetch. There were fifteen of them, Mark IVs. Dust surrounded the tanks, their tracks squeaking loudly over the roar of the engines, the boom and chatter of their guns. How far were they now? Two hundred and fifty yards? By God, they looked close, but still the gunners held their fire.

'Go on, boys!' said Sykes, beside him. 'Give it

to 'em!'

Tanner could feel sweat running down the sides of his face, and his heart was thumping in his chest once more. *Any moment now...*

'Fire!' the troop commander yelled, and a moment later, three of the tanks were hit, rolling to a standstill in smoke and flames. Another tank was hit, and backed away before grinding to a halt. Bren and rifle fire pelted the wrecks, even though they could achieve little, and the remainder, which kept coming forward. But when two more were hit just a hundred yards from the edge of the bowl, they began hastily to turn and pull back, disappearing soon after behind a low ridge.

The sun was dropping behind the ridge too. Tanner watched the colour gradually change from dun to pink, and from pink to orange to russet, just as it did every day. Earlier, he had wondered whether he would ever see this familiar sight again, but somehow he had survived, he and Peploe and Sykes and, he was relieved to see, most of his men. Only poor Mudge had gone.

Wrecks of tanks and the corpses of those trying to escape littered the desert. Some of the panzers stood trackless but otherwise seemingly undamaged. Others smouldered still, while a large number burned fiercely. Sykes reckoned there were seventy out there; Tanner nodded. He'd take his word for it. As the last of the light began to go, he looked around at the strewn and twisted wrecks of guns and carriers, the dead, still lying where they had fallen, and the piles of empty shell cases. Really, he thought, it was such an uninteresting and unremarkable stretch of ground: a slight hollow, a bit of vetch – no different from hundreds of other patches of this part of North Africa. And yet he knew that what they had achieved that day had been quite remarkable. Somehow, they had taken on Rommel's panzers – the very heart and soul of the Afrika Korps, which had for so long tormented British troops in North Africa – and sent them packing. There were many moments in this war of which he felt personally proud, but this action was about as notable as any in which he had taken part.

The relief, inevitably, had not come at nine that evening, as they had been told, or an hour later, but by ten thirty, Vigar had had enough. They were going anyway. Leaving all but one of the guns, and most of the transport that had remained with them – including Tanner's truck – they had walked out of Grouse, trudging wearily back through the Moon gap into what had been no man's land, and finally, in the early hours, reaching the safety of the rear areas behind the British minefield. There they had collapsed. No one had said much. Most were too numb, too drained, too bewildered even to try to put into words how they felt at having lived through such an ordeal. A brew of tea, a bit of food, and then they had lain on the ground, wrapped in whatever clothing they could find. And nothing, not even the cold night air and the dew, could stop them falling asleep almost instantly.

30

After a week of relentless fighting, a permanent fog now hung over the battlefield. It was a yellowish colour, and with it came a distinct smell of smoke, burning rubber and oil, gunpowder – and rotting flesh. Burial parties from both sides were out every night, but it didn't take long for the dead to get a bit high. The sun and millions of flies saw to that. Vaughan found it quite suffocating as he wended his away along a newly established network of tracks up and down the front line and through the now increasingly gapped minefields. There was one crossroads of tracks he had passed a number of times over the past few days. It was at the edge of the second enemy minefield near the Star track and there, in a tangle of wire, lay a dead Highlander. Every time he passed, the body was still there. Vaughan could not understand why it had been left unburied. And with every passing day, it became more and more covered with dust until now, as he passed it today, on Sunday, 1 November, it looked as though it had been turned to stone.

Vaughan had left Tac HQ that morning with the chief busy in the map lorry making preparations for the final offensive of the battle. Montgomery maintained that the battle had gone much as he had expected, but Vaughan reckoned it had been a damn close-run thing. From what he had seen in his tours of the battlefield, from the intelligence reports and sitreps, and from the discussions he had witnessed, he also reckoned the turning point had come on 27 October – the day Rommel had launched his series of counter-attacks. The actions at Snipe and Grouse by the Rifle Brigade and the Yorks Rangers had stopped a major counter-offensive in its tracks. A further panzer counter-attack against the Australians had also been beaten back, while the RAF had repeatedly hit enemy tank formations that day. Much of the enemy's air forces had also been destroyed on the ground, giving the RAF almost complete air superiority. By dusk on 27 October, it was clear that Rommel had lost his chance of making a successful counter-attack.

The next three days had seen continued fighting, particularly in the north where the Australians had been caught up in vicious battles near Tel El Eisa near to the coast. Vaughan had visited one infantry battalion that had fewer than a hundred and fifty men left – more than seventy-five per cent were now casualties.

Only once had he seen the chief flustered and that was when General Alexander had visited Tac HQ the previous day, with Dick McCreery, his chief of staff, and the minister of state, Dick Casey, in tow. Monty had presented his visitors with his plans for his final offensive, which he had codenamed, with typical vigour, Supercharge. As with the opening of the battle, it was a night-time infantry attack with the armour behind and following, launched in the north through the Australian position. Not so wide this time, either

– just four thousand yards – and neither were there the vast numbers of mines to clear. The RAF would play its part too, pounding the enemy in a sustained round-the-clock bombing before the barrage got under way – a barrage, Vaughan had been pleased to note, that involved more guns over a narrower area.

As far as Vaughan had been aware, the visitors had approved of the plan, but a short while after they had gone, the chief had emerged from his caravan and announced that he had decided the planned attack was too far north. Instead, it would take place further south, just above the existing northern corridor. The objective would be a trig point called Tel El Aqqaqir, which lay beside an ancient desert road, the Rahman Track, that ran south-west across the length of the west side of the battlefield. This had always been one of the main lines of communication for Rommel's forces. Cut it, and the Panzer Army would be cut in half too.

Later, Vaughan had asked de Guingand whether Alexander had said anything to the chief about switching the location of Supercharge.

'That's an indelicate question, Vaughan,' de Guingand had replied. 'If the chief says it was his idea, then it was his idea.' But then he had winked.

Now Vaughan was on his way to check on the final preparations. The light was fading, but as he passed through the formations of armour and infantry and reached the Minefield Task Force, he was glad to see the Yorks Rangers.

'A Company, sir?' said a Yorkshireman, as Vaughan stopped to ask directions. 'Just up ahead, sir. At the head of the column.'

Of course. As always.

Tanner and Peploe seemed pleased to see him, and invited him to stay for a brew and a bite to eat.

'All right,' he said. 'Why not?' He knew he would eat with the chief later but, well, he was hardly likely to stuff himself now.

They sat around a little fire beside Peploe's command truck, which until now had been left out of the battle. His carrier had been one of the many vehicle casualties at Grouse.

'Where's your cook? Er, Mudge?' asked Vaughan.

'Bought it during our scrap with the panzers,' said Sykes.

'I'm sorry.'

'Damn sad,' said Peploe. 'He was a good chap, Mudge. But we got off lightly, you know. Sixteen dead and twenty-four wounded. Incredible, really. At the start of the day I thought we'd be bloody fortunate if any of us got through it.'

'Is this it, now, sir?' asked Hepworth, squatting by the fire to stir the hash that was heating over it.

'I think so. One last push.'

'I thought we'd be left out, to be honest,' added Hepworth. 'Thought we might have done our bit.'

'Argue that one with the Aussies,' said Vaughan. 'They've been fighting without a break since the start. I visited one company yesterday that was down to just twenty-seven men.'

611

'So be bloody thankful, Hep,' said Tanner. 'Anyway, the Minefield Task Force is a cushy one. A bit uncomfortable, perhaps, but I'm sure it'll be easier this time round.'

Away to the west, the sun was casting a golden glow like a veil behind the permanent pall over the battlefield. Soon, as they drank their char and ate their hash, they heard the drone of aircraft rising from the east, and then they were over, wave after wave, dark crosses in the sky, coming to pound the enemy positions.

Ripples of explosions peppered the horizon.

'Now that,' said Tanner, 'is hellfire.'

By half past nine the following morning, the armour in their lane had successfully passed through and the Minefield Task Force was dissolved. Ordered to retrieve their carriers and trucks – including Tanner's new Bedford – they had moved forward behind the din of battle, and for the next two days had followed the armour and the air force as they relentlessly pounded the enemy.

The level of destruction had surprised even Tanner. The dead lay everywhere, amid discarded ammunition boxes, empty shell cases, burned-out tanks, half-tracks, trucks and smashed aircraft, but one scene had disturbed him more than others. It had been on the evening of 2 November, as they had driven through the site of a fierce tank battle earlier. Already, the heavy breakdown tractors were busy towing knocked-out Shermans and Crusaders clear, and ambulances were scouring the desert with stretcher parties. Tanner had spotted the crew of one trackless Crusader on the ground around it, and as thousands of flies had swarmed into the air at his approach, he had immediately recognized one of the dead. Harry Rhodes-Morton lay clutching a letter, a dried pool of blood staining the sand dark brown. Tanner stooped and took the piece of paper from his hand. It had not been from a lover, or even his parents, but from his younger sister, writing about life on the farm, about an argument she had had with her best friend, and hoping he was all right. There was a sketch of his horse, too: *I've been riding Mr Kitts as much as possible but he's still pining for you, Harry, so you better hurry up and beat the Germans and get back to him.*

Carefully, Tanner put it into his pocket. When the battle was over, he told himself, he would send it back.

As dawn was breaking on Wednesday, 4 November, the Rangers were emerging from their night-time leaguer just to the east of the Rahman Track – not all that far from Kidney Ridge. For an hour, as they brewed up and smoked, they listened to the infantry attack and yet another artillery barrage a short distance to the south. Suddenly, at around seven, the barrage lifted and a strange calm descended. No guns boomed, no aircraft roared overhead. All they could hear was the crackle of small arms. Then, from the east, a low thunder began, a rumble that grew louder and louder. Suddenly, a hundred yards to their south, the British armour emerged, bursting into their corner of the desert in a massive swirl of dust and smoke, like a tidal wave, and pushing on across and beyond the Rahman Track.

'Jesus,' muttered Tanner, as he sat in his truck drinking tea and smoking. 'Will you look at that?'

'Gladdens the heart, don't it?' grinned Sykes. 'We've got the bastards beat.'

Orders arrived soon after for them to press on and mop up any enemy resistance, help corral prisoners, then work their way towards Daba. Later that afternoon, some fifteen miles east of Rahman Track, they cut across a column of Germans hurrying towards the coast road. A few bursts of Bren fire soon halted the half-dozen trucks, but as Tanner and Peploe strode over to the lead truck – a British Morris, as it happened – it was clear that the decision to surrender had been far from unanimous.

An exhausted-looking major and a *Hauptmann* barely able to contain his anger were stepping out.

'Do you speak English?' Peploe asked the major.

'*Ja*,' he replied. 'A little.'

'Then tell your men to get out of the vehicles and lay down their weapons.'

The *Hauptmann* now interjected and berated the major.

'Hey,' said Tanner, grabbing his shoulder, and in that moment, the German, with a speed that almost caught Tanner out, swung a lightning fast left hook, his clenched hand speeding towards his jaw. Tanner only just managed to duck and, with equal speed, produced an upper cut that crunched into the man's head, causing him to stagger backwards and collapse, unconscious, on the ground.

For a moment, the major stared, open-mouthed, then Peploe said, 'Please tell your men to lay down their weapons.'

But Tanner had walked away. That left hook. It had jarred something in his mind, almost a *déjà vu*. The German had swung his fist in exactly the same way that Tanja's murderer had done, but that night Tanner had been too drowsy – too drunk – to dodge out of the way. But why would someone go for a left hook first, rather than the more obviously stronger right hook? *Because they're left-handed.*

Of course! Tanner put a hand to his head. He had not got to know all the operatives at SIME, but he had met most of them. And there was only one, as far as he knew, who was left-handed. *No,* he thought. *It can't be.* Behind him, the prisoners were clambering out of the trucks, throwing their rifles, pistols and other weapons into a pile, the cocked Brens on the Rangers' trucks pointing at them. Tanner was oblivious to this. Wandering away, he lit a cigarette, then went over in his mind the events of the week he'd spent at Red Pillars. *Christ, I've been a fool.* Why hadn't he seen it earlier?

'Sir? Sir?' Brown was standing beside him.

'What? What is it, Browner?'

'Time to go, sir. We've got to get moving.'

Tanner nodded. 'What about the PoWs?'

'Some other troops have arrived, sir. They're taking them.'

In the truck the men were happily going through some of the booty they had acquired: pistols, knives, even sub-machine guns, like the

615

MP40 Tanner carried. Sykes had picked up an Italian Breda. ''Ere, look at this one, sir!' he said, showing it to Tanner.

Tanner barely glanced at it. 'Good for you, Stan,' he said.

'You all right, sir?' asked Sykes. 'You had a nasty turn or something?'

'You could say that,' said Tanner. 'I've just realized who killed Tanja Zanowski.'

Later they reached the large landing grounds, from where so much of the *Luftwaffe* and Regia Aeronautica had flown since the beginning of July. More prisoners were being rounded up as they arrived there – mostly air-force ground crew by the look of it. The place was utterly wrecked. Bomb craters littered what had once been a vast, flat, open aerodrome, while wrecked aircraft lay everywhere: blackened skeletons and smashed, contorted hulks of aircraft. Others looked to be almost airworthy. They drove past a row of Messerschmitt 109s, which had obviously been undergoing minor repair – a few pieces of engine cowling were missing – but which had been hurriedly abandoned as the front had collapsed.

The battalion leaguered soon after, by the sea where the men could swim and clean themselves for the first time since the battle had begun. Afterwards, as they prepared supper, Tanner sought out Peploe.

'Sir,' he said, 'could I have a word? In private?'

'Of course,' said Peploe. 'I was going to ask you the same. You've barely said a word since we took those Jerry prisoners.'

They walked along the beach. No bombs were falling, no small arms were chattering. Even the skies were quiet. The only sounds were the faint laughter of the men, the clang of cooking pans and the lap of the sea breaking on the shore.

'I can hardly believe it,' said Peploe. 'All this peace and quiet after the near-constant din we've been living through for the past fortnight. I can still barely believe we're in one piece.'

'It's been a hell of a battle,' agreed Tanner. 'I really think that's it and we won't be coming this way again. God knows how long it'll take, but I reckon we'll knock them out of North Africa this time.'

'Incredible. And when one thinks how we were all feeling back in July – it all seemed so touch and go then.'

Tanner was silent for a moment. Then he took out his cigarettes and passed one to Peploe. 'But it's because I don't think we'll be back in Cairo again that I wanted to talk to you, John.'

'Is it Lucie?'

'No, no – no, it's not Lucie. It's to do with what happened when I was away from the battalion. The work I was doing with Vaughan.'

'All that hush-hush stuff you were involved with?'

Tanner nodded. 'Yes.' He had decided earlier that he would tell Peploe everything, and now he did.

'My God, Jack,' said Peploe, when he had finished. 'I had absolutely no idea that this sort of thing was going on.'

'Neither had I. And it's a world I'd rather not

know about, frankly. But you see, this afternoon, when that Jerry officer tried to hit me, the penny suddenly dropped. I saw something that had been staring me in the face ever since Tanja was murdered. And the more I've thought about it, the more I know I'm right. I know who the mole was. I know who this Orca bloke really is.'

'What are you going to do about it?'

'I want to find Vaughan. I want to tell him and I want to make sure this bloke gets what's coming to him. Those SIS characters – they're clever, all right, and some of them are very clever, but they're mostly a bunch of amateurs, really, making it up as they go along.' He paused. 'I have to find Vaughan. I have to make sure that justice is done and that this bastard doesn't wriggle out of it and get away scot-free.'

Peploe looked out over the darkening sea. Away to the west, just a thin strip of light remained on the horizon – light that was almost blood red against a strip of gun-metal cloud. 'All right, Jack. Why don't you take your truck and try and get to Tac HQ now?'

'Tonight?'

'Yes. We're going to be here until morning. Go now. It's not that far, is it?'

Tanner reached Eighth Army's Tactical Headquarters more than two and a half hours later. The journey was less than forty miles but there had been, inevitably, plenty of traffic on the coast road. Still, it was before nine o'clock when he got there.

'It's Major Vaughan I'm here to see,' Tanner

told the sentries. 'Tell him it's urgent.'

He was kept waiting ten minutes, then led down to the mess. There was laughter and talking from inside the tent, but Tanner kept his distance. It wasn't his place to pry. Then the flap opened and Vaughan was walking towards him. 'Jack,' he said, 'what the hell are you doing here?'

'Sorry, Alex, but it's important.'

'So's my dinner with General von Thoma.'

'Von who?'

'The commander of the Afrika Korps. He was captured earlier. The chief's invited him to dinner.'

'Look, Alex, I couldn't give a stuff about some Jerry general. This is about Tanja.'

'What? What are you talking about, Jack?'

'I know who killed her. I know who Orca is. I've worked it out.'

He explained about the dust-up with the German captain earlier, and about how once he'd worked out who the mole was, everything else had fallen into place.

'My God, Jack,' said Vaughan. 'You're right. You're bloody well right.'

'So don't you see, Alex, that you've got to get back to Cairo? You've got to make sure he's brought down. That justice is served.'

'Yes,' said Vaughan. 'Yes, I do.'

'Talk to the chief. Get yourself back to Cairo. Promise me.' Tanner looked him in the eye. 'You owe it to Tanja.'

'Yes, Jack, I will. It's a good time to ask.' Vaughan smiled. 'He's understandably in rather a good mood.'

Tanner shook Vaughan's hand. 'Good, and let

me know how you get on.'

The following morning, having made it back to Daba, Tanner was summoned to see Vigar.

'This has just come through, Jack,' said the colonel, passing Tanner a thin piece of signal paper.

Tanner read the message: FROM ARMY COMMANDER TO OFFICER COMMANDING 2 YORKS RANGERS STOP LT J TANNER TO REPORT TO EIGHTH ARMY TAC HQ 12 NOON 6 NOV 42 STOP EXPECT ABSENCE 48 HOURS STOP

He read it again, his heart quickening.

'What d'you make of that, Tanner, eh?' said Vigar. 'What the devil are you up to?'

'It's a very long story, sir,' said Tanner. 'It's to do with the secondment I had to SIS and C Detachment. It's a matter of seeing justice done.'

Vigar sighed. 'I don't know, Tanner. If Monty's asked for you, who the hell am I to argue? An order's an order, but when you get back, it would be good to have you stay with us, all right? No one can deny you're a fine soldier, but it doesn't look good if you keep buggering off. Wouldn't want people to think you're getting special treatment.'

'No, sir. I completely understand. And you have my word, sir, that I don't want to leave the battalion again.'

'All right,' said Vigar. 'Well, you'd better get going, then. Just make sure you get back as soon as you can, all right?'

Tanner saluted and left him.

He had got a lift to Montgomery's headquarters, where he had met Vaughan, and together they had driven to Burg El Arab, then got seats on a Hudson to Heliopolis. By three o'clock that afternoon, they were back in Cairo, sitting in a car that had been sent specially from GHQ to collect them.

It seemed Vaughan had told the Army Commander everything, much as Tanner had told Peploe.

'The timing couldn't have been better,' Vaughan had told him. 'I've never seen him in a better mood. Of course, everyone's absolutely thrilled about the victory, but it must be particularly intoxicating for the Army Commander. Anyway, I knew he was pleased with us ADCs – he'd told us so earlier. To be honest, I think he prefers us to most of his generals. And when I told him what had been going on, he absolutely insisted that you come with me.'

It struck Tanner as slightly unreal to be driving calmly through the city he now knew so well. Everything was so familiar, and as they entered the curving, leafy boulevards of Garden City, it was as though the days of intense heat and intrigue in August had been just a week ago, rather than three months earlier. It was cooler now – far more pleasant – although the sun still shone strongly, and the sky above was as deep a blue as ever.

As they pulled up outside Red Pillars, Tanner looked up and saw the kites still circling – did they ever stop? They went up the steps and into the hallway, and there was Abdu on his little trolley, greeting them like old friends. 'How are you, sir?' he said cheerily. 'All well, I trust?'

'Fine, thank you, Abdu,' said Vaughan. 'Is RJ in?'

'Yes, sir. The chief is here.'

Up the stairs, two at a time, a brief greeting to Daphne, then down the corridor and a light rap on the door.

'Come!' said Maunsell's familiar voice.

As they opened the door and stepped back into Maunsell's office, Tanner wondered what they were going to say. He and Vaughan had not really discussed it. 'We'll go to RJ and see what he has to say,' Vaughan had suggested, as they'd motored to Burg El Arab. It had seemed as good a plan as any.

'Alex, Jack!' said Maunsell, standing up and greeting them effusively. 'The heroes return! I hear great deeds have been performed and Field Marshal Rommel is on the run.'

'It seems so,' said Vaughan.

'Sit down, sit down,' said Maunsell. 'Drink?'

'Thanks,' said Vaughan. 'A Scotch, if you've got one.'

'Of course. Jack?'

'Please, RJ.'

He went over to the drinks tray, which sat, as always, on the side-table, and poured three generous measures. 'So,' he said, handing them their glasses, 'what brings you back here?'

'It's about Orca,' said Vaughan.

Maunsell eyed them. *Yes?*

'You haven't caught him, have you?'

'No, we haven't – although, of course, the most

important factor is that the Cobra circuit has long since been broken, and the Panzer Army is on the run. It's a source of frustration, obviously, that he's still out there, but it's hard to see what harm he can do.'

'No, but he's also a murderer. Justice needs to be served.'

'I agree.' Maunsell smiled. 'But you didn't come all the way here to tell me that.'

'No,' said Tanner. 'You see, we reckon we know who Orca is.'

'You do?' said Maunsell. 'How on earth?'

'Simple, really,' said Tanner. 'He's left-handed. I suddenly realized that the man who hit me the night Tanja Zanowski was killed had used his left fist. He didn't need to do that. It would have been easier to hit me with the right, but he didn't.'

'And I remembered the autopsy report,' said Vaughan. 'He had held her down with his right hand and cut her throat with the left. I don't know why I didn't think of it before.'

'And then I started thinking,' said Tanner, 'and I began to put two and two together. I thought of who had known about our suspicions of the tailor, Moussa, and the speed with which Tanja was able to send her signals. You see, she told me what she had sent, and when I put it all together, I realized there were very, very few people who could possibly have known what she had been told. But what nailed it was what happened when Tanja was arrested. That meant it *had* to be someone within SIME. I discounted Sansom and Astley because they weren't privy to the kind of intelligence the operatives had and, in any case,

623

they're right-handed. Admittedly, I couldn't account for all the operatives here, but I was pretty sure who our man was. When I spoke to Alex, he confirmed it, though.'

'It's conclusive, RJ,' added Vaughan. 'There can be no doubt.'

'It's Maddox,' said Tanner.

'Paddy?' Maunsell said, an incredulous expression on his face. 'You think Paddy Maddox is Orca?'

'I know he is. And there's also the death of Eslem Mustafa. As soon as Alex told me what had happened, I wondered who had seen him in his cell that day. A hidden piece of glass – I'd put good money on it that Maddox brought that in and killed him himself.'

Maunsell frowned. 'Paddy *was* the last person to see him alive. Neither Rolo nor Tilly had managed to break Mustafa, but then Paddy offered to try. None of us thought there was anything suspicious in it at the time – it was a small piece of glass, after all, and could easily have survived being laundered.'

'I hadn't thought it suspicious either, RJ,' said Vaughan. 'Not until I saw Jack last night. Then suddenly it seemed so obvious. We never suspected him so we never saw the clues.'

Maunsell sat back in his seat, tapping a finger thoughtfully against his chin. 'Good Lord,' he muttered. 'What a betrayal. And what fools we've been. But you're right – Paddy *must* be Orca.' He leaned forward and pressed the intercom on his desk. 'Daphne, can you send Paddy Maddox in, please?'

'He's just left, RJ. He was standing by your door, about to see you, I thought. I told him you had Alex and Jack with you, and he hurried off out.'

Tanner was on his feet immediately, making for the door, Vaughan and Maunsell just behind him. 'When did he leave?' he asked Daphne, as they reached the landing by the stairs.

'Thirty seconds ago – literally just now. Why – is anything wrong?'

None of them replied. Instead they ran to the stairs, hurrying down to the hallway, out through the door, down the steps, Tanner with his Sauer in his hand. *Where the hell is he?* Across the street, a car was moving off.

'There!' shouted Tanner.

The driver who had brought them was still waiting, so they jumped in, Tanner beside the driver, Vaughan and Maunsell in the back. 'That Morris up ahead,' said Tanner. 'Follow it.'

'Quickly!' added Maunsell.

Along Tolombat Street they sped, soon gaining on the Morris, but as Maddox's car turned out of Garden City and right on to Sharia Kasr El Aini, they briefly lost sight of it in the heavy traffic, before catching up with it again.

'I can't get a clear shot,' said Tanner. 'He's just too far ahead of us.'

'Come on, man,' Maunsell said to the driver, 'put your foot down.'

'I'm trying, sir,' said the man. 'It's the traffic.'

It began to thin as they headed south out of town.

'Where the hell is he going?' muttered Vaughan.

They were gaining on him, and Tanner now leaned out of the window and fired a shot, but missed. Maddox swerved, and then they were entering Old Cairo, and their quarry was turning towards the quayside. A cart cut across them, tyres screeching – they managed to avoid a collision. They had lost ground, but ahead Maddox was now in trouble as a truck, emerging from a side-road, barred his way.

'We've got him!' shouted Vaughan, but Maddox was getting out of the car and running. As soon as they ground to a halt behind the Morris, Tanner was out and running after him. He could see Maddox ahead, glancing back, the cool façade that he usually wore now gone. *Where's he heading?* Tanner's chest was tightening, his legs straining. Now they were nearing the wide open space of the quayside, with its warehouses and rows of stalls.

'Stop!' shouted Tanner. 'Maddox, stop!'

But Maddox ran on, turning down beside one of the warehouses. *I can't lose him now.* Quickening his pace, Tanner gained a few precious paces to come within twenty yards of Maddox, then stopped and aimed his pistol, his arms outstretched. What was it? Thirty yards? Getting towards the maximum range for a pistol. Tanner squeezed the trigger once, then twice, and saw Maddox flinch as a bullet hit his shoulder. Now he turned, aimed and fired, but Tanner sidestepped and the bullet missed. Shocked Egyptians were hurrying clear, and Tanner, his pistol still in his outstretched hands, said, 'Maddox, it's all over.'

Still Maddox ran on, but his pace was slowing

626

and Tanner soon gained on him.

'Stop!' shouted Tanner again, at which Maddox turned and once more aimed. This time Tanner knew he could not miss. Firing first, he hit Maddox square in the stomach. He staggered backwards, dropped his weapon and fell to his knees. Tanner hurried towards him, standing over him, pistol pointing straight at him.

'Why?' he said. 'Why, Maddox?'

There was blood on his lips and a line of it now ran from his mouth and down his chin. His hand, clutching his stomach, was bright red.

'Three reasons,' said Maddox, swaying. Tanner was now conscious of Maunsell and Vaughan beside him. 'I'm Irish, not British. I've been working against the British for years.' He held up two fingers. 'Second – the money. The Germans paid me lots of it.'

'And the third?' asked Vaughan.

Maddox smiled. 'The third. Because,' he said, 'it was exciting. Pulling the wool over all your eyes. It's been fun.' He spat the words, so that a spray of blood fell down his shirt and suit.

'I trusted you,' said Maunsell.

'Don't you know the first rule of espionage,' said Maddox, 'never to trust anyone?' He coughed, looked at them strangely, then collapsed on the ground, dead.

Three days later, Tanner was sitting at the top of the massive escarpment that overlooked Sollum and marked the Egyptian and Libyan border. Progress had been rapid in the two days since he had rejoined the battalion. Mersa Matruh had

627

been retaken, so too Sidi Barrani, and now, here they were, stopping for the night and about to enter Libya once more.

'Let's hope it really is the last bloody time we come through here,' said Sykes, as they looked back along the coast and the vast desert stretching away from them. 'I mean, pukka view and all that but, frankly, I know this place better than I'd ever wanted to.'

Peploe now came over to them. 'I've just heard the news.' He grinned. 'We've invaded Algeria. Us and the Yanks.'

Tanner smiled. 'Bloody hell,' he said. 'We really are going to beat them, aren't we?'

'Maybe this time, yes. Apparently Monty's saying the race to Tunis is now on. Last one there's a rotten egg.'

They laughed. Tanner took out a cigarette, strolled over to a rock that was jutting out amid the ochre soil and brush, sat down and looked out to sea. It twinkled peacefully in the evening sun.

He'd been glad to get away from Cairo again. There was something rotten about the place, he had decided. Of course, it had been good to see Lucie, but after the battle the city had seemed so – what was the word? Decadent? Artificial? Slightly sinister, if he was honest. He'd never said to Vaughan what he'd realized about Maunsell and Bowlby – that Tanja had been set up. They'd known there was a good chance that Orca would kill her, which was why they'd done so little to protect her. Tanja had understood that too. There had been no plans for her – except to let Orca do away with her. Problem solved: Tanja would have been an awkward embarrassment. Maunsell had admitted as much. They had hoped to catch Orca in the act, but had failed – he'd arrived through the back of her apartment block without being spotted and had left the same way.

Tanja. He wondered whether he hadn't been a little in love with her himself. Such a tragedy, he thought, for all that she had done, and yet there was so much tragedy in this world. It seemed strange that he, with no family and no home, should continue to survive the war, when young men like Harry Rhodes-Morton, who had had all those things, should be cut down. The mood had been euphoric since the end of the battle and yet he knew that tens of thousands of families across the world would have been receiving telegrams telling them their son or husband or brother was wounded, or missing, or dead, a casualty of a battle that had been fought over a scrap of un-remarkable desert in a land far, far away.

Ah, well. It didn't pay to brood. Cairo, Alamein – Egypt. That was now in the past. The tide had turned, it seemed, but the war wasn't over yet. *Not by a long way.*

Historical Note

Most of the book is set around a framework of real historical events. At the beginning of August 1942, the North African campaign really did hang in the balance. The British Eighth Army had suffered a catastrophic defeat at Gazala and Tobruk, had been pushed back all the way to the Alamein Line, and Rommel appeared to be knocking on the door of the entire Middle East. In Cairo there had been panic, with thousands of documents being burned at GHQ in what became known as 'the Flap'.

What neither side appreciated at the time was that that was a battle too far for Rommel, whose dramatic victory at Tobruk had made him somewhat lose his head. The vast lines of supply he now faced were crippling, while, of course, the British could now bring all the supplies they needed, and more, almost straight from their backyard.

There was, however, a crisis of leadership, and despite General Auchinleck's undoubted abilities, it had been the right decision by Churchill and General Brooke, the Chief of the Imperial General Staff, to remove him. The Auk, as he was known, had earlier sacked Ritchie as Eighth Army commander and taken over the role himself, as well as maintaining his position as Commander-in-Chief, Middle East. It was too much and there was little doubt that some fresh energy and new faces were needed. Whether General Gott would have been as successful as Montgomery proved to be at the battles of Alam Halfa and El Alamein, will never be known, because he was killed in much the way described.

The facts of his death have only recently come to light. For more than sixty years the original news blackout on the incident was largely maintained. A few years ago, I had several long conversations with Hugh 'Jimmy' James, the pilot of the Bristol Bombay in which Gott was killed. He had finally tracked down the leader of the six Me 109s who had shot the aircraft down. The British 'official' story was that two Messerschmitts had happened by chance to be overhead at the time so had shot the aircraft down, but Jimmy had always known there had been six aircraft and that they not only shot out both engines but returned and shot up the Bombay again, once it was on the ground. Herr Claude, the German pilot, also told Jimmy that when they touched down again a short while later, they were met by a senior officer who said, 'Congratulations. You have just killed the new commander of the British Eighth Army.' At the time, Jimmy had still been struggling across the desert to get help. The British did not know then that General Gott was already dead. So, it must have been an assassination.

However, loose radio security would almost certainly have been to blame, rather than an enemy spy circuit operating in Cairo. The

Egyptian General Pasha El Masri was real enough, as was the agitation in May 1941. It is also true that various Axis legations were operating in Cairo until closed down after the El Masri affair, including the Romanian Legation. The Muslim Brotherhood and the Ring of Iron were also both very real anti-British movements. It is therefore not at all implausible that an Axis spy circuit could have been set up at that time, and it is also true that the most successful intelligence operations were those whose information could work hand-in-hand with another source. The British had decrypted many German coded messages in what became known as Ultra; but if Ultra warned of an Axis supply convoy crossing the Mediterranean, then reconnaissance aircraft would always be sent over too. Secretly obtained intelligence is no use if the enemy then discovers that it is being leaked.

Both SIME and the ISLD were real Middle East divisions of MI5 and MI6, as were the other SIS operations mentioned. Many of the characters described were real too: Maunsell, Bowlby, Kirk, Rolo, Tilly, and even the Field Security officers, Sansom and Astley. Trying to work out the labyrinthine structure of these myriad operations and how they interconnected was quite tricky, because very little has been written about it, and what official documents remain involve careful piecing together. Maunsell, however, did write an unpublished memoir of his days as head of SIME. He did favour Christian names and informality, was both tall and rather urbane, and left a reasonably detailed description of both Red Pillars (and the doorman, Abdu), and their counter-intelligence methodology. 'Sammy' Sansom also left a memoir, of which the Eppler Case is its central triumph. That was, in reality, the only Axis spy circuit ever discovered operating in Cairo and was every bit as cack-handed as described. Most SIME 'operatives' – as Maunsell called them – struck me as being rather hit-and-miss as well. Clever and dedicated they might have been, but they were operating with none of the high-tech gadgetry of today's spooks – no GPS, no thermal imaging, no Internet or computer hacking.

Cairo itself was very different from the city of today. The *belle-époque* central area must have been lovely: wide streets, beautiful buildings, fabulous clubs and hotels, and lots of open space, such as at Gezira and Ezbekiyeh. The traffic was terrible, as described, and Cairo must have been a constantly hot, smelly and over-populated place, pullulating with human and animal kind. All the main places and buildings described were real.

The lights and excesses of Cairo also served as a stark contrast with the harsh desert life. Despite the millions of flies, the desert did offer a pretty healthy lifestyle, particularly if you were on the British side. For most of the time, British troops had plenty to eat, fresh air and exercise. It got to most people eventually, but life was more bearable during this period because of the proximity to the Nile Delta and the Canal Zone, and because of the consequent ease with which supplies could reach the front. The Axis troops, in contrast, were living off minimal rations, and struggling to get enough of just about everything. The incredible logistic effort that marked both Montgomery's first battle at the end of August – Alam Halfa – and what became the second battle of Alamein were in marked contrast with the tiny scratch force that had beaten back the Italians in the early days of the desert campaign.

The desert today is largely unchanged, and wandering over the old battlefields, it is still possible to find pieces of shrapnel, old tins, shell casings and dug-up mines. It is also a far more varied landscape than most people realize. Vaughan's criticisms of Montgomery's battle plan for Alamein are largely my own, based on research I did a few years ago for a non-fiction account of the last year of the North African campaign. The battles depicted followed pretty much the course described in the book, even the raids on Benghazi and Tobruk – fiascos from the outset and horribly over-ambitious. They were never going to work, just as Vaughan and others feared. The second raid by C Detachment is entirely fiction, but the hospital building and accompanying villas still stand; so, too, does the underground bunker that served as Rommel's headquarters in Mersa Matruh.

The actions of the Yorks Rangers are based very heavily on those of the 2nd Battalion, the Rifle Brigade, and the memories and diaries of the late Albert Martin were a crucial source. There was no Grouse, but there certainly was Snipe, in which the Rifle Brigade covered themselves with glory. Charles Coles, former skipper of MTB 262, provided some important detail about coastal MTB operations. He also took part in the doomed Tobruk Raid. A number of other veterans – Jimmy James included – have provided me with a large amount of material on living, operating and fighting in the desert war and of life in Cairo too. To them, my thanks.

I would also like to thank the following: Oliver Barnham, Peter Caddick-Adams, Tom Coulson, RSM Darren Gathercole, Martin Holland, Phil Lord, Steve Mulcahey, Hazel Orme, Bill Scott-Kerr, James Shopland, Jake Smith-Bosanquet, Mads Toy, Patrick Walsh, Katrina Whone and all at Transworld. And also Rachel, Ned and Daisy.

The publishers hope that this book has given you enjoyable reading. Large Print Books are especially designed to be as easy to see and hold as possible. If you wish a complete list of our books please ask at your local library or write directly to:

Magna Large Print Books
Magna House, Long Preston,
Skipton, North Yorkshire.
BD23 4ND

This Large Print Book for the partially sighted, who cannot read normal print, is published under the auspices of

THE ULVERSCROFT FOUNDATION